Something to Talk About
(*Heart of it All, Book One*)

Beth Donaldson

*To Tim, the most wonderful husband
a girl could have.*

To Nick, officially the Best Son Ever.

Love you both so much.

"What you don't see with your eyes, don't witness with your mouth."

Jewish proverb

"Some say our national pastime is baseball. Not me. It's gossip."

Erma Bombeck

PROLOGUE

Overheard in the 50 Shades of Style Salon at Serenity Day Spa:

That man will screw anything in a skirt.

I heard Jessie Stevens is gonna leave her husband for him.

Oh, please. He's never with anyone more than once.

True. They don't call him the One Date Wonder for nothing.

And if he's ever gotten anywhere near Jessie Stevens I'll eat my hat.

I wonder how many there've really been? Everyone says something different.

Enough to give him a serious case of the cooties! (laughter)

Too bad, really. He's friendly, polite…and cute! He'd be a real catch if he wasn't such a skank.

Hon, only women are skanks. Men are…what are men like him called, anyway? Dicks? Gigolos? Sleazebags?

I think I like skank better. (more laughter)

He's pretty hot for a skank.

Oh, girlfriend, do not *go there.*

Hush up. I can fantasize if I want.

Well, at least you won't catch anything that way.

1

"Isn't this fabulous?" Fran Bishop gushed, pointing at a booth. "You could put in some planters, and maybe a fountain!"

"No fountains!" Glad and Holly chorused. Fran affected a pout, then pointed at one of the statues on display. "How about him, then?"

The statue was a remake of Michelangelo's *David*, and not a very good likeness. The detailing was minimal at best, and the stark white of the polymer was no substitute for marble.

"The proportions are a little off, don't you think?" asked Glad, eyeing a certain part of the statue's anatomy. Holly and Fran both began to giggle at the tiny plastic penis jutting out from the junction of his legs.

"Seriously, I don't need a statue or a fountain. I need to get that mess cleaned up before I even think about anything else," Glad reminded them, and they moved on to the next booth.

The late February thaw had surprised the community of Mill Falls with a glimpse of spring and shocked Glad when she moved into her new home five days ago. The back yard looked nothing like the pictures the real estate site had offered; the 'dreamy retreat' had morphed into an ugly nightmare of overgrown bushes and strangling vines.

"I really am sorry," Holly said as they examined a display of lawn tools.

"It's not your fault," Glad insisted. Her best friend since college and a resident of Mill Falls, Holly had discovered a house for sale right after Glad had accepted her new job as assistant director of the public library. Between tying up loose ends and the weather, Glad couldn't make it up to Ohio to see the house. Trusting Holly's judgment, she made an offer sight unseen, only too glad to leave her life in the greater D.C. area behind.

"I still can't believe you never looked in the back yard," Fran, one of Holly's besties and Glad's new hairdresser, snorted.

"Why would I?" Holly protested. "It was covered in snow!"

"It's fine," Glad assured her. "I love the house, and I'll deal with the yard. It'll just take a little time." And she had plenty of that, nothing *but* that.

After Glad had shown her the mess, Holly had suggested they attend an upcoming lawn and garden show and get some ideas, and here she was going from booth to booth, her mind boggled by the endless array of plants, outdoor furniture, garden structures and accessories. The place was packed; even though the temperatures had plummeted back to freezing and March had roared in with another eight inches of snow the other day, Ohio was ready for spring to arrive.

"There's so much to do out there I can't even imagine where to start," Glad said. "But I have to do something. I can't leave my yard looking like that."

"Just hire someone," Fran said blithely, then exclaimed, "Here they are! This is our local company. Ken! Kennnn!" She rushed to a large corner booth, waving her hands.

"I'm going to duck into the restroom," Holly said. "I'll meet you back here in a minute."

"Okay," Glad said, and followed Fran to the booth. The banner on the front read "Green Spaces, Mill Falls Ohio". The booth was bursting with artfully placed color, including a gorgeous potted dogwood tree at the front corner, somehow in full bloom. Dogwoods had always been a favorite of Glad's; she usually preferred the white blooms, but this sweet pale pink was amazing. She carefully traced a silky petal with one finger.

"Like it?" asked a deep, husky voice.

Glad started and looked around. A man was under the dogwood, his long fingers pushing into the soil. She watched him take several strange looking spikes from his pocket and insert them into the holes made by his fingers.

"It's lovely. What are you doing?" she asked, curious.

"Keeping this thing blooming," he said.

4

"Freezing temps and flowering trees don't exactly mix." He poured some water on, then looked up at her.

Sepia brown eyes, wild black hair, a full beard and mustache. Not at all the type of man she usually found attractive. But...

"So. Looking for something?" he asked, eyes assessing her.

I could look at you all day. "I-I'm just-"

He raised a thick black brow and slowly smiled. And she felt her cheeks turn as pink as the dogwood blossoms.

"Glad, honey, come here!" Fran waved her over. "This is Ken Anderson, the owner of Green Spaces. You know, that huge greenhouse operation south of town? Ken, this is Glad Donahue. She just bought a house on Lincoln."

Glad shook hands with Ken and he said, "Saw you admiring the dogwood. They're always a nice choice."

"I'd love one, but first I need to clear out a space for it."

"She's got troubles!" Fran proceeded to fill Ken in on all the jobs that needed to be done at Glad's house. Then Ken was handing her a business card, a brochure and several other items with the reminder to "Come see us, anytime."

"Ken Anderson is a really nice guy, and he runs an honest business," Fran told her as they walked away. "They're a little more expensive, but worth every dime."

"I don't know," replied Glad evasively. Yes, the yard was a lot of work, but she could do it; she wanted to. Work was what she needed right now; it kept her mind off other far less pleasant things. Like the past.

Holly appeared out of nowhere and chimed in. "Oh, honey, just bite the bullet and hire it out. Trust me, you don't want to be pulling weeds all summer when you can be sipping margaritas and wearing a bikini."

Glad laughed, took one more look back at the dogwood tree. That glorious pink glowed above the heads of the crowd.

And set off the deep black hair of the man watching her walk away. She caught her breath and warmth flooded her. Okay, he seriously needed a haircut and a shave but he was...wow, was he ever.

Her arm was nearly pulled from its socket by an excited Fran. "Look! Teak! I need this!"

"More teak," Holly groused, and grinned at Glad.

And they moved on.

"You've had a great first month," Chris Harmon, her boss and the director of the library, said. "Your PR ideas must be working, because program attendance is up and circulation bumped up too this month."

"Great!" Glad was pleased. She'd been worried most about the marketing aspect of her new position and had worked her butt off, often staying late or putting in extra time on weekends to make sure the library was being promoted all over town. And it looked like it was paying off. Hopefully the statistics would continue to improve. "Working here is really great. The patrons are so nice and most of the staff have welcomed me right in."

"I'd ask who hasn't, but I probably know." Chris stuffed some papers into a folder and sighed. "Every crop has a bad apple or two. They'll adjust."

"Well, I'm not planning on leaving anytime soon, so I hope you're right. I love it here."

"That's good news." Chris pushed the folder aside and looked at her. "In fact, that's real good news, because I'm thinking about retiring sometime next year."

Glad felt her mouth drop. "What?"

"Retiring. I'll have my thirty in and my wife wants to move to Dallas to be closer to our son and the grandkids." He looked at her again. "It's early days yet, but I think you may turn out to be a good candidate for director here."

"Me?" she squeaked, shocked.

"You're young, but you've got a steady, practical head on your shoulders. You've been doing a great job so far; the board loves you-"

"Not Marie Stahl," Glad corrected him. The board president had protested her hiring strenuously, somehow convinced that at thirty-two and unmarried Glad was as flighty as a teenager and one breath away from running amok.

"Marie Stahl hates everyone," Chris said. "But she'll be done with her board duties in a couple of years."

"You know that won't stop her from hassling us every moment," Glad said wryly.

"Probably not." Chris chuckled. "But I am serious about this. Keep up the good work, keep your nose clean, and I'll have no qualms about recommending you. As long as you want the position, that is."

Her, a library director? Yes, definitely. This was success, proof positive that in spite of everything she'd persevered and come out on top. That she'd won.

She smiled at Chris, confident. "Of course I do."

The afternoon hours were quiet. Chris had taken off after lunch, leaving Glad with a vague excuse of "somewhere to be", which likely meant he was heading for the driving range in Glen View. She didn't blame him; the weather today was almost spring-like after two days of chill and rain and she'd like nothing better than to get outside. Hopefully the weather would hold over the weekend so she could start working in her back yard. She wasn't looking forward to it, but she knew she had to get started back there. Of course, she had to finish steaming off all that awful wallpaper on the first floor, and paint, and maybe she could rip that carpet out as well. Holly had mentioned something about a 'big garbage day' the first week of each month-

Her office phone buzzed. "This is Glad," she answered.

"We've got a problem." It was Marci, the head of Circulation.

"What's up?" Glad asked, stifling a groan.

Apparently one afternoon's worth of peace and quiet was too much for a girl to ask for.

"Can I come to your office?"

"Sure."

A minute later Marci entered, a browsing basket in her arms.

"What's going on?" Glad asked.

"Ellie was shelving over in the DVD section and she found this." Marci put the basket on Glad's desk and tilted it towards her. Inside was a small clear bag with a chunky, whitish substance in it. Glad's eyes widened.

"That's a problem."

"You can say that again," Marci said, running a hand over her short cropped hair. "I nearly fell over when I saw it."

"Did either of you touch it?"

"No. Ellie came and got me and we used a DVD to push it into the basket."

"Did anyone else see it?" Glad asked. "Patrons? Other employees?"

"Not as far as I know."

"Where's Ellie now?"

"In the sorting room. I told her to keep this to herself. She's a good worker, she won't blab."

If true, that made Ellie the sole person on staff who didn't gossip. Glad considered the baggie a moment, then reached for the phone.

Two minutes later Cathy Douglas and Deb Jacobs, heads of Youth Services and Reference, respectively, entered her office. Jim Wheeling, in charge of building maintenance, was also present.

"We have a problem." Glad tilted the basket

forward. Gasps went up, shocked gazes turned to hers.

"A page found this tucked into the DVDs this afternoon," Glad informed them.

"What is it?" asked Jim. "Coke or meth or what?"

"I have no idea," Glad said. "I've called the police and they're sending an officer over in a bit to pick it up. I guess we'll find out soon enough."

"Where did it come from?" Deb asked.

"I don't know."

"But...why would someone leave something like that here?" Cathy asked.

"It's a drop," Glad said. A round of gasps went up and Glad continued, "It appears that someone has figured out the library is a great place to hide things. This could be a one-time thing or it could turn into a regular location for the pushers."

"But," Deb looked horrified, "we don't have drug dealers in Mill Falls!"

Glad understood their reluctance to believe. Mill Falls was a thriving town with tree-lined streets, historic homes, excellent schools and a lovely downtown shopping area that surrounded a large, park-like square where concerts and festivals were held during the year. It was hard to accept that such an ugly truth was rearing its head here.

"There's drug dealers everywhere," Glad said softly. "Even here. It could be someone local or someone from Akron or Cleveland looking to expand their business."

"You want us to search the building?" Jim

asked.

"Yes. Quietly. Don't alarm anyone. If you find anything send me a text. I will look through the coffee shop and meeting room area, then help Marci and Cathy with the rest of downstairs. Jim, can you help Deb in Reference and Archives?"

"Yes I can." Jim got up from his chair and the rest followed.

Glad stood. "I know it's close to closing time and it's the last thing you want to do, but please be thorough. Check every drawer and shelf, especially top and bottom as they are out of normal sight lines." She fixed each manager with her firmest gaze. "One more thing. I'm sure you understand the importance of keeping this information to yourselves for the time being."

They all nodded, understanding. Gossip rushed through their small community like spring runoff in the Mill River and the last thing the library needed was for this to be blown out of proportion. Drugs in the library would be a public relations nightmare.

"All right. Let's do this."

The search turned up nothing more, but Glad still had work to do. She wrote up a report and waited after hours for the police department to pick up the drugs and for the sheriff's department to conduct a search with the county drug dog. The dog acted excited around the same spot in the DVDs where the drugs had been stashed, but did not highlight any other area.

It was nerve-wracking and exhausting. And now Glad would need to work tomorrow, keeping an eye out for unusual activity. Unless there was a bona fide emergency Chris did not set foot in the library on weekends. And unfortunately, the Mill Falls Police Department did not have the manpower to post someone at the library all day long.

Glad got out of her car and trudged up her back steps. She stopped a moment on her small back porch and took in the yard. Large, overgrown bushes and a mass of trailing vines choked the space so thoroughly she could barely see the ground beneath. The tree behind her garage looked dead; too bad, because she liked its craggy branches drooping down. She had no idea what lay beyond it. She'd been too busy since she'd moved in-and a little afraid, to be honest-to venture to the far back.

It was a huge mess and would take months to get in any sort of shape. But it was home. It wouldn't cheat or lie, humiliate or abandon her. No one would take it away from her either.

If she could only say the same for her dignity. Glad sighed and shook her head. Past was past, and better to keep it behind her where it belonged.

The phone started ringing inside. Glad unlocked her back door, dropped her bag on the kitchen table and answered. "Hello?"

"You look like you need a drink!" said Frank Delacroix, her next door neighbor. He missed nothing.

"Would you think badly of me if I asked for two?" she asked.

"Never that. Get yourself over here, doll. We've got beer and salsa waiting for you!"

"Terrific! I'll be over in a minute."

"Hurry up, already!" He hung up.

Glad went upstairs, smiling. Her next door neighbors were two of the nicest people she'd ever met. Frank owned Serenity Day Spa in town, was an avid gardener and nosier than a bloodhound. His partner Sal Amico divided his time between working at the local Urgent Care and as an EMT. Both had welcomed Glad to the neighborhood with open arms and clucked over her like a couple of mother hens.

She entered her bedroom, slipped off her sensible work pumps and took off her suit du jour with a heartfelt sigh, then rummaged in her drawers for something comfortable. Jeans and a faded black tee would do. She stuffed her feet in her worn-out tennis shoes, grabbed a jacket and walked next door.

Frank and Sal never stood on ceremony, so when she pushed open their kitchen door she was greeted with "-libraries are full of old women with buns and glasses, hunched over their books all day long," from Frank and Sal's guest, a big man with his back to her.

Glad put on her sweetest smile. "Am I interrupting?"

Everyone turned to the door. She caught a glimpse of surprised brown eyes, felt her breath catch then Sal was pulling her into a bear hug.

"Here she is! How's tricks, sweetheart? Beer?"

"Definitely!" *Oh, my God, it's him! The guy from the garden show!*

And he looked better than she remembered.

Glad managed to refrain from jumping up and down in her excitement, but it was a close call: all her girly parts were currently standing on their toes, singing hosannas.

"Salsa's on the island," Sal said, then turned back to the fridge. Bottles clinked in the door and he selected one for her.

Frank hugged her, then turned her to face their other guest. "Happy you could make it, doll," he said. "This is Mike Kovalski from Green Spaces. Mike, this is our new neighbor, Glad Donahue."

And her fledgling hopes crashed and burned in front of her eyes. Her mystery man was the infamous One Date Wonder. This was beyond unfair. Why couldn't he be someone else? *Anyone* else?

She'd heard plenty of Mike Kovalski in the short time she'd been in town. The local gossip mill, which had a thriving branch in the Circulation department of her library, tossed his name around on a regular basis. He was a heartless playboy, charming women into his bed right, left and sideways. He'd slept with, depending on who was gossiping, anywhere from twenty to sixty women, and never the same one twice. Pretty amazing record considering he was relatively new to town as well; he'd only been around about six or eight months.

Close up he was taller and broader than she remembered, burly and tough looking. Definitely not a man she'd normally find interesting; his looks were too dark and intense. But that thrill of attraction remained, coursing through her as his warm, rough hand took hers and shook it briefly. She'd have to get over that, and quick. Glad swallowed her disappointment and managed a polite smile.

"It's nice to meet you," she said.

"Pleasure's mine," he said. "I think we've met before."

"Yes-" And Sal came to the rescue, stuffing a beer bottle in her hand and directing them to the island. "Sit and eat! That salsa isn't getting any younger!"

"So you're Glad, like...happy?" Mike asked as they sat. "Were your parents hippies or something?"

She'd fielded questions like this forever. "No."

"Tell him your full name, doll," Frank said grinning.

"I'd rather not."

"What, is it bad?" Mike asked. "Tell me."

"No. And if you tell him," she said, staring Frank down, "I will make you sorry you were ever born." She turned to Sal, eager to change the subject. "What's in the salsa tonight?"

"Mangoes. And a little pinch of habanero. Sweet and hot, just like you."

Glad laughed, delighted. "I don't know about hot, but I'll take sweet." She tried a bite. "Ooh! Nice." She took another.

"Careful," said Mike. "Those habaneros catch up with you."

She glanced across the island. His dark gaze was steady on her face and she felt...admired. It was a little disconcerting.

Who was she kidding? It was a *lot* disconcerting. She shouldn't be attracted to a philandering man-whore. Even if he did have big, broad shoulders and, dear God, chest hair sticking out at the neck of his shirt. She was a complete sucker for chest hair.

"Glad's from D.C. originally, just like you," Frank said to Mike.

"Virginia, actually," she corrected. "Leesburg."

"I grew up around Potomac," Mike said. "We're practically neighbors." He took a chip and met her eyes again. "I haven't seen you around town."

Had he wondered about her, too? Glad thrilled inside, then quickly remembered what a bad idea that was and replied, "I haven't been here long. I got my job, a friend found my house and I moved in about a month ago."

"And swept it right out from under me," he said with a rueful smile.

"What?" she asked, confused.

"The house. I called to see it and it was already contingent."

He'd wanted to buy her house?

"You moved fast," he went on, his gaze fixed on her.

"I don't mess around."

"I'll bet." He studied her, just long enough to make her squirm, then said, "So. What do you do for a living?"

Glad glanced at Frank and Sal before replying. They were both grinning like Cheshire cats, waiting for the hammer to come down. She looked back into Mike Kovalski's deep brown eyes, put on her sweetest smile and said, "I'm a librarian."

2

Mike decided then and there to kill Frank Delacroix at his earliest opportunity. The man had trapped him with that innocuous talk about downtown, which led to talk of the library, which led to Mike putting his size thirteens right in his big mouth just as that living dream from the garden show walked into their house.

Now he looked steadily at Glad Donahue, fighting his embarrassment while noticing her eyes. They were a warm, bourbon brown like her hair, with some flecks of green and gold.

"You're a librarian," he said, still locked on to her eyes. What did they call eyes like hers? Hazel? He wasn't sure.

"Yes. I'm the assistant director at Mill Falls Public Library."

Shit. Okay. Stay calm. She doesn't look pissed off exactly, so...

He put down his beer. Cleared his throat. "Well. All right."

"If it makes you feel better, I do wear reading glasses," she said.

"But no buns. At least not yet," Frank added.

Mike gave Frank a heavy look then turned back to Glad Donahue. Chose his next words with care. "I'm obviously mistaken in my assumptions. Will you accept my apology?"

She blushed a becoming shade of pink. "I-well, it's just an opinion. You're entitled to have one."

"So I am," he agreed, and picked up his beer bottle again.

"Just like I might have the opinion that men with long hair and beards look... seedy," she said.

"Seedy?" Okay, so he hadn't had a haircut since November, but his hair wasn't that long, not really. And he liked his beard!

"It's just an opinion," Sal remarked, grinning from ear to ear under his perfectly trimmed facial hair.

"Does she tell you that you look seedy?" Mike asked him.

"Never," Sal said.

"But Sal keeps his beard nice and neat. Yours is totally out of hand," Frank pointed out.

"I trimmed it last week!"

"It's practically the end of March, doll. Spring is springing and all that. Shave it already!"

"I'll shave when I'm good and ready," he growled at Frank.

"Pax, you two," Sal said, then he turned to Glad. "These two bicker like a couple of old biddies at Bingo night."

Glad laughed. She had a low, sexy laugh. And a lush mouth he was dying to kiss right now. Just once, to see if she tasted as good as she looked.

Mike mentally shook himself. It would hardly be good manners to reach across the island and plant one on her. Even less mannerly would be drawing notice to his sudden and growing erection, were he to stand and make that move.

"So, any good stories from the library this week?" asked Sal.

Glad smiled. "Just one," she said.

"Let me guess. The Perv returned!"

"No-"

"Can't be," Frank interrupted. "He moved away, remember?"

"Who's the Perv?" Mike asked Frank.

"Local wacko that used to flash his junk around," Frank said. "My turn! Edna Frees and her Chihuahuas stopped by!"

"Edna-oh! The little old lady with the gigantic purse?" At their nods she went on, "I knew it! I knew there was something going on there!"

Mike chuckled along with the others. Edna Frees had the heart of a trickster behind her sweet elderly lady façade.

"I tell you," Frank said, "if she brings those little bastards into Serenity one more time I'm going to lose it. She takes them out when she thinks no one's looking-"

"-and they piss and shit everywhere," Mike finished. Last fall Edna let her dogs out for "a little walkies" at Green Spaces and it took Mike and six other staff members over an hour to corral them. The male, Mickey, was sweet and docile. The female, Minnie, tried to take a bite out of his boot whenever he got close. While he'd wanted to blister their elderly owner for letting her dogs loose in a public space, he bit his tongue. Edna was his landlady.

"Thank God she hasn't brought them to the Urgent Care," Sal commented, then said to Glad, "Wait! I know what it is! Surprise in the bathroom!"

"Bingo!" Glad laughed and clinked her beer bottle to his. Mike was charmed all over again by that sexy laugh, those pretty eyes and her wavy hair glowing brown and amber and copper under the pendant lamps.

"What was it this time?" asked Frank.

"One of the pages said the men's toilet up front was clogged yesterday afternoon," Glad began. "So Jim went to fix it and next thing I know he's calling me to come in there. So I go in and he says 'watch your step' and he's standing in the middle of a puddle holding a big purple thong with a pair of pliers. And-"

"Wait. What?" Mike interrupted, lost.

"Ohh, nice!" Frank said, laughing.

"Holy shit! A thong?" Sal asked, shocked.

"In the men's room?" Mike asked, still lost.

"And I said 'where did that come from?' and he said 'that's what was clogging the toilet' and then-"

"OHHH!" Mike, Sal and Frank chorused as one.

"And then Lazlo Park came in and used the urinal," she finished.

"You know Lazlo?" Frank asked him.

Mike nodded. Who didn't? The man was a regular menace. He lived in Mike's neighborhood, walked his scrawny old dog everywhere, yelled obscenities at passing cars and kids from his front porch and dropped his trash bags at other houses so he didn't have to pay for garbage pickup. Lazlo had given him a wide berth since Mike busted him at 4 a.m. recently, trying to drop his trash in Mike's cans.

"He whipped it out right in front of you?" Sal asked, scandalized.

"Like I wasn't even there. And let me just add that he does *not* wash his hands after. May I have another beer?"

"If I had a day like that I'd be doing shots," Mike said.

"We had another reason for having you over," Frank said to him.

"Are you ready to put in that lilac?" Mike asked, grinning. Frank hated lilacs.

"Do not start with that," said Frank. "Really, we called you over for her." He waved his bottle in Glad's direction.

If that only meant what he wanted it to mean. Mike turned to her. "What can I do for you?"

"It's nothing, really-"

"It's her yard," Sal interrupted gleefully, dumping avocados, a lime and a jalapeno pepper on the island. "It's a bit of a mess."

"It's a hellhole," Frank corrected him, "and she needs your help-"

22

"And you know that West bitch-"

"-who thinks she owns Green Spaces-"

"-wouldn't give her the time of day," Sal finished, pulling a big knife out of his block.

"Caroline wouldn't give you an appointment?" Mike asked Glad.

She shook her head. "Frank and Sal recommended Green Spaces, so I went there last Saturday to inquire about landscaping and, well, she wasn't exactly nice. She told me you all were booked through the summer and then just walked away."

"Great," Mike sighed, exasperated. He'd have to talk to Ken about Caroline's attitude problem. Not that it would do any good; Ken thought Caroline was a star employee even though she was regularly snappish with customers, especially female ones, and downright rude to the other employees. She'd hit on him hard the first week he'd worked there; it had taken three rejections before she'd finally taken the hint and he'd been on her shit list ever since.

Glad went on, looking mortified. "It's okay! I mean, I'm sure you're busy..."

"I'll take a look," he said. "It can't be that bad."

"Oh, yes it can," Frank said, crunching on a chip.

"You don't have to," she said.

And pass up a chance to get her alone? Oh, no. He was all in.

"Yes, I do." He stood. "Because if I don't I'll never hear the end of it from these two. Let's go."

23

***

Glad took Mike next door. "The house isn't pretty inside," she warned him. "I've been stripping wallpaper out of the living room."

"Let me guess. Giant cabbage roses."

She laughed softly and he smiled at her. "No. Eagles and bears and pine trees."

"Nice."

"It was pretty scary in there." She risked a glance. He was taking in the front façade, eyes roving over the siding and shakes, the porch and front door. She saw admiration, and more than a little regret in his eyes.

"So. You like Thai food?" he asked as they started up the steps.

"I love it," she said.

"You want to go get some when we're done here?"

Glad tripped and grabbed the rail.

"You all right?"

She faced him. "I'm fine. Did you just…"

"I just asked you out." He smiled and her heart stuttered. She really needed to get over this attraction. Think man-whore. Man-whore.

"That was fast."

"I don't mess around, either. What do you say?"

Glad forced a laugh and waved him off. "No, thank you!"

Mike followed her up to the porch. "Why not?"

"I wasn't in town three days before I heard

about the One Date Wonder," she said, sticking her key in the deadbolt. Behind her Mike huffed out a breath.

"That's just gossip."

"There's plenty of that around this town. Especially concerning you."

No answer; he just stared at her, his brow furrowed. Glad opened the front door and changed the subject. "I think this door is original to the house. I'd like to get a screen door for the front, so I can catch a breeze in the summer."

"Good idea," he said, running an appreciative hand around the leaded glass panels as he stepped inside. Then he stopped. "Huh. I expected this to look more like Frank and Sal's house. It's totally different."

He sounded okay; she relaxed a bit. "My realtor told me most American Foursquares don't have a central hallway. It breaks the house up, but I kind of like it."

"Me too. Man, this is great trim work." She watched his big hand trace the detailing around the living room doorway and shivered. What would it feel like if he traced her 'detailing'?

No, no, no. Do not even think of going there.

Thankfully Mike didn't notice her discomfort. He was now staring at the floor in disgusted awe. "Nice carpet," he commented.

"You don't like forest green shag?"

"Does anyone like shag?" He took one step into the living room, where Glad's furniture was pushed to the middle and a rented steamer stood waiting. "Where's that wallpaper?"

"All gone. My bookshelves are much

happier now." She pointed at the impressive shelving that flanked the fireplace.

"They're pretty sweet. Does the fireplace work?" he asked as they continued down the hall.

"I don't know. I haven't tried it yet." Glad glanced up at him. His alert, interested eyes were taking in everything, tracing moldings and trim, admiring the woodwork on the stair rail.

"Oh, wow." Mike stopped and gazed up at the leaded glass window at the half landing. It was a classic Mission design in muted gray, amber and green.

"Try to imagine it without the wallpaper."

Mike took in the silver and gold fleur-de-lis patterned paper and grinned. "That's awful."

"You didn't see the eagles and bears. Oh, and my dining room is pink and yellow roses, with pink shag."

"Pretty," he commented. Smiled at her and her stomach fluttered.

He's not saying that you're pretty. Get over it.

"What's in there?" He pointed back at the front room opposite the living room. Its glass paneled doors were shut.

"Nothing."

"And nothing in your dining room either. Lot of empty house for one person," he said.

"It is," she said. "But I'm in love with it. Every detail," her fingers traced over a pattern of acorns cut into the trim over the kitchen doorway, "every little extra, like the laundry chute and the leaded glass... it's exactly what I wanted."

Mike stepped into the kitchen. "Yikes.

26

There's no way you wanted *this*."

Glad grimaced, looking at the dated cabinets, the harvest gold eighties appliances and puke yellow flooring. "It's pretty awful, but everything works. I can live with it for a while."

"I redid the kitchen in my rental," he said, opening and closing a cabinet door. "It's not that hard. You can buy stock cabinets, lay down some vinyl…"

"So you do kitchens as well as landscaping?"

He smiled. "Just to keep busy over the winter. Landlord didn't care, and one of my guys does carpentry on the side. He helped me out."

"Where do you live?" Glad opened the back door and went down the steps into the yard.

"I'm on Academy Street-" he stopped and sucked in a breath. "*Oy, vey!*"

"I told you!" floated over. Glad spied Frank's bald head popping up over the privacy fence.

Mike stepped into the yard and surveyed the mess, chuckling. "This is *bad*!"

"Welcome to the jungle!" Sal yelled out their back door.

"You'll probably find Jimmy Hoffa back there somewhere!" Frank added. Sal guffawed, his rusty laugh echoing in the evening still.

"Oh, hush up!" Glad scolded, mortified.

Mike walked farther into the yard, looked all around him. He checked some branches on the tree behind the garage and examined several other plants. He turned back to Glad.

"How big is the lot?"

"Almost two acres."

"Nice. Is it all fenced?"

"I think so, but it's pieced together. There might be gaps."

"You attached to any of this?" he asked, indicating the plant life.

She shrugged. "I guess not. I've only been here a little while."

"Good." He mumbled to himself as he carefully moved into the far back of the lot. Glad caught "pear" and "weigela" and something that sounded like "berberis" but couldn't make out any more. Mike reappeared and broke a twig off the dead tree. He peeled it, nodded his head and looked around for another minute, then returned to the back steps. Glad held her breath.

"Well, I'd like to say I've seen worse, but honestly, I can't remember when."

"But I can fix it, right?" Glad asked.

"By yourself?" he asked, shocked.

"Yes."

He looked her up and down. "You're kidding me."

"I'm not helpless," she said, annoyed.

Mike shook his head. "Listen. This is a bitch of a project. See those vines? That's wisteria. It's all rooted, running and tangled above and below ground. You could pull it up for a year and it would still keep coming back. Your Seckel pear is in bad shape, maybe dead, there's an overgrown barberry back there that you do not want to tangle with, plus the thistle, the briars...geez. I don't think there's one blade of actual grass back here." He put his hands on his hips. "I strongly recommend you get a crew out here before this really starts greening up."

Glad waved a hand. "I can handle cleaning this up."

Mike blew out a harsh sigh. "Girl-"

"She's gonna kill herself!" Frank proclaimed from next door, then the screen door slammed shut.

Mike glanced next door, then back at her. "I agree with Frank. This is too much for one person to handle."

Irritated, she snapped back, "For heaven's sake, I'm capable of more than just hunching over books!"

Mike winced and Glad felt a brief moment of shame for digging at him. Then she squashed it. Too bad. She'd spent years getting past her weaknesses. She wasn't about to walk that path again.

"I'm not questioning your abilities," he said. "I'm just stating a fact. This is a tough job with a lot of injury potential. I don't want you to get hurt."

"Hey!" called Sal's gravelly voice from next door. "The guac won't stay green forever!"

"We're coming!" Glad called back, then she looked at Mike. "I understand your concerns," she said stiffly. "But I'm doing this on my own."

"Fine." Mike dug out his wallet and handed over a business card. "You run into trouble, and you will, contact me. We'll work something out."

She ignored the card. "I don't need you."

"I got that." He stepped forward and tucked his card into her jeans pocket. "Keep it anyway.

Just in case."

His fingers slowly left her pocket but his heat lingered and she felt claimed, possessed. Glad looked up; his dark eyes fixed on hers, held her in thrall. A long, silent minute passed. She couldn't think or move, could barely breathe. It would be so easy to just reach out and-

She forced herself back to reality.

"As I said before, no thank you." Before she could think twice about it she pulled his card out and boldly stuffed it into his pocket. Tit for tat.

It was warm in there. Oh, boy. Her fingers were right next to his-

She yanked her hand away. Mike raised a brow and smiled. She felt heat in her cheeks and cursed herself.

"We'd better get back," she said.

Mike studied her face a moment longer, then stepped away.

"After you."

3

"Mike, you got a sec?" Ken Anderson, his boss and the owner of Green Spaces, waved him to his office. Mike put down the fertilizer bags he was hauling and headed over. Despite being hired on to do landscape design, Mike was expected to work in the greenhouses as well, at least until the design end of the business required more of his time.

In addition, he had been put in charge of a crew consisting of a largely silent former marine named Greg Turk, a thirtysomething smart-aleck named John Fonzi and a weathered, skinny little man who looked old enough to be his grandfather but could outwork him any day of the week.

Harry Phelps was a character. He had strong opinions and wasn't afraid to share them, proclaiming his dislike of his crew boss on day one, calling Mike a 'goddamn mop-headed Kike' among other things. Mike had ignored the slurs, knowing he needed to prove himself to the older man and, over time, Harry's opinion had mellowed somewhat. Now most days he would grunt a hello to Mike then take turns bitching at Fonz and Turk to get off their dead asses and do some work for a change. They were an interesting group, and he wouldn't trade them for anything.

Mike stepped into Ken's office. "What's up?"

"Close the door, would you?" Ken asked.

Okay, that was a little odd; Ken never shut his door. Mike closed it and took a seat.

"I need to ask you something kind of personal," Ken said, settling himself behind his desk. "And I need you to tell me the truth."

"Shoot."

Ken cleared his throat. "How many women have there been?"

"Excuse me?" He couldn't have heard what he just heard.

"Since you moved here. How many women have you been with?"

Mike studied Ken a moment. "Are you talking dates, or women I've slept with?" he asked warily.

"The women you've slept with. Just a number, I don't want names or details."

Okay, he was officially worried. "Three."

Ken's mouth dropped. "*Three?*"

Was that a lot? "Uh… yeah."

"That's the truth? You're not lying to me?"

"No. What's going on?"

Ken sighed, exasperated. "Jesus Christ in a sidecar." He looked at Mike and shook his head.

"You know what the number is around town, Romeo? Try thirty."

"Thirty…"

"That you've screwed around with thirty different women."

Mike's jaw hit the floor. "*What?*"

"Some err on the side of caution and figure you've only done about twenty, and there's a few nuts that swear you're up to sixty or more. I was figuring ten or fifteen myself, but either way, you currently own the crown as the biggest sleaze in Mill Falls history."

Mike knew his mouth was hanging open. But it just wouldn't shut. Twenty? Thirty? *Sixty?* What was going on here?

"Ken, I-"

His boss slammed a hand on his desk. "Damn it, Mike! You've been here, what, eight months and your reputation's gone to hell in a bowling bag overnight! What were you thinking?"

"I wasn't-"

"Obviously! Don't you know anything about Mill Falls yet? Gossip's like breathing here! Shit gets blown out of proportion so fast it'll make your head spin! Don't tell me you don't know that!"

"I don't!" Mike protested, feeling his face flame hot. But suddenly it was making sense, things clicking into place so fast he could barely keep up. The funny looks, the catty remarks, the whispers and pointing in the grocery and other places around town. The dirty looks from the husbands and the assessing looks from the wives.

And those dismissing comments from Frank and Sal's sexy new neighbor. He knew people talked around this town, but he'd had no idea how much. Yes, it all made sense now.

"What the hell did you think was going to happen when you're skirting around like that?"

"I just...I don't know, I was bored! I just wanted to relax and have some fun, so I went out with a few women. I didn't know it had escalated like that, Ken. I swear."

"I didn't know it was this bad either. Not until this morning."

"What happened this morning?" Mike didn't want to know. He really didn't.

"I got two calls. One from Sam Jeffers and the other from Jim Delaney. They both wanted out of their contracts."

"We just signed them. I've almost got the drafts done. Why?"

"They don't want you around their wives."

Mike stared at Ken, speechless.

"This is serious, son. Gossip's out of control." Ken stopped and gave him a grave look. "I like you, Mike. You're one damned fine landscape architect and I think you've got a lot to give Green Spaces. But I can't lose business over you."

Mike went cold. "Are you-do you want me to go?"

"I want you to straighten your shit up. Green Spaces has a solid, seventy-year reputation as a family business. We're a fixture in this community! Christ, the wife and I hand out communion at church on Sundays! We're good, upstanding people and you're slapping us in the face with your behavior."

"Ken, I'm so sorry. I never intended for this to happen."

"I'm sure you didn't, but you screwed up and you need to fix it. I'll give you thirty days to shut this gossip down or you're done here."

Mike clamped down hard on the panic rising in his gut. "I..." he foundered, "I'm not sure what..."

"I'll tell you exactly what. Stop picking up bar bimbos and get yourself a real girlfriend. Someone regular, you know, a nice girl."

A nice girl. *Oy* freaking *vey*. "I don't know if I can do a relationship." Definitely not now. Even though he hadn't thought much of Rachel lately, the fallout from her betrayal was still bitter in his heart.

"Who said anything about a relationship? Just find a girl you like and be with her a while. Six months maybe. Show the town you're respectable, you know? Then when the gossip dies down and business picks back up, you can break things off. Easy, right?"

Easy? Nice girls didn't do easy. Nice girls expected things like weekends spent antique shopping. Or at craft fairs. Yeesh. "I'm not sure about this."

"Listen, people fall in and out of relationships every day. This isn't any different."

It was totally different. It was using someone for his own gain. It was pretending he felt something he didn't.

But if he didn't do something drastic, he'd

be standing in the unemployment line. He had no choice. "Okay. I'll do it. I'll figure it out."

"That's what I want to hear!" Ken pushed away from his desk and stood. "It'll be fine! And don't forget, meet me at the library at three. We've got that meeting with Chris Harmon about their beautification project."

"What if they don't want me, either?" Mike asked.

"They don't have a choice. The bequest specified us." Ken's face brightened. "And you know, this project could make a real difference."

"How?"

"Well, it'll make you look better, for one. This is a big job, a job for the whole community. Do it well and you'll get noticed in a good way."

And it wouldn't hurt Green Spaces or Ken's wallet, either, Mike supposed. "I'll do my best."

"Of course you will! I'm counting on it."

***

After prowling the stacks all day Saturday and steaming wallpaper on Sunday until her arms felt like they would fall off, Glad went to work the following week worn out. She met with Chris and the police on Monday over the drug incident and learned there were no leads to speak of. They were advised to install security cameras, a measure Chris vetoed immediately.

"Board won't go for it," he said. "Too much money, they say it every damn time."

On Tuesday, she met with more officers of the law, Lord County liaison officers this time in charge of community service sentencing. Mill Falls Public Library would soon be receiving its first offender to work off time.

Jimmer Hall was a small-time troublemaker in his early twenties. His prior offenses received not more than a slap on the wrist, but he'd recently upped his game, breaking into the cemetery while high as a kite and spray-painting a gravestone for shits and giggles. He'd been heavily fined and sentenced to a hundred hours of community service, to be performed at the library.

Glad wasn't impressed with their candidate. Jimmer Hall was wiry and lean with gauges in his ears and tattoos on his forearms. He'd protested her insistence he wear long sleeves to work, seeing nothing wrong with the naked, spread-eagled woman on his left arm or the fiery snake-eating devil-skull...*thing* on his right.

"We see a lot of young children in this building, Jimmer," she said. "Those images are explicit and disturbing and could frighten them."

"Who gives a shit about some kids?" he asked with a surly smile Glad recognized at once. He was testing her, convinced he could best a mere woman. So not going to happen.

"We do," she said coldly. "Our children are very important to us. We take their welfare and happiness seriously. While you are performing your community service in this building you will keep them covered at all times."

"What if I don't?"

"Then you can do your time in the county lockup."

Jimmer Hall scowled and grumbled but finally gave in with a "whatever." Glad was not looking forward to the next five weeks.

Today she was buried in paperwork, writing month-end reports and looking at budget figures when her inside line rang. Youth Services. "What's up?" she answered.

"It's Cathy. I'm in a pickle."

"What's the matter?"

"Well, you know it's spring break, and we've got that big dance party scheduled this afternoon and Sandy was supposed to help me with it-"

"Let me guess," Glad interrupted. "She called off sick." Sandy was, without a doubt, the laziest staff member in existence. Glad would have happily fired her, but she was related somehow to Marie Stahl and was untouchable to that extent. It was frustrating beyond belief, the hold that old woman had over this place.

"Close," Cathy said with a sigh. "She sprained her ankle. And Lou is out of town this week with her family. And I thought maybe since you used to be a children's librarian…" She trailed off.

Glad considered. On one hand, she had no desire to show the world just how bad a dancer she was and could spend this next hour finishing up her paperwork. On the other, she was so tired of paperwork. And though she loved being an administrator, she did miss her days working with children.

"What time does the dance party start?" Glad asked.

"Two o'clock."

She had a meeting with Chris at three to go over plans for a beautification project. The library had received a healthy bequest from the Stone family two years ago to be used for landscaping and outside improvements. Thanks to bad timing and other events, the project had stalled. They would be meeting with the board in two weeks' time to present a new plan.

"I can fit it in," she said to Cathy. "But I'll have to run home and change first. This suit is not conducive to dancing."

"Oh, thank you! Thank you so much! You've just saved me such a headache!"

"Keep your aspirin handy," Glad said dryly. "Once you see me dance you might need it."

***

Mike parked in the library lot and turned off his truck. He was early. Not that he was so eager for the meeting, but because after that talk with Ken this morning he hadn't been able to face anyone and pretend things were normal. He had some free time so he took a long lunch and drove the back roads of Lord County with his windows down, the chilly, early spring air blowing in and the music up. Way up.

Everything he'd spent the last eight months working for was in jeopardy. A few dates, a few rounds in the sack and now his job was on the line.

He was angry. Frustrated. But mostly he was shamed.

Granted, this was all his own fault and now

he was paying the price. He hadn't thought beyond his own pleasure, hadn't considered the consequences of dating in a small town where gossip was a way of life. After how his last commitment turned out, the very thought of getting into a relationship again made him sick. Getting manipulated, used and tossed aside for the dream man, not to mention losing the esteem of his friends and family over the lies she had told had made him understandably wary.

He'd left his life in tatters back in D.C. and came to Ohio determined to squash his pain by living free and easy. No strictures, no commitments, no problem. He soon discovered there were plenty of single women interested in what little he had to offer, and it had been fun at first. The first three dates had gone straight to the bedroom after the initial drinks or dinner and the encounters had been, if not memorable, certainly enjoyable. But when his fourth date casually threw out that she'd heard how big his dick was and couldn't wait to try it out, he'd hesitated, then stalled when it came time to take her home.

Seven other dates followed, and while each woman had her charms, he hadn't gone any farther than dinner and maybe a kiss goodnight. He'd tried to go farther a couple more times, but the thrill of a one-night stand had dissipated as quickly as it had come. And after the last disaster with Felice Swanson, he'd called it quits on dating altogether.

But the gossip mill apparently hadn't let *him* go. Assumptions had been made, stories had been told. And embroidered beyond recognition if

Ken's hearsay was to be believed. Mike guessed that, in addition to the three, the others had probably lied to their friends because they didn't want to be seen as lacking the charm or sex appeal or whatever it was that would land him in their beds. Women could be just as prideful and full of shit as men, sometimes.

What a mess. A Grade-A clusterfuck, as Harry Phelps would say. He had to figure something out, had to get through this somehow. He didn't want a girlfriend, didn't want to have to go through the motions of a relationship with a person he had no intention of committing to. The pitfalls of that particular avenue were legion; if he didn't do everything exactly right failure was a big, messy guarantee.

But he hadn't thought up any better alternative and miracles didn't happen in modern times. He really had no other choice.

"Girlfriend it is, then," Mike murmured, then blew out a sigh. He checked the clock on his dash. Two forty-one. He'd better get in there and figure out where he was supposed to be. Maybe he'd have enough time to take a few pictures or do a couple sketches. He grabbed his notepad, tucked his smartphone in his pocket and left the truck.

He'd never been inside the Mill Falls Public Library before. Two huge oak trees stood on the front lawn, providing shade and making a big statement. He knew they were the celebrated Mighty Oaks, the oldest trees in Mill Falls. He stopped for a moment, noted a significant amount of broken and dead branches high up. He was no

41

tree expert and it was too early in the year yet to tell but there could be trouble; the trees could be diseased or dying from old age. They'd have to get someone up there to make an assessment.

Mike stepped through the library doors and was assaulted by noise. Granted, he hadn't been in a public library in a long time, but he was pretty sure you were supposed to be quiet once you walked in one.

Not so here. It wasn't loud, but people were chatting and laughing, the self-check machine was beeping and there was music coming from down the hall to his right. Sam Cooke, if he wasn't mistaken.

Mike drifted down the hall, curious. There was a large meeting room down here and it was packed with kids and grownups, twisting the night away. He recognized Cathy Douglas and many others, from meeting them through Green Spaces, gyrating around with a mob of children of all ages and sizes. And off to the left… a thrill coursed through him and he smiled.

Dressed in snug jeans and a Wonder Woman t-shirt, that Kentucky bourbon hair pulled back in a ponytail, Glad Donahue was holding the hands of a young boy, twisting with him, back and forth. The boy was giggling madly and she beamed down at him as she guided them around.

The song ended and he watched her kneel for a big hug from the boy, then wave goodbye as he turned away to his mother. Then she and Cathy Douglas were at the front of the room again, ready to lead the group in a new dance. Oh, gag. The Macarena. But the kids seemed to be excited about it. Cathy started the demo, Glad followed.

Tried to follow. She stopped, started, stopped again, and then announced, laughing, "Don't watch me, watch Miss Cathy!"

Mike checked his watch as he walked away from the room. Ken should be here soon and he should go wait for him. But he'd much rather stay and watch Glad butcher that awful dance.

He'd almost reached the lobby when it hit him and he stopped cold. Right back there, in that Wonder Woman shirt, doing a really bad Macarena, was the solution to his problem.

Glad Donahue was a perfect choice. They'd already met; she was smart, funny and sexy. He definitely wouldn't have to pretend he was interested. And she was a librarian. If that didn't qualify as 'nice' he didn't know what did.

But even though he was sure the attraction between them was mutual, he'd failed utterly the other night. She believed the gossip and wouldn't fall into his arms at the snap of his fingers.

Could he do it? Could he get her to see past his reputation and want to date him? It was risky and he couldn't afford to make a mistake. Everything was riding on this.

But he had one hell of a motivator. And he'd never been one to back down from a challenge.

4

"Glad Donahue, please report to the conference room immediately," came Chris's growly voice over the PA system.

Glad looked sideways at Cathy. The group was silly dancing, courtesy of Jim Gill. "Is it three?"

"No. Two fifty. You'd better call him, at least," Cathy said.

Glad ducked into the hall and dialed the in-house phone.

"Where are you?" barked Chris.

"Outside the meeting room-"

"How come you're not in here? The meeting's started!"

It was supposed to start at three, but she decided not to point that out. Chris lived by his own watch. "I'm helping Cathy finish up a program. I'll be there as soon as we're done."

"I'm sure Cathy can handle her own programs just fine."

"Not when she's understaffed, like today."

Glad heard other voices through the phone. Good grief, had he put her on speaker? Someone said "three o'clock" and Chris said to them, "I'm not Big Ben over here! If everyone's present, the meeting starts!" Then he said, "Cut it short and get up here."

The line clicked loudly in her ear. Glad winced and returned to the dance party.

"Can you live without me?" she asked Cathy.

Cathy eyed the group. "I'd rather be run over by a herd of buffalo, but-oh! It's fast again!" she called to the group. The kids and grown-ups started wiggling faster. "Can you help me set up the limbo poles before you go?"

"Of course."

Five minutes later Glad, still in jeans and her t-shirt, made it to the Conference Room. She knocked once and entered. Chris was schmoozing with Ken Anderson of Green Spaces…and a freshly shaven Mike Kovalski.

She knew he would be here today and had convinced herself she could handle seeing him again. And she would have been okay, would have been perfectly fine, then he went and turned the tables on her.

She'd thought he was sexy with a beard? Shaving that face turned his sexy meter up to eleven. Her heart started pounding hard and she cursed herself.

"I'm sorry I'm so late," she apologized, stepping into the room.

Mike and Ken both stood and she was charmed. Chris, ever a paragon of manners and gentility, only gave her a sideways look.

"What the hell kind of getup is that?" he asked by way of greeting.

"I needed comfortable clothes for the program," Glad said smoothly.

"You look ridiculous."

"I'd look even more ridiculous dancing around in a suit."

"You better hope Marie Stahl doesn't see you." Chris gestured across the table. "Have you met Ken Anderson?"

"I have," she said, shaking Ken's hand. "It's nice to see you again."

"Same here!" Ken said, beaming at her.

"Miss Donahue," Mike said, his slow smile coming on.

"Mr. Kovalski," she replied, doing her best to ignore the thrill his smile gave her.

"You two know each other?" Ken asked.

"We've met, yes," Glad said, then busied herself with sitting down. If she could get through this meeting without looking at him, she'd be fine.

Like that was going to work. He was sitting right across from her, all rough, tough, sexy, six-foot something of him.

Do not *go there! Danger, Will Robinson!*

"Great! That's just great!" Ken said happily. He really was a nice man, Glad decided. Bluff and hearty and always had a smile on his face. And considering he had to be in his fifties he was still fit and only had a small sprinkling of gray in his hair.

"I asked Glad here because she will be your

contact person for this job. If we get board approval this time," Chris said.

"This time?" Glad asked, masking her surprise. *She* would be in charge? Was he joking? Or was this some kind of test?

Chris rolled his eyes. "This will be the third attempt, since our receiving the bequest from the Stone estate, to have the library grounds landscaped in accordance with their wishes. The last time was just over a year ago. Ken and I had a plan, a great presentation..."

"And Marie Stahl shot us down," Ken said, grinning. "But we've got an ace in the hole this time." He whacked Mike on the shoulder. "We'll win her over, no doubt about it."

Mike gave a small smile but said nothing. His big fingers fiddled with the pencil on the table in front of him and his eyes held hers. She shivered and turned her attention to Ken.

"If you want to win over Marie Stahl, you've already lost," Glad said. "She loves to say no. I recommend you go after the other board members instead. If your presentation can convince them, they'll outvote her."

"I'm not presenting this," Ken said. "Mike is."

"And you'll be doing the initial speech and standing by to answer questions," Chris said to her.

She put on her best smile. "Of course!"

Chris grabbed a paper roll and spread it out on the table. "These are the plans we had drawn up. With just a few alterations, I think we can-"

"I draw my own plans, thanks," Mike said

after a dismissive glance at the paper.

Chris looked at him. "We paid thousands for these plans. We're not going to just dump them."

"You paid thousands for landscaping plans done by someone who doesn't know jack shit about landscaping," Mike said.

"Rafe Caldwell's firm is very highly regarded for library design!"

"Rafe Caldwell is an interior designer. Landscaping is a totally different animal. You see this?" Mike pointed at the design. "Your slope is running towards the building."

"So?"

"So you put all those pavers down, make yourself some nice little paths out there and then you get a good thunderstorm and what happens? Water builds up and comes in through these exit doors. Water damage can be costly. And, over time water retention weakens your foundation. And I'll bet..." He flipped over the top sheet. "Of course. No added drainage. So you've got an even bigger problem."

"These plans are perfectly fine!" Chris blustered. "And we're using them whether you like it or not!"

"Then find yourself another boy. I refuse to put my name behind a shoddy project like this."

Glad looked sideways at Chris and grimaced. Chris's face was slowly turning purple and his fingers clenched into fists. An explosion was imminent.

"You think you know everything, don't you, you cocky son of a bitch," he growled.

"I know my job," Mike countered coldly.

"Now, Mike, we can work with this," Ken said, trying to diffuse the situation.

"You *will* work with this!" Chris insisted, furious.

Mike's brows smashed together and he opened his mouth to reply. Glad got there first. "May I say something?"

Ken jumped in, desperate. "Of course!"

"There's no seal from the zoning board on these plans."

"So?" Chris said, still glaring at Mike, uncomprehending.

"So Rafe Caldwell never got these plans approved by the city. We can't use unapproved plans. Furthermore, assuming Mr. Kovalski knows his job-"

"Of course I do," Mike growled at her.

"And considering he won an award for landscape design in D.C., I'd take his word for it when he points out flaws in this design which will end up costing us far more, in money and headaches, down the road."

"So now you're a landscaping expert, too?" Chris asked, sarcasm heavy in his voice.

It took every bit of her self-control to keep her voice calm and her expression sweet. "I'm a librarian. It's my job to stay informed. I don't know much about landscaping, but I'm sure it's wise to have proper drainage around a building's foundation."

"Are you finished?" Chris asked, his voice impatient and clipped.

"Not yet. There's also the matter of copyright infringement."

"What?" Chris and Ken asked together.

Glad pointed to the drawing. "There's a copyright mark right here."

"Which means you can't alter the design without permission," Mike said.

"And altering at this point would probably cost you as much as new plans," Glad added.

"You people copyright this shit?" Chris asked, amazed.

"I can't answer for every landscape architect, but I have," Mike said.

"And if Mr. Kovalski was unethical enough to put his name on another person's work it would go beyond infringement to fraud, which is a felony," Glad finished.

Silence.

Ken Anderson looked baffled. Chris was no longer purple, but still looked positively irked. And Mike…

Mike was smoldering, frankly admiring her.

Wonder Woman, he mouthed. Her heart stalled in her chest.

Chris finally spoke. "As you can see, my Assistant Director has a gift for gab."

Oh dear. Had she gone too far? "Well-"

Chris ignored her and grumbled, "Of course we want everything to be above board. So we will start over, with a new design. But there are certain elements that the board has deemed necessary that must be included."

"Such as?" Mike asked.

"A water element of some sort. Sufficient room for benches or other seating." Chris checked some papers. "You also need to leave some open lawn space for outside performances." He looked at Glad. "Anything else?"

"Can we get a space for a children's garden?" She asked.

"A children's garden?" Mike asked, brow furrowing.

"A space where our youngest patrons can plant vegetables, flowers...where they can learn to care for and value other living things. I happen to know Miss Cathy is very interested in such a space."

Mike regarded her a moment. "We can probably work that in. Anything else?"

"Well, since you ask, I'd love that pink dogwood from the garden show right outside my office window."

Mike smiled. "Would you."

Ken chuckled. "You and half of Ohio. That tree got more talk-they even took a picture for the Akron Beacon-Journal!"

"That side of the building isn't in the plan," Chris reminded her.

"I know. But a girl can dream, can't she?" Glad asked, smiling at him.

"When's the next board meeting?" Ken asked.

"Two weeks," Chris said.

"Is that enough time?" Ken asked Mike.

"If I start today. I need a site plan with utilities marked, dimensions, grading... everything you can get me ASAP."

"Done," Chris said, then waved a hand in her direction. "Glad, why don't you take Mike

51

around? Show him the place. Brainstorm some ideas or…whatever."

Whatever. Oh boy. The images that word conjured up.

"Nice boss you've got there," Mike commented quietly after the Conference Room door closed behind them. "He treat you like that every day?"

"Of course not," Glad said, which wasn't exactly a lie. "He just hates it when things don't go according to plan. He'll blow up, but two minutes later he's okay, like it never happened."

They left Administration and walked towards the Circulation desk.

"So. Looks like we'll be working together."

"I-um…" she cleared her throat. "Yes." She groaned inside. Some conversationalist she was turning out to be. Every time she looked at Mike Kovalski her mind went fuzzy and all she wanted was to throw herself at him. His sexuality was potent and deeply affecting, but no good could possibly come from it. If she wanted to be the director here someday she had to be professional all the time, no matter what.

"Is this your first time in the building?" she asked. Yes, work talk was a nice, safe neutral territory.

"Yes, it is." He said, his dark eyes assessing her. She felt a flare of heat deep inside. So much for neutral.

"Well, welcome to your library, then."

"My library?"

"The library belongs to everyone," she said, feeling eyes follow them. Great, now the staff had something new to talk about. "So is there anything in particular you need to see in here, or are you more interested in the outside?"

"I want to sketch the areas that look out directly on the property. Can we hit those first?"

"Certainly." They passed the Circulation desk. Glad heard whispering behind them and shot a pointed look over her shoulder. The whispers switched off and she was momentarily gratified.

She motioned to her left. "There's a wall of windows along the reading lounge-that view looks out over the main lawn to the south-"

"Great, great. Hang on." He snapped a quick picture with his smartphone, then drew a rapid sketch on his pad, penciling in the windows and the three maple trees at the property line, writing a few quick notes in some kind of strange shorthand. "Okay, take me there."

Glad led him to the windows. Mike took another shot then held his smartphone out flat for some reason. He checked it, made a notation then drew the view from each, making more notes. From right to left. Glad did a double take.

"Is that Hebrew?" she asked.

"Yes." He made some more notes. "I did my time like every other good Jewish boy."

"Why do you use it here? Keeping your nefarious plans a secret?"

He smiled. "Something like that."

"I was kidding."

"I'm not. I've had plans stolen."

"Really?"

"Landscaping is competitive. People do all sorts of crazy stuff to win awards, to be the best. After one of my designs got featured in DC Home Magazine, I became a target."

"The big brick house with all the green and white landscaping?" she asked, not thinking.

"I was right," he said, smiling down at his notes.

"About what?"

"When you mentioned my award. And now this. You looked me up."

Arrgh! Why had she just opened her mouth? "Well-of course I did! We're investing heavily in a project for the entire community."

"And?" he asked, smiling still. The devil.

"I needed to make sure that investment is going to pay out." She looked quickly around and said in an undertone, "And I really didn't like the other design, so I was hoping you did better work."

"Then I'll do my best to satisfy you."

She wasn't going to read into that. It was a perfectly innocent comment.

Right. His eyes were stripping her and Glad felt her pulse thrumming in her ears, felt that slow spiral of heat begin to build inside. She wanted him. Bad.

No. She would not go there. Would. Not. Glad stepped back, crossed her arms and turned her attention to the view outside. Next to her, Mike began sketching the view from the last window.

"So tell me what you thought about it. The

magazine spread," he said coolly, like the past thirty seconds had not occurred.

"It looked amazing. I don't really know how to describe it."

He looked at her. "Tell me what you saw."

Glad closed her eyes a moment and recalled the photos. "Green. A river of green flowing around that brick island. It made me want to follow it. And the white florals at the front of the house... they're like foam or spray, like when a wave hits a breakwall-" She stopped. "Sorry. My imagination ran away with me."

"That's exactly right," he said, sounding impressed. "It's a river. How did you like the back?"

"It was lovely," she said, remembering the peaceful feeling she got as she'd looked at the spread. "But some of the pictures were small. I couldn't see all the detail. Can I ask something?"

"Shoot." He stopped drawing and looked at her.

"Why wasn't there more color? I mean, I love green, but there wasn't much else."

"Customer preference," he said. "The lady of the house didn't want color at all. We compromised a bit, and there's always a little color going on, pink in the spring, white in summer and so on, but the focus is mainly green."

"The lady of the house," Glad mused, and jumped in. "Dr. Kovalski's wife."

He stilled. "Yes."

"Is it just a coincidence?"

His forehead creased and Glad saw a flash of sadness in his eyes, quickly masked. "She's my mother."

"So you're the son of one of the most respected heart surgeons in the nation."

"Yes."

"You didn't want to-" she stopped; his black brows had suddenly smashed into each other in the middle of his forehead.

"No. No interest in medicine whatsoever."

Okay, that wasn't a popular topic. "So how did you end up in Ohio?"

"Ken offered me a job."

"But D.C. is so big," she said. "There must have been a lot more job opportunities for a heck of a lot more money. I'd think tiny Mill Falls wouldn't offer much in comparison."

"You'd probably make more money in D.C. too, but that didn't stop you from moving up here, did it?"

"Well, no, but there were reasons-"

"I had my reasons too," he interrupted curtly. "Can we leave it at that?"

5

Oh dear. "I didn't mean-"

"How about we move on?" he interrupted again, his voice tight. "Can you show me where the exit doors are?"

Irritation radiated off him like heat from a fire. Glad dropped her gaze and murmured, "Of course. This way."

Glad led Mike to the first exit door, feeling small. She hadn't meant to offend him, but she'd certainly succeeded. She wanted to know, wanted to ask, but she had a feeling her questions would only make him angry. They were silent as he sketched, then they moved to the Youth Services department and she busied herself looking at a display while he sketched the view there.

Cathy Douglas, the department manager, bustled out of the nearby stacks, her arms piled high with non-fiction titles. She dropped the stack on the desk and grinned at Mike, obviously delighted to see him. "Hello! It's so nice to see you again!" she said.

"How'd the cherry trees do over the winter?" Mike asked her, smiling, tension gone.

"We tied and supported them like you said and nothing broke!"

"Great!" he said. "I was hoping they'd make it."

"They're going to be gorgeous this year! I can't wait to see how much yield we get. You're a genius!" She turned to Glad, her eyes bright. "Thanks again for helping out today. Those kids had a blast, and I think little Jack Keller is in love with you."

"Is that the boy you were twisting the night away with?" Mike asked her.

Glad stared at him. "How did you-you saw?"

"I heard your party music when I came in the door. Sam Cooke is a beast."

Oh, God. Kill me now.

"Yes, that was Jack," Cathy confirmed, laughing. "He asked me if you were coming back at least three times while we were doing the limbo."

Glad managed a smile. "He's a sweet little boy."

"And a total flirt." The phone rang on the desk and Cathy moved to answer. "Duty calls! Youth Services Department, how can I help you today?"

"Such accolades for you," Glad said lightly as they moved away. "Are you a genius?"

"In many ways, at many things," he replied, raising an eyebrow.

"I'm going to ignore what you just said."

He laughed softly.

Glad walked them past the downstairs study rooms, the audio visual materials and then they moved to the stairs that led up to the Reference Department.

"Hang on. I need this." Mike got out his smartphone again, tapped it and held it out on his palm in the direction of the big windows.

"What is that?" she asked.

He tilted the screen so she could see. "It's a compass. It actually uses GPS for positioning, but I liked how it looks like the real thing." He closed the app and jotted some notes on his pad.

"Why do you need to know direction?" she asked.

"Sunlight. It angles different in summer. When I draw my plans I'll arrange the setting so the plants that can take the most exposure are in the open, sunniest spots. And there's more. The brick will absorb and radiate heat, the glass will reflect the light… it all comes into play."

Okay, she was totally impressed. "What kind of plants will we be getting?"

"Not sure yet. When I finish the first draft I'll have a list of possibilities for you. Nothing too exotic, nothing toxic, stuff that looks pretty but is easy to maintain. You're contracting with us for maintenance, right?"

"I would imagine so." Glad led him towards the Reference Desk. "There's some views from the Archives Room as well. Hi, Deb."

Deb Jacobs, head of Reference, twirled around in her chair and patted her sleek graying bob. "I'm here to save the day!" Her eyes traveled to Mike and lit up. "Mike Kovalski! *Shalom*!"

"*Shalom*, Deb." Mike smiled at her.

"Mike and I know each other from temple," Deb said to a curious Glad. "Though I haven't seen you there much lately."

"Guilty," Mike said. "Green Spaces is pretty busy right now."

"I believe it. Are you getting the grand tour?"

"Yes. We're going to be landscaping soon."

"Finally! This property sure needs a facelift!"

"I'd like to show Mr. Kovalski the views from Archives," Glad told her. "Oh, are there prints out today?"

"Of course!" Deb grinned, then her face froze. "Uh-oh, trouble at ten o'clock."

"Miss Donahue!" barked a voice from behind them. Glad grimaced.

"I'll meet you in Archives," she said, and turned to face Marie Stahl, the president of the library board of directors. "Good afternoon, Mrs. Stahl. How can I help you today?"

Marie Stahl hobbled closer, then stabbed in Glad's general direction with her ever-present black cane. "What is the meaning of this nonsense?" she demanded.

"I'm sorry?" Glad asked, confused.

"Denim!" Marie Stahl hissed, stabbing the air again. "And that ridiculous shirt!"

"I was assisting Miss Cathy with her dance party earlier," Glad said, groaning inside. "I needed comfortable clothing."

Marie Stahl puffed up like a bullfrog. "That *costume* is completely inappropriate for a library administrator! Go change your clothes at once!"

"I'm sorry, I can't right now." Marie Stahl's mouth opened and Glad held up her hand. "I'm giving a library tour at the moment. But I'll be done soon and then I'll have time to change. Now, if you'll excuse me-"

The killer cane slashed through the air again. "That wild Kovalski boy has no business in this establishment!"

"Mr. Kovalski is a tax-paying citizen of Mill Falls," Glad reminded her.

The old woman turned beet red. "I will *not* have that-that *philanderer* besmirching our good name! He has no right-"

"The public library is open to all," Glad interrupted, her temper fraying. "We are a center of information and ideas and we welcome everyone regardless of their *pastimes*. Excuse me, please. Mr. Kovalski is waiting for me."

Glad turned her back on the board president and walked stiffly to the Archives and Local History Room. The door shut silently behind her and she breathed a sigh of relief.

The room was a treasure trove of maps, books and artifacts, quiet and soothing. A couple of patrons were doing research at the open tables, presided over by Brandon, the local history librarian. Deb and Mike stood at the windows; he was sketching and Glad overheard "bequest from the Titus family estate" as she joined them.

Deb smiled, but her eyes were anxious.

"How did it go?"

"Fine." She wasn't about to discuss the board president in front of patrons. "Are we ready to see the prints?"

Mike made a few final strokes. "Done. Yes."

Deb led the pair back to the workroom and turned on the lights.

"Oh, wow. These are beautiful," Mike said.

Spread out on the tables were a dozen or so prints of flora. Some were pen and ink outlines, others were in full color. The group admired the prints in silence for a moment.

"How many of these did you say you have?" Mike asked.

"Three hundred and twelve," Deb said.

"Have you gotten an appraisal yet?" he asked, picking up a magnifying glass and peering at something on a full-color *Gladiolus* print.

"We've contacted a group in Cleveland. Someone is coming out on Monday. What's so interesting on that print?" Glad asked.

"This *Gladiolus* is dated 1883," he said, handing her the glass and pointing at a spot on the print. "You could have some real value here."

Glad looked at the mark, then at Deb. "Are they all this old?"

"Some are even older," Deb said. "We're doing a dozen at a time and keeping the rest in the vault, and we've set up a database to organize them. We're thinking of framing some to hang around the library as well."

"If you have prints of plants we'll be using, it would tie the projects together," Mike suggested.

"What a great idea! Glad, what do you think?"

"Sounds good," Glad said absently, still admiring the *Gladiolus* print.

"Glads for Glad," Mike murmured, and she looked over. He was smiling, pleased with new discovery and she cursed inside. She gave him a withering look and turned her attention to the *Rosa Lutea* print to her left.

"Will you call me when you get the next batch out?" Mike asked Deb, handing her a business card. "I'd love to see them all, if that's okay."

Deb agreed, thrilled with his interest. Mike and Glad returned downstairs and she escorted him to the front door.

"Do you need me outside?" she asked.

"I don't think so. I'll take some more pictures, and I'll be back some morning soon to compare the light. Thank you for the tour," he said.

"You're welcome."

Mike looked past her. "That lady's waiting for you by the check-out desk," he said softly.

Glad didn't have to ask who he meant. "Of course she is. Run while you have the chance."

He smiled, but his eyes were concerned. "You in trouble, girl?"

"Nothing I can't handle."

He didn't look like he believed her, but he let it go. "Thanks again for taking me around."

"You're welcome. It's a pleasure to show off my place."

"You'll have to come by my place soon."

She gulped. "Your… place?"

"Green Spaces," he said with a sly grin. "Once we win approval from your board-"

"If we win."

"Oh, we will, girl. I've got *ideas*. And once the deal's done, we'll have a lot of decisions to make. We'll really start blooming outside in May, but if you come sooner the greenhouses are open. We've got lots of flowers. Orchids, roses, even some…*glads*… if I recall correctly."

She would not blush. She would not blush.

Damn it. Yes, she would.

"Goodbye, Mr. Kovalski," she said through gritted teeth.

He smiled. "I'll see you around, *Gladiolus*."

Glad scowled at his back as Mike left the library, then turned back to the desk and nearly groaned aloud. Marie Stahl was no longer alone; her nephew Scott stood chatting with her. Glad had a feeling her day was about to get worse.

***

Overheard in the town square, across the street from the Mill Falls Public Library:

What the heck's that boy doin' over there?

Takin' pictures, looks like.

That's that Kovalski from Green Spaces. You know, the one with the dating problem.

(laughter) Guess that's one way to put it.

I wonder if the library's finally gonna get some landscaping done? He's their bigshot landscape guy, right? From D.C.?

Yep. My neighbor got her yard done last fall.

64

He did a real nice job.

Well, that place could use a little sprucing up-what's he doing now?

Looks like he's gettin' ready to climb one of the Mighty Oaks.

I climbed the left one on a dare back in grade school.

Yeah, and you almost fell out the damn thing coming back down.

That's right! Whole life flashed in front of me, I tell you what. Never did that again.

There he goes!

He's gonna fall.

No way, he's as sure footed as a mountain goat. Look at that fella climb!

Must be all that sex keeps him limbered up.

(laughter) I bet it does!

***

"-and he asked me out to dinner right in front of her," Glad groaned as she pulled her mat from the back seat. She rooted around a second and grabbed her bag. "Talk about awkward."

"Please tell me you said no," Fran said.

"Of course I said no! The guy gives me the creeps!"

"What guy?" Holly asked from behind them. Fran turned around.

"Scott Stahl. He asked her out this afternoon."

Holly's face fell. "Oh, God. You're kidding."

Glad shut her car door and locked it up. "I

wish. And he did it right in front of Aunty Marie," she said as they walked towards the Rec Center entrance. "I about died of embarrassment."

"He asks me out every six months or so," Holly commented. "He thinks he's a real ladies' man, all smooth…it's all I can do not to laugh in his face."

Fran pulled the door open. "He still asks me out, and I've been married for eight years now! Like he could hold a candle to Todd."

Glad's mouth dropped. "You're kidding!"

"Not a bit. The guy's addicted to rejection, I swear. You're just the newest target. But don't worry," she said as they passed through the second set of doors, "he's mostly harmless."

Mostly? That was reassuring, Glad thought as they moved towards the studio room where their Pilates class was held. This was her second class; Holly had told her about them just last week and Glad had signed up for the new session right away. She loved the workout; it was challenging and relaxing at the same time. And as a bonus, she'd made a new friend since joining the class. April Fonzi, their instructor, was a petite powerhouse with a sunny disposition who taught art at the local elementary school. She also belonged to one of the book clubs sponsored by the library, volunteered pretty much everywhere, walked people's dogs…her schedule was so full it was a wonder she had time to sleep.

Their path took them by the observation windows to the pool. At this time of night there was usually a class going on in half the pool and the other half was open for lap swimming. Glad loved to swim but there was rarely a lane open when she was available; regular swimmers reserved spots a month or two in advance.

"Wait, wait-" Fran grabbed her arm. "Look who's here." Glad stopped and followed Fran's pointing finger to a swimmer just approaching the pool. He was tall and broad and-oh, no. It couldn't be.

"The neighborhood bad boy himself," Fran purred.

Glad took him all in, from his bare feet to the swim trunks that hugged him like a second skin to his amazing back and impressive shoulders. Yum.

"Would you look at those arms," Fran murmured. "What a gun show."

Holly grimaced. "Well, he's miles ahead of Scott Stahl, but I wouldn't go near that revolving door. He's probably got more germs than-"

"Oh, he's just sowing his wild oats or whatever," Fran said. "And no matter how many women he's done, he's still smoking hot. And he's so friendly and helpful out at Green Spaces-have you met him, Glad?"

Glad couldn't respond. Mike Kovalski had turned to his lane and her mouth had gone completely dry. She wanted to stop staring but her eyes were frozen in place. That promise of chest hair she'd spied the other night was a thick, lush reality of black swirls running down from his neck and disappearing under his trunks. Glad felt her fingers reaching, wanting and she curled them hard at her sides, nails biting into her palms.

Mike stepped onto the platform, pulled his

swim goggles down and launched himself into the water. He surfaced and crawled rapidly towards the opposite end of the pool. He was fast, powerful…undeniably sexy.

"Honestly, you two are pathetic!" Holly pulled at their arms, laughing. "We're going to be late!"

"That chest hair is so worth being late over," Fran said, and they hurried to the studio just as April was clapping her hands.

"Okay, ladies! Time to begin!"

***

Mike loved swimming, had loved it from his first lesson at age three. He'd give his mother credit: she couldn't swim a stroke and stayed away from the water like plague, but she'd made certain all her children learned.

His siblings Ben, Lyddie and Sarah had all abandoned the water for other interests, but Mike had stuck to it, going into competitive swim through their local recreation center, then joining his high school swim team. He wasn't a hotshot like some-one of his teammates had gone all the way to Olympic trials-but he was solid and dependable, race after race.

Of course it hadn't been good enough. Nothing ever was. But the water didn't care if he won or lost, didn't care that he got expelled from Hebrew school, didn't care what he did for a living or whose son he was or how royally he'd screwed up his life. The water soothed, comforted, forgave and forgot.

Mike pushed himself hard tonight, starting with an easy crawl to warm up and progressing into butterfly, counting his strokes and moving quickly from one end of the pool to the other and back. Back and forth, stretching, pulling himself along, flipping, pushing, stroking back. And thinking, always thinking.

How could he win Glad Donahue over? The more he'd considered it today, the more certain he became that she was the one. There was something about her, something that had fascinated him from the first time he'd seen her, back at the garden show. He still remembered how she looked by that dogwood with that tangle of bourbon-colored hair and the prettiest eyes he'd ever seen. How he hadn't been able to stand because he'd gone hard just looking at her, how he knew she'd turn back for one last look and his total satisfaction when their eyes met through that crowd.

And he'd been more impressed by her today; she was intelligent and well-spoken and that was a definite plus. But there was more: a kindness, a genuine warmth in her person that drew him like a moth to a flame. Oh, she tried to keep her distance, tried to keep that professional mask in place. But he'd seen right through it.

She didn't want to like him, but she did. She was attracted, but she wouldn't go down easy. Her stubborn nature-and his reputation-stood in the way and he'd have to work his ass off just to get a yes out of her for a first date.

But maybe that wasn't a bad thing. Maybe, as potentially humiliating as it could be, the gossip of him chasing after one woman, the inevitable speculation that he was in love or some bullshit like that would cast him in a more favorable light. Buy him some time.

Mike took a break midway through his workout, treaded water and checked the clock. He was making good time tonight. Maybe he'd stop at Far East on the way home and get a quart of their specialty, a spicy coconut soup he loved. Actually, everything he'd ever tried on the large and varied menu had been great and he was happily addicted, stopping there once or twice every week.

Mike pulled his goggles back down and started swimming again. Counting his strokes to the end of the lane, counting back. After several more laps he flipped and changed to backstroke. Took it easy, cooled down for five laps then hauled himself out of the pool.

The locker room showers were occupied, as usual. Mike was convinced the Rec paid people to stand under them all day; he'd never once seen an open shower the whole time he'd been in Mill Falls. He stripped down and toweled off, slipped into his comfortable black track suit, packed up and left.

Mike walked past the locker rooms and a couple of empty studios. Then a wave of feminine giggles came from a room to the left. Curious, he approached.

"...into a back bend," he heard as he stepped into the open doorway. It was some kind of exercise class but he couldn't figure out what. In his world exercise meant either swimming or weights. This class was neither. There were mats, and these weird little balls that were partially deflated, which made no sense.

The instructor was April Fonzi, a young woman around his age and sister to Fonz from his crew. Petite and pretty, friendly as a puppy and watched over like a hawk by her four overprotective brothers. He wouldn't have minded taking her out, but Fonz probably would have skinned him alive so he'd steered clear.

April was demonstrating a new position, balancing her feet on one of those balls while she went into a back bend, which made even less sense. Now all the women in class were positioning themselves to do the same thing. Mike scanned the room absently, wondering what the heck was going on when a familiar figure caught his eye.

Well, well. If it wasn't Glad Donahue. In form-fitting workout pants that accentuated the curve of her hips and butt, and a snug t-shirt following the line of her breasts down to a lean waist. Did she ever look good.

Dinner forgotten, Mike leaned against the door frame and watched her steady herself, then slowly rise into a back bend while still balancing her feet on the ball. Very impressive; he was about a hundred percent certain that despite his strength he couldn't do that move to save his life.

Fran Bishop, one of Frank Delacroix's hairdressers down at Serenity, had her mat next to Glad. She could barely get into a back bend and collapsed, laughing. Some of the other students were wobbling, some were falling off.

71

Only a few managed to hold the position and none as steady as Glad.

He watched, fascinated, as April came over and spoke to her, then placed a hand under the small of her back. Glad lifted one foot off the ball and very slowly raised it until it pointed at the ceiling.

A jolt of desire hit him hard. *Oy!* Was it possible to have sex in that position? Mike didn't know, but if he ever got her in bed he was going to find out. He was riveted, imagination on overload. She looked like a sculpture, fluid and perfectly curved and he wanted nothing more than to step between her legs, grab hold of that sexy butt and lose himself inside her. He felt a huge ache deep down and willed his arousal to go away before he embarrassed himself. It would be an easier task if he just left, but he couldn't stop watching her. Wanting her.

***

"Yes," April said, approving. "Beautiful, Glad."

"Looks like we have a voyeur," came from somewhere to Glad's left. Fran.

Glad's eyes rotated to the doorway. Mike Kovalski was there, leaning against the wall with his arms folded across his chest. And damn if he didn't look just as good upside down. And then he smiled. What a smile. Sweet, sexy, devilish…wait.

Was he smiling at *her*?

Her focus tanked. She wobbled.

72

"Steady!" said April. Too late. Glad crashed to her mat and stifled a groan. Great. First dancing around like an idiot, now this.

"Oh, honestly," April blustered, and stalked over to the door. Glad saw her waving her hands at Mike, shooing him away but she couldn't hear what was said over the laughter around her.

***

April went after him like a nesting bird after a hawk. "Get lost! Beat it!"

"Come on, April-ow!" She'd smacked him with the towel she carried around her neck.

"You're a big hunk of distraction, Mike," April said and smacked him again with the towel as he backed away from the door. "Now go on. Shoo!"

"Ow! All right, all right!" But he was laughing, enjoying himself. He retreated into the hall and April marched back to her class. Mike picked up his bag, took two steps and heard "Five minutes left! Time for a little relaxation!"

He could wait around five more minutes.

6

"Are you in?" Holly asked Glad and April as they all left the Pilates studio.

April groaned. "I wish, but I'm babysitting."

"I don't know how to two-step," Glad said, worried. Fran and Holly, both kid-free on Thursdays thanks to Scouts, were discussing going out to a local roadhouse on that night. A popular band was playing and it was a hot spot for dancing.

"You don't have to dance," Fran said. "The Hill is a great time whether you do or not."

"Especially on Thursdays," Holly added. "It's Ladies' Night. Cheap drinks!"

"Trust us, every cute cowboy in the county will be up there, and then some," Fran promised.

"And you're so pretty, they'll be all over you like bees on honey," April added.

Glad laughed, digging into her purse. "Well, thanks, but I don't need a man in my life." Where were her keys? She dug some more.

"You do too," Holly commented.

"For what?" Glad asked, distracted. Holly didn't answer and Glad looked up at three grinning faces. "Oh! You guys!"

Fran burst into laughter. "She's blushing again!"

"Would you cut it out?" She laughed in spite of herself. She knew her friends meant well, and the teasing and promises of set-ups was par for the course. And it wasn't that she never wanted to date again, but she definitely wasn't a one-night stand type. And after the humiliation of her last boyfriend she wasn't sure she should get into a relationship anytime soon.

"Anything to save you from Scott Stahl," Holly said sweetly.

"Oh, no!" April said. "You've been Stahled?"

Everyone laughed at that and Glad searched through her bag one last time. "I need to go back. My keys must have fallen out of my bag."

"You want us to wait?" asked Holly.

"No, I'm fine."

"So you'll come?" Fran asked.

"Yes, I'll come. What time?"

"We'll pick you up around eight," said Holly.

"Okay. I'll see you tomorrow night." Glad turned back and hurried back towards the studio. A quick search produced the keys, laying behind the chair she had put her bag on. Glad scooped them up and left the studio, headed for the exit.

Mike Kovalski was standing at the doors, texting something on his phone. He slid it in his jacket pocket as she approached.

"Evening, Gladiolus."

From his mouth her given name sounded like a caress, but... "Please don't call me that."

"It's your name, isn't it?"

"It is," she admitted, "but I don't want to hear it."

"Why not? I like it."

"Well, I don't." She pushed at the exit door and he moved behind her, held it open with one arm. Gentlemanly of him, she supposed.

"Okay, no big deal," he said easily. "I don't use Micha unless I'm signing something important."

"Your real name is Micha?"

He nodded. "Named after the rabbi in our synagogue. My parents thought I'd follow in his footsteps. But I had other plans."

"I don't know anything about Judaism, but you don't seem..."

"I'm not," he said, laughing. "I'm wicked, wild and unmanageable, or so Rabbi Micha told my parents when he kicked me out of his lessons. Now tell me how you got your name." He pushed open the second door.

"My mother loved flowers," Glad said.

"And?"

She passed by him fully intending to ignore the gentleman act. But it was...nice, actually. She could not remember the last time a man had held a door for her.

Manners won out. "Thank you."

"You're welcome. And?" he pressed again, falling into step with her.

"And she was totally drugged up with pain meds when she had me."

"Ah. Well, it could be worse, right?"

She stopped, annoyed. "How, exactly?"

"You could be a larkspur. Or a daffodil," he pointed out. "Daffy would be a bitch of a nickname."

She stared at him, then felt herself smiling. "I guess you're right. I never thought of it that way."

"Does your mom still live around Leesburg?" he asked.

Hoo, boy, how to answer that? That she had no idea where her mother was, if she was even alive. That she'd been abandoned at age nine in the middle of February. That even though her mother had been pretty lousy, all things considered, Glad prayed for her return and cried every night for a solid year, her face pushed into a pillow so none of her foster siblings would hear. Because any sign of weakness would be exploited.

Mike Kovalski didn't need to know her history. Past was past and she'd moved on.

"She's gone," Glad said.

His face fell. "Oh. I'm sorry."

She shrugged and looked away.

"So...do you come to the Rec every Wednesday night?" he asked, changing the subject.

"Yes. Mondays, too, sometimes." Why had she told him that?

"That's some class you're taking."

"I like the part where I fall down best."

He grinned and her heart skipped a beat. He was too darn sexy, that was all. "Seriously," he said, "if I ever managed to get into one of those positions they'd need the Jaws of Life to get me back out. I don't know how you do it."

"Years of practice. I'm glad they offer Pilates here. I really like this class. April is a great instructor."

"And she can snap a towel like nobody's business, too," Mike said. "I think she left a welt!"

Glad laughed and he smiled down at her. She felt herself getting warm.

"So. You feel like some Thai for dinner?"

She started, stopped in her tracks. "Again?" she asked, incredulous.

"I figure someday I'll catch you in a weak moment."

"Do you eat there every day or something?"

"No, but I totally could. Come on, girl. Let's head over to Far East and get a little coconut soup, a little Pad Thai…you know you want some."

"I don't want to go out with you."

"Well, how about just having dinner, then? As friends?"

She looked at him, spied the black curls trying to escape from the neck of his t-shirt and swallowed hard. "We're not friends."

"We could be. I'm friends with a bunch of women."

"I'll bet."

"Not like that," he said, exasperation crossing his features.

"So you're telling me you'd be fine with being *just* friends. No kissing, no touching, no possibility of lovemaking."

As soon as the words were out of her mouth she winced. That was so *not* the thing to say right now! She felt her cheeks heating under his steady gaze.

"Do you want to make love?" he asked quietly.

Oh, God, did she ever. "I-no." She saw his speculation and blundered further, unable to stop herself. "And even if I did I'm not into younger guys, so you're out of luck."

"I'm plenty old enough to handle you, girl."

Glad opened her car door and stuffed her mat inside, her entire body burning with embarrassment. And something else. "Just stop it, okay?"

He grinned. "Anyone ever tell you that you blush a lot?"

She looked up at him, annoyed. "No. No one ever in the whole history of my blushing life has ever said that to me."

"Well, Miss Sarcastic, just for future reference, I'm twenty-eight. How old are you?"

"None of your business."

"None of your business," he mused, regarding her. "That tells me... pushing forty.

Her mouth nearly hit the pavement. "I am *not*-I'm only thirty-two!"

"See? Just a few years," he said, smiling. "That's nothing.

"I can't-you don't-just-no, okay?" she stammered, staring at her feet.

"Why won't you look at me?"

"Because   you're   making   me uncomfortable."

"And   you   blush   when   you're uncomfortable."

"Yes." And she'd blushed more since meeting him than she had in years, but she wasn't about to tell him that.

"I'm not that bad of a person. Just forget all those stories you heard and have dinner with me. Once we get to know each other a little better--"

"Why would you want to know me better?"

"I just do. I think there's a really nice person under that prickly hide of yours."

"Or maybe I'm a total bitch."

He laughed. "No, I don't think so. My bitch radar hasn't gone off once since I met you. That's a good sign."

"You have bitch radar."

"Top of the line."

She huffed and rolled her eyes.

"How about this? We can hang out, have a beer on your porch."

She looked hard at him. "I live next door to the biggest gossip in town, remember?"

"Then a beer in my back yard. No one gives a crap in my neighborhood."

"Right. They'll be running my license plate in two minutes."

He laughed. "Okay, I'm getting desperate. Here come the puppy-dog eyes." He stared at her and fluttered his lashes, looking absolutely pathetic. "Please? We don't have to stay in town. We can go buy some beer, get some takeout, drive out into the middle of nowhere and hang out in my truck."

He was too cute, damn it. She bit her lip to keep back the sudden urge to giggle and shook her head. "No!"

He groaned out loud. "Why are you making me work so hard?"

"Why won't you accept that I don't want to go out with you?"

"I think you do."

"I don't."

"You won't. That's totally different." He sighed. "You sure? We'd have fun together. You know we would."

She looked up at him. A long minute passed; Glad could feel the currents pulling at them, could see the want in his eyes. But she couldn't go there. She had to keep resisting. It was for the best, even if it wasn't any fun.

"Yes, I'm sure."

He rolled his eyes and relented. "Fine. But I'll give you fair warning: I'm going to try again, and I hope you change your mind. I'll see you around." He walked away, pulling his keys out of his pocket. His truck *blipped* and he got in and started it up, headed out. Glad stared after him, bewildered and aware of a shift inside, a niggling feeling that everything in her life was about to change.

***

Overheard in the Circulation Department of the Mill Falls Public Library:

You'll never guess what I saw last night! The One Date Wonder was walking our new Assistant Director out of the Rec!

No way!

Are you serious?

Totally! He walked her all the way out to her car!

Must be he's trolling for another notch on his bedpost.

Or maybe she is.

Huh?

Think about it! We don't know anything about her. She might be as slutty as him.

Shhh! Not so loud!

***

"I want to send some flowers, Doris."

"Really?" his coworker said. She sipped her coffee and took a delicate bite of the coconut cupcake Mike had just presented her with. He was a firm believer in using food as bribery and Doris had a serious weakness for coconut cupcakes from Angelo's Bakery downtown. "Mmm. So good. Thank you."

"You're welcome."

Doris took another bite, chewed and swallowed, patted a napkin against her fire engine red, lipsticked mouth. "Flowers aren't your usual M.O."

Did anyone in this town *not* listen to gossip? "I'm turning over a new leaf."

"Oh?" She didn't look like she believed him.

"And I need your help." He gestured around

82

the Green Spaces floral center. "I know my flowers, but I'm not any good at putting stuff together. I don't know what women like."

"That's not what I heard." Doris gurgled a laugh. Mike felt his cheeks warming. She was old enough to be his mother and she was teasing him about sex! This was torture, plain and simple.

"Come on, Doris," he pleaded. "I really need your help. Please?"

Doris sighed and shook her head, drummed her red-lacquered nails on the counter. "Coconut cupcakes and begging? Hard to resist."

"I'll get on my knees right here," Mike said, dropping to the concrete floor.

Doris leaned over the counter and grinned. "Very nice. She must be something else."

His salvation, if he played his cards right. "Yes, she is."

"Then get up already. We've got work to do."

One hour later a perfect arrangement was on its way to the Mill Falls Public Library. Doris had quizzed him brutally, raised one plucked eyebrow sky-high when he told her the name of his quarry then helped him put together a gorgeous mix of blooms and greenery. Mike wrote a message on the back of one of his business cards and stuck it on the plastic fork Doris had inserted.

"You don't want it in an envelope?" she asked.

"Nope." He wanted everyone to see it, wanted to hear that gossip mill grinding all the way across town.

"Miss Donahue?" A perky voice said over the line. "You have a delivery at the Circulation Desk."

"I'll be right out."

Glad shrugged into her jacket and left her office, turning over possibilities in her head. She normally received personal packages at home, so it was probably something real exciting, like a free calendar from their office supplier, or yet another coffee mug from some book vendor or other. She rounded the corner to Circulation and stopped. Gasped out loud.

The most beautiful flower arrangement she'd ever seen in her life sat on the front counter. Glad approached, staring at the stunning floral mix of greens and creamy whites and the single, perfect pink rose at the center. Wow.

"This is for me?" she asked softly, shocked.

"That's what the delivery guy said," the clerk responded, giggling.

"Well, that *is* pretty," came from off to the right.

"Green Spaces knows their stuff," said someone else.

"That's got Doris Henley all over it. She's a genius with flowers."

Aware that an audience was forming, Glad stepped close to the counter and read the card, written in a spiky script and stuck in one of those plastic pitchfork things.

Consider Yes. Mike

"Oh," she squeaked, going hot from head to toe. Giggles and whispers flowed around her and her blush intensified.

"I-um, thank you," she managed. She picked up the arrangement with shaking hands and retreated to her office. Put it on a small table near her window and dropped back into her chair, stared at it.

What in the world was this about? She'd rejected the man, twice, and now he was sending her flowers. Talk about persistent.

She was flattered, no question about that. But there was no way she could go out with him. Sure, he was sexy as hell and she spent far too much time thinking about him. Wondering how he kissed and whether he would be tough or tender in the bedroom were thoughts constantly simmering on the back burner of her mind.

But she couldn't go there, couldn't allow herself to be used by him even though it would probably be some seriously good sex. She wasn't going to act on her reckless thoughts and give the Mill Falls gossips more fuel to burn. Especially not with the potential of the director's job down the road.

But...

There was a knock at the door. "Come in?" she said, still staring at the arrangement.

It was Cathy. "Let's see it-ooh!" she breathed happily. "Very nice! So are you saying yes or what?"

"I've already said no. I don't understand," Glad said, shaking her head.

"What's to understand?" came from the

85

doorway. Deb stood there, admiring with her hands on her hips. "Oh, how pretty! I just knew it!"

Cathy turned to Deb. "Me too! The way he looked at her-"

"What are you two talking about?"

"He likes you!" the women chimed together.

"What-no, he doesn't!"

"Let me see, let me see!" Marci bustled in. "Oh, how lovely. What a nice surprise! Does that Doris do good work or what?" She stepped close. "'Consider Yes'? What does that mean?"

"It means he asked her out, she turned him down and he's asking again!" Cathy informed, gleeful.

"Actually, this is number three," Glad confessed.

A collective gasp went around.

"Well, I must say I'm impressed," said Marci. "Am I right? Is she the first woman he's actually gone after himself?" She looked at the other two for confirmation.

"I think so. Seems everything I heard about, they all asked him," Cathy said.

"They were a bunch of bimbos," Deb said, sniffing at the bouquet. "He got them out of his system and now he wants the real thing. I just knew he was a *mensch*. You know he's been by again to look at the new prints from the Titus bequest?"

"Christ, a guy can't get shit done with you all having a hen party in here! What's going on?" Chris asked, barging in.

"Glad got flowers," Cathy said, giddy.

"So?"

Glad waved at the arrangement and pinched the bridge of her nose. This story was probably halfway across town by now. Chris examined the flowers, then peered at the card.

"Mike? As in Kovalski?"

"Yes."

"Huh." Chris eyed her speculatively. "Well, if you go out with him, do us all a favor and pick some place out of town so we don't have to hear about it. And you three get back to earning your paychecks, all right?" He left, muttering under his breath.

"He's right. We need to get back to work." Deb took one last sniff of the bouquet. "It's so lovely. I think I'm jealous."

"I'm totally jealous," said Marci. "I haven't gotten flowers from Joe in ages."

"So what are you going to do?" Cathy asked.

Glad looked up at the three women hovering by the door. She shrugged, at a loss.

"I honestly don't know."

7

"We saw you and Mike Kovalski walk out of the Rec together last night," Holly said as the three women headed for the front doors of The Oak Hill Tavern, known far and wide simply as The Hill, a country bar and roadhouse that literally stood at the highest point of Oak Hill Road. It was situated close to the county line and got patrons in from all over to hear great bands and dance the night away.

"He left at the same time. We weren't together," Glad said.

"Anything happen?" asked Fran, pushing her new hairstyle, a complicated razor cut with perfect blonde highlights, behind her ear.

"Like what?" Glad asked, immediately on guard.

Fran groaned. "You're going to make me crazy. Like did he ask you out or not? Tell!"

"He asked me out," she admitted.

Holly rolled her eyes. "Of course he did."

Fran squealed. "When? Where are you going? What-"

"I said no."

"You said *no*?" Fran stopped in her tracks.

Glad nodded. "And then he sent me flowers today."

"He did?" Holly's mouth dropped open, then she and Fran began giggling in tandem.

"This isn't funny! What does it mean? Why would he do that?" Glad pulled her phone out of her little bag and opened the picture she had taken. "Look at that thing!"

Holly and Fran looked. Both women gasped.

"It's so pretty," Glad said, agonized.

"Wow. He's really going all out," Fran commented. "He must like you for real."

"Seriously," Holly agreed. "That's the bouquet of one smitten man."

"Frank and Sal said the same thing." Her neighbors had spied the bouquet and bombarded her with questions when she'd gotten home earlier. "I told them I'm not interested but I don't think they believed me." And saying it out loud like that, she didn't believe herself, either.

"Girlfriend, you are totally interested. I saw you staring the other night," Holly teased.

"It doesn't matter if I think he's attractive or not," Glad said. "He's a man-whore!"

Holly laughed at her. "That he is. But apparently he's into you. Maybe he wants to settle down! Stranger things have happened."

"You are so lucky. All that tall, dark Jewish hotness running after you." Fran sighed. "Those bedroom eyes, all that chest hair-"

"Oh, man." She did not need a reminder about the chest hair.

They reached the front entry, paid their reduced cover-it was ladies' night, after all-and went in. The Hill was busy, customers milling about, drinking and talking over each other while the band did sound checks.

"This place is huge!" Glad said, marveling over the large hardwood dance floor surrounded by groups of people at tables or standing in sociable knots.

"It's awesome. You'll love it!" Holly promised.

"Should we get a drink?" Glad asked over the noise.

"Wait until the band starts up!" Fran said. "Everyone'll clear out and head for the dance floor."

They weaved through the crowd, slowly making for the long bar along the left side. Then the microphone squealed and someone announced "Welcome to the Hill! Let's get the party started, people! Put your hands together for Harvest Moon!"

The audience cheered wildly and the band broke into their first tune, a Big & Rich cover. Fran was right, the crowd thinned amazingly fast as couples took to the floor. They could easily make it to the bar now-

A hand closed over her hip and Glad shrieked as she was pushed onto the dance floor. Before she could orient herself that hand slid around her waist and she was pulled up against a wide chest.

Mike Kovalski's chest, to be exact.

"Fancy meeting you here," he said.

"What do you think you're doing?" she asked, trying to wiggle free. No luck.

"Dancing, what else? Did you like the flowers?"

"They were lovely. You can let go now." She pushed at his chest.

Mike held her tighter. "Not a chance, girl."

"I don't want to dance with you," she protested, but she could feel herself weakening. Curse him for being strong and warm and smelling so good and…oh, boy. Those eyes. She was in so much trouble.

"Yes you do. Put your hand up here, on my arm. That's right. Now we're going for a walk. Me forward, you backward. Quick, quick, slow-ow!-slow."

"I told you I-"

"Don't try to lead, and don't look at your feet. Look at me."

"That's not a good idea." If she looked at him again she'd be lost the rest of the night.

"You'll do better if you don't look down. Trust your partner. Quick, quick, slow, slow. That's right. Now put a little swing in those hips."

"What?"

"Ow-okay, don't do that yet. Quick, quick, slow, slow."

"Why are you doing this?" she asked, bewildered.

"Because I like to dance. And you just happened to be right there when the music started."

"Really." She gave him a disbelieving look and he laughed.

"Okay, so it wasn't a coincidence. I saw you come in and I wanted to grab you before some other guy did. Since you ignored my flowers-"

"I didn't ignore them!"

"You didn't thank me for them, either. I'm hurt. I worked hard on that arrangement."

She looked into his sorrowful eyes and a big chunk of her resolve broke off and crumbled to dust. "I'm sorry. It's very beautiful. Thank you. I just-I already told you no, twice-"

"Don't remind me."

"I don't know what to say."

"I'm good with yes."

"I think saying yes to you would be dangerous."

He grinned and Glad realized what had just come out of her mouth. Good Lord, would someone just slap some duct tape over it? She fished around for something better. "We're going to be working together. We need to keep things professional."

He turned her expertly, weaving them through the crush as the band played on. "That project isn't going to last forever. I like you, and you like me no matter what lies you tell yourself. We need to get to know each other better."

She was losing herself in his eyes. Oh, she wanted to get to know him better, all right, but that so wasn't a good idea. "Should we?"

"Yes, because-what?" Another man had tapped his shoulder. Mike shrugged and released her and Glad was swung away by a cowboy with more enthusiasm than grace. The band launched into a fun Josh Turner tune next and she found herself with a new partner who had obviously had a few and kept telling her how pretty she was. Then another man stepped in, another song or two and several partners went by and suddenly she was back in Mike's arms.

"Because if we get to know each other you'll discover I'm a nice person," he continued, as if they'd never parted. "And maybe you'll realize you misjudged me a little, too."

"Are you telling me none of those rumors are true?"

"No, but it would have been nice to have the chance to defend myself."

Glad felt a dig of shame. She, who normally prided herself on getting the whole story, had rushed to judgment over gossip. She felt small and petty.

"I should have asked for your side of the story."

"You and everyone else in town."

"So what's your side?"

"Not now." Mike moved a bold hand down over her hip. "You're getting a lot smoother. Give me a little sway. That's it."

"You really shouldn't-touch me like that," she said, breathless.

"Why not?" His eyes held hers.

"I don't like...well...I mean... Can we change the subject?"

He grinned. "We can talk about whatever you want."

"Okay. Um…where did you learn to dance?" she asked.

"I learned the two-step right here. But me and my sibs all went to ballroom dance classes."

"So you can waltz?"

"Foxtrot too, and a few others. I'm a man of many talents."

"I don't think I should respond to that."

Mike laughed out loud. The band finished their Brooks & Dunn cover and cranked it down to a slow song. Eric Church this time.

"One more?" Mike asked, stopping them in the middle of the floor.

She shouldn't. Really shouldn't. "I'm a little tired-"

"I'll hold you up." He wrapped both arms around her, leaving her little choice but to put her arms up around his neck.

Really, it was either that or leave her arms flapping around in the breeze. It wasn't like she *wanted* to hold him this close or feel his arms around her or burrow her nose in his chest hair that poked out from the neck of his soft, cozy feeling flannel shirt…

Stop it!

"Having fun?" he asked into her ear.

She shivered. "Of course not."

"You sure about that?" he asked, his breath warm against her and she shivered again. He chuckled. "It's all right, girl. You keep making me work. I'm starting to like chasing you around."

Glad moved her head back and looked up at him. He met her eyes, then dropped his gaze to her mouth. She felt herself leaning forward, wanting his kiss more than anything on earth-

"Oh!" Glad shrieked as she was wrenched away from Mike and pulled into the drunken embrace of the biggest, scariest man she'd ever seen. He was several inches taller than Mike and easily twice as broad, bald and bearded with mean little eyes and hands the size of dinner plates.

"My turn," he said, giving her a leer.

"Um, okay," she said nervously. He spun her clumsily away.

"Where'd you come from?" he asked after they steadied themselves, holding her in a crushing grip. "Haven't seen you here before."

The stench of whiskey enveloped her. She could get a buzz from the fumes alone. How was this guy even standing up? "I live in town."

"Uh-huh. Where?"

"I don't think I know you well enough to give you my address."

"Come on," he growled, spinning her. "You can take ol' Larry home and give him a try."

"A t-try?" she gulped, not wanting to know.

"I got a big one. Biggest you'll see, I bet." His huge hand smacked on her bottom, squeezed hard and Glad gasped. "Like that?"

"You're hurting me," she said, desperately trying to stay calm. "Please let go."

"Huh-uh. I'm thinkin' you need a real man between your legs tonight."

Oh, boy. If she couldn't get out of this somehow she'd be in big trouble later on. Tamping down her panic, she gave him her most withering look.

"I need you to let go."

Nothing doing. He squeezed her bottom again and laughed.

"Ow! It hurts!" She shoved at him. It was like trying to move a mountain. "Stop!"

"Nope. I'm gonna do you like that all night!"

"The lady told you to stop."

Glad squeaked in surprise. Mike Kovalski was there, his expression as hard as his grip on ol' Larry's arm. He flexed his fingers and the man's hold on Glad slackened. She twisted herself away and Mike pushed her behind him with his free hand.

"This is my dance," Larry said, his little eyes narrowing to slits.

"Go find another partner. You're done here," Mike said coldly.

The nearby couples took notice and edged away; a wave of exclamation spread across the floor as the anticipation of a fight began to build. Larry yanked his arm free of Mike's grip.

"Outta my way."

"Can't do it, man."

Larry sighed and shook his head at Mike like he was the stupidest person on earth. Glad felt Mike's hand pushing at her, wordlessly telling her to back the hell up because he was about to get his ass handed to him. She panicked and reached for the back of his shirt.

"Please, don't-"

Larry hauled back and swung. Mike sidestepped but not quite fast enough and that huge fist skidded across his cheek. There were shouts of alarm. The band stopped playing. Mike staggered; Glad heard herself shriek then he stepped forward and landed a hard punch to Larry's gut. The air whooshed out and Larry's mouth hung wide as he gasped for air.

Mike turned and grabbed her arm. She gasped; he had an open cut below his eye and blood was running fast down his face. "Mike!"

"Move," he growled and steered her into the crowd.

"But-you're hurt!"

Mike shoved her at Fran and Holly. "Get her out of here!" he barked.

"Look out!" screamed Holly and Mike whirled around.

Glad had no chance to see what happened. Fran and Holly pulled her away just as Jason Taylor, the owner, flew out from behind the bar, swearing a blue streak. He and the bouncers rushed in, the crowd closed the women out and they were at the exit and outside.

"Wait!" Glad cried. "I can't just leave!"

"He knows what he's doing, hon. Come on," Holly said.

"Holly's right," Fran said. "Once Hairy Larry Jones gets fixed on something-or someone-it's almost impossible to shake him off. You're better off disappearing right now."

"But-"

"Mike Kovalski can take care of himself," Holly said.

"Can he ever," Fran said as they got in the car. "I wish my hubby would fight for me like that. Not that I want him to get punched or anything, but that was seriously romantic. Gossip's going to have a field day with this."

Glad gasped. "No! No, please, don't tell anyone-"

Holly stuck her key in the ignition. "Honey, a hundred people saw what happened in there. There's no keeping that quiet."

Glad dropped her head against the seat with a groan. Gossip. So not what she needed.

Holly backed out of their parking space and grinned over her shoulder at Glad. "Welcome to Lord County, girlfriend. You sure made a heck of a first impression."

***

Overheard at Stone's Hardware downtown:

Heard there was a fight up at The Hill last night.

Yeah, with Hairy Larry Jones.

Jones is out of the tank again?

Yep, and meaner than ever. I heard he was putting the moves on that new library lady and Kovalski stepped in.

Never thought librarians were partiers.

I never thought anyone in his right mind would take on Hairy Larry Jones.

Say what you want, Kovalski's got balls. You wouldn't catch me within a hundred yards of that psycho.

He was at Urgent Care getting his face stitched up around nine, nine-thirty. My cousin works there, she saw him. Said he was all bloody.

It's like I always say, women are nothin' but

trouble.

He must really like that librarian. What's her name again?

Donahue. Glad Donahue.

***

"Well, Miss Donahue? What have you to say for yourself?"

"About what?" Glad asked politely. It was just after opening and Chris had called her into his office for a meeting. Glad had hoped it was library business, but one look at the Marie Stahl's face and her hopes sank. Damn gossip.

"About your behavior!"

Glad looked from Marie Stahl to Chris and back. Could she worm her way out of this? There was only one way to find out.

"My behavior?" she asked coolly.

Chris cleared his throat, obviously uncomfortable. "You see, Glad, umm-"

"Of all the decent, upstanding people in this town you could choose to spend time with and you're out gallivanting with that Kovalski boy!" the old woman interrupted, banging her cane on the floor.

Keep your cool. Don't let her see you rattled. "What are you talking about?"

"Do you deny you were out with him?"

"Yes, I do. I was out with some girlfriends last night."

"Then why did I receive multiple phone calls about our assistant director in the arms of that-

that *landscaper* at The Oak Hill Tavern last night?" Marie Stahl looked smug.

"We danced together," Glad said, keeping her voice even. "When you dance with someone you get held in their arms. And for your information, I danced with several other gentlemen there as well. It was perfectly innocent."

Marie Stahl's mouth pursed like she was sucking on lemons. "Indeed? And I suppose that fight was perfectly innocent, too?"

Shit. Okay, she needed to ramp up from innocent to ignorant. "Fight?"

"Do you deny that you were involved in that scuffle?"

"I don't know what you're talking about," Glad lied. "My friends and I left early. We weren't fighting."

"The fight was with that Kovalski boy-"

"I do not get in fights with men!" Glad exclaimed, faking outrage.

"-and that hooligan Larry Jones!" Marie Stahl spat out, banging her cane down again.

"I have no idea who that is," Glad said forcefully. "I cannot *believe* you think I'm the kind of person that would pick fights in a bar with men!" She let her voice catch and tremble. "I'm a decent woman! I would never do something like that!"

"Now, Glad, I'm sure she didn't mean any offense," Chris tried, looking at her strangely. He was on to her, but he wasn't about to let the old woman know it. He looked at Marie Stahl and gave an apologetic smile. "You know, gossip can get twisted awfully fast around here. People hear what they want to hear, and see what they want to see."

"My source is reliable."

"Was your source present at the time?" Chris asked quietly.

"Certainly not! He doesn't fraternize with the sort of *people* that frequent that establishment!"

Chris didn't answer that, just gave Marie Stahl a considering look. She grumbled and huffed, banged her cane a few times, then stood.

"Well. Be that as it may-Miss Donahue, I have told you before and I will tell you again: you cannot be too careful with your reputation. There is no such thing as privacy in a small town like this. If you don't want to hear gossip about yourself, don't hang around situations that create it. You would be well advised to stay away from that bar *and* that philandering landscaper. Good day." She hobbled out in high dudgeon.

Chris stared down at his desk and drummed his fingers. Finally, he said, "I wouldn't exactly call this keeping your nose clean."

Glad cringed. "I'm sorry."

"I'm not saying you can't have a personal life, okay? But men getting in bar fights over you is pushing it."

"They weren't-it was all so sudden-"

"That's not acceptable behavior for a library administrator. In fact, it's probably not acceptable for any professional, but I'm going to overlook it. This time."

Pointing out that she hadn't actually done anything wrong would be useless right about now, so she swallowed her protest and said, "It won't happen again."

"It better not." Chris sighed. "Glad, I'm a firm believer that your private life is your business."

"Thank you."

"But whatever's going on between you and Kovalski, you need to take it behind closed doors, you get me? That old bitch is batshit crazy, and if you think she'll forget this, think again."

"There's nothing going on, Chris."

"Nothing?" He didn't look like he believed her.

"Nothing," Glad repeated firmly.

8

"…your waterfall will run on a loop, so you're not wasting excess water. We'll have to clean it, winterize it and such, but maintenance on these things is pretty minimal." Mike forwarded the slide show to the next screen. "Here, here and here," he said, pointing, "you've got the arbors you wanted, in addition to the benches and we'll have *Clematis* and other climbers…"

Truly, Glad was trying to pay attention. The images Mike was showing the board were impressive and it was easy for her to visualize how it would look when the project was done. The library grounds would be a showplace, bursting with color and beauty. Even in winter, as he'd just explained a minute ago, there would be red osier dogwood, evergreens and winterberries to attract the eye.

He gave a good speech, and she could see the board members nodding and smiling as he explained the benefits of his plan. But his words went in one ear and out the other. She couldn't focus on anything but him.

She hadn't seen Mike since the incident at The Hill, but rumors had flown fast in the days that followed. She'd been eyeballed and questioned by one person after another, including a very concerned Ken Anderson at the post office yesterday. Thankfully no one at the library beyond Cathy, Deb and Marci had dared ask any questions and she'd put them off with a vague insistence that she didn't feel like talking about it. Really, the only person she wanted to talk to about that night was Mike. And therein lay her problem.

She'd been worried that he'd been seriously injured but paranoid about what the gossip would do if she called or went to Green Spaces to check on him. So she'd simmered in inertia; the only contact a brief message forwarded from Chris with questions about availability of a big screen, computer hookups and so on. And tonight he'd only given her a cool, proper hello before the meeting started. He was keeping things professional. She wished she could say the same for herself.

His cheek sported a fading bruise under his left eye and a dark line of stitches. If it bothered him at all he didn't show it. He smiled at the board members, made a joke or two and presented the library project like it was any other day.

But it wasn't. He'd gotten in a fight, pitted himself against a nasty adversary who outweighed him by a hundred pounds or more and who could have put him in the hospital.

For her. He'd done it to protect her.

He'd said when they got to know each other better she might realize she'd misjudged him. She'd misjudged him, all right. She'd never known a man in her life who would look that level of pain and trouble in the eye and wade straight in. Mike Kovalski had a core of steel under that casual façade, a sense of honor and chivalry that was surprising to find in this day and age.

And it only made him more attractive. Despite telling herself repeatedly that she needed to *not* go there, she'd spent the weekend replaying the scene and fantasizing like the romantic dork she was, imagining him showing up at her door and sweeping her upstairs to make love despite his bruises and pain. Oh yeah, she had it bad.

"That's it for the landscaping plan," Mike finished. "Questions?"

A few questions were asked, Mike answered, replayed a few slides by request and they were done.

"This is very impressive work," said Tom Smithers, the Vice-President. Glad smiled, pleased. If Tom Smithers was on board, they'd very likely get approval whether Marie Stahl liked it or not.

Mike nodded. "Thank you. When will you be making your decision?"

The group looked at Marie Stahl. She pursed her lips and said, "We'll have to table this discussion for next month."

Murmurs went around the table. Glad and Chris eyed one another. What was this about?

"Next month?" Mike asked, his brow furrowing.

"We simply don't have time to finish this business tonight."

"What's to finish? Either you want this or you don't," Mike said. "Right now, Green Spaces is scheduling into August. As of today I've got twelve jobs lined up, waiting on this decision. If I'm going to be doing this project, I need you to sign off on it by the end of this week so I can arrange things."

"You'll have to wait," Marie Stahl said coldly.

"Then you'll lose. By this time next month we'll be locked in for the whole summer. I won't put off my other clients for you."

In the bureaucratic world of libraries, decisions were rarely made quickly, but Mike was throwing down the gauntlet, take it or leave it. Glad shifted in her seat and tried to appear calm. Finally, Tom Smithers said, "I think the other business tonight can wait. We really need to get the landscaping decision off the table."

"I agree," said Candy Watson. "We've put this off long enough."

"Thirds," said John Toth.

"All in favor of proceeding to discussion?" asked Tom. Ayes came from every chair except one.

"I do not agree!" blustered Marie Stahl.

"Marie, we've got nothing else on the table

that can't wait another month. Let's just get it done already," Tom said.

The old woman banged her cane down. "As your president I protest-"

"We've cast the vote, let's get on with it," said Mickey Swain. "I've got to help my kid with his science project after this."

"Mr. Kovalski, thank you for coming in tonight. We'll let you know our decision in the next couple of days," Tom said.

"Great. Thank you." Mike disconnected his laptop from the projector cable. "Before I go, I have one more item to bring to your attention."

"What's that?" asked Candy Watson.

"The Mighty Oaks are in trouble."

A ripple of alarm went through the room. "What do you mean, they're in trouble?" asked Chris.

"The cores are rotting and the root structure is visible at ground level in several spots. They're a safety hazard and need to come down before they fall down."

The room erupted.

"Impossible!"

"Those trees are over three hundred years old!"

"We can't take them down!"

"They're historic landmarks!"

Marie Stahl banged her cane down. "Mr. Kovalski, you cannot be serious."

Mike calmly tucked his laptop into his briefcase and moved towards the door. "I'm dead serious. Both cores are soft with rot, they have hollow channels and they're both leaning to the northeast and pulling the ground up behind them. They're on their way down. It's only a question of when."

"If you're looking to get more business out of this, young man-"

"Green Spaces doesn't take down large trees," Mike interrupted, looking irritated. "Manny Cruz in Glen View is your best choice. He's an arborist, he's got the proper equipment and he values safety above all else. I strongly recommend you get him out here before the weather gets any warmer and severe weather starts popping up."

Alarmed discussion went around the room, with Tom Smithers finally saying, "This comes down to the safety of our patrons over everything else. If they need to come down, we have a responsibility to make sure it happens. We'll get Mr. Cruz to come out and do an assessment and go from there."

"I'm not sure if this is a decision the library can make," Glad commented, then looked at Chris. "Aren't the trees mentioned somewhere in the town charter?"

"She's right," Chris said to the group at large. "This may have to go before council."

"We'll all be in our coffins by the time Barstow makes a decision," Mickey Swain groused. Mayor Barstow's avoidance skills were legendary.

"True enough," Tom Smithers said, and stood. "Well, Mr. Kovalski, this is a blow, but thank you for bringing it to our attention." He shook Mike's hand and opened the board room door. "We'll be in touch."

Glad punched her code into the security panel and left the library. The meeting had run past closing as the discussion over the Green Spaces plans got heavy. Marie Stahl was opposed to the entire project and said at one point she utterly despised that "wild, womanizing philanderer" and would be damned if she allowed him in her library again. In the end, however, she was outvoted six to one in favor of the project moving forward.

Glad was mentally exhausted and wanted nothing more than to drop into bed and sleep for a solid week. But she and Chris were meeting first thing tomorrow to finalize things before they contacted Green Spaces.

Of course Chris had taken off the second the meeting broke up, leaving Glad to wait on chatty board members before she could lock up. And now she was alone, walking into the dark back parking lot. She really needed to bring up exterior lighting at the next board meeting-

A large dark colored truck was parked next to her car. Glad slowed, shifted her keys so that the business end was gripped tight between her fingers. Not invincible, but she could do some damage if she had to.

A shadow moved on the tailgate and she stopped midstride. Okay, she didn't have to be brave; running was a perfectly respectable, viable option. She backed up a step and the shadow moved again.

"It's me," Mike said. "Relax."

"Oh." She sighed with relief. "I know this is little Mill Falls, but you never know anymore."

"True. And there's not one light back here. You should park closer to the building if you're going to be the last one out at night."

"Sorry, those spots are for patrons. We valued employees get the deluxe back lot with potholes and dumpster views."

He smiled, a flash of white in the dark and Glad felt that blasted attraction in her curl around and begin to purr. It was impossible to shake and while she knew she should try harder, she wasn't sure she could, here alone with him in the dark.

"I'm glad you're here, actually," she said. "I want to thank you for saving me the other night."

"I'd say anytime, but I really don't want to go to Urgent Care again." He held a hand up when she opened her mouth. "Enough about that. What happened?" he asked.

"At the meeting?"

He nodded and she laughed softly. "And here I thought you were waiting to protect me from the boogeyman."

He smiled again. "I can swing both."

Zing. She took a slow breath. "There was lots of discussion, and opposition from a certain board member of course, but the project was voted to go forward."

Mike slammed his hands on his tailgate and launched to his feet. "Yes!" he exalted.

"Chris and I have to work through some details in the morning, but he'll probably call Green Spaces tomorrow afternoon. After everything is signed, we'll have to wait a couple of weeks for the funds to get released and then you're good to go."

"Oh, great!" He pulled her into a bear hug. "We're doing it, girl. We're making it happen!" He swung her in a circle and she gasped in surprise.

Just as quickly she was plunked back on her feet. "Sorry," Mike said, releasing her. "I just-"

Their eyes met and time stopped. Glad was mesmerized, wanting him but not brave enough to open her mouth. But her brain still worked; it sent impulses down her arm, one nerve to the next until it reached her hand and fingers. They moved forward, found his shirt, curled into it and tugged.

"Girl," Mike said roughly. He put a hand on the back of her neck, pulled her against him and kissed her.

Oh, goodness. Sweet and minty and so warm. Want blazed deep and spiraled out and Glad melted against him, ran her fingers up his chest and into his hair. She felt his big hands close over her hips and roam around to her bottom. Mike squeezed through her skirt and a bolt of heat went right to her core; she moaned into his mouth and he squeezed again as he tasted her, explored her with his lips and teeth and tongue.

Feeling brave, Glad moved one hand down and slid it under his shirt. Thick, wiry-soft hair met her fingertips and she felt him tense under her hand, felt a sudden surge of heat against her. He was rock hard, rubbing against her and she slid her fingers higher, deep into that chest hair and sucked on his lower lip.

Mike growled into her, locked an arm around her waist and kissed her harder. His free hand stroked up, pushed her blazer aside and cupped her breast through the thin cotton of her blouse. Glad titled her head back, gasping, lost to sensation as Mike's mouth moved to her neck, licking and sucking at her sensitive skin.

Oh, *yes*. She'd fantasized about this for weeks, but the reality far outstripped anything she'd imagined. Helpless, she gripped his big arms and held on, rocking with him as his hips ground against her, slowly and sensually, stoking that fire inside. She wanted him, here, now and she didn't care who saw or gossiped or-

A car alarm blared to life nearby and they both jumped. And reality returned in a heartbeat. What was she doing???

Glad took a shaky breath and extricated herself from Mike's embrace. He was breathing hard, eyes blazing and she could feel the force of his will pulling at her, wanting her back in his arms, in his bed, all night long.

"I'm so sorry," she said, pulling her blazer back into place, struggling for a little control. "I don't know what-"

"We both know what." His voice was husky and strained and she shivered all over.

"I shouldn't have kissed you," she said, fumbling with her keys, desperate to get away from what she so desperately wanted. "It was inappropriate and unprofessional and I apologize. It won't happen again." She yanked

her car door open and slid inside, reached for the door handle. But before she could close it his voice floated in, heavy with promise.

"Oh, yes, it will."

She really didn't understand it.

Glad lay in bed, thoughts of Mike and that amazing kiss keeping her wide awake. What was it about him that wouldn't let her go? She'd always been attracted to sleek, well-groomed men that wore suits and drove high dollar sport sedans.

Like Evan. She'd ignored the red flags and invested herself, but she'd trusted in vain. After the utter humiliation of their November breakup, she shut her heart away and focused on work, determined to find fulfillment in a single life. Work might not keep her warm at night, but it was steady and mostly predictable. And she'd found a certain level of comfort in that stability, in charting her own course and standing on her own two feet.

And then Mike Kovalski happened and she was lost in an intense desire that was a little scary, if truth be told. He'd broken through her reserve with no effort whatsoever and flipped every switch to on, full steam ahead. The man kissed just how she liked it, just the exact right depth and pressure to scramble her brain and make her want to shuck her clothes, bypass the foreplay and get to the good stuff *now*. And she'd affected him too; his heat and hardness proof positive he wanted her.

Mike wasn't like Evan or any of the other men she had dated, as few as there had been. He was rugged and callused and probably the only designer name in his closet was Carhartt. No doubt he knew his way around a toolbox and wouldn't balk at doing stuff she disliked, like shoveling snow and dragging trash to the curb. And she liked that and she liked him in spite of his hotly rumored tomcatting ways.

But no matter how nice he could be, no matter how tempting his kiss, she knew she wouldn't be able to trust him. Worse, being with him would send her reputation straight down the toilet and it would be goodbye to any chance at promotion. Reality sucked, but in the long run she was better off staying far away from Mike Kovalski.

9

"Jimmer's not doing much," Marci groused to Glad over lunch on Tuesday. "If I stay in the vicinity he'll work, but the minute I walk away he's goofing off or hitting on Ashley or one of the other pages…they're all atwitter because he's the local bad guy. Like that makes him cool somehow. I don't get it."

"Do I need to talk to him again?" Glad asked. Their young offender was in his second week of the program and, while he showed up on time and kept his tattoos covered, his attitude was poor and he was lazier than a pet raccoon.

"I guess, if you think it will help."

It probably wouldn't help a bit. Glad was swimming in unknown waters; her court liaison was vague about how much actual work was required of offenders. It seemed to Glad like they didn't care what Jimmer did so long as he logged in his hours and she signed off on them. But it was frustrating. Pointless, even: why bother placing him without any clear expectations? What could he possibly learn from the experience except that community service was a joke?

Marci swallowed another bite of her sandwich. "I can't wait until his time is up. He gives me the creeps."

"I know what you mean." Jimmer's behavior, while not disruptive or offensive, was definitely weird. He was watchful and jumpy and, though she tried hard not to judge, she was suspicious of him just the same.

"Where is he this afternoon?" she asked, crumpling up her napkin and chip bag.

"Reference. He's supposed to be cleaning the shelves back in the 900's."

Glad brushed her teeth, dropped her lunch box back in her office and headed for Reference, pausing here and there to say hello or help a patron find an item. It was quiet upstairs today, only a few regulars on the computers and Glad headed back to the 900 section, stuffed with history tomes and maps and travel books, in search of Jimmer Hall. She rounded the far stacks to the 970's and sucked in a shocked breath.

Jimmer Hall was up to something all right, that something being Ashley the page's seduction. The girl's shirt was open and Jimmer's hands were busy groping at her breasts through her bra. The pair was panting heavily, totally uncaring as to their surroundings. Glad strode down the aisle, furious.

"What-in the *hell*-is going on here?" she ground out. Ashley gave a little shriek and tore herself away from Jimmer's embrace, but not before Glad saw the ruddy swell of his erection pressed against the girl's hand.

"Miss Donahue, I-"

"Button your shirt, young lady," Glad hissed at her, then rounded on Jimmer, who was casually stuffing himself back into his jeans. "You will be in my office in five minutes, or you'll be heading back to lockup in ten. Do you understand me?"

Jimmer smirked. "Sure. Whatever."

Glad glared at him a moment, then turned on her heel and marched out of the stacks, taking a frantically buttoning Ashley with her.

"Miss Donahue, I swear, I didn't mean for it to happen," the girl blubbered.

Glad rounded on her. "*Shhh!* Do you want everyone to know what you were up to back there?"

"No!" the girl whispered, mortified. She trotted to keep up with Glad and in a minute they were at Marci's office. Glad knocked once and ducked her head in.

"My office?" she asked.

"Oh, dear," Marci said, and got up.

Glad marched Ashley down to her office, Marci hurrying after them. As soon as the door closed Ashley burst into noisy tears.

"I'm so sorry! Please don't fire me! I'm so sorry!"

"What happened?" Marci asked Glad, bewildered.

"Let's just say Ashley and Jimmer were getting to know each other better in the 970's."

Marci gasped. "Ashley! What were you

thinking? What would your mother think?" Ashley's mother and Marci had been best friends since high school.

"I'm so sorry! I'm so sorry! Please don't fire me, please!" The girl couldn't seem to say anything else.

"I'll be writing up an incident report," Glad said, "and a copy will go into your personnel file. You're a good worker, Ashley, and we like having you around. I'm not going to fire you."

"Oh!" The girl's face cleared.

"However, starting now you are on probation. I expect you to show up on time, do your work and stay far away from Jimmer Hall when he is in the building for his service hours. If Jimmer approaches or harasses you at any time, for any reason, you need to leave the area and report it to the nearest manager or librarian. Any more stunts like today and you'll be out the door in a heartbeat. Do you understand?"

Ashley nodded, crestfallen, and scrubbed at her cheeks. "I'm so sorry," she said again.

A knock sounded at the door.

"That will be Jimmer," Glad said. "Can you finish with Ashley in your office?"

"Of course." Marci went to the door and flung it open. "You rotten little punk!" she snarled in his face as she pulled Ashley out the door behind her. Jimmer sauntered in and plopped himself in a chair.

"That old witch is riled up," he sneered. "What's her problem?"

"Mrs. White is Ashley's godmother," Glad informed him coldly. "She and Ashley are very close. You put your hand in a hornet's nest, Mr. Hall."

"I didn't do anything wrong," he said belligerently. "She's over eighteen, and she wanted it. You've got nothing on me."

"Exposing yourself in a public building is a crime. So is engaging in sexual conduct."

"I wasn't fucking her!" he hollered.

"Be that as it may, I'm going to have to report your behavior to your court liaison."

Jimmer surged up from his chair, hands balled into fists. "You can't do that!"

Glad stood as well, willing herself to be calm and controlled. "I am required to report any deviance to the liaison. It's the law. And now I'll ask you to leave the premises for the day."

"I haven't finished my time yet," he argued.

"Too bad. Go home. I'm sure your liaison will be in touch."

Jimmer Hall stared at Glad a long minute, his face contorted with rage. Then he hollered, "You fucking bitch. You fucking *bitch*!" and stormed out, slamming her office door behind him. Glad followed at a safe distance, cringing as his curses echoed. Why was it things like this happened when Chris was out of the building? She always seemed to get all the crazies on her watch.

Jimmer slammed out of the front doors and stalked down the front walk and Glad returned to her office, ignoring the exclamations and whispers that followed her. She closed her door behind her, dropped back into her chair and pressed a shaking hand to her head. Breathed deep and slow, calmed her racing heart. In that moment when he'd leapt to his feet Glad had been sure he was going to launch himself over the desk. She'd kept it together, stayed cool.

He was, in Marci's words, a rotten little punk.

But he'd managed to scare the crap out of her, just the same.

Wednesday brought meetings, phone calls and general aggravation from the county courthouse. Glad was required to fill out several forms and spell out in detail what had gone wrong with Jimmer Hall's placement at the Mill Falls Public Library. The court liaison was not happy with Jimmer's failure to complete his community service, to say the least and several long, involved phone calls were required before the officer was satisfied that the library had held up their end of the agreement. By Thursday afternoon, Glad was thoroughly sick of hearing the name 'Jimmer Hall' and a headache was brewing when there was a knock at the door.

"Come in," she answered, rubbing her temples.

Marci poked her head in. "Busy?" she asked with a grin.

"No," Glad said. "Believe it or not, I'm finally done. What's going on?"

Marci entered, followed by Cathy and Deb. Cathy had a handful of napkins and Deb carried a plate of pastries in her hand.

"What's this?" Glad asked, surprised.

"A party!" Marci exalted. "You're our hero!"

Deb put down the plate on Glad's desk as the women sat opposite. "I don't know what you did or who you bribed, but I am so happy Jimmer Hall is gone. Dig in!"

Glad took a piece and tried it. The pastry was flavorful and sweet, the raspberry filling sublime. "This is wonderful. What is it?"

"Rugelach," Deb said. "My Bubbe's recipe from way back."

"It's heavenly," Cathy sighed, taking a second bite of her piece.

"So have you heard anything from the court liaison?" Marci asked.

"Just that he won't be returning here," Glad said. "They wouldn't tell me anything else."

"You mean he didn't go to jail?" Cathy asked.

"I don't know," Glad said. She ate her last bite of rugelach. "And I've got to admit I'm a little nervous. He was so angry when I kicked him out."

"Jimmer's not going to come after you, honey. He talks tough, but inside he's just a chickenshit punk like the rest of them." Marci wiped her fingers on a napkin and said to Deb, "Thanks for taking me off my diet. I needed that."

"I'm always thinking of your welfare," Deb said, and pushed the plate towards Glad. "Go on. Eat that last one. You deserve it."

"So," Fran said as she clipped away split

ends and other damage, "have you seen Mike around lately?"

"Should I have?" Glad asked. It was a week since they'd kissed in the parking lot. Seven solid days of nothing. Not a call or a visit-not that she'd expected one, and she'd told herself over and over it was for the best, but still. Not even a sighting! She'd even peeked at the swimmers on Monday night, hoping he'd be there. Of course, he wouldn't be allowed to swim with an incision even though there was enough chlorine in the Rec Center pool to bleach half of Mill Falls snow white. Nothing. Zilch. It was beyond frustrating, trying to casually bump into someone who'd dropped off the face of the earth.

"Come on! He sent you those amazing flowers, got in a fight over you…girlfriend, you so need to go out with him, to thank him for his valor if nothing else. And gossip says he's a god in bed, so you know you're going to have a good time." Snip, snip.

"I'm not really a one-night stand kind of girl."

"Come on, let me live vicariously through you!" Fran begged.

Glad laughed and shook her head.

"Seriously, I think he really likes you," Fran stated. Snip, snip. Comb and compare. "Trust me, he hasn't acted like this about anyone else. Hold still."

Glad stared into the mirror and Fran clipped into the long layers around her face.

"And even if it is just a one-nighter, who better to have it with? He's cute, there's the chest hair thing, and rumor has it he's got a nice package."

"Fran!" Glad laughed, even though she burned with embarrassment. "You're married!"

"And very happily so," Fran said. Snip, snip. "But that doesn't mean I don't notice a hot ticket every now and then. Bend down."

Glad obediently lowered her chin. Fran began to comb and cut the length at the back of her head.

"If I were single, I would not push Mike Kovalski out of my bed," Fran pronounced. Snip, comb, compare, snip. "In fact, I think I'd chain him there for a week straight." A bell rang and Fran glanced at the security monitor that showed the front entrance of Serenity Day Spa. "Ooh. Speak of the devil."

Glad glanced up. Mike Kovalski was shaking hands with Frank. Oh, boy. Her girly parts began waving their pom-poms around in her core.

"Does he get his hair cut here, or... something?"

"Not as far as I know. But they do the landscaping out front. Bend down."

Glad put her chin back down and Fran clipped more away.

"I could seriously look at him all day."

"When you've got scissors next to my head, you'd better be looking at me!" Glad said. Fran laughed out loud and clipped a few last strands.

"Okay, time to style." Within minutes she had blown out Glad's hair to shining perfection.

"Why can't I do this at home?" Glad

complained, admiring herself in the mirror.

"I've got mad skills, hon." Fran pulled off the protective apron Glad wore over her clothing and Glad got up. Fran walked her out to the front desk, chattering the whole way.

"Admit it," she said to Glad. "I can tell you like him."

"I admit nothing."

Fran snorted and totaled up Glad's bill for the day's services. "If you take my advice-and I know you won't-I'd go for it if he so much as looked at me sideways. Twenty-six today."

Glad handed over some cash. "I just don't think I'm that kind of girl."

"Doll!" Frank Delacroix was heading in her direction, followed by Mike Kovalski. Frank threw his arms open and hugged her tight. "You look fab. Love that cut on you."

"Fran's got skills," Glad said. "You really should pay her more." She took her receipt from a grinning Fran. Tried to avoid looking at Mike Kovalski, but her eyes betrayed her.

He was watching her, his eyes hot and the memory of their kiss flooded through her. Glad went warm all over and looked away.

"She bankrupts me as it is," Frank groused, and turned back to Mike. "You see what kind of flak I have to put up with in here?"

"Try a day in the field with my crew," Mike said to him.

"I would put those guys to shame and you know it."

"You'd have them all getting manicures."

Frank grabbed one of Mike's hands. "You

could stand one, that's for sure. You know what a nail brush is, don't you?"

"I was in the field this morning-"

"And you've got hair on your knuckles! Haven't you ever heard of waxing?"

Mike snatched his hand back. "Hey, I'm a man. The only hair removal I do is on my face. Sometimes not even that."

"Don't I know it! You're like a fucking gorilla! You've probably got hair on your ass!"

"My ass is my business," Mike interrupted, grinning.

"*Oy, vey!*" Frank moaned, putting Glad's arm in his. "Let me walk you out, doll. I need to look at something beautiful for a minute."

"What, I'm not pretty enough for you?" Mike said, laughing as he followed them outside.

"You're a beast. Why would I look at you when I can look at her?" Frank threw at him.

"Why indeed," Mike said. "I'll get those new contracts over to you this afternoon. Nice to see you again, Glad."

Thankfully he didn't wait for a response, because she was absolutely tongue tied. God almighty, why couldn't she act like a normal person around him?

"I think you like him," Frank said as they moved to her car.

Glad shook her head. "No. Not at all."

"Then why are you blushing? Honestly, doll, you blush more than anyone I've ever met."

"I've always been this way. And just because I blush doesn't mean-"

Frank guffawed. "I saw those looks you two

were giving each other. You like him and he likes you right back. Add in those flowers and that bar fight and you're headed straight for love, baby!"

"Stop it," she groaned.

Saturday dawned clear and perfect and Glad decided to ditch the last of her painting-the dining room-in favor of yard work and began clearing a path from her back porch to her back fence line, yanking out those stinging wisteria vines, pulling up crabgrass and other assorted weeds, clipping and digging and filling yard bag after yard bag.

She was running full steam and feeling great about her progress even though the path to the back fence was only about four feet wide. No need to call in the professionals. She knew one end of a rake from the other and could pull up vines and weeds with the best of them. She was a librarian. She could handle anything, could make this yard into a showplace with no help from Mike Kovalski.

Mike.

She'd lost more time at work and sleep at night than she wanted to admit, playing that kiss over and over in her mind. And he'd even invaded her dreams, a sexy presence that had her waking up aching and longing for him. One dream in particular, where he'd held her down in a field of flowers and entered her had her on the verge of orgasm when she woke.

It was crazy. It was ridiculous. She'd never be more to him than a checkmark, a notch on the old bedpost, so to speak. He just wanted her because she'd said no and he probably was used to women falling over themselves for him. She needed to stop thinking about him and keep her focus where it belonged: on work and promotion and getting her house and yard shaped up.

If only it were that easy.

By mid-afternoon she had cleared back to the fence and took a break, staring over into the large park that bordered some of the properties on her side of the street. Frank and Sal had told her they had the best seat in the house for the July fourth fireworks show, and there was a big festival in the park over Labor Day weekend, the highlights being the Great Founder's Day Race for children five and under, a parade and a community softball game before the annual Founder's Day Ball.

She pulled one last vine away from the chain link, thankful she'd reached the fence at last. But there was still more to do; she needed to get the whole fence line clear, according to the snippy letter she'd received from the city just the other day. She picked up her gloves and clippers from where she'd dropped them, intending to keep on, then spied a dark apparition to her right.

That must be the barberry Mike had been talking about, a mass of twisted, wickedly thorny branches about eight feet high and at least six feet wide. Glad walked over to it, curious.

It was pretty, in a threatening sort of way. The branches were knobby and there were tiny flower buds that looked ready to burst into bloom any day. And it was growing through the fence, waiting to catch some unwary traveler in its thorny embrace. No wonder she'd gotten that letter.

She'd get that job out of the way first, she decided, then clear off the rest of the fence line. And then she'd take all those bags to the curb, sink into a bubble bath and stop thinking about Mike Kovalski once and for all.

Glad carefully cut the first few branches and pulled them through the chain link. She stepped in a little farther and cleared out some more. This wasn't so bad. You just had to be careful and watch what you were doing. She reached over to clip another.

A thorn tore into her shirt and pierced her arm. Glad jumped and dropped the clippers. "Ow!" She pulled away and her hair snagged on a branch. She reached up to free it and was immediately caught by a half-dozen more thorns. "Son of a-ow!"

It was like the tree had come to life and closed around her. No matter which way she turned she was caught in a tangle of wicked, scratching thorns. She tried one mighty lunge backwards, but to no avail: the tree held on and snapped her back. Desperate, panicking, she flailed out; a branch answered with a slap to her face and stayed there, one long thorn stuck in her cheek and another dangerously close to her eye. She couldn't move. She didn't dare.

10

"You coming out? Good band up at The Hill tonight," said Fonz.

"No, I'm too tired," Mike said, closing his office door and heading towards the exit. Okay, his office wasn't much bigger than a closet, but it was his own and that was pretty sweet. He let Fonz go out first, then locked the back door behind them.

"And besides, I don't think Jason Taylor wants to see my face up there anytime soon." The owner of The Hill had shoved Mike against his truck and roundly cussed him out in the parking lot after the fight, using some of the most creative combinations of swear words Mike had ever heard. Taylor had a fiery temper, but he ran one hell of a bar.

"I still can't believe you took on Hairy Larry Jones," Fonz said as they walked out to their trucks. "He could've killed you!"

"But he didn't." Mike held up his key fob

and the F-150 gave him a *blip*.

"Good thing," Fonz said. "I'd hate to have to train a new boss."

Mike laughed and opened his truck door. "You on this weekend?"

"Nope. I'm at church. See you Monday!" Fonz headed for his truck, a vintage 1956 Ford in mint condition with a faded out 'Fonzi Construction' sign on the door. It had belonged to his grandfather, the founder of the Fonzi Construction Company in Glen View and the truck was, in Fonz's words, his sole inheritance. Mike hadn't pried, but he knew Fonz's decision to leave the family business and work in landscaping while doing finish carpentry and custom woodwork on the side had not gone over well.

Fonz had recently purchased ten acres out on McCarthy Road and was rehabbing the structure that stood there-an old church-to be his future home. Mike had gone to check it out a few weeks ago and, while he appreciated Fonz's talent, he wondered if his crewman was in over his head on that job. The structure was solid, but the inside was a complete wreck.

Mike drove out of the Green Spaces lot and headed towards town. He turned his mind back to the incident up at The Hill and the fallout. To his happy surprise, the gossip generated was favorable as Larry Jones was not well liked in the county. Several people had come up to Mike since that night and high-fived him or shook his hand; defending Glad Donahue from a crazy drunk being seen as a noble act. Not that he'd wanted to get punched in the face, but it turned out to be good press and he'd take whatever he could get.

It wasn't enough, though. He needed to get Glad Donahue out on a date, pronto. Ken had told him today another client had been wavering, then proceeded to pester him for another fifteen minutes about Glad and his progress, making suggestions until he thought he might scream. The rest of today panic had clawed at his gut like a hungry beast. Mike wasn't stupid; he knew if Ken lost any more business he'd let him go no matter how good he was. He needed something positive to happen.

He stopped for the railroad tracks and waited for the freight cars to pass. Considered his options for the rest of the night. Go home, eat something, hang out awhile then go to bed. Or he could get a six-pack and just show up on her doorstep. Ask her about the progress on the library project, talk plants or something.

Maybe even kiss her again like he'd been fantasizing about for the last week.

She'd completely shocked him that night after the board meeting, reaching for him like she'd been unable to help herself. And he'd been unable to resist giving her what they both wanted. Things had gotten hot fast and he'd ached for a long time after she left him.

It was probably for the best they'd stopped. After all, he was making a play for respectable and screwing the assistant director against her car in the library parking lot wasn't exactly a classy thing to do. Not that it stopped him from wanting to do just that.

Yeah, he had it bad. He was challenged, frustrated beyond belief but enjoying the chase all the same. And he knew some part of her was, too.

The last car passed and the gates went back up. Mike drove to the next intersection and turned right on Center Street and headed east. Towards Lincoln Street and her.

***

How long had she been here? There was still plenty of daylight, but the shadows in Glad's back yard were lengthening. She'd been desperately listening for any nearby human sound and had called for help a dozen or so times, but no one had shown up. You'd think someone would be coming or going, but her neighborhood remained quiet. And Frank and Sal, blast them, had gone out of town for the weekend.

Her body was aching and stinging and she wanted nothing more than to drop where she stood. But the thorn embedded in her cheek and the one poised to impale her eyeball kept her on her feet.

She should never have tried to do this herself. And when she got out of this mess, if she got out of this mess, she was going to march right inside and set up an appointment with Green Spaces, her pride be damned. Let Mike Kovalski and Frank and everyone else laugh and say 'I told you so' a million times over. She totally didn't care anymore. She'd had it with yard work for the rest of her natural life-

Was that a car engine? Yes! Right out on the street! Was it stopping? She couldn't tell. Glad listened hard. The engine was idling close by. Maybe it was the neighbors across the street. Maybe a visitor.

"Come on," she begged the noise. "Shut it off and get out of the car. Please."

The car shut off. She waited. A door slammed and she sucked in a huge breath.

"Help!" she screamed. "I need help!"

Running steps. "Where are you?" a man's voice called.

"Back here! By the fence!" *Thank you, God. Thank you, thank you, thank you!*

Rustling and snapping sounded behind her. Sweet relief.

"I'm stuck," she called out, trying not to cry. "I think my clippers are down under the-"

"Mother-arrgh! Didn't I tell you to stay away from that thing?"

Could it get more embarrassing than this? Probably not. Life was so unfair. "I was just trying to-"

"Did I, or did I not tell you specifically to leave the barberry alone?" Mike Kovalski growled from behind her.

"You told me," Glad said, feeling stupid.

"And what part of that didn't you get?"

"I'm sorry," she said in a very small voice.

"Woman, you're a danger to yourself," Mike grumbled, circling the tree. "How you ever got this far in life I'll never know."

"I just wanted to-ow-do some yard work."

"How's that working out for you?" he asked, peering at her through the branches.

"You're good at laying on the guilt, you know that?"

"I'm Jewish. I cut my teeth on guilt. And here's some more for you," he said, rounding the tree so he stood opposite her. "Tell me why it is that instead of putting your I-can-do-it-my-damn-self pride aside for a minute and listening to the professional, you decide to come out here and get in trouble? You know how many gray hairs you're giving me right now?"

"I'm sorry, okay?"

"You don't have to do everything yourself, you know. It's okay to need someone every once in a-oh geez. Don't cry!"

"I'm not crying!" Two fresh tears spilled out, making a liar out of her.

Mike came back around the tree. "Hang tight, girl. I need to grab a couple of things and I'll be back."

Glad waited, heard his truck door open and close and then Mike came back into view, wearing a canvas jacket. He zipped it up and put on safety glasses. Heavy work gloves went on then he picked up a big pair of loppers and went to work on the tree.

"Why are you cutting those out? The problem is me!"

"The problem's always you," he muttered.

"That's not true!"

He gave her a look full of meaning, but only

said "I need space to work. You're tangled to shit in there, in case you haven't noticed."

"You're mad at me, aren't you," she said as he cut some bigger branches away.

"I'm not mad." He cut some more, his face set in concentration.

"Yes you are," she gulped. "I'm so sorry. Thank you for saving me. Again."

"You're welcome. Now stop that crying. You're killing me." He tossed all the cut branches into a pile, then switched to a smaller pair of clippers and trimmed a few more branches back. Then he came close.

"I want to get that one by your eye first. You ready?" he asked.

"Yes." She closed her eyes. Mike's gloved hand gently covered her face, protected it while he snipped the thorn away. He clipped a few more times and dropped his hand. She opened her eyes again. "What is it?"

"I'm going to take this one out of your face now. It'll probably sting." He reached over.

"Okay-ow!"

"I'm sorry. It's gone. Hold still." Mike reached behind her head and clipped some more. He was so close she could count the tiny stitch scars in his cheek. Nine of them, small and perfectly spaced along that dark pinkish line below his eye.

"You got your stitches out," she said.

"This morning." He cut another branch.

"Does it still hurt?" she asked.

His eyes met hers for a second. "A little."

"I'm so sorry. I didn't want you to get

punched. And I shouldn't have left you."

Mike pulled a branch away and tossed it aside. "You did the right thing. Larry Jones is certifiable."

"But you got hurt and it was my fault."

"Then you owe me one," he said, clipping some more. "Okay, step to your right." Glad obliged, Mike clipped one more branch and she was free.

"Hang on." He stuffed his clippers in his coat pocket and carefully pulled away the twigs and other pieces still stuck to her clothing and hair.

"Good thing you were wearing long sleeves," he said, "or you'd look like a pincushion right about now." He took off his glasses.

"Thank you so much. I don't know what I would have done if you hadn't come by." She looked at him. "Why did you come by?"

"I wanted to see you."

"You did?" She felt suddenly warm inside. He'd wanted to see her, talk to her...kiss her again, maybe?

"And I find you up to no good, like usual." He growled his response but his lips were curving into a smile.

"Thank you, again."

"You'd better clean up those scratches," he said. "I'll take care of this mess. And maybe afterwards we can have a beer."

"Okay-wait. I don't think I have any left."

"Ah, so the librarian's a lush. Wait 'til I tell the guys."

"Stop it!" She laughed. "I'll just go down to that convenience store on Gibson-"

He handed over his keys. "No need. There's some in my truck."

***

"So we're set on the design, clearing, excavating and utility work is on the schedule for May and we've got plants mostly picked out," Mike said to Glad nearly two hours later. He closed his notebook, pushed his battered book of garden plants aside and made one last notation on his smartphone. "Now it's time for the real question. Did you learn your lesson today?"

He pocketed the phone and his chair groaned beneath him; a tiny bistro-style chair that had no business supporting a big guy like him. She'd probably thought it was cute, but in reality it was a rickety piece of crap he expected would collapse under him any second.

They were on Glad's back porch in the growing dark. She'd showered and dressed her injuries while he cleaned up the branches and moved her legion of yard bags to the curb, then they had their plant discussion over beers and snacks. The quiet conversation was pleasant and nice, a perfect way to spend an evening. He could easily see them talking this way years from now.

Years from now?

"What do you mean?" she asked, putting down her empty bottle. Mike refocused.

"Are you going to let me handle this?" he asked.

She didn't answer him.

"You're in over your head, girl."

She frowned down at the table. "I was doing all right."

Was she serious? "You were trapped back there!"

"It was just an accident, a fluke!"

He put some steel in it. "Gladiolus-"

"Okay, okay! You're right! Are you happy?"

"Yes." He noted her stiff posture and clouded eyes. "Why is that so hard to admit?"

She shrugged. "I just like to do stuff myself, that's all."

"I think there's more going on here than that."

She shrugged again and looked away.

"Glad. It's okay to need help sometimes. To need someone."

"I don't...I prefer to not depend on anyone but myself."

He eyed her for another long minute. There were shadows in her lovely eyes that spoke of a lifetime of disappointment and grief. "You want to tell me about it?"

"Not really."

He tried his most charming smile. "You might as well spill. I'm nosy as hell and you know how persistent I can be."

"I'd rather not go there right now. Can we change the subject?"

Mike nodded. He'd let her keep her secrets for now, but there was no way he was giving up. "So you'll leave this job to the professionals?"

She narrowed her eyes, then smiled a little.

"I suppose."

Was she teasing him? Didn't matter; watching her hair ruffling in the breeze and smelling her, all clean and citrusy, was taking all his attention. Was it orange? No. Grapefruit. He inhaled again, trying not to be too obvious about it, but man, did she ever smell good.

"You suppose?" he asked.

She blushed a bit and said, "Well, since I gave you back your card I don't…"

Mike raised a brow, pulled out his wallet and tossed three cards on the table.

"Three?" she asked.

"One for home, one for work, one for your purse." Mike pulled out his smartphone again and checked it. "So. How's Thursday morning? My crew's free. We can be here by eight, rain or shine."

"All right."

"Good. Great." He made a notation and closed the app. "Now what do you want back here?"

"Want? Oh," she laughed a little, "just one of everything. But what I can realistically afford is not much. Probably just grass and a few perennials."

"We can do more. We can make this any way you want. I promise you, I can turn that nightmare into paradise."

"Well-"

"You've seen my work," he reminded her. "Tell me what you want. Dogwoods, lilacs, ornamental grasses, a patio, fire pit, Koi pond…name it. I can do it."

"I can't afford anything fancy."

"We'll work something out." He gave her his most intense gaze. "Let me in. I want this."

And he wanted her, right here and now. Wanted to kiss her again, wanted to skim off those low-rise jeans and take her on this crappy little table, pull her legs over his shoulders and-

Glad leaned back in her chair, looking wary. "I-I'll have to think about it."

Mike forced himself to relax. If he kept pushing her, she might start getting defensive again and he'd lose ground. He put on an easy smile and chose his next words carefully.

"Sorry. I get excited, you know? I see a space and all the potential it has and the ideas just flood in."

"You're certainly passionate about your work." She smiled again.

"I am." He moved to put his wallet away and the chair groaned under him again. He shot to his feet, alarmed.

"It's not going to break," Glad said, giggling.

Mike regarded the little chair. It was definitely listing towards the right. "I don't trust it. Don't you have anything bigger?"

"Bigger doesn't necessarily mean better," she said primly.

"When you average around 235, bigger is always better," he assured her, leaning against the railing. He'd be damned if he ruined their progress by sitting down again. Nothing killed romance quite like landing on your ass in front of a girl you were trying to impress. Sadly, he knew this from past experience.

"So I won't see you tooling around town in a little sports car any time soon?"

Mike snorted. "Do I look like I'd fit in a sports car?"

She laughed softly. "I guess not. Is it comfortable?" she asked.

"You'll find out soon."

Glad's eyes flew to his. "Are we going somewhere?"

"Not tonight." He activated his phone. "Give me your number."

"My number?" She looked panicked.

"So I can call you next week. For a date."

"I-well-"

"You owe me," he reminded her with a patient smile. She opened her mouth once, twice, then rattled off her mobile number and he stored it, fixed it as speed dial number one. Now it was time to leave her hanging. He pocketed his phone and pushed off the rail.

"Where are you going?"

"Home," he said, starting down the steps. "I've got some work to do."

"Work-haven't you done enough today?" she asked with a little laugh.

"There's no rest for the wicked," he said. He unlocked the F-150 and opened the door, and smiled as her soft voice reached him.

"Wicked is an understatement."

11

Glad made coffee, yawned her way to her front porch and picked up the Sunday paper. Though she kept up with the news as part of her job she had little interest in politics or sports, but the plethora of ads and inserts in the Sunday edition were always fun to look at. She paged through them and sipped her coffee, not really seeing any of the sale items. Instead memories crowded her head and every one of them had to do with Mike.

He'd asked her out, multiple times. They had kissed. He'd rescued her from a pawing drunk and her own back yard. He'd sent her flowers and he had her number and they were going on a date sometime soon.

Should she do this? She knew she was risking a lot by agreeing to a date. Gossip would follow, perhaps another Marie Stahl inquisition. She should probably just call things off.

But...she didn't really want to.

Okay, she was weak. Her hormones were running the show. Mike Kovalski was sexy and funny and he made her feel good. One date wouldn't kill her. Some good sex wouldn't kill her, either. Based on that single kiss, she had a feeling Mike took good sex to a whole new level.

But it wasn't just the sex. She was starting to care about him.

No. She would not fall for that man. Would not give over to love again, especially not with someone who was just 'sowing his wild oats' as Fran had put it.

Glad's phone began chirping on the coffee table. Who in the world called at seven-thirty on a Sunday? "Hello?"

"Are you up?" asked Mike.

"Of course," she said, trying to ignore that thrill inside.

"Then good morning," he said, the warmth in his husky voice vibrating to the very core of her. Glad squirmed in her seat, taking far more pleasure in how sexy he sounded over the phone than she should.

"Good morning to you, too."

"Almost. I'm still in bed."

"Oh?" she managed. The vision of a hairy chest and tumbled bed sheets nearly gave her heart failure.

This was ridiculous. She needed to calm down. Needed to just relax. This wasn't a big deal, people talked on the phone while they were still in bed, possibly naked...

"Worked on your yard design 'til late. But I'm getting up soon. We've got a reservation for

143

eleven. I'll pick you up around 10:45."

"Ten-wait. Today?"

"Yes."

"We're having our date this morning?"

He chuckled into her ear and she shivered down to her toes.

"But you said you'd call me next week."

"This is next week."

"Well, I guess, but I wasn't expecting-where are we going?"

"Someplace nice. Wear a dress."

"Are you wearing a tie?"

"Yes."

Okay, that meant someplace very nice. She'd only been out a couple places in town, and a couple more in Glen View with her friends, but none of them were dressy establishments.

"Where are we going?" she asked again.

"Not telling."

"That's not fair."

"That's all you get, girl." He chuckled again. "Ten forty-five. I'll see you."

***

Mike adjusted his tie, looking in the long mirror on the back of his bedroom door. He definitely wasn't a suit-wearing type of guy, but he had attended enough family, synagogue and work events to understand that a man needed a good suit. His body had changed in the last few years, had grown broader and bulkier and a few months ago he'd sucked it up and spent the money on a new suit, then had laid down the extra and had it tailored to his frame. He still laughed whenever he thought of going into the tailor's fitting room and stripping down for measurements. The little man had taken one look at him and said "Son, you're a lummox!"

Lummox indeed, but he couldn't help that. Unlike his older brother or sisters, Mike had taken after the Russian side of the family. From the few pictures he'd seen, his Russian ancestors were all tall and burly, even the women. His Zayde and Bubbe swore that his great-grandfather was a giant and, while Mike didn't actually believe that, the lone photograph the family had of him showed a large, strapping man with a beard that came halfway down his chest, holding a double bladed axe that would surely make even the toughest character think twice before messing with him.

He shrugged into his jacket and regarded himself. Not bad, considering. The scar on his face was permanent, but his doctor assured him it would fade somewhat over time. He'd mentioned plastic surgery as an option during their follow-up visit and Mike had laughed in his face. As if.

Mike checked his look one last time and left the house, nerves stretched and jangling. There was a lot riding on this date. He didn't like the pressure, didn't want to go out in town and endure the staring and talk. But he didn't have much choice. Sunday brunch at the Mill River Inn was the place to be and, since it was Easter today, the place would be packed. He needed every eye on them, needed everyone to see him on a respectable date with a respectable woman. He'd called Annie Scott, the manager of the inn, last night and begged her to find him a good table in a prime spot. She'd groused and grumbled, but as he'd performed a miracle makeover of her property last fall, she said she'd figure something out.

He hoped he didn't blow it. He needed to be charming and witty and cover how anxious he was about the whole thing. He needed Glad to have a good time. He needed her to want to see him again.

***

She told herself she didn't need to impress him, or anybody, but Glad changed her outfit six times before she was satisfied, settling finally on a knit dress in a dark peach that draped nicely and showed off her curves to advantage. It had a modest scoop neckline, a slightly less modest vee in the back and long sleeves, a big plus as she had two ugly scratches on her left arm from her tangle with the barberry yesterday. Thankfully, the wound in her cheek was healing well and there was only a tiny scab that wasn't too noticeable.

She managed not to poke herself in the eye with the mascara wand, dusted her cheeks with a hint of blush and put on a tinted lip balm. She'd never been good with makeup; she'd tried to do a smoky eye a few months ago and wound up looking like something out of *The Walking Dead* for all her effort. Simple was definitely best.

She glanced at the clock. Ten-forty.

Hoo, boy. He'd be here in five minutes. Glad checked her appearance again, briefly thought about changing her dress again, then squelched it. She liked this dress and knew it looked good on her. But she allowed herself a second to wish she'd had time to shop for something new and positively stunning. After all, this was her only chance to blow the One Date Wonder away.

Okay, she could admit it. She knew this date had to be a joke, that it wouldn't mean anything more to him than any other of his nine million dates. But fool that she was, she was looking forward to it. She wanted to go out with Mike Kovalski, to bask in the glow of his admiring gaze. Glad rolled her eyes in the mirror as she put on earrings.

"You're an idiot," she said to her reflection.

A door slammed outside. He was here! Glad touched a bit of perfume to her neck and wrists, stuffed her feet into her heels then dashed to her full-length mirror.

She looked like crap!

"Relax," she told her reflection. "You look perfectly okay, everything is fine."

Her doorbell rang and Glad headed for the stairs, heart pounding in her chest.

12

Around the main dining room at the Mill River Inn:

Easter Sunday is such a wonderful day. The Inn is so lovely, and it's just packed today!

It's always packed for Easter Brunch. Seems like everyone in town is here.

Did you see the spring flowers on the tables? So gorgeous.

Did you try the ham? I don't know what they do to it here, but I can never get my ham to turn out like this.

Did you see her? That lovely Miss Donahue from the library's here.

Who is she with?

Him.

Him who—oh, well, well, well! If it isn't the One Date Wonder himself.

Did you see him holding her hand? I can't believe it. She's not his type at all. She's nice!

Well, he saved her from Larry Jones, after

all. You heard about that, right? Wound up in the Urgent Care, got stitches and everything!

So maybe she's just thanking him by going out to brunch.

I'll just bet she thanked him, all right.

***

Okay, this was easier than he'd thought it would be. He was still a little nerved up, and it felt like every eye was on them, but so far things were going well.

Better than well; Mike was having a good time. A really good time. Glad Donahue was smart and funny and easy to talk to. And hotter than hell in mid-July, which was a definite plus.

That dress. Those legs! *Oy, sheyn!* Those legs in high heels! He'd always been a leg man and she had about the finest pair he'd ever seen. When he'd helped her up into his truck he'd had to act the gentleman and pretend he didn't notice when her dress slid up and gifted him with a closer look, had to make small talk when he really wanted to scoop her up, take her back into her house and find out what other surprises were in store for him.

Nervous, he'd reached for her hand as they walked to the front doors of the Mill River Inn and she'd given it with a shy little smile. And he quickly discovered he didn't want to let her go. Didn't want to stop touching her and found himself laying a hand across the small of her back when they were waiting for their table and again while they cruised the buffet line. And she was okay with it.

He didn't have to try. Didn't have to pretend at all. He was having fun and he found himself relaxing, able to enjoy the moment and the surroundings and, quite possibly, the best date he'd ever had in his life. He would have no problem continuing this. More dates. More time with her. And yeah, sex.

His insides clenched at the thought. Oh, he wanted it and bad. But they'd have to wait a little bit. Third or fourth date maybe, so she wouldn't think he was only after a score. Damn his reputation and all its consequences.

"Is that bacon I see on your plate?" Glad asked as they returned to their table.

Mike grinned. "Maybe."

"I guess that means you're not orthodox, then?"

"I'm about as far from that as you can get," he said, placing his napkin on his lap. "I go to synagogue when I can and try to be observant. But I don't keep kosher. I eat dairy and meat together. I like bacon. And a rack of ribs every now and then." He paused and looked around, then leaned forward as if imparting a great secret and stage-whispered, "Don't tell my mother."

Glad giggled. "I won't."

"I sure wish there was a good Jewish deli close by. Some days I could kill for a knish, and I dream about rugelach. My Bubbe made the best one, with raspberry filling and-"

"Icing on top," she finished. "And it's really good. Deb Jacobs made me some last week, as a sort of thank you for getting rid of Jimmer Hall."

"I've heard of that little snot. Doesn't he have a bunch of tattoos?"

"And a lip ring, and gauges..." Glad shuddered.

Mike shook his head. "If I showed up at my parent's house looking like that, they'd call the cops on me."

She smiled at him. "Are you close with your family?"

How to answer that? "I...was."

"Did you have a falling out?"

"Yes." He stabbed a piece of potato. Ate it and stabbed another.

"I'm sorry. It's not my business."

"It's fine." He cleared his throat. "We talk on the phone a little, but I haven't seen anyone since I moved up here. It's hard. I miss them."

She looked at him, her eyes sympathetic. "I know we don't know each other that well, but I'm a good listener if you want to talk."

The offer was unexpected and oddly touching. "As am I," he finally said.

She regarded him. "Is this some kind of 'I'll show you mine if you show me yours' moment?"

A sudden image of her naked settled in his conscious. He gazed into her pretty eyes and smiled and she turned as pink as the lilies on their table.

"Champagne?" asked their server. Perfect timing; he really needed a change of subject or he was going to embarrass himself. Mike raised his brow and Glad nodded. The server poured them each a measure and moved on. Mike lifted his glass and touched it to Glad's.

"What are we toasting?" she asked.

"Us."

She smiled and took a sip. He tried his. A bit too sweet for his taste, but drinkable.

"So what's with all the hats?" he asked, putting the glass down. Many of the women in the room were wearing hats, in all colors and varieties.

"It's Easter."

"It's Passover."

"There's room for both, I think."

He liked the idea of that. "So what do hats have to do with Easter?"

"Haven't you ever watched *Easter Parade*?"

"I don't really like musicals."

"Neither do I," she admitted. "But in the movie-and I guess this is an actual tradition-all the ladies and gentlemen walked down Fifth Avenue in New York City on Easter. And the women would all be sporting new bonnets. I don't really understand why, it's probably a social, 'hooray it's spring' kind of thing. It has nothing to do with Jesus rising from the dead."

"Well, fancy seeing you here!" Ken Anderson interrupted, beaming. Mike stood and shook hands, kissed Ken's wife, Mary, on the cheek.

"Glad, you remember my boss, Ken, and this is his wife Mary."

"It's so nice to meet you," Glad said, shaking hands with Mary and smiling at Ken.

"Don't let us interrupt! We just wanted to say hi!" Mary said cheerfully.

"Got to eat and run," Ken said. "One o'clock

comes fast." And they moved away to the buffet line.

"Green Spaces is open today?" Glad asked, surprised.

"Just for the afternoon. You'd be surprised how much business we do, with families in town and such. People around here really get the gardening itch come April."

"Do you have to work today?"

He nodded. "I wish I didn't. I'd much rather hang out with you."

She glowed and Mike was charmed all over again. He could spend the whole day looking at her, memorizing the planes of her face, picking out all the shades of bourbon in her hair.

And kissing her again. He was totally down with that.

"Oh, boy," she said, suddenly looking uncomfortable.

"What's the matter?"

"Brace yourself," she muttered, and Marie Stahl, on the arm of her nephew Scott, the biggest blowhard in Lord County, stopped at their table. Mike stood.

"Miss Donahue. I see you choose to ignore my advice," the woman said.

"I choose to live my life as I see fit," Glad said sweetly. She turned to Mike, a hint of anxiety in her gaze. "You remember Mr. Kovalski, I'm sure."

"A pleasure to see you again," Mike said, smiling his best.

"It is certainly not!" Marie Stahl said tartly. "Young man, you are a disgrace!"

He couldn't help it. He laughed out loud. The old woman puffed up like a toad and her nephew patted her arm.

"Let's get to our table, Aunty," Scott said to her. "Everyone's waiting for you." He nodded briefly at Mike, then gave Glad an appraising look that raised Mike's hackles. But he only said, "Nice to see you again," and led his aunt away.

"That was interesting," Mike commented as he sat. "Want to tell me about it?"

Glad rolled her eyes. "She thinks being board president makes her God Almighty. She's high on her power and likes to make everyone's life miserable, especially mine."

"Actually, I was talking about Scott," Mike said.

She grimaced. "Oh, he asked me out the other day."

Something dark twisted in his gut. "And?"

"And I'm not interested," Glad said, then leaned closer and half-whispered, "He asked me right in front of *her*! It was so awkward!"

"I'll bet." He smiled. "And now here you are with me. Is this awkward?"

"No. It's…nice."

"Agreed." He picked up his champagne glass, intending to toast her again when a sneering voice floated over his shoulder.

"Parading your latest 'ho at Easter brunch? That's ballsy, even for you, Mike."

***

Glad stiffened as a gorgeous blonde

154

approached their table. She was perfectly made up, dressed to the nines and her face had that faintly surprised look that screamed BOTOX. She held out her hand and Glad took it automatically.

"I'm Felice. One of Mike's other *friends.* Just wanted to welcome you to the One Date Wonder Club."

She hadn't expected this, and from the look on Mike's face he hadn't expected it either. What to do? If Felice expected a scene, Glad could certainly oblige her: she'd learned some dirty tricks growing up in foster care that would put her opponent down for the count. But she didn't think the Mill River Inn management would appreciate a girl fight in the middle of their dining room. She tried another tack.

"Oh, there's a club?" she asked, putting on her best smile. "Do we have monthly meetings? A secret handshake?"

Mike made a strangled sound that could have been a cough. Felice narrowed her eyes and regarded Glad. "Cute. And I'm sure you think you're special, that he really likes you, that there's something between you that's different. But you're not. Once he gets what he wants you'll be tossed out on your can just like the rest of us."

People at the nearby tables were watching this little drama play out, including Marie Stahl. Glad could hear whispers above the general din of a dining room and had no doubt this would come out during the next board meeting, and her director interview down the road. Well, in for a penny, in for a pound.

"Does he at least stop at the curb or do you have to tuck and roll?" she asked. "Just so I'm prepared later."

Felice stared at her, flummoxed. "You're as messed up as he is," she pronounced, and stalked away.

"Nice to have met you," Glad called after her, then turned back to Mike. He was smiling at her like she'd just handed him the moon. "What?"

"I promise, I come to a full stop."

She picked up her champagne and tapped his glass with hers. "That's good. It's tough to stick a landing in four inch heels."

He laughed. "Girl, you are something else."

***

"I'm not sure another date is a good idea."

Mike wanted to howl and bang his head on something. He'd apologized, they'd finished brunch without any other problems and he'd thought everything was okay. Apparently not.

They were standing in Glad's front yard. He'd helped her down from his truck, getting another sweet flash of her legs, and had intended to walk her to her door and get another one of her mind-blowing kisses. Looked like that wasn't going to happen now.

"I know you got spooked by that scene with Felice, and I'm sorry-"

Glad waved an impatient hand. "Didn't you

see them all staring? Didn't you hear them?"

Mike cringed. Of course he had, he'd created that mess, hadn't he? But he'd hoped she hadn't. Foolish, naïve hope.

"People gossip. I can't control that. And since ninety-five percent of it is crap anyway, I ignore it." Which was true most of the time. These last few weeks were an exception, unfortunately. You had to listen to gossip if you wanted to spin it to your advantage.

"Well, I can't ignore it."

"Why do you care what people-who have nothing better to do with their lives-say about you?" This was edging towards an argument and Mike forced himself to breathe, to stay calm. He could not afford to get pissed off over this.

"I care because I'm the face of something a lot bigger than me. You can do a job; landscape someone's yard, hand them the bill and move on. It doesn't matter if you like them or they like you, they want you because you're the best. My world isn't like that. I have to work with these people, wait on them and help them every single day, over and over. I'm not allowed to walk away, even when I can't stand the sight of them." She put her hand on his arm. "Mike, I had a great time with you today. You're fun to be with and I hope we can stay friends."

He was in no mood to be placated. "I don't want to be just friends."

"Why not?" She looked hurt.

"Because I like being with you. You're smart and funny and sweet-"

"Thanks."

"And I'm seriously attracted to you. I want you. And you want me."

She looked away. "That's not true."

He snorted. "After the way we kissed the other night? Stop lying to yourself."

Glad crossed her arms and stared up at him, huffed. "So what if I do want you? So what if I get all weak and stupid whenever you're around?"

Heat flared deep inside. Weak and stupid sounded *great*. "So we've got something big between us, girl. You're not the only one who feels like that, you know."

For a second he thought he had her. Her lips parted and a tiny moan came out. Then she shook her head and stepped away from him.

"It doesn't matter," she said, obviously flustered. "My position...I have people looking to me for example. I can't afford to have my name dragged in your dirt."

Another face, another lifetime flashed into his conscious and Mike saw red. "My *dirt*? Who do you-" He stopped himself before he said something he'd regret and turned away, willed himself to calm down. It was just a word. He used it every day, no big deal.

I deserve diamonds, Micha. All you've got to offer is dirt.

"I-I'm sorry."

He took a deep breath and turned around. She looked confused, wounded. Not good. "No, I'm sorry. It wasn't you."

"Okay." She still looked wary, and so pretty in the midday sun. He needed to turn this around and decided to risk some truth.

"Listen. This is my dirt, as you call it. I've gone on eleven dates since I came here."

"Okay."

"And I slept with three of them."

She looked shocked. "That's it?"

"People lie," he said. "Women tell fish stories just like men. I slept with three women and they talked. The other women, the ones I didn't sleep with? Well, I guess they didn't want to be left out, so they started talking too."

"And that Felice person?"

He knew what she was digging for. "She was one of the nos."

Glad raised her brows. "Maybe that explains the attitude?"

Mike shook his head. "She was a huge mistake. I found out her divorce wasn't final during appetizers and by the time dinner showed up I had a headache from listening to all her crap. She wanted to follow me home and when I told her no she went ballistic and started screaming at me. She was the last."

"The last?"

"I stopped dating after her. That was right before the garden show. I was busy with that and my kitchen and had no idea that what was going around was so bad. I noticed some people giving me weird looks here and there and I didn't think anything of it at first, but then..." And that was as far as he was going because if he didn't shut up he'd be telling her all about Ken and the agreement and everything would fall apart.

"Why didn't you say something?" she asked.

"Who's going to believe my truth when the gossip is so much better? I just wanted to live a little, have some fun. I didn't know things would get so out of hand but they did and I'm stuck with it." He sighed. "And I'll probably be stuck with that stupid One Date Wonder moniker the rest of my life, too. But that isn't who I am."

"Who are you, then?"

"Just a man like any other. I work and sweat and drink beer and scratch myself in public." He gave her a small smile. "And I want to kiss you again. So bad I can taste it."

Her eyes went wide and a faint "oh" slipped out.

"But I'm not going to. I'm going to back off and give you some space." Mike reached over and took her hand in his. "I'm not just in this for a fuck, Glad. I like you and I'd like to see you again. Will you at least consider another date?"

She looked at him a long minute. Had he pushed too hard? He didn't think so, but you never could tell. After that close call at brunch, he wouldn't have been surprised if she ran away screaming. But she hadn't. She was still here, still letting him hold her hand and it felt pretty nice.

"I'll think about it," she finally said.

Yes. Score another run for the home team.

"That's all I ask."

160

13

"Mike Kovalski, eh?" asked Fran, giving her a nudge.

Glad rolled out her mat. "What are you talking about?"

"It's all over town! Everyone knows you went out with him! Tell!"

Holly plopped down next to them and undid the straps that held her mat together. "I am so bummed I missed it! We were going to go to Easter brunch, then Alex was sick over the weekend and-"

"Is he okay now?" Glad asked, concerned. Alex was Holly's son, a precocious seven-year old who could worm his way into the hardest of hearts. Holly's husband, a local football hero and US Marine, had died in Afghanistan six months after the child was born and Holly swore that Alex was the only thing that kept her from going completely insane with grief. Glad could still see a few shadows in Holly's eyes, but her friend had come out of those dark days stronger than ever.

"He's fine today, went back to school and everything." Holly rolled her mat out and sat next to Glad. "So was he any good?"

"What-no!"

April clapped her hands at the front of the class. "Time to begin, ladies!" The twelve women in class obediently lay back on their mats and began the pre-workout breathing, slowly stretching their arms and legs in time with each breath.

"He's lousy in bed?" Holly hissed over, scandalized.

"Five, six, seven, eight! Now left!"

"We didn't have sex," Glad hissed back. "We just went to brunch. That's it."

"Breathe in, one, two, three-"

"But he has sex with everyone," Fran said, not bothering to keep her voice down.

"Shhh!"

"Breathing, Fran!" called April from up front.

"He doesn't have sex with everyone," Glad whispered, aggravated.

"Okay, time to start our hundreds!" April said. The group got into position, sucked in, curled up and started counting.

"Does-too-" Fran gasped between breaths.

"Does-not-" Glad managed. She'd been doing Pilates for over five years and the hundred still started to kill right around fifty.

April moved the group into roll-ups next. Glad focused on keeping her shoulders down and her stomach in, breathing steady.

"So why didn't he want to have sex with you?" Fran whispered.

"Fran, hush!" Holly hissed. "It's none of your business!"

"Well, for heaven's sake!" Fran said out loud. "If she didn't have sex with Mike Kovalski, what *did* she do?"

The entire room went quiet and every eye went to Glad, who was currently bowed over her legs, touching her toes. And she wanted to stay that way forever, so she wouldn't have to look at anyone. Her face burned hot.

"Fran," came Holly's exasperated voice, "I love you like a sister. But your volume control really sucks, you know?"

"Ladies," April tried.

"I don't know about anyone else, but I'd like to know the answer to that," came from one corner.

"So would I," commented someone else.

"Ladies, please," said April, trying to get her class back under control.

Glad straightened to a sitting position, totally exasperated. They wouldn't give it a rest until she said something, she knew. Fine. "Mike Kovalski and I went to brunch. We ate. We talked. We had a nice time. He drove me home, he asked for a second date and I said I'd think about it. We didn't have sex. We didn't even kiss. That's all there is and I'm not going to talk about it anymore." She rolled herself down to her mat and lay there, staring at the ceiling.

"The One Date Wonder asked you for a *second* date?" came a shocked voice from over on the right somewhere.

Glad growled, rolled over and got to her feet. This would never end. She picked up her mat and began rolling it up, refusing to look right or left, ignoring the murmurs all around her.

"Hon, I'm sorry," Fran said, contrite. "Don't go."

Glad fastened the straps around her mat and picked up her ball. "Don't worry about it."

Holly stood. "Are you okay?"

"I'm fine." She left the exercise room and headed outside. Stuffed her mat in the back seat of her car and dropped into the driver's seat. Stared out the windshield at nothing.

The best thing to do was to tell Mike to back off. The gossip for one date was bad enough; she couldn't imagine how it would get if they actually started seeing each other. It could kill any chance she'd have at gaining the director's position. The board would want a paragon, someone people would respect, not someone who jumped in bed with the local lothario.

It was for the best. Definitely.

Glad sighed miserably. 'For the best' totally stunk.

***

Staying away from Glad was harder than he thought it would be. After enduring the third degree from Ken on Monday, not to mention several digs from his crew about buns, glasses and giving up his bachelor ways, Mike wanted nothing more than to see her, spill all and bitch about it over dinner like she was his girlfriend already. But by the time he reached the railroad crossing that night he remembered he was giving her space and he went home instead, frustrated.

Tuesday and Wednesday weren't much better. Thoughts of her crowded his mind alongside the worry that things weren't moving fast enough to save his job. He was getting closer to the end of April than he wanted to think about and the worry of it burned in his gut, kept him awake in the night.

He briefly considered going to her house last night and coming clean, telling her the truth of the situation and begging her to just pose as his girlfriend for the summer. But even if she agreed, which was highly unlikely, he couldn't depend on the gossip mill not ferreting out that little tidbit and then everything would blow up in his face.

And now here he was, stepping out of the Green Spaces truck on Thursday morning at number fifteen, Lincoln Street, getting ready to see her again after three days. He was nervous. Excited. Worried. Excited some more. It was totally nuts.

"Front doesn't look bad," Turk commented, coming around from the driver's side.

"Front's not the problem," Mike answered.

Fonz and Harry came up from the other truck. "Who gets to play today?" Fonz asked.

"Not you," Harry grumbled. "Tired of that hippity-hop pop star bullshit you put on."

"Aww, Harry, you know you secretly like it," Fonz teased and narrowly missed getting a cuff upside his head.

"All right, all right." Mike fanned out four playing cards, face down in his hand. Each man picked one, then they turned them up together.

"Yesss!" Fonz exalted. He had the ace, which meant he picked the music for the day. Mike handed over the player and Fonz began scrolling as they walked up the driveway and into the back yard.

"Hot holy shit," came from Harry.

"Damn," Turk muttered. "Fucking wisteria."

"Tell me about it. And there's a barberry in the back besides. But we shouldn't have much problem. I don't think there's anything worth saving back here, so we'll just raze it all," Mike told them, walking them into the mess. "No water or sewer lines back here, power lines are at the street-"

"Hello?" came from behind them. Oh, that voice. Everything in him began to heat and hum. Three days was too damn long.

"You guys get started," he said and waded back through the mess to Glad. Mike heard murmurs behind him and watched her cheeks turn a faint pink as he approached. Man, she was pretty. Even in that stiff gray suit with her hair pulled back and...

"Sneakers?" he asked, staring at her feet.

"I walk to work most days," she said. "It's only a few blocks."

"I see. So. How's it going?" he asked, losing himself in her eyes.

"Fine. You?"

"Fine. Miss me yet?"

She sighed. "About that."

Uh-oh. Mike tensed.

"I've been thinking..." She looked away. "We're both busy people and I've got a lot on my plate right now and...I really don't have the time to...date anyone."

"Anyone, or just me?" he asked. She blushed and he pressed her. "So you won't take a chance on something that could be great."

"It's not you, I just-I need to focus on my work, okay?"

Damn gossip! Mike regarded her, frustrated, as the music started behind him. Black Eyed Peas. Harry would be bitching all day. "I thought you were tougher than that, Gladiolus."

"It's not you, it's-"

He cut her off with a wave of his hand, irritated. "Whatever. We'll probably be done here this afternoon. I'll have to get your signature on the work order sometime today. Should I stop by the library?"

She swallowed and dropped her gaze. "That would be fine," she said quietly. "So what are you removing?"

"Everything. We're razing it."

Her eyes flew up to his, panicked. "But-not that tree behind the garage, right? And what about that bush thing right there?" She pointed at an ancient, overgrown weigela.

"We're getting rid of it all and starting over. It's for the best."

"I like the tree!"

"Tree's dead, ma'am," Turk muttered as he walked past, pushing a wheelbarrow full of tools.

167

"You hired us to clear this out," Mike reminded her. "It's a little late to cherry-pick."

Her chin tilted stubbornly. "But I want the tree!"

"The tree's dead. You're not getting it."

"It's not dead! There's some buds-"

"Do we need to do this the hard way?"

"No!" Glad dropped her bags and bolted past him to Fonz, who was fiddling with a chainsaw. "Stop right there!" she yelled. Mike sighed, exasperated, and went after her.

Glad stood with her arms wide in front of the pear tree. "Don't you dare cut this tree!"

Fonz held up his hands. "Lady, I just do what the boss tells me. The thing's dead. You're better off getting rid of it."

"You will not-"

"Out of the way, Fonz."

Fonz gave him a look and stepped back. Mike reached out, grabbed Glad and slung her over his shoulder like a bag of mulch. She screamed out loud.

"Put me down!"

"No." He walked them away from his open-mouthed crew, wrapping an arm around Glad's legs to hold her steady.

"Mike Kovalski, you put me down *now*!"

"You asked for this, so just shut up and enjoy it." Mike scooped up her purse and tote in his free hand and kept walking. Laughter erupted behind them.

She struggled mightily against him. "Enjoy-oof-I did not-you are going to be so sorry-"

"I can't wait," he growled. Then he saw

Frank Delacroix staring out his kitchen window next door. "Morning, Frank!"

"Oh, my God-"

"You need a library card to check out that reference material!" Frank called. Mike laughed out loud.

"Frank! Help me!" Glad commanded.

"You're doing fine, doll!" Frank yelled after them, then shut the window with a bang.

Mike carried her down to the end of the driveway and unceremoniously dumped her on her feet.

"Do you manhandle all your clients like this?" she asked. Oh, she was mad. He smiled down at her. She was one of those women who got even hotter when she was riled up.

"Only the ones who give me trouble. Now go do your work thing since it's so damn important." He fluttered a hand at her. "Go on. Shoo."

"Don't you tell me-"

"I'll carry you all the way downtown if you push me anymore this morning." And he would and he could tell she knew he would. They were toe to toe and she stared up at him, furious and frustrated and he was so turned on he could barely think.

"If you think I'm going to just roll over and take being treated like this, you-"

"This?" he asked, and laughed. "This is nothing. Just a little fun," he promised, cupping her cheek in his hand.

"Fun? Are you kid-hello?" She pushed his hand away. "I'm mad at you right now!"

He put it back. "You're not mad at me. You're mad at all those gossips that won't let up on you." He traced along her jaw and felt her tremble. "I heard about Monday night. I'm sorry."

"Doesn't anybody mind their own business in this town?" she groused.

"Not where we're concerned," Mike said. "We're the hottest topic since..." he grimaced, "since me. *Oy*."

"If it wasn't for you I wouldn't be in this mess."

"I know." He ran his thumb lightly over her lower lip. "And I'm sorry, but I'm not sorry, either. I like having you in my mess, Glad."

"You...like..." Her lip trembled under his thumb and he stroked it again.

"Yes." He tilted her chin up and lowered his head.

"Don't kiss me."

"Wouldn't dream of it," he said, and brushed his lips over hers.

"I thought you were giving me space," she said breathlessly.

"I am. If I wasn't, I'd kiss you like this." He slid his hand behind her head and dove in.

Glad only resisted for a second, then she was clinging to him, kissing him back, sending him right out of his head. She was so sweet and fit in his arms like she was made for him. He could kiss her all day-

A wolf whistle and a "Lawdy-Lawd" in Turk's Tennessee twang snapped him back to the present. So much for acting professional on the

job. Mike ended the kiss and released Glad.

"Wow," she sighed.

"Wow is right." Mike handed over her bags, amazed at his self-control. "You sure you want to give that up?"

"I... well, I..." She murmured, a dreamy, confused look on her face. He wanted to kiss her again.

"Quit looking at me like that," he said instead.

"Like what?" she asked, still unfocused.

"Girl. You need to go to work now." He turned her around and gave her a little push. And then, because he just couldn't help himself, he smacked that curvy bottom of hers. She came out of her reverie in a heartbeat.

"Ow!"

"Go on. You're going to be late."

"You enjoyed that, didn't you?" she tossed over her shoulder as she walked away.

"You bet," he called after her, watching her swaying hips with covetous eyes.

"Hey Romeo!" Harry's crotchety voice yelled from the back. "You gonna get off your dead ass and do some work today or what?"

***

"...and we thought we could make it up to you," Holly's voice said over the phone that night. Glad was walking around her nearly bare back yard, amazed at the transformation. The wisteria had been eradicated, the barberry was gone, the fence line was clear.

"Where?" she asked, fingering the bark of the pear tree. Mike had left it standing but pruned a large amount of branches away. It looked a little scraggly and funny, but it was still here and she'd nearly cried when she saw it tonight.

"At El Nino's. The patio's going to open Saturday night."

"It's still kind of chilly for that, isn't it?"

"It's supposed to be in the seventies on Saturday. And trust me, there'll be so many people out there it'll feel like July even if it's freezing out. Please come. The scouts are on their spring campout so Fran and I have a free night, April actually has time off, and Jayne-you remember, Alex's sister-is coming out too. Her divorce was finalized last week and she says she wants to party. This is number two, and I really hope she doesn't go for three. She has the worst luck with relationships."

"Jayne is going out?" Glad asked, surprised. The one time she'd met Holly's sister-in-law, the woman had seemed like the farthest thing from a party girl.

"Believe it. And as much as I love her, I'd rather talk to you. Jayne's bound to be waxing on about her ex and the divorce and..." Holly made a disgusted sound. "We all knew it was coming, they were a disaster from the start. She has the worst luck! Anyway, Fran and I want to make it up. We know how private you are and we pushed your boundaries too far."

"You don't have to make up for anything," Glad said. "I just have to get tougher, that's all."

"We love you just the way you are, hon. So

will you come?"

"I have to work, but I can meet you there afterwards. Is that okay?"

"Great! We'll see you Saturday!"

"I found out something interesting about our friend Jimmer from Ashley," Marci said to Glad Saturday morning as they did their stacks perusal, recommended by the police. The department managers and administration each checked different areas several times a day.

"What's that?" she asked, running a hand along the top shelf of DVDs.

"That Jimmer requested the library for his community service," Marci said, feeling behind a stack of horror films. "What do you think about that?"

Glad stared at Marci a moment. "I think," she said slowly, "that's quite a coincidence."

"And it would explain his weird behavior, right?" Marci asked.

"It could," Glad allowed. Had Jimmer Hall been the drug connection? They hadn't discovered any more drops since that first one in March. Was it because there hadn't been any more, or because Jimmer had put himself in the position to intercept them? She'd likely never know, unless drops started appearing again.

They finished the DVD section and moved into music, opening drawers and feeling behind the rows of CDs. It was tedious work, but much easier to do before patrons were in the building and you had to pretend you were actually looking for an item or reshelving something.

"Should we tell the police?" Marci asked after a minute.

Glad went to her knees and opened the bottom drawer. "Yes. It doesn't prove anything, and they can't do anything about it since Jimmer's in the county lockup, but we should definitely put it on record."

"So maybe there won't be any more drops."

"Maybe," Glad allowed, sweeping her fingers behind the CD cases, "but don't depend on it. I was in a large system before and drops were regular things. We intercepted a bunch, but God knows how many we missed. Once a dealer finds a good spot, they'll keep coming back. And sadly, libraries are great places to hide things."

"I wish we had security cameras."

"You and me both."

Building closed for the day, Glad escaped to her office and changed out of her suit into a pair of jeans and a cute brown and pink printed paisley top. It was one of her favorites and well suited to the gorgeous weather outside. She tucked her suit into the small cabinet in her office that served as a closet, set the security panel and left the library.

El Nino's was just off the large downtown square on Miller Street, a three block walk from the library. It didn't look like much from the front, but the large patio out back was the place to be in warmer weather. Cars were cruising the parking lot for open spots as she crossed the street and the inside was filling up fast. Glad made her way out to the patio, looking for her friends.

"Here!" Holly called, waving frantically from the far side of the bar. Glad ventured over, sliding through the crowd to where three women stood. April had indeed made it out and she listened patiently while Jayne Spence, a lean, athletic woman with pretty blue eyes and strawberry blonde hair went on about the legalities of her divorce.

"So glad you could come!" Holly gave her a hug and dropped her voice. "Thank God, this is killing me."

April hugged her as well. "Are you mad at me?"

Glad laughed. "Why would I be mad at you?"

"It's my class!" Then she added in a whisper, "Some of those women are just bitches."

"You remember Jayne, right?" Holly asked.

"Yes. It's nice to see you again," Glad said warmly.

Jayne Spence nodded and smiled.

"Where's Fran?" Glad asked.

Holly shrugged and looked back over the crowd. "She texted me and said she was bringing a friend so she might be a little late. Don't worry, she'll-oh, no."

Beside Glad, April stiffened and cursed under her breath while across from her Jayne's eyes widened and she murmured, "Here comes trouble." Glad looked towards the entry, then did a double take.

Fran was there all right, navigating the

crowd, waving at them. Her hair was teased out and she was wearing more makeup than usual.

But she wasn't what was drawing everyone's attention. Strutting behind her was a tall, blonde, blue eyed bombshell. She wore skinny jeans, a silky shirt that Glad was certain cost more than she earned in a week and stiletto heels. The crowd parted before her like the Red Sea before Moses and every male eye in the place fixed on and followed her progress.

"God," Holly murmured, "that's all I need right now."

"Who is she?" Glad whispered.

"Heeeyyyyy!" Fran flung her arms wide and hugged Glad and Holly together. "We made it!" She released them and patted the arm of the woman next to her. "Glad, this is Liz Meyer! We've been friends since Kindergarten! Liz, this is Glad Donahue."

"Hi," Glad said, smiling. "It's nice to meet you."

"Hello," the other woman said coolly.

"Do you live around here?" she asked.

Liz huffed. "This godforsaken hole? God, no!"

Glad was taken aback. "I like Mill Falls-"

"*You* would," Liz said, her eyes raking over Glad's casual attire with disdain. Glad stared, unable to think of anything to say that was even remotely polite. Fran jumped into the gap, her smile wide.

"Liz's mom lives in Glen View still," she said as Liz nodded her hellos to April, Jayne and Holly. "She's up visiting for the weekend! Isn't that great?"

Glad smiled at Fran. "Sure," she said. Liz Meyer didn't seem very friendly, but it was obvious Fran adored her. Glad resolved to try harder.

Liz turned back to her. "So what do you do?"

"I'm the Assistant Director of the library."

"You're a librarian?" Liz asked.

"Yes, I am."

The other woman's pouty mouth curled into a sneer and she barked a laugh. "Where's your bun and glasses?"

"Left them at the office," Glad shot back.

Liz raised one perfect brow, smirked, then turned to the group. "Let's do a shot and get this party started."

"I'd rather not," Glad said.

"One isn't going to hurt you," Liz said.

"Come on, hon, try it!" Fran giggled, pushing her at the bar.

The other women crowded in and Glad stifled a groan. She really didn't like hard liquor, especially not tequila. "This isn't really my thing," she tried.

Liz rounded on her. "So what's your thing, then? Sitting home every night and reading books?"

And just like that, her resolution went right out the window.

"Actually, I do read a lot," Glad replied. "It's my job to read so I can offer the best recommendations to our patrons." She smiled and clapped her hands together, as if struck by an idea. "In fact, I could recommend a great book for you right now!"

"Oh really?" Liz said on a laugh. "What?"

"The newest Miss Manners guide. Call number 395. We carry it in hardcover, paperback or digital. Which would you prefer?"

Liz Meyer's face froze, Fran gasped and the group went quiet. Glad did not care. She wasn't about to get pushed around by this rude, arrogant, sneering woman. Right now those sapphire blue eyes narrowed with dislike as Liz took fresh measure of her adversary. Glad stood her ground and kept her smile pasted on. Finally, Liz huffed and turned her gaze to the bartender. She smiled at him and said, "We'll be doing shots. Do you have Patron?"

He nodded. "How many?"

Liz raised a brow at the group.

"Just try one," Fran urged, looking anxious.

Glad folded. "Okay. I'll do it for you."

Fran gave a little squee. "Awesome!"

"Aren't you brave," Liz said in a syrupy sweet tone. "Six," she said to the bartender, and he began to pour.

Groaning inside, Glad stepped to the bar with the others. She licked her hand, sprinkled her salt, licked again and picked up her shot. Downed it fast and grabbed the lime wedge.

The tequila burned all the way down, hit her stomach and set it on fire. Glad sucked her lime, fought back a wave of nausea and carefully placed the shot glass back on the bar.

To her left, Jayne was coughing and April was fanning the air in front of her mouth. Holly put her lime wedge in her glass and began to giggle. "That was so good!"

"You are so insane," Glad told her. Holly hugged her.

"Let's do another one!"

"Honey, I don't like--"

"But you're like a pro!" Holly exclaimed. "You didn't even flinch! Come on!"

"Holly-"

"You never struck me as the tequila type," said a deep voice behind her.

***

Glad jumped and faced him. "Oh! Hi, Mike," she said.

"Hi yourself," Mike said. "I'm impressed."

Her cheeks were rosy, but he'd bet that was the tequila burn. He held her gaze, losing himself in her pretty eyes for a moment. Then she stepped close and sniffed the air. "Do I smell rosemary?" she asked.

He grinned. "And lemon balm and thyme and sage…we were transplanting herbs all afternoon. You like it?"

She inhaled deep and sighed, "Yes," and he knew he was in trouble already.

"Are you going to introduce me?" interrupted her friend, a devilish grin on her face.

"Of course," Glad said. "Mike Kovalski, this is Holly Spence."

"A pleasure," Mike said, shaking Holly's hand. "Don't you live in my neighborhood?"

"I'm on Orchard Lane," Holly said.

"You've got a boy, right? Alex? I helped him get his chain back on his bike the other day."

"That was you?" Holly glowed suddenly. "Alex told me. Thank you."

"You're welcome. He's a nice kid."

"You fixin' to get them beers anytime soon?" asked Turk from behind him. Glad gave Turk a friendly smile, but her friend Holly looked like she'd seen a ghost.

"Nope, getting friendly with the locals instead," Mike said to him, then turned to the bartender. "Four Dortmunders."

"Bottle or tap?"

"Tap," Mike answered. "Talls." The bartender nodded and began to pour and Mike turned back to Turk. "Happy?"

"I will be when I start drinking it," Turk said. Then he focused on Holly, his gaze intense. "Well, well, will wonders never cease. Hello, Angel."

Holly said nothing. Instead she turned fiery red and walked away. Glad stared after her, then turned back to Turk. "I take it you know each other?" she asked.

"In a manner of speakin'," he said softly, and held out his hand. "Greg Turk, ma'am. We weren't properly introduced the other day."

Glad shook his hand. "Where do you hail from, Mr. Turk?"

Turk laughed. "Mr. Turk? He's my granddaddy. I'm Greg the fourth, born and raised in a Tennessee holler," Turk answered. "I've spent the last twenty years traveling a bit."

"Military?" Glad asked.

"Yes, ma'am," Turk answered with a pleased smile. "Marines. How did you guess?"

Glad regarded him. "You look like you've lived the kind of life most people can't handle."

Turk grinned and turned his attention back to Mike. "Smart and beautiful. I'm not sure you deserve her, boy."

"I'm not sure I do, either," Mike said, and stepped aside for a giggling, teased-out blonde.

"Hi Mike and friend! I'm Fran," she said to both men, then turned her attention to Mike. "You're even cuter than my hubby, you know that?"

Mike laughed. "Thanks. I think."

"So are you and Glad an item?" she asked.

Mike took two beers from the bartender and handed them to Turk. "Well, I'd like to be," he said with a disarming smile, "but she says no." Ignoring Glad's gasp, he took the other two beers from the bar and handed one to Fonz, who was busy chatting up his sister.

Fran made a *tsk* noise with her tongue and turned to Glad. "Oh, hon! He likes you! And you like him! Don't let him get away!"

"I know, right?" Mike asked. "We could be great, but she doesn't want to give us a chance." He smiled ruefully and shook his head at Glad, enjoying the panic on her face.

Holly Spence reappeared at Glad's side, looking composed again. "Really, what are you waiting for? You like him, go out with him!"

"Umm, remember that talk about boundaries?" Glad asked.

"We just want you to get back out there and

try again. There's plenty of nice, single guys to choose from!"

"Like me! I'm a nice, single guy," Mike said, grinning.

"I'm a nice single guy, too," Greg Turk offered.

Mike scowled at him. "Go give Harry his beer already."

Turk grinned. "Just yankin' your chain, boss. I prefer blondes." And he gave Holly a sizzling look that had her turning red all over again.

"Is that so?" drawled a sultry voice.

A designer blonde stepped into the group. Gorgeous face, perfect body, killer smile. Mike had seen that kind of smile before and his bitch radar turned on, full alert.

Next to him Turk stared while the blonde gave him a slow perusal. "I haven't seen you around town before," she purred, placing a hand on his chest. "I'm Liz Meyer."

"Greg Turk, ma'am," he said.

Behind him, Mike heard something that sounded something like "effing bitch" and he tensed. Things might get ugly. Then the blonde turned her attention to him.

"And you're the One Date Wonder I've heard so much about," she said, stroking his arm and smiling up at him while keeping her other hand on Turk's chest.

Even if he'd been the slightest bit interested, that was the *wrong* thing to say. Mike nodded and tried to move away but her long, French manicured nails curled into his shirt and held fast. She smiled at him again, looked over at Turk and said, "Why don't you both drink up so we can get out of here and have a little fun together?"

Mike choked on his beer and stepped out of her reach, coughing. Turk's eyes bugged and he said, "*Both* of us?"

"Why not?" she asked, giving them each a smile full of promise.

He wasn't sure if the blonde was serious or not but it didn't matter; he didn't want any part of this. Mike backed away another step and reached blindly behind himself. Where was Glad? His hand found an elbow and he tugged. "Um, thanks, but I'll pass."

The blonde appraised him again, stepped right up to his chest, licked her pouty lips and said, "Trust me, I'm a lot more fun than a *librarian*."

14

"Oh!" Glad gasped as Mike unceremoniously hauled her to his side.

"Thanks, but I'm good," he said.

Glad took in Liz's calculating gaze and slid her arm around Mike's waist. Mike looped his free arm around her shoulder. "Sorry," she said sweetly.

Liz looked Glad up and down, disdain all over her face. Then she rolled her eyes and said, "Whatever," and turned her attention back to Turk.

"Do you need me to protect you or something?" Glad asked, smiling up at him.

"You better believe it," Mike said. "She scares the shit out of me."

Glad watched Liz Meyer loop her arm through Turk's and pull him away from the group. "You should probably go rescue that poor man."

"Are you kidding?" Mike asked. "I'm not

getting anywhere near that." He looked after Turk and shook his head. "And besides, he's a marine. He can handle anything."

"Liz Meyer eats guys like him for breakfast," came a voice from behind them and Glad turned. Holly's face was pure misery, watching Turk be led away by Liz.

"Hon? Are you okay?" Glad asked, putting a concerned hand on Holly's arm. The other woman shrugged her off.

"I'm fine. I just need another drink." She smiled brightly at Glad. "Let's do another shot!"

"Are you sure that's a good idea?" Mike asked.

Holly gave Mike a dirty look. "It's a great idea. Now how about you go away too?"

"Me? I didn't do anything!" Mike protested.

"Just go," Glad said. "We'll talk later."

"Hon, you haven't had very many boyfriends," Holly pointed out. "Can you tell a good man from a poor one?"

"I-well, I-of course I can!" Glad stuttered. Then she giggled loudly. "Okay, maybe not!"

Some part of her conscience realized that the second shot Holly had talked her into, followed by a beer was starting to work against her. But another, bigger part of her brain was having too much fun to pay attention.

"Maybe that's the problem!" said Fran excitedly. "Between Asshole Evan and those couple other guys, you don't have much of a base to compare with, you know?"

"Who's Asshole Evan?" came a voice over her shoulder. Glad jumped and turned to face a grinning Mike.

"Hey, girl," he said.

"Hey, boy," she said back, and giggled some more. She just couldn't seem to stop. And she couldn't stop looking at him, either. Man, was he ever cute.

"So who's Asshole Evan?" Mike asked Holly and Fran.

Holly groaned dramatically. "Her cheating ex from when she lived in D.C."

"A complete tool," Fran chimed in.

"Total asshat," Holly agreed.

"Who I am not talking about right now," Glad said, mortified.

"Oh, all right," Holly groused, "but I think we're on to something here. You really need more experience in the man department."

Glad's mouth dropped. "I do not!"

"Oh, yes," Fran said. "You need more dates!"

"So," Mike drawled, "maybe you girls should find her some other guys to go out with."

***

The look on her face was priceless. "What- were you eavesdropping?"

He grinned. "Of course I was."

"I can *not* believe-"

"How else can I find out all that stuff you won't tell me?" he interrupted. She scowled at him and he laughed out loud.

186

"Are you *serious*?" Fran asked, her mouth wide with shock. "You want us to set her up with other guys?"

"No!" said Glad.

"Yes," corrected Mike.

Holly and Fran looked at one another and dissolved into laughter. Glad looked totally dismayed. He traced her cheek with a finger.

"Girl, you know I want to be with you. But I don't want you to just settle for me."

"Mike, I-"

"Seriously!" He made a general gesture with his beer glass, enjoying her discomfort. "The man of your dreams is out there somewhere! He could be right here on this patio!"

"But, Mike-"

"This'll be fun!" Holly interrupted gleefully. "I already can think of one guy!"

"Me too!" said Fran.

The two fell to whispering. Glad turned to him and hissed, "You do *not* play fair."

"I do not," he agreed. "And I cheat at Monopoly, too. Just so you know." He looked down at her and smiled. "You look so pretty tonight."

Her cheeks stained pink. "I-I do?"

He fingered a lock of her hair. "Oh, yeah. Pure gorgeous-"

A loud round of giggles grabbed their attention. "Yes!" Holly said to Fran. "He'd be perfect!"

"You picking out some good ones?" Mike asked. Glad punched his arm.

"Don't encourage them!" she begged.

"Oh, there's so many to choose from!" Fran said, excited. "We can't wait to get started."

"Well, don't set her up with anyone too great, okay? I want to win this thing."

Mike turned back to Glad. She stood there, her beautiful face so woebegone he had to laugh.

"This isn't funny!"

He lifted her hand and kissed it. "Everything's fine," he said, smiling down at her. "But don't have so much fun you forget about me, okay?"

He walked away under a wave of giggles and talk, pleased as hell. He collared Fonz and pulled him away from April and a thin, tawny-haired woman next to her. "Come on, we need to go rescue Turk."

"I guess that's goodbye," the woman called after them.

"I'll be back," Fonz threw over his shoulder, then glared at Mike. "I was in the middle of something!"

"Good to leave a woman hanging once in a while," Mike said, still high on his confidence. "She wants more, she'll come back around."

Fonz didn't answer and Mike looked at him. "What's the problem, man?"

"I've loved Jayne Spence since we were kids," Fonz said quietly, and shook his head. "She's never come back around."

***

Glad was having a great time! She'd talked to so many people tonight! People she never would have talked to! There was what's-his-name with the toupee! And that funny biker lady with the spikes on her bra top! Glad wished she could get away with wearing something *that* awesome!

She'd talked to the girls-but not that bitch Liz-and to a couple of people she knew from the library. She'd talked to Holly some more about getting a dog, or maybe a cat, or was it a bird? She couldn't remember.

But it was getting late. She needed to go home. And the floor was starting to tilt to the left. That could *not* be a good sign. Where was the exit?

Glad began making her way across the patio, smiling giddily, and saying goodbye to complete strangers. Then she ran into a wall.

A tall, broad wall with black hair and the darkest, sexiest eyes she'd ever seen.

"Wow. You're *cute*," she said. "Have we met?"

The wall smiled. "Yes, we've met."

"Would you like to be friends?" she asked.

"I'd like that," the wall answered. "You all right, girl?"

"I think I need-" she hiccupped, "to go home."

"I think you need to go home too," the wall said, gripping her arm and steering her towards the exit. Glad tripped over the threshold and began giggling, then snorted out loud. How much had she had to drink, anyway? Who cared? She felt great!

"Did I just say that out loud?" she asked the universe.

"Sure did," said a voice next to her. Glad stopped and finally managed to focus.

"Hiiiya, Mike! What are you doing out here?"

"Same thing you are," he answered. "Did you drive tonight?"

"I...no?" she looked around, uncertain. Had she driven? She didn't think so. "I walked?"

"How about I drive you home?"

She smiled at him, her smoking hot savior. "That's-*hic!*-probably a good idea."

***

"Does this count as a second date?" Glad asked, smiling up at him.

Definitely not. He preferred his dates to be sober. "No. Just driving you home."

"Okay. I like you. Do you know that? I do. You're so nice to me," she said.

Mike gently moved her on. "I'm sure lots of people are nice to you," he said.

"You'd think that, wouldn't you?" Glad poked a finger in the general direction of his chest. Missed by a mile. "But nope. My families didn't like me, boyfriends-*hic*-were a bunch of fakers-"

"Families?" he interrupted, confused.

"Bunch of fakers." She stumbled and righted herself. "You know who's a real big faker? That Liz. Did you know her boobs are fake?"

"Really?" Mike tried to act surprised.

"Yep, they're fakes! *And-*" she looked around, hiccupped, then leaned against him and stage whispered, "-you know what else she is, besides being a big faker? She's a total-*hic!* Made me do a shot," she accused, then tripped over a pebble.

"Steady, girl." Mike slid his arm around her waist. Glad hiccupped loudly, turned pink and giggled. She peered up at him like she wasn't quite certain of his identity, then smiled.

"You're so cute. Waaaay cuter than-*hic*-Asshole Evan. I wish you really liked me."

"I like you a lot," he reminded her patiently.

She blew his assurance off with a drunken wave. "Sure you do. You kiss me like that and-*hic*-first chance you get you push me on someone else. How come you don't want to go out with me anymore?"

"What do you mean?" he asked, confused.

"You want me to go out on all those *dates.*" She wrinkled her nose like she smelled something bad. It was totally adorable.

"I just want you to be sure," he said.

She sighed loudly. "Fine." Then she narrowed her eyes at him. "You know what I'm gonna-*hic*-do? I'm gonna make you jealous."

It came out blurry, like jell-ish, but he knew what she meant.

"How are you going to do that?"

"I'm gonna go out with those other guys. And have fun, and maybe even have *sex,*" she said belligerently. "So there."

Shit. He hadn't thought about sex. The thought of Glad in bed with anyone else...

No. Don't think about that right now. He dug out his keys.

"All right, let's get you in the truck, here." He unlocked the passenger door and opened it.

"Okay-oops!" Glad missed her step and nearly went face first against the floorboards. "That's a high one!"

Mike took her by the waist and hoisted her up, settled her in the seat. She dropped her purse and clumsily reached for the seat belt. Missed.

"Let me help you out, here," he said. He pulled it across, clicked it into place... and froze. Glad's hand was stroking through his hair. Twirling it, wrapping it around her fingers. Torture.

"I love how your hair feels."

No! Stop! Oh, crap, she wasn't stopping. "Glad-"

"And your lips. You're the best kisser I ever kissed-"

Mike lost it. He leaned forward and took her mouth, hungry and deep and she curled her arms around his neck. Mike knew she was drunk and probably wouldn't remember this tomorrow but his willpower had checked out the second he laid eyes on her tonight. He would have done anything to kiss her again.

Glad sighed against his mouth as he slowly let go. "Magic," she whispered.

"Yes, it is," he agreed.

"Mike, I..." She sighed, closed her eyes and was out.

***

192

Glad woke early, head pounding like a 70's disco and mouth dry as an old corn cob. She was in bed, tangled in her sheets and had no idea how she'd made it this far.

Wow. What had happened last night? A few scattered images fluttered across her brain: Holly giggling and hugging her, April spilling her margarita, Mike tucking her in-

Mike tucked me in???

"Oh my God," she whispered, frantically sitting up. The sheet fell away. Okay, she still had her clothes on, so nothing had happened.

Right?

Glad groaned and tried her faulty memory. Nothing. What had she done last night? What had *they* done last night? Nothing? Something? Would she remember it if they had? She groaned again and rubbed at her forehead. If she could only remember something, just a piece of it she'd know for sure. Let's see... they'd gone to El Nino's... shots...Fran and Holly were setting her up...

Glad groaned over that and thought some more. She'd talked to some woman with a spiky bra top on...Liz Meyer's sneering face...Mike...kissing...

Yes, they had kissed at some point. Was that all? Wouldn't she remember if they'd had sex?

She rolled herself into a tight ball and squeezed her eyes shut. Maybe, just maybe, if she slept some more she'd remember. Better yet, maybe this would all go away.

She woke much, much later. She still felt like crap and wished she could sleep the entire day away. But someone was making noise outside, doing... something.

Glad dragged herself out of bed, took a shower, brushed her teeth and changed into fresh clothes. A tiny bit better. Maybe some coffee.

Her stomach revolted at the thought. Okay, no coffee. Fresh air would do her good, though. She went slowly downstairs and out to her back porch.

The noise was coming from her back yard. Mike was cutting some kind of outline in the soil with some kind of tool. A spade? Her brain had turned to mush.

Mike looked up as the screen door opened and gave her a grin.

"Well, well. Awake at last."

"Shut up."

He laughed. "How's that hangover feel?"

Glad didn't answer, just waved him away and sat down, hands firmly over her eyes.

"You're looking a little peaked." His voice got closer.

"I'm feeling a lot peaked."

She heard a faint thump. He climbed the steps to the back porch. "Here."

Glad lowered her hands. Mike placed a can of ginger ale, a sleeve of saltines and an apple on the table. He sat across from her and leaned back in a chair that looked nothing like her cute little bistro chair. It was wood and metal, large and heavy-looking.

"Where did that come from?"

"I brought it over. I need something a little bigger. Eat."

"I don't think I can."

"You need to. Salt and sweet settle everything down." He took a jack knife out of his pocket and cut the apple into several pieces. "Trust me."

Glad took a piece of apple and bit off a little. When that stayed down she tried more. Then a saltine found its way into her hand.

"You don't have to feed me," she muttered.

"I know." Mike gave her another piece of apple and opened the ginger ale.

"Why are you being nice to me?" she asked.

"Because you need someone to be nice to you today."

"Oh." She bit her lip. Had to know. "Mike?"

"Glad?"

"Did...did we..."

He raised a brow. "Are you kidding? I could barely get you up the stairs!"

"Why didn't you just leave me on the couch?"

"Because you insisted you had to sleep in your bed."

"I insisted?"

"Actually, you yelled it. Right in my ear. I might have hearing loss, thanks to you."

Glad put her head on the table and covered it with her arms. "Oh, no. Mike, I'm so sorry."

"When I get the bill for my hearing aid, I'll send it to you," he said gruffly. "Drink some ginger ale."

She lifted herself back up and took a sip of the ginger ale. Looked at him a long moment. "You look different."

He grinned. "Do I?"

"Wait. You cut your hair!"

"Yes, I did."

"It's short!" She stared at him.

"Summer cut. It's getting too warm out for all that hair."

"You look so...different." Just as sexy, but definitely different.

"You don't like it?" he asked.

"It's fine. I just..." Her fingers tingled with the memory of that deep black silk against her fingers. Sure, hair grew and he'd probably have his wild man look back by winter, but...

"I made sure they left enough," he said.

"Enough for what?" she asked, confused.

"For you to run your fingers through. You seem to like doing that."

Okay, he'd just read her mind. Glad felt herself getting hot. "Did I..."

"Yes."

"Oh." She picked up another slice of apple, unable to look him in the eye. "Did I do anything else? Anything bad?"

"I don't know. But you were lit up and talking a lot, about a lot of stuff. Nothing bad," he added when her eyes widened. "Just stuff, like asking me if I wanted to be friends, how you want a cat and a dog... harmless. Then you sort of staggered up to me awhile later and said you needed to go home."

"Like you're my taxi service," she said, shaking her head.

"And on the way out to my truck you gave me the lowdown on Liz Meyer's fake boobs-"

Glad gasped. "I did not!"

Mike laughed. "You did."

"Oh, no!"

"Oh, yes. Next time I want to know anything I'm getting you liquored up." He grinned. "So. Tell me about Asshole Evan."

"Was I talking about him, too?" she asked, dismayed.

"You told me I was cuter than him. Definitely a win for me-unless that was the tequila talking."

Glad studied him. "You're totally different looking. He was blonde and lean. A lawyer. Very polished. You're..."

"Not."

She smiled. "You clean up all right. And you're so much more...manly."

"Really." His eyes darkened and her heart thrummed a happy little beat. "How manly?"

"Fishing for compliments?"

"All I can get." He smiled wolfishly. "Bring it on, girl."

She blushed. "Well, you're big and burly and really strong."

"A lot of guys are."

"Okay, fine. You remember when we met up at Serenity that day and Frank was giving you grief?"

"Yeah."

"If Evan lived in Mill Falls he would be a regular there. Getting manicured, manscaped, massaged, the whole bit. He loved all that pampering."

Mike snorted. "I might be down for a massage every now and then, but there's no way I'm letting someone rip hair off my body. That's just wrong."

"That's what I mean. You're manly. You do man stuff like take out the garbage and mow the grass and shovel snow-"

"Damn right." He made a fist and pounded it against his chest. "And I make fire. Fire good."

Glad laughed. "And you probably wouldn't dream of, say, letting me get out and fix a flat tire in the rain."

"Of course not-wait. He did that?" At her nod he snorted. "What a dick."

"Well, God forbid he got water spots on his Gucci loafers," Glad said. "Never mind that I was in a dress and heels."

"Did you break up with him then?"

She sighed and shook her head. "I wish I would have. It would have spared me so much humiliation."

15

Mike suspected he knew the answer, but he asked the question anyway. "He cheat on you with someone?"

Glad nodded. "She was one of my coworkers. A good friend, or so I thought." Her lip curled. "They were involved a long time before I found out."

"So what happened when you did?"

A dark shadow passed over her face. "Oh, the usual. There was drama and I got burned."

Mike waited, but nothing else came. "Drama…" he prompted.

She shook her head. "It doesn't matter. It's over and done with."

Not if she couldn't talk about it. Did she still love the guy? He sounded like a complete jerk, but you never knew.

"Same here," he replied. "Except I was dumb enough to get engaged before I found out."

"What happened?"

"He was a doctor. A plastic surgeon. He was rolling in money and I didn't have anything but dirt."

He saw the comprehension in her eyes. "She told you…"

"That she deserved diamonds and all I had to offer was dirt."

"Bitch." Glad took another sip of ginger ale and ate the slice of apple.

"Thanks."

"Did you love her? Never mind, of course you did. You wouldn't have gotten engaged otherwise."

Mike looked at Glad, not sure how to answer. Had he loved Rachel? He'd been angry over her betrayal, was still bitter about the lies and the fallout, but had he really loved her?

"I thought so," he finally said. "I had a crush on her for a long time and when we started to date it was like a dream come true."

"Was she beautiful?"

"Oh, yeah. A stunner. And she knew it, too." He reached over and took a piece of apple. "She was really into her appearance, you know, always wearing designer clothes, every hair in place."

Glad looked down at herself. "I bought this shirt at Target."

"Girl, you've got nothing to worry about." He ate the rest of his apple slice, thinking. Rachel had been perfect on the surface, but underneath lived an insecure, mercurial personality in constant need of assurance and praise. She flirted with every man she came across and always acted surprised when he got jealous. Glad might not be perfectly turned out, but she was genuine, sweet and warm and that counted for far more in his book nowadays.

"She was tough to be with," he finally said. "Wanted to be the center of attention twenty-four seven. Looking back…" He sighed. "She led me like a dog on a leash and I let her do it. Jumped through her hoops, bought her a ring, the whole nine yards. Then she suddenly got cold feet and said she needed some space. I gave it to her and a few days later all hell broke loose. She'd told her mom I'd cheated on her, and that I got rough with her when she confronted me and now she was scared of me."

"Oh, no."

"I was called to my parents' house and everyone was there. Rachel made a big scene, poor little her and they just ate it up." He sighed. "A lot of shit went down, a lot of accusations were made and no one wanted to hear what I had to say. At the end my mother walked up to me, slapped my face in front of everyone and told me to get out of her house and not come back."

"But…you're her son!"

"Didn't matter. She believed Rachel. Everyone did." Everyone except his Bubbe. She alone had been steadfast and strong by his side. Then she'd died in her sleep three weeks later and in her grief, his mother had blamed him for it. He knew it wasn't true, just as he knew she hadn't truly meant to say something so awful. But his mother never filtered her mouth and the words came out, rained down like broken glass and those bitter shards sliced him to the bone.

A warm hand slid over his and he took it, held on. Glad looked at him, her eyes at once sorrowful and kind. And he knew, suddenly, that she got it. That she understood who he was because she was exactly the same. Alone.

"I'm sorry," she said.

"Me, too," he said.

***

Overheard at Mimi's Diner:

I saw him at El Nino's last night. With her. They did a shot at the bar.

Librarians do shots?

Apparently. They must be wilder than they look.

Did you see them in the parking lot? She looked pretty tipsy!

Aw, people can tie one on now and then, no big deal.

Now, I don't know how true this is, because it sounds kind of weird to me. But. *I heard her friends are setting her up with other guys, and it was his idea!*

What? What would you do something like that for?

I don't know. Like I said, it's just a rumor.

***

"Have I got a man for you!"

"Do you," Glad said absently, staring out the Archives window at the landscaping activity below her. Today was day three, complete with

202

heavy machinery and she had to say Mike Kovalski looked good in a hard hat.

Scratch that, he looked great. Downright spectacular. In fact, the only thing that might be better would be him wearing nothing *but* that hard hat. Oh, yes. Nothing but that hairy chest and that hard hat and…mmm…

"Yes!" Holly said into her ear, breaking her reverie. "It's Jeff Williams!"

"The principal at your school?" Holly was a first-grade teacher in the Glen View district. "Isn't he married?"

"They split up a while ago. He's not officially divorced, but he's definitely on the market."

"I don't know about the whole married thing." Glad glanced at the clock. She had five minutes before the Archives Room opened. She loved the utter quiet of this room. And the view from the windows.

"He's practically divorced. It's fine, I promise," Holly assured her.

"Okay. What does he look like?"

"Sort of…nerdy cute."

"Nerdy cute?" Glad asked, heart sinking. This didn't sound good.

"Trust me, hon, you'll like him. He's smart and funny and nice. Brown hair, blue eyes. He's not big, you know, not like Mike Kovalski is big, but he's still got some muscle on him. Oh, and he wears glasses. But not the nerdy coke-bottle types, the sexy types."

"The sexy types?" Glad asked, but Holly wasn't listening.

"He drives a fun little convertible when the weather's nice. I think it's one of those Sky Roadsters. Oh, and he's seen you around, so he knows who you are. And he said he's interested."

"You've already talked to him about this?"

"Of course! I wanted to get right on it. I gave him your number already. He'll probably call you this week."

"I don't think I'm ready for this."

"Why not? You're not together with Mike, right?"

"No."

"And he did tell you to date other guys, right?"

"Yes, but-"

"He's got a point, hon. It's a good idea to check things out, kick the tires and look under the hood before you commit. Especially if you haven't, um, gone for a drive in a while."

"That is the worst comparison I've ever heard."

"I teach first grade. What do you expect?"

Glad stared out the window at Mike and sighed. "I don't understand any of this."

"It's a unique approach, I'll say that much. And I'll say this too: maybe the rumors are wrong. Maybe he's a genuinely nice guy."

"Since when are you all Team Mike?" Glad asked.

"I'm not, I swear. But it's kind of sweet, how he's all hung up on you."

"He's not hung up on me."

"He is! He was watching you the whole time we were at El Nino's on Saturday night."

"Speaking of Saturday night," Glad said, "what's up with you and Greg Turk?"

"Nothing," Holly said, too quickly.

"Come on, spill."

Holly huffed. "After he let Liz Meyer climb all over him I'm not touching him with a ten-foot pole. The jerk."

"He didn't leave with her, did he?" Glad asked.

"No, but it doesn't matter. I'm through with him."

"What happened between you two?"

"Nothing!"

"Holly, we've known each other fourteen years. You can't fool me."

"I-well, we-oh, look at the time! Recess is almost over! I've got to go get my class." "You're not getting out of telling," Glad threatened her. "I'm going to bug you about this, night and day, until you do."

"And you will, too," Holly groused. "Fine. Come for dinner tonight and I'll tell all. But now I have to go get my class."

"Oh, sure, use a bunch of first-graders as a shield."

"I'll take whatever I can get."

Holly's little rental house was on a quiet side street near the Rec Center. She'd been a tenant there for nearly five years. After her husband's death she'd left the Marine base where he was stationed and returned home to be closer to their families. She'd tried to live with both sets of parents for a while, then tried a tiny apartment in

Glen View before finding this house. Glad loved the cozy rooms and Holly's innate sense of style and organization.

Holly was also a great cook and dinner had been fabulous, a homemade lasagna, salad and breadsticks loaded with asiago cheese. Now they sat in the back yard, sipping the last of their wine while Alex finished his homework inside.

"So tell me what's going on with you and Greg Turk," Glad said.

Holly sighed. "Man. He-oh, man. It was last fall. Me, Fran, April Fonzi and some other girls went out to Mack's-you know, that microbrew bar with all the pool tables in Glen View."

"Isn't that a biker hangout?"

"It was once. Now there's college kids, a few bikers, but it's mostly locals. Anyway, we went out there. And he was there, with John Fonzi, Big Jim Ascher and a couple other guys, shooting pool in the back. Somehow or other, probably because of Fran's big mouth, we got roped into playing with them."

"And you got Greg Turk."

Holly nodded. "I was feeling reckless, and he was pretty hot looking, and I bet him on the game."

"What did you bet?"

Holly flushed. "Ten minutes in his truck."

Glad gasped, totally shocked. Sane, practical Holly? The girl who always had a plan, always had her head on straight? "And?"

"And…I lost."

Glad stared. "And then?"

"Well, it was a little cramped, but he had a bench seat, so we managed."

Glad nearly dropped her wine glass. "Holly!" she hissed, scandalized. "You had sex with Greg Turk in his *truck*?"

Holly nodded. "Right there in the parking lot."

"How did-what about-weren't there other people around?"

"There is not one light in that lot. Plus, he was parked over in the corner. And it'd been so long, you have no idea. I didn't care, I wanted it. I wanted him. I think I lost on purpose."

"Wow." Glad shook her head, still in shock. "A truck?"

"Haven't you ever had sex in a truck?" Holly asked, grinning.

"No. Just in the bedroom."

"Girlfriend, you need to get out more. That Mike's got an F-150, right? I bet if you told him you've never done it in a truck he-"

"Stop it!" Glad blushed at the thought and the thrill it gave her.

Holly laughed at her, glanced back at the house to make sure her son wasn't eavesdropping, then whispered, "The sex was amazing. I mean, *wow*. That man knows his way around a woman." She fanned herself with one hand.

"What happened after that?" Glad asked.

"Nothing. When it was over I panicked. I threw on my clothes and left him there. And I've taken great pains to avoid Mack's Billiards and Brews ever since. I haven't seen him at all. And then he was at El Nino's last Saturday night and he looked so *good*."

"He called you Angel," remarked Glad. Holly did look angelic, with her golden blonde hair and spring green eyes. But the attitude beneath was pure devilish.

"He did that night, too. And I didn't know his name, so I called him Cowboy. That twang…I thought maybe he was from Texas or something."

"Did anything happen Friday night? I don't remember much, to be honest."

"No, and I want nothing more to do with him." Holly stared into her darkening yard. "But something tells me I haven't heard the last of Greg Turk."

***

"You're getting a new crewmember starting today," Ken said.

"Don't I have enough?" Mike asked.

"It's Jake," Ken explained. "Dumb ass flunked his GMAT exam. Can you believe that shit?"

"Graduate exams are tough," Mike said, noncommittal. He knew Ken had high expectations of his only son. Mike had only met Jake Anderson a couple of times and didn't know him at all, but his first impression hadn't been positive. Of course, people's impressions of him weren't exactly positive lately either, so Mike didn't have much high ground to judge from.

"He had plenty of time to study, but he had

to go party and get laid instead. Like that's more important than making something of himself. His mother's furious, and I don't know what in hell to do with him anymore."

"So you're handing him over to the-what did you call it? The 'biggest sleaze in Mill Falls history'? Isn't that like throwing the fat in the fire?"

"Well, I haven't had any cancellations lately, so you must be doing something right." Ken's brow furrowed. "About that cutoff…"

Mike waited. Ken scratched at the back of his neck, obviously uncomfortable.

"It's up soon," Mike reminded him.

"How's it going with that librarian?" Ken asked.

"Slowly. I'm giving her space right now." And the space was killing him. He hadn't so much as caught a glimpse of her in a week.

"Is that a good idea?"

"Absence makes the heart grow fonder."

"If you say so. If it were me I'd be all over her. Flowers every day, shit like that."

Mike suppressed a sigh. Bad enough he'd gotten himself in this fix; he really didn't want, or need, Ken's well-intended but unwelcome meddling.

"Don't worry about me and Glad Donahue. I've got a plan and its working." At least he hoped it was working. Giving her friends carte blanche to set her up on dates was a hell of a risk, but if it worked out how he was pretty sure it would, she'd be back in his arms-and in his bed besides-very soon.

Had she gone on any dates yet? Mike wasn't sure he wanted to know the answer to that.

"So she's playing right into your hands?" Ken asked.

"Something like that."

"Good to hear."

"Ken? Renny McQueen from Sunrise is on the phone."

Mike turned. Caroline Anderson stood directly behind him. She gave Mike an odd look, then said to Ken, "He wants to talk about some order you two split."

Ken sighed. "All right. Tell him I'll be right there." Caroline gave Mike another strange look and walked away. What bug was up her ass today?

Granted, Caroline always had a bug up her ass. And she'd been extra pissy with him since Ken had finally spoken with her earlier this month about her poor customer service.

"Jake'll be out with your crew this morning. I know it's a pain, but I'm hoping you'll be a better influence on him than Joe or Terry. You value education and you do good work."

"Well, thanks, but fair warning: I'm not a mentoring type. I'm not going to hold his hand or give life-changing lectures."

"Ken snorted. "Just keep him busy. That's all I want."

Mike headed out for the trucks, aggravated. Ken's son was a complication he did not need right now. Jake Anderson was certainly capable of a full day's work and if he were any other man Mike would be more than willing to give him a chance. But Mike knew the Andersons had spoiled all their kids and Jake's good looks and popularity had only served to turn him into an arrogant, self-absorbed, six-foot-two pain in the ass.

And there he was showing off for Fonz and Turk, twirling a shovel around, heedless of his vicinity. Mike sighed and approached, grabbed his arm when the shovel came back around.

"What the—hey!"

"You want to twirl a baton, go join the band," Mike growled. He pulled the shovel away and tossed it in the truck bed. Turk and the Fonz both barked a laugh.

"Who died and made you God?" Jake snarled. Mike ignored him and moved towards the next truck. He wasn't in the mood for this posturing horseshit.

"Uh, Jake, 'God' there is the crew boss," Fonz said behind him.

Jake huffed. "No fucking way."

"Way," Mike said over his shoulder. "You got a problem with that, go cry to your old man. Otherwise, get in." He unlocked the second truck.

"You don't tell *me* what to do."

"Shut up," Harry Phelps materialized out of nowhere and cuffed Jake upside his head.

"Ow!"

"Where to, boss?" asked the Fonz, grinning.

"4680 Lee Road. See you out there." Mike opened his truck door, everyone bundled in and set out.

That morning Jake mulched his beds so

sloppily that a total re-do on the part of the team was required. Add to that his snarky comments and his lousy attitude and Mike was aggravated to shit. When they stopped for lunch, a hasty break while parked on the side of Wells Road, Mike took Turk and Harry aside.

"Thanks to Wonder Boy, we're behind," he told them. "I'll need you two to go on ahead to the State Road job and I'll take him and Fonz to the Berkshire development. We should be out to State by three-"

"He's at it again," Turk said.

Mike turned around. Jake was twirling a shovel around again. Mike growled low in his throat and stalked back to the trucks, at his wit's end. Turk and Harry followed.

Jake was boasting about one of his college conquests to Fonz.

"...and then she said 'I don't care if your roommate joins us' and I was like 'whoa, okay' and then she-"

CRACK.

Splintered pieces of taillight fell to the ground.

"You idjit!" Harry bellowed.

"Sorry, man." But Jake didn't look one iota sorry. Mike yanked the shovel from his hands for the second time that day.

"Get in the truck," he ground out.

"I don't have to-"

Mike's temper flared. He stepped forward and pointed the business end of the shovel in Jake's face. "Get in. The truck. Before I use this damn thing on you."

"Better do what the boss says, boy," Turk said quietly.

"This is bullshit," Jake grumbled, but he slunk away and got in the truck.

"On second thought," Mike said, tossing the shovel into the truck bed and turning back to Turk and Harry, "maybe Jake should go with you two."

It had been a bitch of a day. Mike headed back into town, grumpy and sweaty. He changed at home then headed for the Rec Center and the blessed relief of the pool. He needed lots of laps tonight to work off his frustrations. Then he needed to see Glad after she got out of her Pilates class. Talk to her. Just be around her for five minutes and let the balm of her company soothe his ragged edges.

He was starting to crave time with her. Starting to miss her. He was playing with fire and he knew it and he really ought to step back, keep things in perspective. Glad Donahue was the kind of woman you could get used to, the kind you found yourself picking out china patterns with and that was not where he needed to go. He needed to focus on the goal, on winning her over and saving his job. Even though he hadn't had any kind of answer this morning, Ken appeared to be rethinking his ultimatum. But Mike knew he wasn't out of the woods yet.

He got to the Pilates room just as class ended. The women filtered out as he approached the door, a few giving him sideways looks. Then

Fran and Holly stepped out. No Glad.

"Hey, Mike! How's it going?" asked Fran.

"Fine. Is Glad-"

"She's on a date," Holly said, grinning at him.

"Oh." Mike tried to keep his face neutral. Failed. "Who with?"

"Holly's principal," Fran supplied, hooking her arm with his and giving him a knowing smile. "He's cute, but I like you better."

Holly took his other arm and they walked towards the exit doors together. "You just like his chest hair," she said to Fran.

"If anyone deserves a man with good chest hair, it's Glad," Fran pronounced, then patted his arm. "Don't be jealous, hon. Jeff Williams has nothing on you. I've seen him without a shirt."

"Good to know," Mike said, amused. He stepped forward and opened the exit doors for the women. They passed through with smiles and thanks.

"Maybe we should go check up on them," Holly said when they got outside. "Far East is right down the street. You want to?"

Mike felt a hot stab in his gut. Okay, it shouldn't matter where she ate, it was a free country. But the fact that he'd asked her to go there with him, twice, and she'd turned him down twice, and now she was out with some other guy at the very place...

Oh, for the love of...was he jealous over a restaurant? No, he couldn't be. He needed to lighten up and focus, here. Where Glad Donahue ate dinner did not matter. What was Fran saying?

"...leave them alone. You know how she blushes; she'd probably die if we showed up. Let's hit Mimi's instead. You want to come, Mike?"

"No, thanks. I've got to head home."

"All right. See you!" Fran called as she and Holly moved off. Mike went to his truck and climbed in. Started it up.

Speaking of food, he hadn't eaten yet tonight. What was he going to do for dinner?

He had some leftovers in the fridge. He could get a pizza from Shakespeare's.

Or he could stop a few blocks down and pick up some of Mama Lin's coconut soup.

16

"...but of course, now that I'm in a condo I don't have as much room but a guy needs a big screen, you know?"

Glad smiled and kept her interested face firmly in place. Jeff Williams was perfectly nice, behaved like a gentleman and drove a nifty little sports convertible. He could hold his end of a conversation, he was well read and interested in a variety of subjects and he was even good looking in his way. No sparks whatsoever on her end, and despite what Holly had said, she didn't think there were any on his end, either.

But that was fine. He was still nice and easy to talk to, and she'd almost be having a halfway decent time, except for one little thing.

The Ex.

Jeff's soon to be ex-wife dominated the conversation. She popped up over and over again, Jeff making reference to The Ex in so many sentences Glad had lost count.

Jeff really liked the charm of Glad's older home, but The Ex had wanted new.

The Ex had loved the Sky Roadster, even though she was convinced it was some kind of midlife crisis thing.

Far East had been one of their favorite restaurants in town.

The Ex had almost the same shade of hazel eyes as Glad.

And the killer: *Are you about a size eight? Yeah, I figured you were about the same size as The Ex.*

And they hadn't even gotten their appetizers yet.

"Coconut soup," the server said, putting down a fragrant bowl in front of Glad. And "Sushi Roll" was placed in front of Jeff. Thank goodness. She could at least have something to do while her date waxed on about his wife.

Glad put a spoonful of soup in her mouth. Lemongrass burst over her tongue, followed by savory heat and coconut. She swallowed and sighed.

"Good?" Jeff asked.

"Heavenly," Glad said, and dug in again.

"That was one of The Ex's favorites. She liked the Moo Shu Chicken too."

Glad spooned in more soup in lieu of an answer. If the dinner she'd ordered was as good as this soup, she could make it through this evening. She wouldn't even have a problem coming back here in the future for more of this fabulous cuisine.

Just not with Jeff Williams, that's all.

The bells at the door tinkled. She looked over and nearly choked.

Mike stood at the podium, looking at a menu. Mama Lin, the proprietor, came out of the back and fussed over him.

"You got haircut!" she pronounced, scandalized. "You get shorter, shorter, soon you be bald!"

"Not a chance," Mike said, chuckling.

"You want *Tom Kha Gai* tonight?"

"Of course. And some of your Lemon Chicken."

"Vegetable too?"

"Please."

"Okay. Five-ten minutes. Sit." She hustled off and Mike took a seat near the podium. Glad returned her attention to her soup. It didn't taste quite as good with that heaping helping of guilt sprinkled on top. He'd asked her to come here with him and she'd refused. And having him show up tonight and see her here with someone else felt wrong somehow.

Like she was cheating.

Ridiculous. It was just a restaurant like any other. She could come here if she wanted, whenever she wanted with whomever she wanted. And besides, this dating crap had been his idea.

Glad spooned in another mouthful of soup. Her phone chirped faintly in her purse.

"You can answer it," Jeff said, deftly picking up another piece of his sushi roll with chopsticks. "I don't mind."

"I'm sure it's nothing." Glad fished in her

purse and pulled out her phone. The text was from Mike.

i see you went with the soup

Good grief! She rolled her eyes.

"What's the matter?" Jeff asked.

"Just Holly," Glad lied, "wondering how things are going." She rapidly texted back *yes* and sent it.

Her phone chirped again. Glad glanced down at the phone.

did you order the Pad Thai

"She is so nosy," Glad said. "I'm sorry."

"People do it all the time," Jeff said. "No big deal. I check my phone constantly too." As if to prove it, his phone pinged and he pulled it out of his jacket pocket for a quick check. Glad sent back a quick reply:

Stop texting me I'm on a date

Her phone chirped again and she shoved it in her purse. But not before she saw the reply:

date schmate

"I am not answering that," she said, just loudly enough for that certain nosy person by the podium to hear.

It chirped again. Glad spooned in another mouthful of soup and slid her eyes towards the door. Mike was grinning down at his phone, ignoring her. She frowned and spooned up the last of her soup. Their server appeared as if by magic, picking up the empties.

Her phone chirped again. Jeff laughed. "She's really nosy," he said.

"One of her most annoying qualities," Glad said, refusing to even look in Mike's direction.

But her periphery noted that Mama Lin had returned to the podium. That Mike was taking the bag, paying her and leaving the restaurant. That he was gone.

"Pad Thai," said their server, plunking down a loaded plate in front of Glad. It looked great and she knew it would be delicious.

But her appetite had gone, followed Mike right out Far East's front door.

***

It was official. He'd crossed that invisible line that separated a caring individual from a nutjob stalker. He did not care.

Mike sat in the plaza across the street from Far East. He'd made it as far as St. John Street before he'd turned around and now he was sitting here, waiting for Glad and her date to come out of the restaurant.

Mike activated his smartphone, typed *are you done yet* and sent the text.

Yeah, yeah, real mature, trying to get her attention like some middle-school kid with his first crush. He'd texted her about ten times already while his dinner grew cold in its takeout bag. He knew that chirping noise would bug the crap out of her, as much as the thought of her with principal boy was bugging him.

He wasn't jealous, not really. He was just...

Fuck. Okay, fine. He was jealous. Whatever. Shouldn't they be done with dinner by now?

His phone pinged. Mike opened the text.

GRRR CUT IT OUT

Mike grinned and hit reply.

***

"So how did it go? Did you have fun? Isn't Jeff the nicest?"

Holly's enthusiasm was a little tough to take at seven a.m. Glad took a sip of her coffee.

"It was fine."

"You don't sound too excited."

"There isn't going to be a second date."

"Aww! Why not?"

"Well, aside from the fact that there was no attraction-"

"But he's cute!"

Maybe so, but he wasn't big and burly and he didn't have those dark sepia eyes-oh, for the love of-could she not go five minutes without thinking of Mike?

"He just didn't do it for me. And I could tell he wasn't into it either, not really."

"Well, you could try it again, right? Sometimes these things take time to build."

Glad sighed. "He wouldn't shut up about his ex, either."

"Oh, lots of guys mention their exes!"

"In every other sentence?" She took another sip.

"Oh, dear."

"I told him after dinner that I thought he was still in love with his wife and maybe he should think about trying to reconcile."

"You didn't!" Holly gasped.

"I did. He couldn't drive me home fast

221

enough."

"Oh, honey. I'm sorry."

"It gets better," Glad said. "Mike showed up."

"Oh, he did?" Holly sounded wary and Glad immediately got suspicious.

"What did you do?"

"Nothing...exactly."

"Nothing exactly what?"

"Well, we bumped into each other at the Rec and...I might have mentioned where you were having dinner."

"Holly!"

"So? He didn't make a scene, did he? Oh, my God, did he punch Jeff?"

"No!" Glad said, exasperated. "He just kept sending me texts, even after he left! I had like twelve texts from him!"

Holly laughed. "What did they say?"

Glad snorted. "Oh, they were real mature. Stuff like 'pick up your phone' and 'are you done yet'. He's such a dork."

"And jealous, too. How cute!"

"If he's jealous it's his own fault. This was all his idea."

"And if you're a smart girl," Holly said, "you'll make sure he doesn't forget that."

***

Mike expected some backlash from Glad after his stalker-thon Monday night but got nothing for his troubles. By lunchtime Tuesday the pain of being ignored got to him and, worried, he put his mind to what Ken had mentioned. It probably wouldn't hurt to send flowers again or a little gift. Something to take the edge off his behavior last night. But what? What could he give her that would really wow her?

Inspiration finally struck on Wednesday. In the narrow window between lunch and their afternoon job Mike and his crew-minus Jake, who hadn't shown up-busted their humps unloading sod in Glad's back yard. After they finished their afternoon job Mike sent his men home and returned to Glad's house to prep the soil, lay the sod out and trim and shape the edges. It was hard, dirty work and he was soon shirtless and sweaty and his arms were crusted to the elbows with soil and grime.

But it would be worth it, a nice surprise for when she came home. And a daily visual reminder that he was the guy for her, not some buttoned-down school principal who drove a sports car. A freaking convertible sports car.

He was man enough to admit it. This whole dating comparison thing was a bad idea. At the time it had seemed like just the thing to do, no big deal, a joke. But the joke was on him now; this jealousy burning him up inside felt pretty damn real. He'd wanted to walk over to that table Monday night, punch principal boy right in the face and haul Glad out of there.

It was driving him nuts, no doubt about it. But he'd screwed himself the minute he'd opened his mouth and he had to see it through whether he liked it or not. But how many more dates would there be? How much longer would this take? And what if…

No. No what ifs. The game had changed and the sole objective was winning the girl. Stoking gossip and saving his job now rode the bench.

He'd win. He had to win.

Mike finished placing the last sod and trimmed the edge where it overlapped the area he'd marked out for a patio. Then he stood, limbs aching and surveyed his work.

Good. Damn good. Sure, it wasn't very big, only about twenty by thirty, but it was a start. Nothing like an instant yard. Maybe next week he could get her out to Green Spaces so she could order some plants and pavers and they could really start moving. Of course, he'd have to figure out when he could fit it in his schedule. May was nearly upon them and he was busy now from daylight 'til dark, most days.

Mike tossed his shirt over his shoulder and picked up his tools. It was getting late. He'd better skedaddle before Glad got home if he wanted this to be a surprise.

***

Glad walked home, wanting nothing more than to get out of this suit and into more comfortable clothes. It was unseasonably warm today and her confining skirt and jacket were locking in her body heat.

Glad paused to remove her jacket. Much better. She draped the jacket through her tote straps and resumed walking. She'd have to consider bringing a change of clothes with her if she walked to work all summer. She didn't want to sweat all over her suits and rack up more dry cleaning charges than she had to.

Man, it was warm out. Thank goodness she only had four blocks to go. Glad moved her tote over to her left hand and readjusted her purse strap on her shoulder. She could never figure out how some women could keep their purse hanging with no effort whatsoever; hers was always slipping off. Maybe she should invest in some shoulder pads or something-

She stumbled midstride and stared down Gibson. Three blocks away an F-150 was idling at the end of Lincoln Street, waiting for some traffic to pass. It was Mike. It had to be Mike. No one else around town had a truck that deep green color.

Her adrenaline spiked and she walked faster. Why was Mike here? What was he doing on her street? Had he been at her house? She'd told herself she needed to ignore him after all those silly texts the other night and that she wouldn't talk to him at all or even spy on him out on the library lawn. Then of course another contractor- who definitely did *not* look good in a hard hat- had shown up to do more preparation, running drainage pipes and connecting them to the sewer line at the street and instead of being able to ignore Mike she wound up wondering where he was and what he was up to.

Another car passed Lincoln and there was an opening. The F-150 pulled out on to Gibson and headed away from her. Drat that man! Glad growled and kept walking fast. He'd been at her house; she'd bet her paycheck on it.

She headed up Gibson and turned onto Lincoln at a brisk pace, tote swinging and purse slipping off her shoulder with every other step. She knew if the neighbors were watching she'd look foolish, tearing up the street like this with her bags bouncing all over. She didn't care. She had to see what he'd been up to.

She reached her property line and looked around out front. Nothing but a few dirt clumps in her driveway. Glad headed up to the back yard, feeling anxious. Had he planted something? They hadn't even talked about trees or bushes or anything yet-oh, my! She dropped her bags.

Where once there was only dirt, she had a fresh rectangle of grass. Grass!

Glad clapped her hands with glee, tore off her sneakers and socks and stepped onto it. Okay, it was wet. Really wet and she beat a retreat to her back steps. Grabbed her phone from her purse and dialed.

"Hey, girl," he answered in that rumbly voice that turned her to jelly.

"You gave me grass," she said.

"I did."

"Grass!" she repeated, giddy.

"What, you thought I was going to leave your yard bare?"

She smiled. "I thought if it stayed that way much longer I might have to move my car back there and put it up on blocks."

His laughter warmed her through. "So you like it?"

"Very much. Thank you."

"You're going to need to keep it watered. Soak it good every other day."

"I will-oh, I'll have to go get a garden hose."

"Just use mine. I left it there."

"You did?" A tender ache blossomed in her chest. Okay, it was just a garden hose, but he was thinking of her, taking care of her. How long since anything like that had happened? She couldn't remember.

"I did."

"This is wonderful."

"It's not much," he said, sounding bashful. Glad smiled into her phone.

"It's perfect. I couldn't ask for anything better, Mike, really. Thank you so much."

"You're welcome, girl."

***

On Thursday morning, Jake didn't show again and the crew left Green Spaces without him. He showed up at the job site twenty minutes after they started clearing the front beds, unshaven and rumpled with a big hickey on his neck and he smelled like stale cigarettes and beer. And Mike's buoyant mood from the evening before evaporated.

"What the hell, man?" Jake asked without preamble. "Couldn't you wait for me so I didn't have to drive all the way out here?"

"The job doesn't wait," Mike said. "This is real life and we work in real time, on a schedule. We can't sit around and wait for you to drag your ass out of some girl's bed."

227

"Who the fuck are you to-"

"I'm responsible. I'm in charge of this crew, this job and everything that happens here. My crew shows up on time, gets the job done and does it well. My crew is presentable, clean and respectful. You are none of these things. You're an embarrassment. Go home."

"What?" Jake was shocked.

"Go. Home." Mike's patience frayed.

Jake's brilliant blue eyes snapped an unholy fire. "You can't tell me-"

"Dude, don't mess with Kovalski," Fonz tried and Jake rounded on him.

"I'm not letting that Jew asshole tell me what-*aiiiyyy*!"

Mike picked up Jake like a hay bale and threw him in the direction of his car. For a moment Jake was an airborne tangle of flailing arms and legs then he hit the ground with an "OOF!" He scrambled to his feet and backed to his car, a stream of obscenities pouring from his mouth. He got in his car, still cursing and took off down the street. Mike shook his head and turned back to his crew.

"I'll give you an eight for form and a nine-point five for that landing," Fonz said, then chuckled at his own joke.

"I had a lance corporal under me during my second tour," said Turk. "One day he gave me a ration of shit and I picked him up and threw him, just like that. I got dressed out by my company commander, but damn. It was worth it."

"And I'm sure I'll get dressed out by Ken when we get back to Green Spaces," Mike said.

Or more than dressed out, he might get fired for manhandling the boss's son on top of everything else. Well, it was too late for do-overs. "Let's get to work."

Mike turned back to the truck, took two steps and stopped when a sound he'd never heard before broke out behind him.

Laughter. Like a rusty nail being yanked from an old board, but laughter just the same. Mike turned and found Harry Phelps, the man who never cracked a smile bent over and busting his gut, hanging onto a stunned Fonz for support.

"Well, I swear," Turk drawled. "That there's a first."

"Never thought I'd see the day," Harry gasped. "You gave that sumbitch *wings*, boss!"

17

"Okay," Fran said, "it's my turn. Jerry's single, responsible, has a steady job and he likes cats."

The three friends had met for after-work drinks at Slade's, a wine bar on the square that had just opened a week ago. The place defied description: the interior looked like the remains of a rummage sale with a line of salvaged church pews along one wall and a mishmosh of tables and chairs, no two alike. The immense bar was also a salvage piece and an old rolling ladder, saved from the days when the building had been a bookstore, was still attached to the wall behind the bar. It allowed the bartender to stash glasses, Slade's merchandise and wine on the floor-to-ceiling shelves that had formerly held all manner of reading material.

The menu was just as eclectic as the décor, consisting of only appetizers, and they ran the gamut from chicken wings to steak tartare. It was an odd little place but Glad was excited to try it out. She loved a good red wine, especially Pinot Noir.

"He's also going bald," Holly said as they approached the bar.

"What does his hairline have to do with anything?" Fran asked.

"What do cats have to do with anything?" asked Glad.

"You're a librarian! Isn't it like some sort of requirement for you to like cats?"

"Welcome, ladies," the bartender said. His piercing gray eyes stopped on Holly's face and he said, "You look kind of familiar."

"I was Holly Klingler in high school," she said. And you're Matt Slade. You played on Glen View's football team with Alex Spence, my hus-*former* husband," she corrected herself with a sad smile.

"I did," he agreed. "He was a good guy. Damn shame what happened."

Holly smiled. "So you came back home, huh?"

"Believe it or not," he said.

Glad studied him. Matthew Slade was dark and dangerous looking with intense gray eyes, tattoos running down his left arm and his hair and beard clipped short. "If you missed the board out front, we're touring California's Central Coast tonight." He passed over a printed list. "These are the specials. The Laetitia Pinot is more expensive but trust me, it's worth it."

"Sold," Glad said as Holly and Fran bent over the page. He poured her a glass of the Pinot

Noir she'd requested and placed it on the bar.

"What's your name?" he asked, holding her with his eyes.

"Glad," she said, fighting the urge to add "sir" after. The man had a commanding air about him that was a little scary. And a little sexy, if she was being honest with herself.

"You work up at the library, right?"

"Yes." She forced some authority into her voice. "I'm the Assistant Director."

He gazed at her a moment longer, then finally said, "Interesting," and turned to take Holly and Fran's orders, a Cabernet and a Sauvignon Blanc, respectively. The women ordered some appetizers and retreated to an open table.

"I had such a crush on him freshman year," Holly said. "I never told anyone because he was an outsider, you know, he didn't really hang with anyone. The kids used to call him Scarface-he's got a scar along his jaw under that beard-but always behind his back. No one wanted to mess with him. Of all the people I remember from school, I never would have pegged him as the wine bar type." Holly brightened and turned to Glad. "Hey, if he's single, you could try and catch him!"

Glad sipped her Laetitia Pinot and sighed with bliss as the full fruity flavor danced over her tongue. He knew good wine; she'd give him that much. "He's not...he kind of scares me, if you want the truth."

"What?" Holly laughed. "Why?"

"I don't know." Glad eyed the bartender

again. He was serving another customer, and smiling, but… "He just looks so intense. Volatile." She shook her head. "I want someone who's a little more laid back."

"Then you'll love Jerry," Fran said. "He's sweet, and dependable, and a really nice guy. Plus, he's my second cousin. What's not to like?"

Glad took another sip of her Pinot and gave up. "Whatever. Set me up. Can we talk about something else, now?"

***

He couldn't stand this anymore. Thursday had been interminable and today wasn't much better. He still had two hours to go before he could get out of here and the clock had stopped moving altogether.

He missed her. He needed to see her. Tonight. Mike ducked into his office and dialed.

"Mill Falls Public Library, how may I direct your call?"

"This is Mike Kovalski from Green Spaces," he said, trying to sound businesslike. "May I speak to the Assistant Director, please?"

There was a moment of silence, then the voice said "One moment" and put him on hold. Classical music came over the line. Mike fiddled with a pencil laying on his desk. Come on, hurry up and answer already. Then the line clicked and a voice from heaven spilled into his ear.

"This is Glad Donahue. How can I help you?"

"It's Mike. You busy tonight?" he asked. "I

233

thought maybe we could have dinner."

"Oh! Well, I'd like to, but…I have a date," she said, her voice sounding pinched.

"A date." Fuck!

"Yes. It's Fran's turn to set me up with someone. For, um, comparison's sake, remember?"

Fuck and double fuck. Mike bunched his hair in his hand. "Yeah," he managed. "Okay."

He heard her take in a breath. "Maybe we could do something together tomorrow?"

"I'm working tomorrow."

"Oh. Well, um…"

A knock sounded on his door. "Mike? A customer needs you out front."

"Shit," he muttered. "I'll be there in a minute," he promised the door, then said to Glad. "Sorry, customers. I'll uh, catch up with you later."

"I…okay. Bye."

He hung up, frustrated. Got up and circled his tiny desk. Grabbed his phone and dialed again.

"Serenity Day Spa," said a velvety voice.

"Fran Bishop, please."

***

She was so killing Fran tomorrow.

Glad stared across the table at her date and tried to act interested in what he was saying but she couldn't focus on anything but the myriad ways she was going to make Fran pay for setting her up with this guy.

Jerry was pleasant enough, his car was clean and he'd held doors for her when they'd stepped into Rambler's, a chain eatery along the commercial strip on the far side of Glen View. He was neat and presentable and she totally respected that he didn't feel the need to hide his balding with a comb over. And she could have handled all that except for that little bomb he'd dropped on the way here.

Jerry lived with his mother. Had never lived anywhere else *but* with his mother. Had even invited her along tonight as she really liked this restaurant, but mother had insisted he go alone. It was a date, after all.

She shuddered inside. Maybe she could get a migraine, or burst her appendix. Anything to get out of here sooner.

Their server appeared. "Hi! I'm Kevin!" he said, oozing that fake cheer that all these chain places seemed to have in abundant supply. "I'll be your server tonight!" He did a quick check inside the menu, then handed one to each of them.

"What are the specials tonight?" asked Jerry.

"Tonight we've got a fish fry with coleslaw and French fries for nine ninety-five! Soup is clam chowder! And our happy hour drink specials are still good, all tall drafts are four dollars-"

"Oh, we don't need a drink," Jerry said.

"I would love a drink," Glad said at the same time. Oh yes, alcohol would definitely help her through this mess. "What's on tap?"

"Let's see. Bud, Bud Light, Labatt, Great

Lakes Dortmunder Gold, Thirsty Dog Twisted Kilt, Shock Top-"

"Dortmunder," Glad said, ignoring the raised eyebrows of her date.

"Great! I'll get this up and be right back for your orders." Kevin walked off.

"I didn't think librarians were much for drinking," Jerry commented, disapproval in his expression.

"Oh, we let our hair down on occasion," Glad said and opened her menu. Gasped aloud.

"What's the matter?" Jerry asked.

"Nothing, uh, there's just so much to choose from," she said lamely, trying to calm her racing heart.

Mike's business card was stuck in the lower left corner of her menu, tucked under the plastic corner piece. Glad glanced over; Jerry was intent on his menu so she slid the card out and flipped it over.

in the bar

Her stomach clenched and fluttered. What was Mike doing here? How did he know-of course. Fran must have told him. Oh, yes. Definitely killing Fran.

She would not go to the bar. Would *not*. After all, she was on a date! Okay, so far not much of a date, but it was still technically a date. Jerry was perfectly nice and she could deal. She'd have a fine time and Mike Kovalski could sit at the bar by himself all night long-

"So," Jerry said, interrupting her reverie, "what looks good to you?"

"I'm not sure yet," she hedged, sliding the

business card onto her lap.

"Well, the salads are always good here, and the last time I took Mother here she really liked the spaghetti. The sauce isn't too spicy so she doesn't get heartburn."

Hoo, boy. This was torture. "It sounds good. Could you excuse me a moment?" Glad asked sweetly. "I just need to use the restroom." She slid off her chair and headed for the bar, Mike's card clutched in her hand.

He was sitting alone at the far end, away from the Friday night drinking crowd, a book propped up on a pile of coasters in front of him and a pint of beer in his hand. Glad dropped the card in front of him and hissed, "What are you doing here?"

He turned a page. "Waiting for you."

"Fran told you I was here," she accused.

"Maybe. How much longer you think you'll be?"

"How much-none of your business! I'm on a date!"

He smirked. "If you say so."

"Jerry's perfectly nice-"

Mike gave her a look. "Glad. He's got six cats and lives with his mother. Do you really want to go there?"

"I-well, no, but I can't just leave! That would be rude!"

Mike shook his head and took a sip of his beer. Turned another page. "Suit yourself. I'll be here another thirty minutes, in case you want a ride home or anything."

She rolled her eyes, agitated. "You don't

need to stick around. I'll be fine."

"And I'll be here for another thirty minutes," he said, unperturbed.

Glad left the bar and returned to her table. Her tall Dortmunder stood at her place and the menus were gone.

"I took the liberty of ordering for you, since you weren't here," Jerry said.

"Oh. How nice of you," Glad said, forcing a smile. Spaghetti would be fine, she supposed. She took a big drink and asked, "So, what do you do for a living?"

"I work down at the propane store on Route 38. I fill up tanks for customers and sell grills and heaters and accessories. Did you know that propane is a byproduct of natural gas? It's also a byproduct of crude oil refinement. It's nontoxic, colorless, odorless…"

Ten minutes later Jerry was still waxing on about propane. Glad's beer was half empty, she was completely glazed over and in danger of falling asleep. The server appeared with more rolls, picked up their salad plates and promised dinner was coming right out.

"So, what do you do in your spare time?" Glad asked, eager for a change of subject.

"Well, my kitties take up a lot of attention. Four of them have long hair, so there's a lot of grooming involved." He dug out his wallet and opened it. "This is Morris. He's an orange tabby, just like the cat on TV. Now this one's Arabella, she gets matted if I don't comb her every other day. And this one's Lucille. She's got seven toes on her-"

238

"Your dinners!" interrupted Kevin. He placed two plates down and disappeared. Glad looked down and sucked in a horrified breath.

"What...is that?" she asked. The smell was horrifying.

"Liver and onions," Jerry said, cutting into his portion with relish. "They make it really good here, fry it up nice. I thought you might need a little extra protein in your diet-"

Oh, God, she was going to vomit.

"Excuse me." Glad bolted, gagging. She stumbled into the bar, rushed past a wide-eyed Mike and headed out the side door.

Oh, thank God. Clean, fresh air. Glad took in deep, cleansing breaths, desperate to chase away that awful stench of fried liver. Her stomach quivered one last time and was still. Then it fluttered anew when a warm arm went around her shoulders.

"You all right?" Mike asked.

"He ordered me liver!" Glad said, shuddering. "Liver and onions! What kind of weirdo does that on a *date*?"

Mike stared at her a moment, his expression shocked. Then he threw his head back and began to laugh.

***

"It's not funny!"

It was hilarious. Mike laughed harder and she whacked him on the arm. "Stop laughing at me!"

"I'm not, I swear." He wiped at his eyes and

smiled down at her. For whatever reason that seemed to piss her off more and he started laughing again.

"Are you done yet?" she asked, crossing her arms.

"Almost. Come on, I'll take you home." He steered them over to his truck, hit his key fob and opened the passenger door. Glad climbed in and he shut the door behind her. Mike walked around the truck, still chuckling.

"Trust me, you'll think this is funny in the morning," he said, tucking his book behind his seat and sliding behind the wheel.

"Oh, no I won't," she growled. "First thing tomorrow I'm killing Fran and you're going to help me hide the body."

He chuckled again, thinking he'd should call and thank Fran tomorrow. Maybe even send her flowers. "You don't want to kill Fran."

"No, but I could. I can't believe she thought- ooh! What a disaster!"

Mike pulled out of his parking space. "It was one bad date. Old Jerry could turn out to be the man of your dreams, despite his questionable dinner choices."

"More like my worst nightmare," she corrected him. "I asked him what he did for a living and he talked about propane for ten minutes! I didn't know anyone could talk about propane that long!"

"Men like talking about gas," he said with a smile.

Glad folded her arms and gave him a look that clearly said she was not amused. He cracked up again.

"Stop that. And then I tried to change the subject and I asked him what he did in his spare time and you know what he did?"

"Got out the cat pictures?" Mike asked.

"Yes! And he talked about his mother's heartburn! How do you expect to get anywhere with a woman when you talk about your mother's digestive problems?"

"You don't." Mike chuckled again. He pulled out of the parking lot and they headed back to Mill Falls.

Mike stared up at her dark bedroom window. "You can't climb up there!"

"Of course I can," Glad scoffed, looking for all the world like scaling a roof was child's play, something she did every day.

"How? You got a ladder?"

"Um…well, actually…no."

"Were you going to fly, then?" he asked. He couldn't believe they'd gotten into this mess. He'd driven them all the way back to Glad's house before she'd realized that, in her haste to leave the liver and onions behind, she'd left her purse at Rambler's. So they'd gone back, only to discover that her date-and her purse-were both gone. She didn't know Jerry's number or where he lived, so he'd let her borrow his phone to call Fran.

Only Fran didn't answer. So he'd offered his place for the night and she'd laughed at him and said no and now here they were in her back yard, contemplating killing themselves.

"You don't need to be sarcastic about it," Glad said, crossing her arms and giving him that stubborn look that did not bode well.

"I'm not seeing another solution, here. Just come home with me. I'll sleep on the couch." Which was a lie, of course, but she didn't need to know that.

She looked at him like she'd just read his mind and shook her head. "I know I can get up there. I just need something…"

Mike took her shoulders in his hands and turned her around. "I don't see any wings sprouting yet."

"Would you stop-wait. I can take my table off the porch," she said pointing.

"It's not tall enough."

"Then I'll put my chair on top and-"

"Absolutely not," he interrupted. "That piece of shit will send you straight to Urgent Care. And I'll be damned if I go there twice in the same month."

She looked hard at him, considering. Then she brightened with an idea. "Well, you're tall enough!"

Mike put his hands on his hips and tried his best to look intimidating. "Tell you right now, I'm not getting on that table."

She waved a hand. "No. You can give me a boost!"

Mike stared at her. "I can give you a boost," he repeated, dumbfounded.

"Yes! It'll work! I know it will!" She hopped on one foot and pulled off one sandal, then the other. Crashed into him.

"You'll get hurt!" he said, steadying her.

"It'll be fine!"

"It won't. You're a klutz."

Her mouth dropped into a perfect O. "I am not!"

"Who fell off her Pilates ball at the Rec?" he asked, raising a brow.

Glad put her hands on her hips. "That was *your* fault!"

"And who tripped up her own steps the night we met?"

"If you want the truth, that one was your fault too."

He grinned, pleased at her admission. Now it was time for the crusher. "And who tripped over a *pebble* in El Nino's parking lot?"

She glowered at him. "I have no recollection of that."

"It still counts. Come on, Glad. Just come home with me."

"I can't do that."

Mike sighed, exasperated. Damn gossip.

"Listen, I want in my house and this is the only way I can think of. Are you going to help me or not?" she asked.

He'd probably regret this, but... "Okay, fine. We'll try it. But if you can't get up there, we're going to my place. No arguments."

"Fine."

Mike bent his knees and laced his fingers together. Glad put one hand on his shoulder and her foot in his hands. "You ready?" he asked.

"Yes."

Mike straightened and was rewarded with a face full of cleavage. Okay, maybe this wasn't such a bad plan after all.

"Sorry," Glad muttered, adjusting herself and leaning away.

He wasn't. "I'm going to lift you higher. You grab the roof and get your feet on my shoulders. Got it?"

"Okay."

Mike lifted her, felt her feet on his shoulders, one by one.

"I've got it!" She grabbed higher and got one knee on the roof, pushed off his shoulder...

"Whoa-wait-Mike!" Her right knee slipped down. A tiny shriek slipped out. "No! Mike! Help!"

Mike made a grab for her flailing left foot and missed. She slipped farther and he felt gray hairs being born all over his head. "Hold still already!" He made a second grab, got her foot and pushed. Glad scrabbled for a better hold and finally got both knees on the roof.

"Oh, thank goodness!" She pulled herself higher, more secure and crawled up to the window. Stopped.

"How do I get the screen off from this side?" She hissed down to him.

"Just tear it," he said. "They're easy to fix."

"But if I can just-hang on," she said, wiggling the screen around. Suddenly it popped

244

off in her hands. "Wow! Did you see that?" she exclaimed.

"Very nice. Now get in there."

Glad pushed the window up all the way, tucked the screen inside and wiggled herself through. Mike heard an "Ow!" and a curse, then a crash, followed by "I'm in!"

She was something else. "Goodnight, Gladiolus," he called up.

Her head poked out the window. "Wait! Don't leave!" She disappeared and he heard the faint pounding of feet inside the house. What did she want now?

The back door opened and she came down the steps. Stopped right next to him and put a hand on his arm. Heat flooded him and his brain shut down.

"I'm sorry I was such a bother."

"It's no problem." She was so close, stroking his arm with her fingers, gazing up at him like she was spellbound. Or maybe he was, standing here looking at her, his breath hitching in his chest. Damn, she was beautiful in the moonlight.

"I really do appreciate the ride home. Thank you."

"You're welcome," he said. "Sorry your date didn't work out." Which was a total lie.

She stared at him, then a strange little smile curled her lips. "Well, if men like Jeff and Jerry are my options maybe I'll just give up and get a dog or something."

Wait. What? *Give up?* "A dog?"

"Sure. I mean, dogs are easier than people, right? All I'd have to do is walk him and feed him and pick up his poo once or twice a week. That's way easier than dating!"

Mike could only stare. Was she kidding? She must be.

"And he'd always be glad to see me, and give me doggy kisses and stuff."

Okay, maybe she wasn't kidding. "Um, Glad-"

Glad smiled and clapped her hands together, obviously delighted with her new idea. "Maybe I can go to the shelter tomorrow and look for one."

Shit. This wasn't looking good. He needed to derail this train fast. "But what about-"

"There's got to be some cute little mutt down there that needs a home! Do you want to come with me?"

"What? No!"

"Aww! Why not?"

She looked hurt and he felt bad. So Mike did the only thing he could think of. He grabbed her shoulders, yanked her close and kissed her.

18

She'd have to remember this I'll-just-get-a-dog-instead strategy. Glad went up on her toes and wrapped her arms around Mike's neck, rejoiced at the re-acquaintance of their lips. She opened for him, tasted hops and malt and a faint essence of mint. Heavenly.

"No doggy kisses," Mike said against her mouth, "and no more dates."

Glad ran her fingers into his hair. "There were only two."

"I can't take it anymore, okay?"

She laughed. "Come on. You weren't really jealous of Jerry, were you?"

"Right down to his damn liver and onions." He nuzzled her and dropped a sweet kiss on her nose. "So are we done with this shit? Can we get on with us, now?"

"Should I remind you this was your idea?"

Mike kissed her again. A little harder, nibbled at her lips and her knees went weak.

"Don't. This was the dumbest of dumb-ass ideas and I don't want to hear about it ever again. I want to be your man. I don't want anyone dating you but me."

"But what about the dog?"

"I don't want anyone humping your leg but me, either."

She laughed out loud and he kissed her, stroked his tongue into her mouth. Liquid heat spiraled out from her core and she squirmed against him. "All-all right."

"We'll take things slow, I promise." He kissed her again, his breath coming short. Glad slid her tongue along his lower lip and he moaned into her mouth. "One-one date-at a time. I won't-push."

Glad pressed closer and moved her hand down below his belt buckle. Traced over the bulging denim with her fingers and Mike dropped his head into her neck with a harsh groan.

"Girl-"

"Push," she whispered.

Mike raised his head. Raw, feral desire burned in his eyes and he took her mouth again. The kiss was demanding and hard and Glad dissolved into a burning pool of want, gasping against his mouth, moaning when he moved down her neck and sucked at the skin over her collarbone. His hands went to her hips, caressed over her bottom and pulled them together. His erection strained hot and hard against his jeans, pushing at her, wanting *in*. Glad kissed him again and Mike's arms tightened around her like iron bands. She felt her feet leave the ground, felt him take a step and she curled her legs around him.

Need trumped niceties; urgency left sweetness and foreplay in the dust. Somehow they got back in the house and upstairs, lost all their clothing in a heartbeat and then Mike took her down on her bed. He closed his mouth over her left nipple and suckled hard while his hand moved to her most private spot. She was already wet and as he slid one finger into her Glad arched against his hand and begged, "Take me. Now."

"Oh, girl-"

"Please." She closed her fingers around him. He was thick and pulsing, heavy in her hand. She stroked him once, twice and he groaned and stopped her.

"Don't-I'm too close-" He dove for the side of the bed, fumbled with his jeans a moment and pulled a condom from the pocket. Glad took it from him, opened it and slid it on with a caressing hand. He moaned out loud and mounted her.

Glad guided him to her and he pushed in carefully, slowly stretched her until she took all of him, gasping against the heat and fullness. Above her Mike moaned out loud.

"God, you feel so good." He took another slow stroke, trembling all over and hissed, "Wanted this-waited-so long." He pushed deep a third time, his breath coming hard and Glad curled her arms around his neck.

"I want to-be gentle, here," he panted, "but I-"

"No," she interrupted, rocking her hips up to meet his. "Hard. I want it hard."

249

Mike moaned and thrust deep, settled them into a vigorous rhythm that had her groaning, raising her hips to meet him, lifting her legs around him, taking him in all the way. She gasped against the intensity of it, the power of his big body over her and inside her and her animal response drove her forward, urging him for more and still more. She was close, her body coiled tighter and tighter with every stroke. Just a few more, just one more-

Her orgasm rocked her from head to toe and she cried out. Heard him growl against her neck as she bucked under him, clenched around him, trapped him inside her. He kept going, pushing her farther and it lasted, sweeter and longer than any ever had. She was shaking, crying out his name over and over, helpless against the tide of it. Then Mike stiffened, shivered and flexed inside of her with a hard, guttural groan. Glad wrapped herself around him and held him tight, as close to heaven as she'd ever been.

***

"Well. Now that we've gotten that out of the way, could you explain to me again this whole taking it slow, one date at a time thing?"

Mike gave a loud, lusty laugh and pulled Glad against him. Kissed her and ran his hand down her bare back to squeeze that delectable bottom.

"I was trying to be a gentleman," he said in his defense, stroking along her thigh. Her skin was so soft and he couldn't stop touching it.

"You had a condom in your pocket," she reminded him, her free hand busy in his chest hair. She sure seemed to like it. And he liked it too; he was rising again just feeling her hand on his body.

"That was hope," he clarified, "not intent."

Glad's long fingers traced him. "So if I'd had a lovely time with Jerry-"

"I would have gone home and put it back in the box with the others. Probably cried."

"You would not!"

"Girl, you have no idea. I've been wound up so tight these last weeks-oh. Mmm. You need to stop that."

"Why?" Glad stroked up his length and he moaned. Man, was she ever good at that.

"I don't-ohh-I only brought one with me."

Glad smiled and stroked him some more. "Well, lucky for you I'm a librarian."

"I am totally down with the sexy librarian thing." And he was, too. He'd hit the sexy librarian jackpot.

"Thanks, but that's not what I meant. We librarians, generally speaking, like to have a plan. We think ahead."

"Which means…"

"There's a new box of Trojans in my medicine cabinet."

"Hope or intent?" he asked, kissing her again.

"Definitely intent."

He smiled wolfishly. "Lucky me."

"Indeed. Go get it."

***

Mike arrived at Green Spaces just after daybreak. He hadn't wanted to leave Glad and that so-comfortable bed, but he had multiple hives to check before they opened for business and his honeybees preferred he bother them in early morning rather than at other times of day.

He yawned heavily as he headed out back to the sheds. He'd only caught a few hours of sleep and knew he'd be worn out by the end of today. But Glad had been worth it. All of the waiting and stress and angst of the last weeks had been worth it.

She was his, finally. They were together. Last night played over and over in his head and he knew he was smiling like an idiot and he didn't care.

They'd gone again after he'd freed the Trojans from their plastic-wrapped prison. Slower and sweeter, exploring each other with their hands and mouths until, at his limit, he'd pulled her on top of him and she'd given him the ride of his life.

And they had talked, and laughed and teased each other and, best of all, made plans. They were going to have dinner tonight. Pick out plants and pavers for her back yard tomorrow. Maybe drive to Amish country next weekend if the weather was nice.

Mike unlocked his supply shed and took out his beekeeper suit and veil. He grabbed his smoker and the bucket that held his other supplies and placed them outside the shed.

"Hey, Mike."

Mike jumped and turned. Jake Anderson stood there, hands in his pockets, looking uncomfortable.

"You're up early," he said. "Or haven't you made it home yet?"

Jake smiled a little, then he said, "I wanted to apologize. For acting like such an asshole the other day."

This was unexpected. Probably his old man had put him up to it, but Mike wasn't going to look a gift horse in the mouth. "Apology accepted. Are you coming back on Monday?"

Jake frowned. "Yeah, I guess."

Mike stepped into his suit and pulled it up. "You don't have to work with us if you don't want to, you know. Your dad has other crews, or you could work in the greenhouses."

Jake shook his head. "It's not that. You guys are all right, actually."

Mike groaned inside and zipped up his suit. The 'poor me' litany was imminent, he knew it. "So what is it then?"

Jake looked around him, taking in the operation. His face furrowed and he frowned and suddenly looked twenty years older and worn out. "I hate this. Not Green Spaces, not exactly, but Mill Falls and my dad's..." He shook his head. "I've busted my ass the last four years, double majored in business and law, graduated early with a three-point eight and it wasn't good enough because it wasn't a four." Jake raked his hands through his hair and stared at Mike. "I mean, come on. Really?"

"Three-point eight's pretty damn good," Mike said, impressed. Contrary to his exhibited behavior, Jake Anderson had a few brains in his head.

"Oh, no. If it's not perfect, it's crap. If it's not what he wants, it's crap. It's like he's got a scale someplace and I'm on one side and all these expectations are on the other and you know that fucker's not evening out." He blew out a breath and raked a hand through his hair again. "Sorry, man. It's not your problem."

Okay, he'd told Ken he wasn't a mentor, but Mike understood where Jake was coming from. That last comment pretty much summed up his entire childhood. "Well, the way I see it you've got two choices. You either keep banging your head against the wall trying to make everyone else happy, or you figure out what's going to make you happy and go for it. You really want to go to grad school, then get back on the horse. Take your GMAT again and pass it this time. Or take the LSAT and go to law school. Or get a job."

Jake looked uncertain. "It's not that easy."

"Yes, it is. You're a grown man. Make a decision and stick with it."

"What if it's the wrong decision?"

"Then start over." Mike looked at Jake, saw the lingering uncertainty and plunged ahead. "Listen. I get where you're coming from. It's not easy to strike out on your own. All my life, all I've been interested in is plants and bugs and being outdoors. When I was a kid I wanted to be a farmer. My parents wanted me to be a rabbi.

Then when I got kicked out of Hebrew school they decided I should be a doctor like my dad. I finally had enough after freshman year, dropped pre-med and went into botany. They flipped out and took the money away."

"You mean they stopped paying for your college?"

Mike nodded. "Wouldn't give me a dime."

"What did you do?" Jake asked, fascinated.

"I applied for every scholarship I could find and got a job. I worked thirty hours a week at a home and garden store and took classes the rest of the time. I shared an apartment with three other guys and slept on an air mattress. Some days all I could afford to eat was a dollar burger at McDonalds."

"Wow." Jake looked impressed.

"My point is this is what I wanted. More than anything. So I walked away from a free ride, pissed off my parents and busted my hump for it. You've been knuckling under, putting your life on hold for everyone else. Well, now it's your turn. What do *you* want, more than anything else?"

A shadow passed over Jake's face.

"I want to forget," he finally said, and walked away.

***

"Why did I find your purse on my doorstep this morning?" asked Fran's voice.

Glad yawned and stretched, then winced. Lord, she ached. But she felt great. "Oh, thank goodness. I didn't know if I'd see it again."

"I also had a message from Jerry telling me to never set him up on a date again. What went wrong?"

"Where do you want me to start? How about the part where he lives with his *mother?*"

"Oh, dear," Fran said.

"You knew that," Glad accused.

"Well...yeah. But he really is a nice guy!"

Glad sighed, exasperated. "Fran..."

"I'm sorry! I really am! How about I buy you lunch to make up for it?"

"Deal."

Glad stepped into Mimi's Diner promptly at noon. Mimi's was a throwback in time with its black and white checkered floor, red vinyl upholstered booths and a long counter fronted with stainless steel. The menu was full of heart-clogging comfort food, the milkshakes were to die for and the waitresses called everyone 'hon'. Glad had loved it from the first and regularly came here with her friends.

The lunch crowd was starting to pour in but Fran and Holly had already snagged a booth in the far corner and waved her over. Glad dropped into the seat opposite her friends and Fran handed her purse over the table.

"You'd better check and make sure everything is there," Fran teased.

"I will," Glad said, opening her purse and examining the contents.

"I was kidding!"

"I put nothing past that man. He invited his mother on our date. She didn't come, but that's

256

beside the point. He invited her."

"Oh, wow," Holly murmured.

"Then he wouldn't shut up about the wonders of propane, then he got out the cat pictures, and then," Glad said, opening her wallet, "he ordered me liver and onions for dinner."

"No way!" Holly and Fran gasped together.

"Way. I almost threw up right there in the middle of Ramblers! And-" Glad checked her cash again. "That creep! He took fourteen dollars out of my purse!"

"I'm sure it was just to cover dinner," Fran said, biting her lip and looking at Holly for help.

"And maybe a little extra for the tip," Holly snorted.

"It's not funny," Glad said, trying her best to stay serious.

"No, of course-not-" Fran collapsed against Holly and they began giggling madly.

Glad crossed her arms and waited for the two of them to finish their laugh-fest. Their waitress stopped by and took Glad's order, eyeballing Holly and Fran like they were crazy. Finally, the giggles died away and Holly asked, "So how did you get home?"

"Mike Kovalski was there. He-"

Fran gave a little squee. "Oh, I hoped he'd show! He called me yesterday and asked where you were going! He's *so* jealous, hon."

"Yes, well-"

"Speak of the devil," interrupted Holly. Glad turned around and beheld Mike at the front counter. The waitress scribbled something on a pad then he handed her several bills. Her stomach flipped and twirled and memories flooded in.

Ride me. Oh, girl, yes. Just like that.

She smiled and, as if he'd sensed her, Mike turned around. His eyes found her and he left the counter and headed in her direction. Heat flooded her and she squirmed in her seat, thrilled at the very sight of her man, tall and broad and so, so sexy.

Mike put one knee on the booth seat, leaned down and kissed her deeply.

"Hey, beautiful," he murmured against her lips. Glad sighed and kissed him back, happy down to her bones. Across the table Fran gave a little squee of delight.

"Are you together now? You must be together! Oh, how exciting!"

Mike broke the kiss and turned to Fran. "Did she tell you about the liver and onions yet?"

Fran and Holly began giggling again. Glad sighed. "Yes, I did. And I still don't think it's funny."

"Come on. Yes, you do."

She felt herself smiling. "Okay, maybe it's a little funny."

Mike kissed her again. "Gotta get back to work. I'll see you at dinner."

"I can't wait," Glad said. Mike kissed her one more time and straightened. "Ladies," he said, smiling at Holly and Fran, and went back to the counter. The waitress handed him two bags with an automatic "Thanks, hon!" and he walked out. Glad turned her gaze back to the two expectant faces across from her.

"So I guess you got a little more than a ride home," Holly commented.

Fran giggled. "She sure did, look at that blush!"

19

Overheard at Slade's:

The One Date Wonder's off the market!

I know! I saw them together just yesterday! Kissing!

I can't believe they're actually dating.

I saw them at the IGA last night. They were looking pretty chummy over by the carrots.

She knows what a sleaze he was, right? I mean, someone told her, right?

Oh, I'm sure she knows. The library is gossip central!

I can't believe a nice woman like her settled for a tomcat like him.

They looked really happy together. Maybe it was love at first sight or something.

Maybe he'll settle down. It'd be good for him.

***

"Should I be turned on by this?" Glad asked.

They were planting grasses in the far back part of her yard and listening to another of Mike's seemingly endless array of playlists. A song by The Miracles had come on and Mike had stopped everything to sing about being a love machine in a scratchy falsetto while swiveling his hips to the music.

He stopped swiveling. "Actually, I was hoping you'd jump me by now."

"We're supposed to be planting all this stuff," Glad reminded him.

"How about I up the ante?"

He pulled his t-shirt off and Glad lost her breath, like she did every time. Heat flooded her and her fingers itched to touch him, to run down his chest and unbutton those low slung jeans and...

"Yeah," Mike said, smug. "That's the look I want."

"You do not play fair," she protested.

"And I cheat at Monopoly, too," he reminded her, pulled her into his arms and kissed her.

This was heavenly, and not just the kissing part. Every second of the last few weeks had been perfect. She and Mike had spent nearly every spare minute they had together, from dinners out to neighborhood walks to grocery shopping and, of course, yard work.

The good citizens of Mill Falls smiled and gossiped, her friends were thrilled, her coworkers regarded her with a pleased sort of awe and Chris had sighed and shook his head. She didn't care. She was happier than she'd ever been, content and satisfied, confident in Mike's affection for her.

"Do we really have to go to your boss's party?" she asked, tickling a finger across his chest.

"It's a Memorial Day tradition," Mike said, rolling his eyes. "Apparently the Anderson clan has been doing this forever and everyone from Green Spaces goes." He released her and checked his watch. "We'd better finish this up and hit the shower if we're going to make it on time."

Glad slid her fingers under the waist of his jeans. "Can we share the shower and be fashionably late?"

Mike grinned like a shark. "Sounds like a plan."

***

Mike drove to out to Green Spaces just after dawn. He wanted to work on the drawings for the Sellers account before his crew showed up. They had three days scheduled at the library starting today; the plants were ready to deliver and they'd be laying out his design over the following days. It was one of the most exciting parts of the job, when the drawings turned into reality.

As he drove his mind wandered back to yesterday. The party had been fun and everyone had loved Glad: Ken, Mary, their kids and relatives and neighbors and friends, Ken's business associates and employees-well, probably not Caroline but she didn't like anyone so that didn't count. Glad had won over his crew, even grouchy old Harry had complimented her later in the day, saying simply, "That girl's all right, boss." High praise indeed.

And she'd charmed him anew every single moment. From that steamy little quickie in the shower to that pretty dress she'd worn, an orange and pink flowered thing that skimmed her curves and made him fantasize about getting it back off her. From her pitching in right away to help Mary Anderson finish peeling potatoes to her willingness to play tag with the younger kids, she'd made herself at home and more than one person had told him what a wonderful woman she was and how lucky he was to have landed her.

And they were right. He was damn lucky. Glad was everything he wanted and more. Sweet and giving and so, so sexy. When he'd stripped that tease of a dress off her late last night and asked if she'd like to try something a little different she hadn't even blinked. And he'd discovered to his delight that not only was sex possible in that Pilates position he'd fantasized about, but the climax had been especially intense. And then she'd shared a few bedroom fantasies they could try if he felt so inclined.

He was inclined all right. He couldn't wait.

It was like that all the time, he realized. He couldn't wait to see her, couldn't wait to kiss her and talk to her and make love to her. While he looked forward to going to work each morning because he loved his job, he looked forward to leaving just as much because now when he left he was going straight to Glad. He couldn't get enough and by all indications, neither could she.

He was pretty sure this was leading right where he'd said he didn't want to go. But he couldn't stop it and wouldn't even if he could.

He was well and truly hooked, no doubt about it.

Mike pulled the F-150 into the Green Spaces employee lot and parked next to the back door. Unlocked the back door and headed for his office.

Something rattled and bumped in the main display area. What in hell was that? Mike walked quietly towards the front displays and the noise got a little louder. A sort of pounding noise that was almost familiar-

A soft groan, then a guttural 'oh, yeah' came from the center display space. The one with the six-thousand-dollar lawn furniture set in it.

Damn it all. If Jake was in here with one of his bar chicks, Mike was going to kill him. He sidled up to the entryway, looked to his left.

It wasn't Jake. Mike stared, shocked to his core.

Was this really happening?

Mike stifled a curse, backed up silently, shut himself in his office and dropped into his chair. He squeezed his eyes shut, tried to block it out but it was no use. The image of his boss, Ken 'Mr. Family Man' Anderson banging Caroline West for all he was worth on that double lounger was seared into his retinas, probably for life.

Okay, considering his own reputation, he had no right to pass judgment. But Ken was cheating on his *wife*! Mike had thought they had

264

a great marriage, a solid partnership. It was one of the things that had drawn him to Green Spaces, that feeling of family and belonging that he had lost in D.C.

But in reality it was all a big sham. Did Mary know her husband was cheating? Mike doubted it, she seemed totally content and devoted to Ken and her family. Did Jake know? Was that why he had such a problem being here, knowing his dad was *shtupping* Caroline right, left and sideways? How long had it been going on? Was this the first time, or was Caroline the latest in a long line of women Ken had seduced?

And Ken had had the balls, the utter gall to lecture Mike on propriety. To tell him to clean up his act and behave himself when he was making a total mockery of something sacred. What a crock of shit.

Mike got to his feet. The drawings could wait, he needed to get out of here *now*. He'd just go back home, or have some breakfast at Mimi's or something. Anything but stay here.

He slipped out of his office and had nearly made it to the back door when voices sounded behind him. He froze, his hand on the knob. If they came this direction he was beyond screwed.

"…come back to my apartment?" Caroline asked.

"I better not," Ken said.

"But I want it again," she said, sounding petulant.

"Oh yeah? I think I can arrange that." Mike heard the unmistakable sound of pants being unzipped and cringed. Then he heard his office door open. What the-?

"Lean over the desk." Ken's voice was gruff.

"But this is Mike's-"

"Green Spaces is mine and I'll fuck you anywhere I want in it, you got me?"

"Sure, okay."

"And besides, how many times did he shoot your pretty ass down? Just think of this as a little sweet revenge, fucking me right here on his desk. How's that sound?"

"Ooh-oh, so good."

The bumping and moaning began again and Mike let himself out the back door. He couldn't risk starting the truck and leaving, they'd be sure to hear it no matter how wrapped up they were. Damn it all. He'd have to disappear out back for a while. Maybe check on his bees or something.

And when he came back inside the first thing he was going to do was find a big, industrial size can of Lysol and spray every square inch of his desk.

"Hey, you're here early!"

Mike hung up his bee veil before he turned around. Ken was grinning, looked just the same as usual. But now Mike saw something new in his gaze.

Worry. Wondering how long Mike had been here. Wondering if he'd seen or heard.

"I wanted to check my hives before I go out this morning," Mike said, keeping his voice light and his expression as neutral as he could manage.

"If I'd known you were coming early, I'd have stopped and got bagels or something!"

Oh yeah. He was worried to shit. As he should be, the faithless fuck.

"I already had breakfast." Mike lied, holding Ken's eyes. He waited a second, then deliberately asked, "Why are you here so early? I thought being the boss gave you the right to sleep in."

Ken laughed, that hearty, good old boy laugh that would never fool Mike again. "Just paperwork. It never ends, you know?"

Paperwork. Caroline would probably have a shit hemorrhage if she heard him refer to her as 'paperwork'.

"So, things seem to be going well with you and the librarian," Ken said next.

Mike nodded. "Very well. She had a great time yesterday." And because he couldn't resist, he added, "She really liked Mary a lot."

"Mary's a good woman."

"Yes, she is."

The two men looked at each other a moment. Then Ken cleared his throat and said, "So everything's great, huh?"

"Fantastic. I'm a lucky guy."

"That's good. All I hear is good about you now. We're getting more landscaping requests all the time."

"Great. I've got some new designs to show you later."

"Cool." Ken cleared his throat. "You, uh, don't have to keep it up any longer."

"What do you mean?"

"This thing you've got going with the librarian. I mean, we're golden. Everyone loves you again, the gossip is gone, and-"

"I'm good," Mike interrupted.

"What?"

"I like being with Glad. I'm happy with her."

"Oh." Ken's brow furrowed a moment, then cleared. "Oh! Well, that's great! Great to hear! Hey, I'll just let you get back to it, then. See you later!" He turned and walked back towards the greenhouses, whistling. Mike gritted his teeth and began stripping off his suit. It was going to be one long damn day.

* * *

"They're here!" Marci crowed over the phone.

"Wonderful! I'll be right out." Glad hung up and left her office, eager to witness this next step in the landscaping process. Over the past weeks the site had been dug out, pavers had been delivered and the outdoor lighting and water feature had been installed. Early this morning a small backhoe had dug several large holes in various spots around the site for the larger trees and a forklift stood ready to move them. Now the plants were being delivered and she could hardly wait to see what would go where.

A few people, library patrons mostly, had gathered on the front walk to watch the unloading process. The first truck, driven by Mike, was backing onto the lot and Glad spied the contents rising high from the bed.

Dogwoods. Two pink, two white. They hadn't been chosen for the library, they'd been chosen for her. She sighed, pleased beyond words. That man. No wonder she loved him.

Her heart stuttered at the thought. Love?

Yes. She loved him. Was completely crazy about him and couldn't be happier. She still didn't understand how it had happened, because they were different in so many ways, but they simply fit together and everything about him felt solid and right.

Mike gathered his crew for a quick meeting, gesturing at the site and pointing at the clipboard he held in his hand. They scattered and he walked over to her.

"I see you went with the dogwoods," Glad said, smiling up at him.

"As ordered," he said. His eyes were solemn.

"What's the matter?"

He shook his head. "Nothing. Just tired."

"Am I keeping you up past your bedtime?"

He smiled a little at that. "I'm not complaining."

Glad studied him. "Are you sure you're okay?"

"I'm good, I promise." He eyeballed her figure and gave her a grin. "Now get out of here before I forget I'm supposed to be working."

The project was an overwhelming success. Most of Mill Falls showed up for the ribbon cutting ceremony and the next edition of the *Mill Falls Herald* was plastered with pictures of the new landscaping at the library. Glad wrote up a breakdown of the improvements and sent it, along with several pictures, to *Library Journal* in the hopes that the national publication would feature their design in an issue slated for the following spring on outdoor spaces.

In addition, Deb Jacobs had run with Mike's idea of hanging the prints that matched the outside plants and fifteen of them, including the *gladiolus*, were being framed to hang in strategic locations throughout the library.

Glad was praised to the skies at the next board meeting-except for Marie Stahl, who grumbled only a grudging 'well done' when prodded by Tom Smithers. Chris was well pleased with her efforts, the staff and patrons loved the garden area and Cathy had already started a 'lasagna garden' with her junior gardeners, planting tomatoes and other vegetables that would be harvested and turned into as many lasagnas as the crew could make later on. Everything in her life was great.

Except…something was bothering Mike. He acted like everything was okay when they were together but Glad sensed tension just beneath the surface. And in spite of her success and all the good coming her way, a dark seedling of worry sprouted.

***

Mike lay wrapped around a slumbering Glad, wide awake.

He had to tell her.

He'd barely slept this last week, guilt and worry plaguing him. Glad knew something was wrong; despite his best tries for normal he knew he wasn't acting the same way. He caught every one of those worried looks she gave him and the unspoken between them was beginning to grow and he hated it. The only time he could really let go was when they made love but even then the worry lingered, pricked at him and made him even more desperate to lose himself in her.

Witnessing Ken's adultery had rocked Mike's foundation. It was a good thing he was so busy with his crew during the day because whenever he went into the main facility and saw Ken, or Caroline, or both of them together he felt angry and sick. Caroline's self-satisfied smirk made it nearly impossible to act pleasant and professional. And Ken was trying too hard. Being Mr. Super-friendly, slapping him on the shoulder, shooting the bull and making jokes all while assessing Mike with his eyes, calculating and suspecting.

Mike kept telling himself it wasn't his place to judge. That Ken and Mary might have a miserable private life. That infidelity crossed all boundaries. Even in his childhood, raised where families adhered to deep religious tradition he'd overheard the occasional whisper of cheating.

And therein lay the rub. Despite his idiocy up here, despite the debacle with Rachel back in D.C., Mike believed in marriage and fidelity, in cleaving to your wife, in the sanctity of family. And yet he'd made a mockery of his own beliefs by screwing around like some Don Juan then allowing himself to be caught up in a ridiculous scheme to save his job. He'd pursued Glad under false pretenses and that lie stood between them, looming as large as Ken Anderson's infidelity.

He had to tell her. He had to come clean. But he was afraid she wouldn't understand even after he explained the whole story. That even if they didn't break up things between them would cool by degrees and one day he'd turn around and she'd be gone and it would kill him.

He loved her. He didn't know how or when it had happened, but he was lost so deep there was no fighting it. He had to figure something out, and soon, because losing her was unthinkable.

"It's just some pavers. What's the big deal?" Caroline huffed, rolling her eyes.

"The big deal is you gave away a two-thousand dollar upcharge!" Mike said, pointing at the list. This was all he needed. Andy Sellers and his wife were some of the pickiest clients he'd ever had to work with and they'd just decided they wanted to change their pavers to a different brand and color. And Caroline hadn't bothered to see if he was available or even checked prices before she approved the change and had the client sign off on it.

"When a client wants to change something there's a process," Mike said, standing and stuffing the Sellers paperwork back in its folder. "I have to check availability, prices, shipment times... Then I sit down with the client and explain it all, including the upcharges if there are any. When the client is fully informed we draw up the agreement and lastly they sign off on it. Since you skipped right to the end without checking things with me-"

"I didn't know where you were!" Caroline interrupted, her face reddening. It was starting to sink in that she'd majorly screwed up. Mike could see the wheels turning. She was going to try and weasel out of this and he'd be damned if he let her.

"If you'd looked at the schedule you would have known I was in my office this morning. I am always in office on Friday mornings."

"The schedule wasn't there!"

"Then you open the schedules folder in the C drive and check there."

Caroline was foundering, her eyes wide and panicked. "Well, you weren't in your office when I checked."

"Really? Because I haven't left my desk all morning. Not once. Face it. You screwed up."

"They're your clients!"

"That's right. But *you* stuck your nose in and messed everything up. You need to tell Ken and you need to get Andy Sellers back here. Today."

"No way!" Her eyes narrowed with unfettered hate. "You think you're the fucking golden boy and everyone has to do what you say around here. Well, I don't!"

"You damn better do what I say," Mike replied, furious. "This isn't a couple of dollars missing from the till. It's two thousand dollars that has to be accounted for."

"So account for it!" she demanded.

"No. I refuse to cover your ass on this. You need to clean up your own mess, Caroline."

"Fuck you! You're not in charge here!" Caroline yelled.

"No, I'm not. And FYI," he growled, leaning over his desk, "fucking the boss doesn't put *you* in charge, either."

Caroline went white. Her mouth opened, then she clamped it shut and stormed out of his office. Mike sighed and dropped back into his chair. Damn his mouth, he should have kept that to himself. Well, too late now. He glanced at the clock on the wall. Just noon. Maybe he should get himself some lunch and disappear the rest of the day-

Footsteps sounded in the hall and Ken Anderson filled the doorway. "What the hell's going on back here?"

20

Glad parked in the main lot at Green Spaces and got out of her car. She'd been patient the last ten days, waiting for Mike to snap out of his funk. But he hadn't.

She had no idea what had happened, but she suspected something was wrong here, at his work. He hadn't talked about work at all lately; usually he had stories to share at the end of the day. He probably wouldn't appreciate her barging in like this, but too bad. She was driving herself crazy with worry and needed an answer.

The main retail area was empty for the moment and Glad weaved her way through the lawn furniture displays to the service desk. Caroline West stood there, looking grumpy as ever.

"I'm here to see Mike," Glad said to her. "Is he here?"

Caroline huffed. "He's in his office with Ken."

"Oh. Will he be long?"

"How should I know?" Caroline snapped. Then her eyes narrowed. "You know, I feel sorry for you. You're so frigging stupid."

"I beg your pardon?" Glad was completely taken aback.

"I said I feel sorry for you. You think Mike's for real when he's just dragging you around town to make himself look good."

"What?" Glad asked, lost.

Caroline's pretty face screwed up with malice. "All the gossip about him? It was driving away business and he got in hot water with Ken. So he hooked himself up with you, Miss Prim and Proper Boring-Ass Librarian. You made him look good again. Mike's not dumb, he knows how important appearances are."

"Appearances," Glad repeated, a hot spike of dread spearing her. This wasn't true. It couldn't be true. Mike cared for her. She knew he did. He must.

Caroline went on. "Oh, and money, of course. It all comes back to the money."

"The...money?" Glad asked. A hot spike of pain pierced her chest. *No. Please, God, no. Not Mike. Please.*

"Yeah. Duh! You know how many contracts he's brought in since he started running after you, acting like your boyfriend?"

"Acting like..." Glad choked. Grief was rising fast, checking in for a long stay, choking the breath out of her. The edges of her vision were going black, her head was whirling. She backed away, needing to escape before she fainted right here in the middle of Green Spaces.

Caroline moved out from behind the desk and came close, smiling in the nastiest possible way. "You are so stupid! None of this is real! It's all business! And now we're rolling in it, Ken's in heaven and Mike's a bigshot. And you?" She laughed cruelly. "You're just a dumb bitch who fell for his lines, that's all."

***

"It's a big upcharge and it needs to be accounted for," Mike said, knowing he was wasting his breath. Ken was going to let this slide, wasn't going to call out Caroline for her mistake and it burned.

"We'll figure something out," Ken assured him. "Let's go over to my office and get Andy Sellers on the phone."

They walked down the back hall towards the main display area. "You think he's going to bend on this?" Mike asked.

"Well, I doubt it, but maybe we can compromise-hey, your girlfriend's here."

Mike spied Glad near the service counter and smiled. "Glad!" he called.

She turned to him. Her face was ghost white and alarm pierced him. "You all right?"

"Anything the matter?" Ken asked Caroline, brow furrowed in concern.

"Nothing-"

"Is it true?" Glad faced Mike. Her voice sounded high and thready.

Mike put his hands on her arms, rubbed

them. "Is what true?"

Glad stepped back and broke contact. Haunted eyes searched his face. "Is it true you and me-all of this was just some…" she gulped, "some ploy for business?"

Mike stared at her, stunned. How-he glanced to his left and saw the victorious smirk on Caroline's face. *She knew. Son of a bitch!*

Ken stepped forward, his best smile on. "Of course not! Why would you think-"

"Did you tell him to get a girlfriend so he'd look better?" Glad interrupted.

"Glad, it's not-" Mike started, then Ken jumped in again.

"He just needed to look a little more respectable! Have a steady girl! You know! And it worked and everyone thinks he's great again! And he fell for you, right? I told him a couple weeks ago he could break things off and he said no!"

"You *what?*" Her mouth dropped wide and Mike felt an ugly rush of panic. This was bad, so bad. He had to do something, had to get her away from here, something.

But Ken was on a blundering roll. "Well-that is-I mean, well, he likes you, right? I mean, he might not have started out that way, but-"

"Ken. You are not helping." Mike stepped forward and took Glad's arm, pulled her away for some privacy. "We need to talk."

Glad looked at him like he was a stranger. She shook her head and pulled her arm from his grip. "No. I don't want to hear any more."

"Glad, you don't understand."

She backed away, her hands held out like she was warding him off. "Don't," she begged.

Mike's throat closed. "Please let me explain. Let me try."

"I believed in you, Mike," she whispered, broken. "I trusted you."

"Oh, girl." He kept following, reached for her but she smacked his hand away.

"That Felice woman was right. I wasn't special. This wasn't different. It was *nothing*."

"Glad, please. We need to talk. I need to tell you the truth."

"The truth?" she choked. "What could you possibly know about that?"

And she ran. Fast.

"Shit. Glad!" He took off after her, made it to the front doors in time to see her climb into her car. Too late. Mike turned and rushed to his office. He needed his keys, needed to follow her. Needed to make her understand.

Mike yanked open his desk drawer, grabbed his keys and stuffed his wallet in his pocket. Where was his phone? He grabbed it off the desk.

"Guess you won't fuck with me anymore, will you?" came a sneering voice from the doorway. Caroline stood there, looking triumphant and Mike saw red. He slammed the drawer shut and rounded the desk.

"You think you've won?" he gritted out, advancing on her. "Think again. This isn't over." Caroline's eyes widened and she backed into the hall, wary.

"You can't touch me," she blustered. "You don't dare."

Mike shut his office door and glared down at her, fury hot in his gut. "You forget, I wasn't raised to do unto others. I take an eye for an eye. Now get the fuck out of my way, you heartless bitch."

Caroline stared at him, her mouth hanging open. Then she turned tail and ran.

***

Glad drove blindly back to town, her mind reeling, the same litany echoing over and over.

Mike. Mike, why?

Glad stumbled into her house, dropped her purse on the kitchen table and tried to go upstairs, tried to make her feet move but ended up collapsed on the bottom step, sobbing. Memories from the past, bitter and buried deep, clawed their way to the surface.

Her mother, concerned only with the next support check so she could party some more. Bouncing from one foster house to the next, hiding her few possessions away so the others wouldn't steal them out from under her. Discovering her college boyfriend had gotten engaged to his high school sweetheart while dating Glad because her father was rich and he'd been promised a position in the family company. Evan and Shari and the baby.

"Oh, my God," she moaned helplessly, squeezing her head between her hands. She'd worked so hard to heal and move on and had finally, stupidly decided to let go, to trust in someone again…

And Mike had broken her to pieces.

"Stupid!" she cursed herself hoarsely. "Stupid, stupid-"

A hard knock sounded on the front door. "Glad, open up."

"Go away!" she yelled at him, scrubbing at her face.

"No. Open the door, Glad."

"I don't want to see you anymore!" she yelled through her tears. Yes. Get mad. Mad was way better than crying.

"Too bad," he hollered. "I'm not going anywhere until you talk to me. I will stand out here all day, and *SHOUT* at the *TOP* of my *LUNGS*-"

He would, too, damn him. Glad wrenched the front door open. "What do you *want*."

"I want to explain." Mike stepped forward, crowded her back into the house and shut the door behind him.

Anger nearly blinded her. "What's to explain? You screwed yourself so you screwed someone else to save your own ass!"

"I didn't have a choice!" Mike thundered.

"You did! You could have told the truth!"

"Truth doesn't mean shit in this town and you know it."

She did know it. But she wasn't about to give him an inch.

"Well then you should have left me out of it! I trusted you, Mike! Don't you know how hard that is for me? I trusted you and you lied to me! You used me-" she gulped, whirled around and stomped back towards the kitchen. Mike followed.

"Please listen to me. I was wrong to do what I did. I was wrong to get you involved." Mike shoved a hand through his hair. "But I was in deep shit and I was scared. I was going to lose my job, lose it because of that damned gossip. Ken gave me until the end of April to get a steady girlfriend and clean up my mess. I didn't want to but I didn't see any other choice.

"And then I walked into the library that afternoon and saw you twisting around with that little boy and doing that stupid Macarena dance. And I just...it was you." His shaking hand reached out and stroked her hair, cupped her face. "It had to be you."

Glad pushed his hand away. "It was all a lie."

"It wasn't. I pushed you hard, sent those flowers and kept bugging you because I needed to land you. But I wanted *you*. I didn't even consider anyone else. And the more time we spent together, the more I wanted to be with you. I still want to be with you."

"Get used to disappointment," she said, forcing herself to be cold. Cold and hard as steel because there was no other way she'd survive this.

Mike sighed heavily. "Glad, I'm sorry."

"It's a little late for-"

"But I'd do it again."

What? "What do you mean?"

"I would. If it meant I could be with you for five damn more minutes, I'd do it all over again. Glad, I..." He swallowed hard. "I'm in love with you."

She stared at him, open-mouthed. Joy flared bright for one moment then extinguished under the crushing weight of her anger and grief. She forced out a laugh.

"You think I believe-oh, wait, that's part of the act, isn't it? Do you get a bonus if you throw out that line?" He let out an anguished breath and she continued, "No? Well, your performance in my bedroom should have been worth a little extra!" She grabbed her purse off the table and flung it against his chest. It bounced off and hit the floor; coins and bills, cards and receipts spilled out.

"Don't do this."

"Take the cash!" She stormed, stabbing a finger at the floor. "Consider it a tip!"

Glad pushed past him, needing to get as far away from him as she could. She heard a low growl behind her then Mike grabbed her. He spun them around and pinned her against the closest solid object. The refrigerator shuddered under the impact; the contents inside clinked and rattled. Then he kissed her, hard, pressing his mouth against hers while she struggled against him, grabbed a handful of his hair...

And then she surrendered to it. Opened for him and kissed him back wildly. Nothing in the world felt as good and perfect as his lips on hers, his arms around her.

For several bittersweet moments they clung together. Then Mike abruptly ended it and pushed himself away, breathing hard.

"That's some act, right?"

And he left her house, slamming the front

door so hard one of the glass panes cracked.

***

Heard all around Mill Falls:
They broke up! Can you believe it?
What happened? No one's talking!
I know! I can't believe no one knows anything.
Trust me, people know. They're just not saying.
Have you seen her around at all? It's like she dropped off the face of the earth.
I've seen him. He looks like someone ran him over with a truck, poor thing.
Poor thing? That cad?
Yes, poor thing. He loved her and something terrible happened and he lost her.
He probably cheated on her.
We don't know that.
Please. Tigers never change their stripes.

***

"We need a night out."

"Holly, I'm really not up for socializing," Glad protested. A week had passed and, while she'd gotten really good at lying to people, telling them everything was fine, that she and Mike just hadn't suited and whatever other cockamamie lines she could come up with, she was still drowning in misery. She tried to stay angry, reminded herself incessantly that a whole lot of nothing was what you got when you trusted someone.

She buried herself in her work and spent evenings ticking off items on her mile-long job list of things to get done around the house. Told herself she'd get over it and everything would go back just the way it had been before. But she didn't want that solitary life anymore. She wanted Mike, even though he was just as big a scumbag as everyone else had been. She longed for his company, ached for his touch, wept every night for the loss of him, of them.

"It's not just you anymore," Holly said, sounding distinctly pissed. "April's boyfriend dumped her the other day and that damn Greg Turk disappeared on me. I could kill him!"

"You're seeing Turk?" Glad asked, surprised. When had that happened?

"I don't know if I'd go that far, but…listen, I need a drink, April needs some support and I know you're still down in the dumps. Let's go to Slade's and cry in our wine glasses. Fran can drive us all home later."

"I am so glad I'm happily married," Fran said, sipping her glass of seltzer, "because you three are pathetic."

"Thanks a lot," Glad said, taking a drink. The Pinot was fabulous and she was finding some comfort being out with her girlfriends. She'd given them the bare bones of the story, but no details. The hurt was still so fresh, a gaping wound that would not close.

But misery loved company; poor April had been unceremoniously dumped by her new boyfriend just two days ago, no warning whatsoever.

"Let's toast to Fran's marriage!" April said, giggling and raising up her glass.

Holly smiled and raised her glass. "To Fran's marriage. You got the last good guy in town and left the losers for us. Cheers!"

The women clinked their glasses and drank, then April said, "I don't know why I ever started seeing him in the first place. Both Luke and John warned me off him, but I didn't listen because I knew better." She sighed and rolled her eyes.

"It must be wonderful to have brothers," Glad said. What she wouldn't have given to have someone at her back while growing up.

April snorted. "I love them all, believe me, and I'm so grateful I was adopted into this family and not some other. But they go overboard with the protective thing. It's like my whole family thinks I'm not capable of making a single decision on my own."

"And then you prove them right by dating Jeremy Swale," Holly said.

April giggled shook her head. "Well, at least I didn't fall in love, not like Glad and Mike." She looked at Glad, her brown eyes sad. "I really am sorry, hon."

"We didn't love each other," Glad said softly, looking down at her glass.

"You so did. Everyone knows that," April said, waving a hand. "But really, Jeremy and I weren't dating that long or anything, and I thought we were having an okay time, but then he shows up at the Rec and just says it's over and he's dating Liz Meyer. And he was such an ass about it," she groused, then straightened and pursed her lips. "*Your company is more a burden than a pleasure.* What kind of jerk says something like that out loud?"

"Jeremy Swale, that's who," Holly informed her, taking another drink. "The way I see it, there's only one solution for you. Revenge boyfriend."

"What?" April, Glad and Fran said together.

"Revenge boyfriend. Find some stud and let him take you out places you used to go with Jeremy. Rub it in! Oh, and have some hot, no-strings sex while you're at it."

Glad forced a smile and tried to ignore the bone-deep ache that settled deep in her. Hot sex. It was all she could do not to groan out loud. Yes, she'd kill for some right now, but the problem with that was the only guy she wanted to have sex with was Mike.

Okay, so she still wanted him, the lying creep. She wasn't going to do anything about it, so what did that matter?

April grimaced and finished her wine. "I don't know about another boyfriend. I mean, sure, I'd like the hot sex, who wouldn't? Jeremy wasn't exactly Mr. Wonderful in the sack."

"How?" Holly and Fran asked together, eager for a little firsthand gossip. Glad sighed softly and tried to look interested.

April held up one finger. "Only one orgasm. The entire time we dated, all the times we did it, I only got one orgasm. Selfish jerk. Liz can have him." She pushed back her chair. "I'm getting another wine. Anyone want a refill?"

Glad declined, as did Holly and Fran and April headed for the bar alone. Holly looked after her for a minute and sighed. "Even though he was a total jerk, at least she had a boyfriend. You know how long it's been since I could even call a man my boyfriend?"

"What about Turk?" Glad asked. "When did you two start seeing each other? And how come you never told me?"

Holly smiled. "You were all lovey-dovey with Mike. And it wasn't much, I mean, he stopped by my house one night out of the blue. I didn't think he even knew where I lived, but he found out somehow. Anyway, Alex was at that sleepover campout with the Boy Scouts and, well, one thing led to another, just like last time."

"Did you manage to have sex in a bed?" asked Glad.

"Yeah, we did it the old-fashioned way, you prude," Holly said.

Glad made a face at her. "So then what happened?"

"He left in the morning and nothing for almost a week. Then we ran into each other in the IGA. Alex was with me. He and Greg just chattered away, instant besties, then I sent Alex on a hunt for some good tomatoes. And Greg asked how come I didn't tell him I had a son and I got a little smart-assy with him and said 'I only introduce Alex to people who want to stick around longer than ten minutes' and- Uh-oh. I'm being summoned. Hang on." She slid out of the pew and headed for the bar. Glad and Fran both turned in their seats.

"Oh, dear," Fran said. "Looks like April's in trouble."

It did indeed look that way. An angry looking Matt Slade said something to April and pointed at the door. Holly took April's arm and weaved them back through the crowd to the table. April looked furious.

"What happened?" asked Fran, worried.

"April pissed Matt off," Holly said scooping up her purse and pulling at April's arm.

"Well, who knew he'd be such a girl about it?" April asked belligerently. She turned her head and glared back at the bar.

"What did you say?" Glad asked, glancing over at Matt Slade. He was following their progress with his brows smashed together over his nose.

"Give me your keys," Holly said to Fran. She handed them over and Holly pulled April away. "We'll wait in the car and you two can finish your drinks." Glad and Fran watched, fascinated, as April, grumbling under her breath, was led outside.

"I can't wait to find out what that was about," Fran said and took a big drink. Then she eyeballed Glad, still sipping at her wine. "How long is it going to take you to finish that?" She shot the rest of her seltzer down in one gulp.

"Are you in a hurry?" Glad teased, taking another dainty sip.

"Yes! Finish that thing, will you?"

"But it's a Pinot Noir. It needs to be savored."

"Glad Donahue, if you don't hurry it up you'll have to walk home. Gossip awaits!" Fran pushed back from the table, agitated. Glad gave up.

"Okay, okay!" She emptied the last of her wine and followed Fran out of Slade's.

***

"Mike Kovalski?"

Mike looked up at a stranger standing next to his booth and sighed. Seriously, all he wanted was some breakfast. He had no desire to talk to anyone or to hear another lecture about what a bad guy he was for hurting Glad. He'd had about all the sideways looks and stink-eyes he could stand.

"That's me," he said, bracing himself for the smackdown.

But the man tossed a copy of the *Mill Falls Herald* on the table instead. Mike glanced at it; it was from a few weeks ago and the pictures of the completed library project filled the front page. He looked back up at the man and raised a brow.

"I'm Renny McQueen," the man said, sliding onto the opposite seat. "I own Sunrise Garden Centers in Cincinnati, and I'd like to try and talk you into coming to work for me."

Mike looked at the man across from him. Was this a joke? It didn't seem to be, the guy looked completely serious, his eyes clear and direct.

"I'm listening," he said.

21

It had been a hell of a day. Mike drove home, noting all the red, white and blue bunting and other decorations around town. Fourth of July was tomorrow and it looked like Mill Falls was gearing up for quite a celebration.

Renny McQueen had talked to him for over an hour this morning and Mike had agreed to go see him next month, when business would be a bit slower and he could get away for a day or two. The job sounded right up his alley and despite McQueen's bulldozing personality, Mike liked him. He pulled no punches and was blunt to a fault, laying the facts right out without apology.

"I know Ken's not paying you what you're worth," he'd pointed out.

"Well, I wanted to leave D.C., so money wasn't my first concern," Mike said.

"Yeah, he lucked out and picked up a rising star on the cheap. But he made one crucial error, my man. He bragged. Ken's never been able to play his cards close. He was at the Expo in Columbus telling anyone who'd listen what a frigging genius you are."

"And what's your verdict?" Mike asked.

"Why the hell do you think I'm up here?" McQueen returned.

Mike stopped for a traffic light and realized that once again he'd gone the wrong way. He'd turned right on Center Street instead of left and was idling in the left lane for Gibson. That habit just wouldn't die and he cursed himself as he turned, passed Lincoln and kept going. Back downtown, west on St. John.

He needed to forget her. Needed to stop this endless cycle of hurt somehow. He turned onto Academy and slowed for his driveway.

Only there was a car in it. A little sporty thing with Maryland plates. Mike parked behind it and stared out the windshield as the door opened and the driver stepped out. Waved and smiled and called, "Micha! Surprise!"

His vision blurred and he stumbled from the truck. "Sarah?"

His little sister flung herself into his arms.

***

July fourth was balmy and perfect for Frank and Sal's annual party. Glad really wasn't in the mood, but she was in even less mood for all the gaiety downtown today. Chris had allowed her to beg off marching in the parade with the library float and this morning she sat curled in Mike's big chair, staring into her unfinished back yard.

He'd been by several times while she was at work; he'd done some plantings the other day and now her patio space was leveled and graveled and a third of the stones were set into place. It would be lovely when it was finished, as would the rest of the yard, but she didn't know if she could ever use it, any of it. Mike had stamped himself all over her property and he hovered here like a ghost. Every sight and scent and texture was him, right down to this chair. She should make him come get it, should have thrown it on the curb or something but she couldn't. It was a piece of him, all she had left of them and, bitter as it was, she couldn't let it go.

Warm, kind arms went around her and Frank said, "You're in a rough patch, doll."

"I know," she blubbered. "I'll get over it, I promise."

"You know he didn't mean to hurt you, right?" Frank asked. "You know that job's all he's got left and he panicked."

"What do you know about it?"

"I know he's practically a pariah."

"What does that mean?"

"Well, I'm only half-Jewish on my mother's side, and we didn't exactly live kosher, but I know how important family ties are. They barely talk to him anymore and it kills him. And now he's lost you besides."

"Are you trying to make me feel bad for him?" Glad scrubbed at her eyes. "Because *he* used *me*, he broke my trust-"

"I know. I just want you to see all the angles."

Glad sniffed and said nothing. Frank dropped a kiss on her head and said, "You need a little distraction. You want some wine?"

"At ten a.m.?" she asked.

"Just a thought," he offered, and kissed her head again. "Seriously, you need to get your mind off this whole thing for a while."

"I agree." She looked over at the fence and spied a string of lights dangling there. "Do you need any help?" she offered.

Frank beamed. "Oh, doll! You will so regret asking that. We need all the help we can get!"

So Glad became Frank and Sal's assistant for the day, moving furniture, hanging party lights everywhere, setting up tables, chairs and a large canopy, picking up bits of twigs and other detritus from the back yard and finally putting an apron on and helping Sal prep endless amounts of food in the kitchen. Guests began arriving in droves around six and Glad shooed Sal out of the kitchen to shower and change while she finished cutting a small mountain of fruit and vegetables and arranged them on trays.

"They look fabulous, sweetheart," he said when he returned to the kitchen. "You, on the other hand, are a sight. Get that apron off and go put on something hot."

Glad smiled and shook her head. "I don't feel hot."

Sal covered her hand with one of his. "You know Mike's probably going to show tonight. He deserves to see you beautiful and sexy and, most importantly, not available. You must have at least one 'fuck you' outfit in your closet!"

"I'll see," she answered evasively.

Sal took the knife from her hand and steered her towards the door. "Seriously, go shower and change or you'll miss all the fun!"

"Okay, okay, I'm going!" she laughed and reached for the door knob. It twisted under her hand and the door opened and she was face to face with Mike.

"Hey, Glad."

Oh, God. Her first sight of him since the breakup and he was beautiful. Sexier than ever and her poor dogpaddling heart gave up and went under. She loved him and she wasn't going to stop loving him for a long time, if ever. But she wasn't about to let him know that. She took a slow breath and forced herself to be calm and collected.

"Mike," she said coolly. "Could you excuse me, please?"

"Oh, sure, we'll just..." He shifted and Glad's breath stopped in her chest at the sight of the young woman behind him.

He'd brought a date.

So much for his confession of love. So much for all the other moments she'd been holding deep in her heart, hoping they'd actually been real like he'd sworn they were.

His date was beautiful. She had long black hair, brown eyes and a sweet expression. Glad's control faltered and she knew her façade was slipping, knew jealousy and hurt was wearing her like an ugly Christmas sweater. But she forced herself to raise her chin high and look Mike straight in the eyes one more time. Cool, disinterested. No big deal.

"Excuse me," she said again, and slipped out the back door. Managed to walk next door with her head high and her posture straight, just in case anyone was watching. Made it into her kitchen, made it up the stairs and into the shower before her control deserted her.

"I can't do this," she said out loud to the showerhead. "I can't." She stuck her head under the spray and burst into noisy, messy tears.

I can't go over there and be around him pretend everything's fine. I can't.

Yes, you can. You're stronger than him and better than this. Just take a few minutes, get over it and get back there.

She wept and cursed him while she cleaned herself and let the spray rinse her tears away along with the soap. She wanted to stay in the shower forever. But that wouldn't do. She couldn't disappoint Frank and Sal after all the work they'd done today. And Sal was right. She had to give Mike a taste of his own medicine, especially now, tonight. She had to look beautiful, sexy, jaw dropping, ass kicking I-don't-care-how-pretty-your-date-is-I'm-perfectly-fine-by-myself-fuck-you-pal kind of perfect.

Glad dried her hair and for once it fell in nice waves around her face. She rummaged in her closet and finally settled on the same sundress she'd worn to Ken Anderson's Memorial Day party. It was a favorite, and very flattering to her figure and complexion. And once Mike saw her in it he'd probably remember what happened after they'd gone home that night. Nothing like a little torture to get the party started.

Glad pulled on the dress, added a spritz of her favorite perfume. Dropped some Visine in her red eyes, slid on some comfortable sandals, fluffed her hair one last time, pasted a smile on and headed back next door.

"Doll!" Frank greeted her, giving her a kiss on the cheek. "You look fabulous. Just-wow!"

"I clean up all right every once in a while," she said. "How's everything going?"

"We couldn't have done it without you. We owe you, big time. In fact, you deserve champagne. Sal's got the good stuff. Come on," he said, dragging her across the party.

***

He watched her in an agony of heartbreak and desire. She stood twenty feet away with her back to him, laughing and talking and having a great time, ignoring him like he'd never existed. And worse, she was wearing the very same dress on she'd worn Memorial Day. The one he'd taken such pleasure in stripping off of her that night. The Pilates sex. Oh, man.

And he couldn't touch her. Couldn't have her anymore because he was a flaming dickhead and an idiot besides.

"What's the matter, Micha?"

Mike looked at his sister and forced a smile. "Nothing. I'm fine."

"You're not fine," Sarah said. "Tell."

"I don't want to talk about it, really." All he really wanted to do was go break something, like maybe his head against a brick wall so he'd stop thinking about her. But instead he had to stand here and pretend that everything was fine, that he was having a good time. Glad thought he'd been acting before? Well, try acting normal when your ex-girlfriend is treating you like you're invisible, having a great old time while you're dying just a few feet away. Someone should hand him a freaking Oscar for this.

"Is it her?"

Mike sighed. He should have known she wouldn't leave it alone. Sarah was as bad as their mother for ferreting out what she wanted to know. "Who?" he asked.

"Her. With that gorgeous sundress on that I *want*. The one from Sal's kitchen."

"Can we please not talk about this?"

"You've been staring at her all night."

"It's nothing."

"Oh, please. I can read you like a book. You like her."

Mike looked away from his sister and finished his beer.

"Micha," she tried again, her voice soft and sympathetic.

"Just-I had her and I lost her, okay?" he ground out. "Can we change the subject now?"

Sarah put a hand on his arm. "I'm sorry, Micha. I really am."

"I know." He looped an arm around her and kissed her forehead. "So tell me more about home. Who's mom trying to fix you up with now?"

"In a minute. I spy dessert coming out and I want some."

His sister had a wicked sweet tooth. "Go on, then. And if he made cheesecake, grab me one."

***

"Hey, sweetheart!" Sal grabbed Glad's arm. "Can you help me out for two secs? I swear I won't ask you for another thing, ever!"

"Of course," Glad said. "What do you need?"

"Just some help plating up these desserts. People are eating me out of house and home!" he groused.

Glad just smiled. She knew Sal loved to entertain and show off his culinary skills as much as Frank loved to show off the house and yard.

"This all looks great," she said, helping him put slices of cheesecake and pie on small plates.

"Hey, can I have one of those?" a man asked. Glad handed him a plate and he thanked her. Then more people showed up and desserts flew off the table for several minutes. Glad helped Sal plate up the rest of the desserts quickly, before the next rush of people came along.

"You think we'll have enough?" Sal asked, worried.

"I'm sure we will," she said. "When I get done here I need to grab something to eat."

"You better be quick. Stuff's running out fast."

"I'm going right now, I promise."

"Oh!" shrieked a voice.

Glad turned and someone fell against her. It was Mike's date; Glad saw her shocked eyes, then felt two plates slap against her front. Glad grabbed the woman's arms to steady her and felt Sal's hand at her back, keeping her from landing on the desserts. The woman straightened, the plates stuck to Glad's dress for one awful moment, then slid down and clattered at her feet. Gasps resonated through several nearby groups.

"Oh, no!" the young woman said, looking horrified. "I'm so sorry! I don't know how-I must have tripped-I'm so sorry!"

"Oh, sweetheart!" Sal exclaimed, dismayed.

"It's-I'm okay, I'm fine," Glad said, groaning inside. Couldn't she just get one break? Just one?

"Oh, I'm so sorry." Mike's date looked truly distressed. "I've ruined your dress, and it's so pretty. Can I pay for a cleaner's? Anything?"

Glad stared at the young woman. For a second a hot ball of pure hate bloomed in her breast. Of course this happened, and of course it was *her* of all people. Why didn't Mike just come up and slap her in the face, too? Give the town something else to talk about?

She closed her eyes and forced herself to relax. It wasn't anyone's fault and she needed to get a grip. Glad took a long slow breath and met the other woman's eyes again. "It was an accident," she managed, backing away from that sweet, upset face. "It'll wash right out, I'm sure."

"Let me give you a hand, sweetheart." Sal was at her side, swiping the worst of the dessert off with a dishtowel. Frank appeared as if by magic, clucking and tutting over her like a mother hen. Her eyes filled. No. Not now. No crying allowed.

"We'll get it cleaned, doll. It'll be good as new in no time," he promised.

Glad took a breath and blindly pushed the helping hands away. "I'm good," she said, her voice wobbling. A tear slipped out and she cursed herself. "It's all right. I'll just run home and change." She stepped away from the crowd and hurried off.

"Fireworks start in about fifteen minutes," Frank called after her.

Glad didn't give a damn. She locked herself in her house, stumbled up the stairs for the second time that night, stripped off the ruined dress and took a quick shower to get the remaining bits of cheesecake and cherries off, then ran the tub and laid her dress in to soak overnight. Then she pulled on an old pair of yoga pants and a t-shirt and laid down on her bed.

BOOM!

The sky outside her window lit up red and white. The fireworks show had begun. She was missing it, but she didn't really care anymore.

What a bastard he was. Using her, lying to her, telling her he loved her and then showing up with a date. A date who was too gorgeous for words and had likely just ruined Glad's favorite dress besides.

Glad rolled to her side, stared out the window and the bright flashes blurred together.

It was never going to end. It would never stop hurting.

***

Sarah was in tears. "Oh, Micha, it was awful! I just wanted to say hello to her, introduce myself and-and I tripped and-"

"I know," he said, putting a comforting arm around her. They were sitting on Frank and Sal's front steps while the fireworks boomed behind them.

"And the way she looked at me, like…like she *hated* me-"

"Trust me, you're not the one she hates, Sarah." No, that honor fell to him.

"I made her cry, Micha!"

Glad was crying? "I'm sure she wasn't-"

"She was crying, Micha. I saw her!" Sarah sniffed loudly and scrubbed at her eyes. "And then she ran home-oh, I feel so *awful.* Do you mind if-can we leave, now? I'm sorry, I'm just-not in the mood for a party anymore."

"Sure." They got up from the steps and headed down Frank & Sal's front walk. At the street Mike cast a glance over his shoulder. Her house was dark and silent.

Crying? Over an accident? Over cheesecake?

Or maybe she wasn't that indifferent, that over him as she'd appeared to be. Maybe.

An idea crawled into his brain, fumbled around for a second then struck a match. It wasn't much, a flicker, but it was enough to make the wheels start turning. And for the first time in weeks he felt something other than pain and emptiness and loss.

He felt…hope.

22

BUMP!

Glad jerked awake. What was that?

She glanced at the clock. One-thirty in the morning. Sometime after the fireworks had ended and she'd finished crying herself out, she must have fallen asleep.

Another bump. Then nothing. Glad lay frozen, eyes wide, staring in the dark, desperately listening.

Scraping, thumping-

A dark shadow settled in front of her window and pulled the screen free. Too late, she realized she was still in bed, paralyzed. And her trusty Louisville Slugger was in the downstairs closet.

Get up! Move, already!

A big hand holding the screen came in and set it against the wall. A long leg followed. Glad slid from the bed and crouched down next to her ever-present stack of paperbacks. Better than nothing, she supposed, but hardcovers were the go-to when you wanted to leave a mark.

She hadn't played softball since high school, but she still remembered proper technique. The intruder climbed in all the way and Glad stood, grabbed a book, hauled back and fired. The book winged off his shoulder and a lively curse filled the room, followed by, "Damn it, Glad, what are you doing?"

She gasped. "*Mike?*"

"How many other guys in town know that screen pops right off?"

Shock turned to rage in a heartbeat. Glad grabbed another paperback and let it fly.

"Ow!"

"How *dare* you!" She wound up and threw another book.

"Glad, hang on-ow-"

She kept throwing. "You lied to me-you broke my heart-"

"What the-Glad, come on." Mike batted away Ernest Hemingway and ducked with a curse as a romance sailed past his ear.

"You said you loved me and then you show up at the party with a-with *her*-"

"It's not what you think!" he said, dodging another tome.

"And then you have the balls to come here and *break in*?" She threw two in quick succession; he only sidestepped one.

"Ow! Cut that out!"

Glad kept throwing. "Who do you think I-you think I'll just-you are SO wrong-"

"She's my sister, okay?" he got out while dodging two more books.

Glad hefted her last book. It was a big trade version of *War and Peace*, nice and heavy and it came in handy as a door stop when she needed one. It would *hurt*. "Oh, sure she is!" She held the book ready and pointed at the door. "Get out, you lying skunk, you big jerk, you-you-"

"Sarah. Is my sister." He held both hands out in front of himself. "She just showed up out of the blue yesterday. I haven't seen her in almost a year. Didn't you hear me introducing her to people?"

No, she'd been too busy avoiding him and pretending to have fun while drowning in misery, no small task. Glad hugged *War and Peace* against herself and tried to calm down. She took a deep, slow breath and let it out. "Why are you here?" she asked, her voice wobbling.

He stepped around the litter of books and moved towards her. "I needed to see you."

Her heart dropped somewhere south of her knees. "You could have rang the doorbell."

"Would you have let me in?" he asked.

"I..."

"I didn't think so, that's why I brought a ladder," he said softly. "Glad, this is killing me. I thought...fuck, I don't know. I thought I'd be at least a little better by now but everything's just getting worse. I'm going crazy."

"You have no one to blame but yourself for that." She stepped back from his reaching hands. "Please don't touch me."

306

"I need to hold you," he said, crowding close. "I just need *you*."

His arms closed around her. She could smell his outdoorsy scent and shivered when he dropped his head against her neck.

"I miss you," he murmured against her skin. "I miss us."

"Don't." He was too close, too warm, too much but she couldn't make herself move out of his arms. His heat soaked into her, making her pulse jump and her breath come short.

"The way you smell, those looks you give me, holding your hand." She felt him reach between them, felt his fingers pull at *War and Peace.* She let it go.

"I miss talking to you," he said, running a slow hand up and down her back. "Laughing with you. I miss sleeping next to you and waking up with you in my arms. I miss kissing you. Making love to you."

She curled her fingers against his chest and shook her head. "We didn't make love."

"Yes we did. I love you, Glad." He sighed shakily and nuzzled into her. Kissed that ticklish skin right under her ear and she jumped.

"I can't-I don't believe it." How did her arms get up around his neck?

"I love you," he said again, softly. "And you love me. I know you do."

He was lowering them onto the bed. She wanted to protest, wanted to stay strong and send him away. But her body had other ideas. She was quivering and aching, longing for his touch and kiss and the feel of him inside her.

"I don't trust you," she managed.

"I know." His lips were soft against her temple. "I lied and I hurt you and right now I don't deserve your trust. But I'm going to do everything I can to earn it back."

They lay tangled together, Mike half over her, his hand slowly stroking over her hip and up to just under her breast. Then he went higher, cupped it in his hand. Ran his thumb over her nipple and she gasped.

"Don't, please," she begged softly, arching against his caress. Heat pooled and headed south and the ache turned into a burn.

Mike found that sensitive spot under her ear again. "I need you, girl," he whispered against it, touched it with his tongue and she moaned out loud.

"Love me," he said, moving his hand down. "Love me tonight. You can go back to hating me tomorrow."

"I don't hate-don't want-" Her breath caught in her throat as his fingers slid under her yoga pants, under her panties, over her most sensitive spot. She should stop him, needed to stop him but she wanted this, wanted him so much.

"I know. Do it anyway." Mike slowly kissed over to her mouth, hovered there and whispered, his lips brushing hers, "Love me." He kissed her, slid one long finger inside, stroked it against her while his thumb worked its magic outside. In seconds she was gasping and moaning, pulling at his shirt, begging him with her hands while his stroked her to a fever pitch.

Their clothing disappeared and after several minutes of frenzied kisses and caresses Mike moved over her, positioned himself. Then he stopped.

"Tell me," he demanded, his voice ragged and husky with want. "Tell me you want this. You want me."

"Mike-" Glad clawed at him, desperate to have him in her but he was immovable.

"I need to hear it." He pressed himself against her, moved up and down over her wet, swollen center and she couldn't stand it. Had to have him, had to admit it.

"I want you, I-Mike, I want you so much-"

Mike thrust deep with a groan and Glad locked her legs around him, hanging on for dear life as he settled into that hard rhythm that drove her out of her mind. She rose fast, came with a high, keening cry that ended on his name.

"Yes," he growled as she shuddered and bucked against him, "I've got you, take it, yes, take it." He drove deep, over and over and her release went on, spiraled out, sent tingles all the way to her toes. But she wanted more, needed more. She pulled at his hips and Mike shifted himself higher so his erection rubbed against her with every thrust. It didn't take long; her second climax shuddered its way in and Mike moaned as she clamped around him, locked him in until he released moments later.

She was weak and this had been stupid, she knew that. But right now, holding his shaking body to hers and hearing him whisper *I love you* against her ear, she didn't care.

"This doesn't change things."

Mike traced a finger down her arm in the dark, trying to ignore the ache in his heart. He knew she was going to say it, but that didn't make it hurt any less.

"We're still-we're not back together or anything."

"I know."

"I'm not sure if I can get past this," she confessed in a whisper. "I don't trust easily."

"You said that before. Why?"

"I don't want to revisit my past."

"But I need to understand. Please tell me."

"I can't."

"You won't."

"The point is I put my trust in you and you broke that trust and I don't know if I can do it again. I'm afraid."

Mike sighed, depressed. "So am I, girl." He gently kissed her hair, breathed her in.

"What are you afraid of?"

"That I'll lose you. That we'll lose this good thing because you won't jump."

Glad shifted next to him. "I won't jump? What do you mean?"

"The trust thing. It's intangible. I'm laying myself bare here, opening myself, not knowing if you'll believe in me or not, if you'll kick the shit out of me or take another chance. This is all on you, you jump or you don't."

She was silent a moment, digesting that. "You're right. But…I need time."

"I understand."

"And I need you to give me some space."

He disagreed. "Glad, if we're going to work this out we need to see each other. Talk things over and figure out what's what. We need to do this together."

"But when we're together…this happens."

"I happen to like this."

"So do I, but falling into bed isn't going to make things clearer."

"No, it won't. But it makes things feel easier. Like talking." He took a deep breath. "I'm going to tell you something no one else knows. At least, I don't think anyone else knows about it. It's not pretty."

"Okay."

"Ken's cheating on Mary. With Caroline."

Glad sucked in a shocked breath. "No. How do you know?"

"The morning after Memorial Day I went to work early, you remember? They were there together."

"You saw them?" she whispered.

"In the flesh. Literally."

"Oh, wow." Glad thought a moment. "So that's why you were acting so weird."

Mike nodded. "Knocked the pins out from under me. I thought they had a solid marriage and there he was with someone else. Maybe it was the first time or maybe he's been doing this kind of shit for years, I don't know. But it brought everything into perspective. I realized how far I'd strayed from how I was raised, what I believe in. I was in love with you, but our relationship started on a lie. I knew I had to tell you the truth, tell you everything. But I was scared to do it because I might lose you. And then…" Then he'd lost her and his world went dark.

Glad shifted and turned to him, slid her arm around his waist. Held him close for a long minute, then tipped her head up and kissed him softly.

"I won't promise you anything," she said. "Just give me some time, okay?"

She kissed him again, a little deeper. Pulled at his back and Mike rolled over her, lost himself in loving her the only way he was allowed.

"Do I get to ask where you spent the night?"

Mike put Sarah's bag in her trunk and closed it. "No."

She giggled. "Like I don't know. Did you get back together?"

"No." Mike thought a moment. "But we might. I hope we do."

"I hope so too, for your sake. And I hope…" Sarah broke off and studied him. "We didn't talk about it."

He knew exactly what she meant. "I don't want to, either. Water under the bridge."

"You know everyone is so sorry about what happened, don't you?" Sarah pressed.

He shrugged. "I guess."

"Rachel had us all fooled. It was so hard to- I knew you'd never be like that, not really, but the things she said-and, well, we've all seen you get mad-"

"That was when I was a kid," he reminded her. "A long time ago."

"Micha, I'm so sorry I ever doubted you."

"I know."

"Everyone is. Dad misses you so much. And...Mom's sorry too." Mike barked a laugh and Sarah grabbed his hand. "Truly, she is. Especially those awful things she said after Bubbe died. And then you just up and left without saying goodbye to anyone."

"Who would have listened?" he asked, irked. "No one wanted me around!"

"But you didn't have to leave! Sure, this is a pretty town, but you didn't have to come all the way out here, to the middle of nowhere-"

"Ohio is more than a flyover state, you know."

"But don't you want to come home?"

"Ohio is home," he said quietly.

"But-"

"I like it here, Sarah. I'm doing what I love and small town life suits me, for the most part. I'm never going to be rich, I'm never going to be a bigshot. I don't care. This is what I want." And Glad. Glad back in his arms, in his life.

"So will you come for a visit? Maybe for mom and dad's anniversary party this fall? I have my own place now, so you can stay with me instead of with them."

"I'll think about it." He hugged her close. "You'd best get on the road if you want to beat traffic."

"All right." She kissed his stubbly cheek and stepped away.

"Drive careful. I love you."

"I love you, too."

Mike watched her pull out of the drive, waved as she drove away. Felt a warm tug in his heart that had been missing for a long time.

Family.

23

"Thanks for meeting me," Mike said, sitting opposite Holly Spence.

"I really didn't want to, if you want the truth," Holly said, gripping her coffee mug with both hands. Probably to keep from bashing his head in with it.

They sat at a corner table inside Common Ground in Glen View. It was packed with students this morning, getting their caffeine fixes before they headed for class. Midstate College had an active summer session with almost as many students on campus as during the fall and spring sessions.

"I'm hoping you can help me out," he started.

"Why should I help you?" Holly snorted. "You hurt one of my best friends. I could kill you right now. She was so happy, finally. I was so sure it was a good thing."

"It was. Glad's the best thing that's ever happened to me. I fell in love with her. And I think she loves me, too."

"So what happened?"

"Glad didn't tell you?" Mike asked, shocked.

Holly shook her head. "She just gave me the basics, and she was so miserable I didn't press her for more." She considered him a moment, then said, "Why don't you fill me in?"

So Mike did. The whole nasty, screwed up story, only leaving out the part about his cheating boss.

"Wow," Holly said when he finished. "You really messed up."

"I know. I want to earn her trust again, and I'm trying, but she keeps holding back. She says trust is a problem for her. But she won't tell me why. She won't tell me anything," Mike said, frustrated.

Holly regarded him. "Does she...did she ever talk about her past with you?"

Mike thought. "Just about-what did you call him? Asshole Evan?"

"Did she tell you the whole story?"

"She told me he cheated and they broke up."

Holly shook her head. "Well, that's it in a nutshell, but there's more."

"Will you please tell me?" Mike asked.

Holly thought a moment, then sighed. "Okay, so Glad and Evan started dating and she took him to her library's Christmas party and he met Shari. Shari worked in the same branch as Glad and they were friends. At least, Glad thought they were friends. Anyway, Evan and Shari started fooling around, but he was still dating Glad. Then Shari got pregnant."

"And Glad found out?"

"Not then. Somehow those two assholes kept things on the down-low. And Glad, being Glad, never shared her private life at work so people honestly thought she and Evan weren't involved anymore."

"So how did she find out?"

Holly grimaced. "Well, the library staff held a baby shower. Glad organized the whole party, made it real nice, they rented out a party room at a local restaurant…and Evan showed up to help Shari with all her baby gifts when it was over."

Mike stared at Holly, speechless. She nodded. "It gets better. Glad and Evan had been out the night before. Hearts and flowers, sex and all."

"Man," Mike muttered, picturing Glad in the midst of her coworkers, facing that awful truth. He couldn't even begin to imagine the pain and humiliation she endured.

"It was a real blow, to say the least," Holly said. "She trusted Evan and he screwed her over."

"Just like me," Mike said, depressed. The hole he'd dug just kept getting deeper.

"She hasn't had the easiest life," Holly said. "Sometimes I'm amazed at how well she turned out, considering everything she dealt with."

"Now that I think about it, she's never talked about her childhood. It's like her life started when she met you in college."

317

Holly smiled a little. "Well, I brought her out of her shell, but she's always been full of ambition. She's always needed to prove herself."

"Can you tell me anything?" Mike asked.

"I probably shouldn't-"

"I need to understand," Mike pressed. "I don't want to lose her, Holly."

Holly looked at him a moment. "She never talked about growing up?"

"No. Never." And that had been a little weird, as he had mentioned his family on several occasions and she'd barely said two words about hers.

Holly sipped at her coffee. "Glad's mom and dad had an affair. She was a freshman in college and he was forty or so. He tried to hush it up because he was married and had kids and he was some bigshot businessman."

"Who is he?"

"Glad's never said. I'm not sure if she knows. Anyway, the guy paid her mom a big settlement and some hefty child support and her mom went through it like water, partying, boyfriends...all Glad meant to her mom was a check in the mail. Then her mom left when Glad was around nine or ten."

"Left?" Mike asked. "I thought she died." He'd assumed that 'gone' meant dead.

Holly shook her head. "She told Glad she was going out one night and never came back. Glad was on her own for almost a week before someone wised up and called social services."

"But...you can't just abandon your kid!" Mike was stunned. The thought of Glad as a sweet little girl, scared and alone for days on end twisted his heart with grief.

"Well, she did. Never heard from again and Glad went into foster care."

"What about her dad?"

Holly shrugged. "He signed away any legal rights, wanted nothing to do with her. His name wasn't on her birth certificate, there wasn't DNA testing...no one could force him into compliance." She frowned down at her cup. "And as far as other family, well, Glad's mom had cut all ties. Her grandparents wanted nothing to do with them."

"But...her mother's behavior wasn't Glad's fault."

"Didn't matter. They didn't want her."

They fell silent, each staring off into space. Mike's chest ached; he wanted to go to Glad, pull her into his arms and never let her go. But he couldn't. He might never again.

"So she went into the system," he prompted after a minute.

"Yes. She hardly ever talks about it. I know she was placed in at least four different homes and they weren't great. Not that she was abused or anything, but they were overcrowded and it was a constant struggle, you know? She said the older kids would take food off her plate if she didn't eat it fast enough, that they stole or tricked her out of most of her possessions-one time she showed me a necklace that had belonged to her mother. Just a gold chain, you know? She told me she had to hide it behind a baseboard so the other kids wouldn't find it.

"She hated living in foster care, so she ended up at the library a lot. Studied like crazy so she could get good grades and prove she wasn't completely worthless. And it paid off: she got a full scholarship, went to college and…well, here we are."

"*Oy, vey*," Mike said, swamped with guilt and sorrow. Even as messed up as his family life was now, he had grown up without any doubt that he was loved and wanted. Glad had received little to none of that. He realized now that she'd taken a big leap of faith, trusting him. And he'd played with her trust like it was a toy.

Holly reached over and touched his hand. "I believe you care about her. And she's miserable without you. But if you're going to win her back you have to prove that you won't let her down. You haven't done a good job of it so far, Mike. You've got a tough road ahead."

"I know. But I love her. She's worth it." He sighed. "I wonder if she still thinks *I* am."

"I'll put in a good word for you."

"Thanks." He smiled, but she didn't return it. She looked troubled. "What's the matter?"

"Nothing, I-oh, what the hell." She met his eyes. "Do you know where Greg went?"

Mike studied Holly a moment. He'd known Turk was interested in her. Apparently things had progressed if she was asking after him and looking worried like this.

"I don't," he said. "I'm sorry."

"He's been gone for weeks."

"He's done it before. I'm not sure, because he doesn't talk much, but I think he might be under some kind of contract with someone. Maybe like the guys who do Reserves?"

Holly looked at him, her eyes bleak. "I was a military wife. I know Reserves doesn't operate like this. Is he doing something bad? Something illegal?"

Mike shook his head. "I don't know. I sure hope not."

***

Glad paced in her bathroom. Back and forth, to the door and back to the tub, counting seconds, trying not to look at the stick on her sink.

Had it been five minutes? No, not yet, she was only up to one seventy-two. She should go do something, get some coffee, make the bed, anything to distract herself. But she couldn't leave that room. Not until it was done and she saw the result.

She had a feeling she already knew the answer. Last night she'd driven over to the Walmart in Ashland and slipped the test in with her other purchases, covering it in the cart while she shopped, paranoid she'd see someone she knew right when the clerk was scanning it because she never got away with anything. But she'd made her getaway, managed to chat normally with Sal a few minutes when she arrived home, then tucked the box in her medicine cabinet right next to that box of condoms that had not been used once that last time they were together.

After a mostly sleepless night she'd given in, got up at five and unwrapped it. And now...

Three hundred. Okay. Five minutes were up. Glad slowly approached the sink and looked down. Two bright pink stripes streaked across the window.

"Hoo, boy," she whispered.

Glad shakily picked up the instruction paper and read the words, even though she'd read them already and knew what her result meant.

One stripe negative. Two stripes positive.

Glad sat down on the edge of the tub and stared into space for another five minutes then rechecked the stick. The stripes didn't change.

She was pregnant. She was going to have a baby. Mike's baby. Their baby. Oh baby. A baby. A baby! She didn't know anything about babies! She'd never changed a diaper in her life! What in the world was she going to do with a baby?

Well, one thing was certain. Hysterics were not going to help. Glad forced herself to leave the bathroom, to walk over to her bedroom and sit on the bed. She called on her Pilates training and took long, slow breaths, in and out.

"Okay, you're pregnant," she told herself. "This is no big deal. Women have been getting pregnant since Eve. You can handle this. You're a librarian. You can handle anything."

And if she said that enough times, she might even believe it.

"You're about five weeks along." Dr. Rose said, then chuckled. "Guess you made your own fireworks on July fourth."

Glad groaned and covered her flaming face with her hands.

"Relax, honey. I'm only teasing you." Dr. Rose pulled off her exam glove and picked up a device from the counter. "Let's take a listen."

"To what?" Glad asked, scared.

The doctor pulled Glad's gown up and pressed the device against her abdomen, moved it around in slow circles. First there was nothing, then suddenly an amplified *wip-wip-wip-wip* came through the device.

"That's your baby's heartbeat," Dr. Rose said, smiling.

"It...is?" A strange, sweet warmth rose inside. A heartbeat. Her baby.

Wip-wip-wip-wip-

"Sounds good!" Dr. Rose turned off the device and pulled the sheet back up. "Have you told Mike yet?"

"How do you-"

"I live down the street," Dr. Rose reminded her. "I was letting Rudy out to piddle right when he was leaving your house the morning after Frank and Sal's party."

Glad bit back another groan. Outed by a Schnauzer, it only needed that.

"I was hoping that meant you were back together," Dr. Rose continued.

"No, we're not."

"Well, this is a game changer," Dr. Rose said. "I'll write you a prescription for prenatal

323

vitamins, and we'll get you on the schedule for monthly checkups, ultrasound, and blood tests."

"Wait," Glad said, panicking. "Can I call for the appointments in a few days?" Dr. Rose looked at her strangely and she continued, "I know you'd never say a word, but if someone else put two and two together... I just need to tell Mike first."

"Okay. But don't wait too long. My calendar fills up quick."

"I won't. I promise."

***

Mike cruised up I-71, his mind in a tangle.

He was impressed, he'd admit it. Sunrise Garden Centers was a huge operation with six retail locations around the greater Cincinnati area and thousands of outlying acres of trees and shrubs. The demand for landscaping was high and there was plenty of money around that city to pay for it. Renny McQueen had taken him all over town, wined him and dined him and made him an offer he'd be a fool to pass up.

But instead of accepting he'd asked for time to consider everything. McQueen hadn't looked too happy about that but he'd agreed to get in touch in a week for Mike's decision.

It was a dream job. He'd be doing a lot more design work and a lot less labor, plus he'd be raking in some serious bucks for it. He'd have more freedom and autonomy.

It was a dream job. It really was. He'd be a fool not to take it, and Mill Falls wasn't that great anyway, there wasn't much to do besides go to bars or work out at the Rec Center. Cincinnati had night life galore, clubs and concerts and plenty of culture if he was so inclined. Yep, a dream job in a great location.

But Glad wouldn't be there.

That ache, familiar by now because it had happened so often these last weeks, radiated out from his core, hot and sickening. Despite everything, he and Glad were not progressing much. They'd only seen each other a couple of times and she seemed more distant every time. He'd called, left messages, did more work in her yard...but it seemed like it was all for nothing.

He had to face it. She didn't want him back, so there really wasn't any reason for him to stay in Mill Falls. He'd kick the job offer around a couple days, email a copy of the contract to his attorney-and best friend-Nico Roth to check over, just to be sure. Then he'd call Renny McQueen and accept.

He wasn't moving forward, and he couldn't go back no matter how bad he wanted to. It was time to move on.

"So, enjoy your day off?" asked Ken. He and several employees, including Mike, had come in before the store opened today. They were rearranging the main display area to accommodate the décor and sales items for the fall season, pushing the display stands into a new configuration. He and Ken were left with the heavy work while the other employees were gathering boxes of merchandise.

"It was fine," Mike said, shoving his stand into place. "You want this one here?"

"Sure." Ken moved his display stand another three feet to the right. "So how'd you like Nicola's?"

Mike stilled and looked at Ken. "Sorry?" he asked.

Ken shoved his stand a little more. "Nice restaurant. McQueen's got good taste. How much did he offer you?"

So much for keeping his interview on the down-low. Mike felt every ear in the room straining their way. "Did he call you or something?"

"Of course he did. He told me back in the spring he was going to steal you away from me." Ken sat on his stand. "So? How much?"

"You're assuming he made me an offer," Mike hedged, uncomfortable.

"Please. He knows you're good and he wants to be the king of landscape architecture in Cincy." Ken shrugged. "If you're interested, it'd be a good move for you."

Mike stared at him. Was Ken telling him to leave?

Of course he was. He had a secret to keep and it would be easier if Mike was out of the picture. "I haven't made a decision yet."

Ken shrugged. "Let me know when you do."

***

Morning sickness? She wished. Try all day, all night sickness. Try living on Gatorade, saltines and plain pasta sickness. And sometimes that didn't even stay down.

Glad was so miserably nauseous during the day she didn't have time to be miserable over Mike. But at night, when the house was dark and silent and she lay down alone and her poor stomach stopped quivering for more than a minute at a time, she still wept, helpless against the memories. They'd been thick as thieves, in each other's pockets night and day. April had been right: they had loved each other.

She knew this was up to her. That she had to decide, and soon. Mike wouldn't wait around forever. And now there was more at stake than just her heart. Dr. Rose had left her a message just yesterday, reminding her that another week had passed and she needed to call the office and schedule her follow-ups. She couldn't ignore her baby's welfare because she was afraid to trust her own judgment.

She had to tell him today. Her fingers shook as she dialed the phone. One ring. Two.

This is Mike Kovalski. I'm not available to take-

She hung up. Dialed the next number.

"Green Spaces, how can I help you?" a friendly voice said.

It was Ken Anderson. Glad gritted her teeth. "This is Glad Donahue calling."

"I-oh! Glad-well-um, how are-um…listen, I'm real sorry."

"I don't want to hear it, Ken. I want to talk

to Mike."

"He's moving hives out back. Should I-can I have him call you back?"

"No, thank you. I'll come out there. Goodbye."

***

Mike smoked the surface of the hive one more time then carefully wiggled the super frame and pulled it partly out. About a third of the foundation had honeycomb in various stages of development. Great, the queen had settled and the workers were making honey. He tucked it back into place.

"Uh, boss?" Fonz said.

Mike looked up. Fonz was pointing back towards the greenhouses. Mike looked in that direction and his heart stopped.

Glad. Standing at the bottom of the path, hugging herself against the morning chill.

"You want to finish up here?" Mike asked. He stood and pulled off his veil, moved down the path to where she stood waiting.

She looked pale and thin, but endlessly beautiful and his heart cracked in two all over again. He wasn't going to stop loving her any time soon, if ever.

"Cold out this morning," he said, pulling open his beekeeping suit. He had a Green Spaces zip hoodie on underneath and he stripped it off and wrapped it around her. "Better?"

"Yes. Thank you."

"Good." He reached a hand forward, then let

it drop. It hurt like hell not to touch her, but she obviously wanted him to keep his distance. "So. What…um, brings you out here?"

"I need to tell you something."

"Okay." He waited. Glad took a shaky breath and it dissolved into a sob. "This is so hard," she whispered, scrubbing at her eyes with the sleeve of his hoodie.

"Tell me," he urged, worried. "Whatever it is. I'll help you. We'll figure it out."

"I'm pregnant."

Mike felt his mouth open, but nothing came out. He stared at Glad, shocked.

"I wanted to tell you first, before everyone else finds out and starts talking," she went on, looking up at him, her lovely eyes huge and scared in her white face.

He couldn't seem to make his brain work. "When-how…"

"It was July fourth. Well, technically July fifth, considering what time you broke into my house."

And they hadn't used a condom. They'd made love three times that night with no protection whatsoever and he hadn't even thought, hadn't even considered this outcome.

"I'm just letting you know. I'm not expecting anything from you."

What? "What do you mean?"

"You don't have to do anything for me. I can take care of things on my own."

"Glad. We're having a baby. I'm the father and-"

"I don't need you, okay? Don't," she said,

holding her hand up when he opened his mouth to protest. "I can't take this right now, so just back off." She spun on her heel and hurried away down the path.

Mike watched her go, helpless, hurt flaying him alive.

I don't need you, okay?

"It's all those hormones." Fonz stood at his side. "Trust me, she needs you." Mike gave him a heavy look and Fonz laughed. "Sound carries like crazy back here, you ever notice that?"

"Can't say as I have," Mike said.

"Clear as a church bell," Fonz said, and clapped his shoulder. "Congratulations, dad."

24

Overheard all around Mill Falls:

You'll never guess who's got a bun in the oven.

I know! I know! Can you believe that?

Is he *the father?*

Well, I guess-but they broke up awhile back, so maybe not.

Oh, he's the father all right. My niece saw it on her chart.

She's not supposed to divulge that kind of stuff! Isn't that right? All that doctor-patient confidentiality-

Pooh. She just happened to notice, that's all.

Well, he may be the father, but he's not sticking around.

No! He's not leaving Mill Falls!

I heard, from a very *reliable source, mind you, that he had an interview down in Cincy and they made him a big offer. Way more than he can get up here.*

That can't be right. He wouldn't leave her, would he?

I guess we'll have to wait and see.

***

"So you're pregnant."

Glad shifted uncomfortably in her seat. Chris stared back at her, a look of pure exasperation on his face.

"I am," she admitted.

"Who's the father?"

Glad's face went hot. "I-it's Mike Kovalski!" Who did he *think* the father was?

Chris huffed. "Figures. Well, at least you know him, he's not some yahoo you picked up at that honkytonk on the hill."

Glad felt her mouth drop at his crudity. "What?"

Chris slammed his hands against his desk. "Do you have any idea of the position you've put me in? Any idea at all?" he snapped, furious.

"Chris, I-"

"I've spent months telling everyone in town about your sterling character and great work ethic and what do you do? You get knocked up by that goddamn landscaper who's been in half the beds in Lord County! The board's flipping out, especially Marie Stahl! She wants to fire you!"

Glad gasped. "Fire me?"

"She can't do it, but that's beside the point!" Chris was turning puce. "Christ in a sidecar, Glad! You might as well stick a scarlet letter on your chest for all the credibility you've lost here!

All the good work you've done, all the potential in you just went to hell overnight. I'm disappointed in you, Glad. Damn disappointed."

"I'm sorry-"

"I don't really care right now. Just get out of my office."

Glad slowly stood, her eyes stinging from his censure. She felt sick and shamed, but also furious. She'd fallen in love and was having a baby. It might be unexpected, it might be inconvenient for a lot of people, but she'd be damned if she let anyone tell her that loving Mike, that creating a new life together was wrong.

She'd guarded herself, held herself back, had coveted success and advancement to prove to herself that she was good enough. That she had been good enough all along.

But everything had changed on that exam table. One tiny heartbeat had shoved her ambitions aside with its *wip-wip-wip-wip*. She didn't need a position, or a flawless reputation to be good enough. She only needed to be good enough for the life growing inside her.

She swallowed down a fresh wave of nausea and girded herself, but before she could speak a sharp rap sounded and the door crashed open. Marie Stahl stalked in, stabbing the air with her cane. "Where is that tramp you hired-there! You! Are!" she growled, waving the cane at Glad. "Young woman, hiring you was the biggest mistake this library has ever made! You're disgraceful, shameless and wanton! What have you to say for yourself?"

Glad faced the old woman, fully intending to keep things professional while she defended herself. She opened her mouth to speak…

…and threw up.

Glad slowly pushed her grocery cart to her car. She'd had a somewhat good day from the eating standpoint as she'd managed to keep down six saltines, half an apple and a can of warm ginger ale.

It was one of the few combinations that seemed to work; she'd learned the hard way that some things weren't good ideas, like the chicken salad sandwich she'd vomited up on Marie Stahl's shoes last week, for example.

That little stunt had produced some unexpected results. Chris had instantly lost his anger, apologized profusely and had become as bad a mother hen as Frank. And Mrs. Stahl, disgusted and horrified by the event, hadn't been seen in the library since, a blessing for staff and patrons alike.

Glad clutched the cart handle as nausea pricked her again. She had an appointment with Dr. Rose on Friday and it couldn't get here soon enough. She was trying hard to stay calm, but she was increasingly worried that something was wrong with the baby. Every pregnancy book she'd sneaked a peek at in the library stacks said nothing about morning sickness being this bad, day after day. She was drained and weak and only managed to get through work each day by sheer force of will.

She had told Holly, April and Fran, Frank and Sal and a few others, but otherwise had kept the news of her pregnancy to herself. Well, at least she'd tried; gossip about her condition had boomeranged through town and returned to her with a juicy little tidbit attached: Mike had a job offer pending in Cincinnati. When she heard that Glad locked herself in her office and cried for an hour.

She'd put him off too long and now he was leaving.

Mike, please don't go. Please don't leave us.

He'd finished the patio, been by to mow the grass a few times, trim her shrubs out front, edge the driveway and sidewalk, take her garbage and recycling to the curb on Wednesday mornings and roll them back later on. Each time he'd dropped his business card through her mail slot, probably so she wouldn't worry over who was stopping by. She was amassing quite a collection.

But he hadn't told her anything about his job; in fact, they hadn't talked at all. Nothing about themselves, their baby, the future. And now he was leaving, probably soon. Would she see him again? Would he visit at all, be there when the baby was born? Would he support his child? Would he even want to know him or her?

Glad shook her head and kept pushing the cart. She didn't need Mike, she had plenty of support from caring friends and she'd make sure her child didn't suffer any lack of love and affection. She wasn't negligent and indolent like her mother. In fact, she was already in love with her baby, whispering to it in the night, telling it stories and singing songs while she caressed her abdomen. Soon she would have a bump, and soon after she'd look like she swallowed a basketball. But first she had to get through this awful day-in, day-out sick stage.

Glad loaded her groceries in the trunk of her car. She should have asked Mike to grocery shop for her. That would be a real help, seeing as how she could barely keep down the vomit smelling all those food smells. The deli counter was the absolute worst-

"Well, if it isn't Little Miss Assistant Director Lady, in the flesh," said a surly voice behind her. Glad started and turned.

Jimmer Hall stood there. His hands curled around the handles of her shopping cart and made tiny pushes back and forth.

"I thought you were still in lockup." Glad kept her cool, loaded her last bag in the trunk and shut it before looking at him again.

"Overcrowded," Jimmer said. "They cut me loose early."

"I see. How nice for you."

"Isn't it." He sneered at her and Glad felt a chill all the way down her spine.

Don't be nervous. He's just a punk. This isn't a big deal.

"You must be happy to be out," she tried.

"You think?" Jimmer shoved the cart forward. It banged against her car and bounced back. Glad gasped and jumped, frightened. "You *think*?" he repeated, grabbing the cart again. He leaned over the handle, squeezing it so hard his knuckles turned white.

"Jimmer, please-"

"Don't *please* me, bitch. We got unfinished business, you and me."

"Only business you got is backing the fuck off, boy," drawled a voice from behind them. Glad jumped and turned just as Greg Turk stepped in front of her and shoved the cart hard into Jimmer's midsection. Jimmer fell back and Glad felt a hand on her arm.

"Hey, Glad," Fonz said, smiling kindly at her. "How's it going?"

"Better now," she admitted, watching Turk plow the cart into Jimmer again. It looked like it hurt and some perverse part of her took great pleasure in that. "When did Turk get back to town?"

"Just this week."

"Where was he? Holly was pretty mad." Turk now had Jimmer pinned in the cart return caddy and whatever he was saying was turning Jimmer's face ghost white.

"No clue. I don't know what he does on those little jobs he goes off to, but, I don't want to know either, you get me?"

Glad nodded. As mild and soft-spoken as he was, she got one big danger vibe from Greg Turk. "I get you. Thank you for helping me."

"Ah, me and Turk are like knights in shining armor. Always on the lookout for ladies in distress," Fonz said, opening her car door. "Let's get you home, okay? I'm sure you've got pickles and ice cream to get put away."

Glad shot him a suspicious look. Fonz grinned. "I've got three sisters-in-law and seven nieces and nephews. I know about these things."

***

Mike pulled into Glad's driveway, killed the engine and bounded up the front steps, furious. Not that he wasn't grateful to Turk and Fonz for rescuing Glad-and probably saving him from jail time by putting the run on Jimmer Hall-but she hadn't called. Hadn't told him a thing, like usual and he was damn sick and tired of living in the dark.

Mike banged hard on the front door. He heard faint shuffling noises inside and then the click of the door locks and her beloved face, pale and drawn, peeked out.

"Oh. It's you." She opened the door a little wider.

"It's me," he growled. "So were you going to tell me sometime, or did you think informing the father of your child that you were assaulted in the IGA parking lot yesterday wasn't that important?"

"Oh, for heaven's sake. I'm fine-"

"You don't think I need to know that Jimmer Hall asshole was threatening you?"

"What difference would it have made? It's over!"

"Is it?" Mike stepped through the doorway and into the house. Glad scowled up at him and he sighed, exasperated. "He's not on a weekend pass, Glad. He is out of jail. If he was thinking at all beyond grabbing your shopping cart, he's got the plate number of your car, make and model... What if he shows up here? Or at your work, or corners you in that damn pitch-black parking lot behind the library? What if there's no one around next time?"

"I think you're overreacting," she said, sounding distinctly annoyed. Too bad.

"Am I? Glad, you're pregnant!"

She drew a shuddering breath and her hand went protectively over her stomach. "Yes. *I* am. Not you."

"What does *that* mean?"

"It means I can take care of myself and I don't need you barging in here-after disappearing for weeks!-and trying to take everything over."

"You told me to back off!" he barked.

"Well, yes, I did, but-"

"I'm not a mind-reader, you know," he interrupted, aggravated still. "I'm trying to respect your boundaries, here. I just want to help."

She looked down. "Just-go away. I'm tired."

"You look like hell."

"Yes, well, morning sickness that lasts twenty-four seven will do that to a person."

That didn't sound right. "Your doctor know about this?"

"I'm seeing her Friday. Everything's fine."

"I want to go with you." *Please say yes. Please let me in.*

"No. I don't need you."

It was the last straw and Mike lost it. "Of course you don't need me. You don't need me to take care of you or help you through this…I was done after the sperm donation, right?" he snapped.

Glad gasped, her face stricken.

"I'm more than that!" he hollered at her.

"Mike-"

"I'm a *damn sight* more than that!"

She flinched as if he'd struck her. Mike swallowed down the lump in his throat and willed himself to calm down.

But it hurt, it hurt so damn bad. He took a slow breath, let it out and decided to risk it. "I know why you're having such trouble trusting me. I know, okay?"

"Know what?" she asked, wary.

"About your past."

"My p-who told you? Holly? What did she tell you?"

She looked afraid and it broke his heart. "That you don't know your dad and your mom abandoned you. That you got stuck in foster care and treated like crap. That you got burned in the worst possible way by a man who said he loved you."

"I-"

"You don't have to hide yourself from me, Glad. I'm not like them. I want you, okay? I want you with me. I'm not leaving you."

"Oh, no?" she retorted. "What about your new job in Cincinnati?"

How did-? Mike opened his mouth to answer, but she rode right over him. "I hear rumors too, you know. And let me just point out, while you're bitching at *me* about not talking to *you*, you didn't exactly lay that one on me, either!"

"I told him no."

She stared at him, obviously shocked. "But why-what do you mean?"

"I went down there, he showed me the place and I told him I'd think about it. Two days later you came to Green Spaces."

He watched the myriad expressions flit across her face. Confusion, disbelief...maybe even a sliver of happy. He sure hoped so.

"But...wasn't it a good job?" she whispered.

"A great job. Big outfit, lots of money."

"So why didn't you take it?"

"Because you're more important than money."

Glad shook her head. "I...I don't understand."

"Well, then let me clear it up for you. You matter more, and our baby matters more and I'm staying here whether you want me or not."

Glad touched her forehead with a shaking hand. "But...you're not...leaving?"

Mike stepped close and put his hands on her arms, rubbed slowly up and down. "No. Not ever, okay? I know you had a lot of jerks let you down in your life. I'm not going to be one of them. I love you, girl. I'm with you, whatever comes."

She just stared, uncomprehending, what little color she had in her face draining away. Mike felt a spike of panic.

"What's wrong?"

Glad's eyes rolled up into her head and she collapsed.

25

Her head felt stuffed with cotton, voices faint, images blurry.

Frantic words.

...Glad, please baby, come on...

Deep brown eyes over her.

...fainted, she's pregnant...

A stranger holding her wrist, his mouth moving.

...start an IV...

A faint prick and she flinched.

...stay with me, girl...

A void.

A man in scrubs bending over her.

"Where am I?" she whispered, afraid.

"You're in the Emergency Room," the man said.

Glad shifted, distressed. "What-how-"

"Lie still, Miss Donahue."

No. No, she needed to get up. Needed to get out of here. She tried to sit up and hands pushed her back down. Then Mike's face moved over hers.

"Relax, girl."

"M-Mike?"

"I'm here," he said softly. "You're not alone. I'm here."

Everything flooded back and she burst into tears. "The baby," she begged weakly. "Did I lose the baby?"

"No! No, I swear," he assured her, taking her hand in his. "You passed out on me. I couldn't wake you up so I called 911."

"There's s-something wrong," she bawled. "I'm so a-afraid there's something wrong Mike I'm so *afraid*-"

"Shhh." Mike gently blotted her tears with a tissue. "You'll be all right. We'll get this figured out."

The doctor pulled up a stool at her other side. "You gave us a little scare, Miss Donahue. I hear you're not eating?"

"Barely anything," Mike said. "And she's sick all the time. That's not normal, is it."

He sounded worried. He looked worried, his eyes stark as he blotted up her tears.

"Is that true?" asked the doctor.

Glad nodded and sniffled. "I-everything I eat or drink...I almost always feel sick."

"Well, it's not common, but it can happen, unfortunately. And when it does it's extremely important to keep you hydrated, eating and healthy. We've got you hooked up to some fluids right now," the doctor said. "And we've contacted Dr. Rose."

"Okay."

"By the end of the first trimester this will go away, which is the good news. But you've got a few weeks before you get there, so we need to make a plan. Let's take a listen down here." The doctor pressed a device to Glad's abdomen, moved it lower and was rewarded with a steady *wip-wip-wip-wip.* "Good, nice strong heartbeat-"

"Oh, thank God," Glad whispered, fresh tears leaking out.

"That's a heartbeat?" Mike asked, surprised.

The doctor smiled. "It is. You want to hear it again?"

"Please."

The doctor obliged. Glad saw a delighted smile spread over Mike's face. "Isn't it...wonderful?" she asked.

Mike lifted her hand to his lips. "The most beautiful sound I've ever heard," he said.

***

Mike held Glad's hand and watched her sleep. She was still pale, but the hospital had run a bunch of tests and the doctor had assured him multiple times that she and the baby were going to be all right.

They had to be all right. Life without Glad in it was unthinkable. He knew they needed to be together, knew his future lay with her, knew he was bound to her.

And that meant doing things right, manning up and taking charge of the situation. She'd probably freak out, but too bad. He was done backing off.

***

Hospitals were torture at best, with nurses bustling in and out, taking her temperature and blood pressure and who knew what else around the clock. And lucky her, she was stuck here another whole day! But at least there was television if she wanted it and a pretty bouquet of daisies Mike had brought up from the gift shop for her to admire. One nurse, a big lummox of a man with kind eyes and a gentle voice had brought her a stack of magazines from the waiting room to read.

And she wasn't completely alone. After seeing her settled and staying the night in a chair next to her bed, Mike had gone home this morning but promised he'd be back later on. Dr. Rose had come by to do an exam and discuss Glad's dietary needs. Holly had visited at lunchtime and Frank and Sal stopped by in the afternoon despite Frank's horror of hospitals.

"How can you stand all that beeping?" he complained after five minutes.

"At least it's not in here," Sal said. "And you don't have to share your room."

"I'd rather be in my own bed," Glad remarked.

"Doll," Frank said to Sal, "if I ever get sick enough to need a hospital you have my permission to take me out behind the azaleas and shoot me."

Dinner arrived, bland and boring but she managed to eat most of it and not be sick. Then she flipped channels and fretted and flipped some more and stared at the clock and turned the TV off and stared at her magazines and finally gave up and closed her eyes.

A soft kiss on her forehead woke her. "Hey, beautiful," Mike said softly. "Sorry I couldn't make it here sooner."

"Busy today?" Glad asked, feeling relief flood in. He was here, finally. Okay, she'd been waiting for him to come back all day. So? She didn't care.

"Very busy. What happened here?" He settled in and they talked about her day, talked about getting her home tomorrow, and about anything else that came to mind.

And he held her hand the whole time.

***

Mike pulled the truck into Glad's driveway and rolled to a stop. "I'm going to unlock the house then come back and get you, okay?" he said.

"I'm a lot better now," Glad reminded him. The time in hospital had improved her constitution somewhat and the strict instructions given by Dr. Rose concerning her diet and getting some bed rest should help even more.

"I know, but your doctor said don't overdo and I want to make sure you can take the steps without passing out or anything."

Glad gave in. "All right, but you need to

relax a little," she said. "I'm not going to break."

It was actually kind of sweet, how nervous Mike was. He'd probably be a basket case when she had the baby, but she'd worry about that later. Glad watched him unlock her back door and disappear inside briefly, then return. His face was set in concentration.

"You ready?" he asked.

"Of course." She slid from the truck and Mike walked her to the back steps. She took a step up and wobbled and gripped his arm hard, muttering, "This is ridiculous. It's just stairs!"

"You'll get better. Don't worry about it." He held the door and they passed into the house. "You want to lay down for a while?"

"No. I'll just sit in the living room." Glad made her way down the hall, wanting her comfy sofa more than anything. But something made her stop just over the threshold.

"Where did that recliner come from?" she asked, confused.

"Let's sit you down, here," Mike said, guiding her to the sofa and ignoring her question. Like that was going to work.

She sat. "That recliner looks just like-"

"I'm going to grab you a ginger ale, unless you want something else?"

Glad pinned him with her best no-nonsense librarian gaze. "Mike. The recliner."

Mike sat. "Okay, it's like this. I moved in."

"You what?" Glad surged forward. Mike caught her shoulders and gently pushed her back.

"I moved in. Well, not everything yet, just a few necessities."

"Like your recliner?"

"I need my recliner. And my drafting table and my bed and clothes and stuff. I'll get the rest of it over the next couple of days. Now, listen," he said, placing his fingers over her ready to protest mouth. "This is for the best. You need someone to take care of you and I'm the man for the job."

"But I don't-"

His brows smashed together over his nose. "Gladiolus."

"You're trying to intimidate me. It won't work."

He kept looking at her, pinning her to her seat with his eyes. Okay, maybe it would. Glad slouched back against the cushions. "I don't like this."

"It's for the best."

Glad tried one last protest. "But I'll be fine on my own-"

"Really? You can barely make it up the stairs right now. You're not supposed to drive anywhere until you get stronger. And what about down the road? Are you going to shovel your driveway this winter when you're out to there pregnant and we get two feet overnight?"

She hadn't thought that far ahead. "Well-"

Mike kept talking. "How about hauling those heavy trash cans to the curb every week? Or mowing the grass? What if you fall? What if you go into labor in the middle of the night?" His voice changed, became suddenly husky. "What about when the baby starts kicking and you're so excited and you want to share it? Or when he won't stop crying in the middle of the night? What about when he takes his first steps or says his first words? You think I want to miss all that?"

"I-"

"Do you really think I don't care?"

Glad stared at him, her mouth working, but nothing came out. Mike reached over and took her hand in his. "I know you don't think you can depend on me. I dug myself a pretty deep hole over here and now I have to get out of it. It's going to take a long time to prove I'm worth anything. But I'm not going to stop trying. I can't. This is too important." He looked suddenly worried. "And...I want to talk about something else, too."

"What's that?" she asked.

"Um." Mike looked down at their hands, then back up at her. "Marriage."

She felt her eyes bugging out of her head. "What...why?"

"Well, for starters, I love you. For seconds, you love me. And we both love our baby. We're a family. We should make it official."

Glad dropped her gaze, flustered. Mike's big, callused hand held hers and his thumb stroked over her skin. "I don't know what to say," she whispered, feeling her cheeks heat. Married? To Mike? Could she? Should she?

A huge part of her wanted to simply let go. Let Mike in, let him take the driver's seat so she could concentrate on having a healthy baby. But could she trust him that far? Would he stick around for the long run? Did he really want to marry *her*?

349

"I don't know what to say," she repeated, looking at him helplessly. "This is so…you moved in without asking me and now this…I'm a little overwhelmed."

"I see that." Something flitted across his expression: pain? But it was gone too quickly for her scattered brain to latch onto. "Listen, I know it's a lot to take in," he continued. "But will you think about it?"

She stared at him, still in shock.

"Okay, consider the benefits," he said. "You'd have your very own, round-the-clock landscaper on call. For free. Think of the money you'll save!"

Glad laughed weakly.

"And if you act now, I'll throw in a bonus: how does a downstairs bathroom sound?"

Her mouth dropped. "A bathroom?"

Mike smiled wickedly. "I can see you're a tough customer, so I'll go one better. How about a whole new kitchen?"

Hoo, boy. She'd give her right arm for a new kitchen.

"It sounds like a lot of work."

"Winter's slow time. I'll need a project. Come on, girl, you know you want it."

"That's a pretty irresistible offer," she allowed.

"So you'll think about it?"

She squeezed his hand. "I'll think about it."

***

The weekend was good; living with Glad

and taking care of her needs gave Mike a huge burst of purpose, confidence and accomplishment. He returned to Green Spaces Monday in a bubble of contentment, ready to take on the world. Then his boss stormed into his office and the bubble burst.

"Where the fuck have you been?" Ken demanded.

"Uh…I needed time off, remember?" Mike asked, mystified. "I gave you the request-"

"Which I never approved because it was last minute," Ken snarled. "You have to wait for goddamn approval! You can't just leave!"

What was going on here? "I'm sorry, but I thought-"

"You don't think! That's fucking obvious!"

Whoa, okay. Something was seriously wrong. "What happened? Is there a problem with one of the contracts? You could have called-"

"What happened?" Ken hissed, slamming Mike's door shut. "You've got the balls-you know what happened, you goddamn snitch. You told her. You told my wife about me and Caroline!"

As Harry Phelps would say, hot holy shit. It was out. Mike took a steadying breath. "Ken. I never said a word to Mary. I swear it."

Ken yanked an envelope from his pocket and threw it in Mike's face. "You're telling me you don't know about this?"

The envelope was addressed to Mary Anderson, postmarked Friday. Mike pulled out the note and scanned it. Then Ken ripped it from his hand.

"You're telling me that's not your signature?" he demanded, jabbing at the paper.

Not even close. "No, it's not."

"Bullshit!"

Okay, he needed to stay calm. But it was tough. "It's not my signature. Go get any invoice I signed and you'll see."

But Ken wasn't listening. "You sent this!" he yelled.

"I wasn't even in town. I had a medical emergency come up."

"That's a crock of shit if I ever heard one."

Calm fled for the hills. "Glad went to the ER on Wednesday night! I was in and out of the hospital for two days! That's why I took off!"

Ken stared at him a moment, then sneered, "How noble of you. Playing daddy with your knocked-up ex. Well here's a little get-well present, Mr. Boy Scout: you're fired."

Mike stopped breathing altogether. "What?" he asked, stunned.

"You heard me."

"I didn't do this," Mike gritted out.

"I don't need your excuses, Kovalski. Clear your desk and get out before we open for business." And he slammed out of Mike's office.

Mike stared at the door, his mind a complete void. Then a soft knock sounded and Fonz let himself in.

"Eavesdropping?" Mike heard himself ask.

"Kinda hard not to, the way you two were going at it. What the hell, boss?"

"I'm no longer your boss." Mike watched his hand open his desk drawer. He watched it pull out his external hard drive. Months of work, some real sweet designs stored on that thing.

"That's nuts! Who's gonna do the design work? What about your bees, man?"

"You can take care of them." Mike tucked his laptop into its carrying case, aware that the numbness was dissipating and a sour mix of anger, grief and panic was taking its place. "You've been out there with me enough." He pulled a planner out of the middle desk drawer and dropped it on the desk. "All my contacts are listed and all the instructions are…" He paused.

He loved working with those bees. Loved studying them.

And two words later they were gone.

You're fired.

"You okay?" Fonz asked.

"Fine." Mike cleared his throat, looked around the office for anything he might have missed. Thank God all his papers and drawings were at home; he'd have a hell of a time carting all that stuff-

Home. Oh, damn.

How was he going to tell Glad?

26

"Welcome back!" Marci pulled her into a big hug. "We were so worried!"

"I'm okay," Glad assured her. "Anything exciting happen while I was gone?"

"Nah. Lazlo was in bitching Friday, and Farmer McHottie came in Saturday and gave us all a thrill-oh, and someone backed into someone else's car in the parking lot yesterday afternoon. Woo-woo, high times at the library."

"Well, at least you got to see the McHottie," Glad teased. The man in question was Jim Ascher, a local farmer who stopped at the library every few weeks to pick up a fresh pile of paperbacks for his mother, usually romances and cozy mysteries. Every once in a while he also dropped off pies for the staff, which were brutally fought over in the break room.

Glad had caught a glimpse of him one time and had agreed with her Circ girls that he was smoking hot with his broad shoulders, tawny hair and bright blue eyes. But her attention had already been caught by Mike and…well, no one else came even close.

"Oh, and the best news? Jimmer Hall is banned!"

"Really? When did that happen?"

"Well, speaking of hotties, Mike stopped by while you were in the hospital and talked to Chris about what happened to you at the IGA. Chris talked to the police and he's banned for life." Marci snorted. "You can't just threaten a library administrator and get away with it, you know."

"Wow. That's…that's wonderful news!" And it was. She'd been too distracted to think much about the incident with Jimmer Hall, but knowing Mike had taken action to protect her felt wonderful.

"For all of us. He's a nuisance." The phone rang and Marci picked it up. "Mill Falls Public Library, how may I help you?" She looked at Glad and smiled. "She's right here."

Glad took the phone. "This is Glad Donahue, how can-"

"Can you come outside?" Mike's voice interrupted. "I'm over by the kids garden."

"Sure," Glad said, curious. She hung up and made her way out to the garden, still beautiful and full of color this late in summer, and found Mike standing alone. His face was pale and bleak, his eyes glittering with anger.

"What's the matter?" she asked, worried.

"Ken just fired me."

Glad gasped. "*What?* That's impossible! He wouldn't-why did he-what happened?"

355

"Someone blew the whistle on him. Sent a note to Mary with my name at the bottom."

"That's ridiculous. You'd never do something like that."

"Yeah, well, I told him so, but he didn't want to hear it. So I'm out of a job."

"But-is that legal? Do you have any recourse?"

"I don't know." Mike sighed hard and grabbed a handful of hair with a shaky hand. "This is crazy."

"Who do you think did it?" Glad asked, moving towards a shady bench at the end of the garden. Mike followed and they sat.

"My money's on Caroline. It doesn't matter, it's over. I need to move on."

"What about that job in Cincinnati?" Glad asked, trying to sound calm when she was anything but. Could the timing be any worse? They'd just started to settle in together! "Maybe-"

"I'm sure he filled it, and besides, with you being pregnant and everything…and I know you love it here."

Glad nodded. "I do. But if you find something good…I can start over."

"You shouldn't have to. I mean, you've worked hard for everything and…" Mike sighed and stared down at his hands. "We're supposed to get married and have a yard full of kids and drive Frank and Sal crazy with all the family chaos. I'm not supposed to lose my job three days after moving in with you."

Glad smiled, warmed to her soul over his

sentimental musings. "We'll be fine. Try not to worry."

"I am worried!" Mike pushed up from the bench and began to pace. "I'm supposed to take care of you and provide for you!"

"How...archaic of you."

Mike blew out a sigh. "You know what I mean, girl. We're pregnant, and I want to get married, but what if I can't find work?"

"Look around you!" Glad said, waving at the landscaping. "You've got so much talent! Your name is getting out there and people want what you've got. Oh-and I got notice that our gardens are going to be on the cover of that design issue of *Library Journal* I told you about! Once that comes out you'll be known throughout the industry. There's no way you'll be out of work for very long."

"But meanwhile I need to take care of you, help you out. I've got some money saved, but it isn't going to last. And winter's coming. Not exactly prime landscaping time."

Glad reached out her hand and he took it. "I'm still getting a paycheck, remember?"

"It's not going to stretch that far-"

"But it will stretch for a while." It hurt to see him like this, grieving and panicked. She stood and took his other hand.

Mike sighed. "Three days in and we've hit rock bottom. I'm so sorry."

Glad slid her arms around his waist and hugged him tight. "Well, if we've hit rock bottom then we've nowhere to go but up, right?"

***

Up turned out to be an understatement. Within a day word had spread throughout Lord County and Mike's phone began ringing. Clients contracted to Green Spaces were worried their jobs wouldn't get done. Clients he'd already serviced invited him out to take pictures to add to his portfolio. And to his surprise some potential new clients, including Matt Slade, the wine bar owner, called and asked to see him.

Within three days Mike knew he was getting in over his head and called Nico Roth, his closest friend, and asked him to come for a visit. An attorney specializing in contract law, Nico was more than happy to help Mike understand the ins and outs of starting his own business. Nico also contacted a firm in Glen View to mediate between Mike and Ken Anderson to sort out the remaining Green Spaces contracts Mike was involved with. Ken wasn't happy about paying Mike a consulting fee, but it was better than being sued for breach of contract by his clients. Mike also assured Ken he would recommend future clients to Green Spaces for plantings. He and Ken would likely never be friends again, but working cooperatively would benefit them both.

Nico stayed for nearly a week, getting to know Glad and their neighbors and Mill Falls.

"I like it here," he said to Mike on their last night. Glad had gone to bed and the men sat on the front porch, sipping Wild Turkey from Mike's bourbon stash.

"So stay," Mike said. "That firm in Glen

View could probably use another lawyer. And you could live a lot cheaper out of D.C."

Nico nodded, his lips pursed. Despite having a solid career and a good track record, he was nearly broke. Two years ago, Nico's parents had foolishly invested their retirement in a scheme that had left them in serious financial trouble. By the time it was resolved, Nico's savings were gone and his parents were forced to sell their home and other assets just to keep solvent. They moved into Nico's house, a modest cluster home in a golf course development, and watched what little money they had left very carefully. The arrangement was far from ideal but Nico never complained; he'd told Mike once that they'd sacrificed so much for him that he could do no less than help them in return.

"It's a nice firm," Nico allowed. "And that Jake Anderson couldn't say enough good things about it."

Mike nodded. Jake had scored a job with the firm as a clerk, doing research for the attorneys while he waited for his law school applications to come back. He was happy, thriving, and had told Mike point blank that neither he nor his mother blamed Mike for the debacle at home.

"Please," Jake had said. "Mom knows it was Caroline. This isn't exactly the first time, you know? She made dad fire that bitch, and they're going to counselling." He shook his head. "I wish mom would just kick dad's ass and divorce him, but she's so traditional."

"Maybe I'll look into it," Nico was saying. "It would be nice to have some breathing room.

Except," he took a sip and gave Mike a sideways glance, "I'd kind of miss your sister."

"Hang on." Mike stared at Nico. "You…and Sarah?"

"We ran into each other after she came back from visiting you. We caught up over lunch and then we ran into each other a few more times and…" He shrugged, looking slightly uncomfortable. "I can't give her anything-I can't even take care of myself-but I sure like her."

"I thought she was dating some guy named Blumenthal," Mike told him.

Nico looked troubled. "They've gone out a few times, I guess. Your mom's over the moon about that. You know how she can get."

"Yeah." Mike didn't need any reminders. His mother had adored Rachel; they had shopped together, served on committees together... Mike wouldn't be surprised if they still spent time together.

"Your mom's never liked me," Nico said. "And you know how hard Sarah tries to please her."

"There is no pleasing my mother," Mike said.

"I know. And she invited Blumenthal to their little thirty-fifth anniversary party, like it's a done deal," Nico said sourly, downing the rest of his drink. "You coming home for that?"

"I might have to, just to see this guy. What's he like?"

Nico huffed. "A condescending, officious little prick."

Mike contemplated this new development

while he finished his drink. Then he said, "Nico, you're my best friend. I don't care if you've got money or you don't. You'll bounce back, and I'd be happy to have you for a brother-in-law. But fair warning: you hurt Sarah and I'll come down to D.C. and kill you."

Nico grinned. "Don't worry about me. Worry about your own stuff, like getting that girl in there under the *chuppah.* She's a keeper."

***

She was in love more than ever.

The last few weeks had been, aside from the nausea, wonderful. After work most nights they'd had quiet dinners then Glad kept Mike company, reading while he puttered in the yard or worked on his designs. Some nights they retired to the front porch together and talked, cuddled close on her old double lounger as the night came on.

She and Mike skipped the Labor Day celebrations downtown and taken a long weekend at a private lakefront cottage near Vermilion that belonged to someone Sal Amico knew. The soothing sound of the waves coupled with leaving the wagging tongues of Mill Falls behind restored much of their camaraderie, and the long, slow kisses they shared while they lay in the hammock together didn't hurt, either.

New gossip awaited their arrival home; a drunk had crashed one of the Founder's Day parade vehicles into the war memorial and there had been a big scene between April Fonzi, Matt

Slade, Liz Meyer and Jeremy Swale at the Founder's Ball that had turned the town on its ear. Glad and Mike both just breathed sighs of relief, happy the gossip had moved away from them, finally.

Mike had been a gentleman, sleeping in the other bedroom so she could get as much rest as possible, helping with the housework and keeping a steady supply of chicken soup-his Bubbe's recipe-on hand to combat her nauseous moments. He hadn't pressed, hadn't pushed her at all. Sometimes she saw the question in his eyes but he did not ask it and, though she was pleased he was giving her time, she was also flummoxed. How long was he going to wait?

"Just tell him you're ready," Holly advised over lunch. "You're done thinking about it and you want to get married. Easy peasy."

"I guess," Glad said doubtfully.

"What's the matter?"

"I don't know…"

"You want it to be all romantic."

Glad flushed. "I'm not expecting him to go down on one knee or anything, but… How did Alex propose? I don't think you ever told me."

"He was on leave and we were in bed in some fleabag motel. Right in the middle of things he stopped and said 'I want to marry you, you know' and I cried." Holly smiled at the memory. "Not a romantic setting at all! Cheap sheets, the air conditioner was rattling…but it was perfect, just the same." She looked at Glad. "Don't expect him to read your mind. The only way to get what you really want from a man is to tell him."

"I will. After I get done with work tonight."

"And you'll call me first with the big news, right?"

"Of course I will."

The afternoon dragged into a slow evening and Glad was making one of her evening rounds, winding her way through a quiet children's area when her phone vibrated. She moved to a less public spot and took it out of her pocket.

It was a text from Mike. It read:

635.9PER 654478219030

What in the world? She stared at it a moment, then it dawned on her. It was a call number and a bar code from something here in the library. Glad tucked her phone away and headed upstairs, curiosity running rampant. She went into the 600's and found the book, double-checking the bar code as she removed it from the shelf. It was *A World of Flowers* by Clay Perry.

A page was marked with his Green Spaces business card. Glad opened the book and beheld a lovely, full-color listing for *gladiolus*. She removed the business card and flipped it over. Another number was on the back: *883.01HOM 654332988433*.

Okay, what was he up to? Glad went to the 800's and found the book. It was a volume of Homer, a page marked with, again, his Green Spaces business card. Glad opened to the page and scanned it, then did a double take about halfway down: *There is nothing nobler or more admirable than when two people who see eye to eye keep house as man and wife, confounding their enemies and delighting their friends.*

She exhaled, suddenly nervous and flipped the card over. It was the same number as the first: *635.9PER 654478219030.*

Glad slowly moved back to the 600's, not certain what she would find.

She'd put it back on the shelf, but now *A World of Flowers* lay in the middle of the aisle. Confused, Glad picked it up. It was bulging oddly and she flipped it open-

A dozen of Mike's business cards spilled out and fluttered to the floor. Glad dropped the book with a shocked "Oh!" then went to her knees to clean up the mess. Stopped cold.

Several cards had flipped over at landing, exposing words written in pen, pencil, Sharpie, orange crayon, letters cut from a magazine...each one was as unique as the sweet messages they contained.

Marry Me. I love you. Be my wife. Say yes...

Warmth flooded in and she felt the last of the defenses she'd built around herself crack and crumble away. She was exposed, naked as a newborn and she should be scared out of her mind but it felt okay, felt right and good. Glad flipped all the cards over, savoring each message, tracing them with her fingers, smiling beatifically. Her doubts disappeared; Mike loved her, absolutely and truly and he wanted her with him the rest of their lives.

A pair of worn boots and jean-clad legs came into her line of vision and Mike knelt across from her.

"You really want me," she whispered.

"Always," he said. "You're getting a raw deal in me, you know. This business idea may fail and we're going to be short of money all winter. Maybe longer."

"I want to be with you," she said. "As long as you're sure-"

Mike nodded and held out his hand.

"Jump," he said. "I'll catch you."

Glad grabbed his hand and Mike pulled her into his arms.

27

Judge Harlan Jones at the county courthouse in Glen View married Gladiolus May Donahue and Micha Lev Kovalski ten days later. Holly Spence, Frank Delacroix and Sal Amico stood as witnesses.

Glad flubbed her lines, Mike dropped the rings and they bonked their noses together when it came time to kiss. But she couldn't have asked for a sweeter ceremony, and he nearly burst with love and pride whenever he looked at his wife.

The news spread through Lord County like fire in a drought, but most of it was good and well-wishers abounded. The next two weeks brought cards and wedding gifts to their doorstep and the couple enjoyed opening them all.

And then the envelope came on a Tuesday, heavy and gilt-edged with *Micha Lev Kovalski* written across the front, a forwarding address sticker pasted over his old address.

"What is it?" Glad asked.

Mike picked the envelope up. "It's from my parents. The official invitation to their anniversary party next month." He opened the invitation and read the card, frowning.

"Is that a bad thing?"

Mike shook his head. "My mother probably invited everyone she knows to this little soiree. It'll be big and showy...after everything that happened last year I just..."

She understood. Mike didn't want to be thrust into yet another situation where everyone whispered behind his back.

"Are we going?" Glad asked quietly.

He snorted and handed her the invitation, along with a handwritten note that had also been enclosed. "Does that sound like a request?"

Glad read the commanding note and smiled. "I take it your mother doesn't believe in the old 'catching more flies with honey' idea."

"No, she'd rather bludgeon them to death."

***

"Here we are." Mike slowed and pulled into a gated street, gave his name to the security guard on duty and they passed through. Glad straightened and peered out the window, then her eyes bugged.

"Oh, my goodness!"

The houses were monstrosities of brick, stone and shingle on manicured five-acre lots. Beautiful, certainly, but...

"Which one is...wait! It's that one!" She

pointed ahead and to the right to a huge, stately brick colonial with familiar landscaping, even prettier with the reds, yellows and russets of late October breaking up the endless green.

"I really did a good job here," Mike murmured, sounding awed.

"You should take some pictures for your new business," Glad suggested, gazing out the windows. "It's so beautiful in fall."

They passed a line of evergreens and pulled into the driveway; Mike cursed and Glad gasped at the same time. "I thought...are we late?" she asked, worried.

There were cars lining the right side of the long drive. A lot of them.

"No, but this is typical mom," Mike grumbled. "She tells everyone one time, then starts calling all her favorites and suggesting they come a little early." He cursed again.

"So...you're not on the favorites list?"

"Guess not." He barked a laugh and parked behind a silver sedan. He killed the engine and stared at the house. Glad watched a myriad of emotion cross her husband's face; longing and hope, bitterness and regret.

"Are we going in?" she asked.

"In a minute. I need to talk to you first." He looked over at her. "I haven't been here in over a year," he said. "Everyone knows I'm coming, and I hope we'll all be civil, but this isn't going to be some Hallmark reunion. And I'm bringing a wife home besides."

"A surprise pregnant wife," she said with a small smile.

They had disagreed on this; Glad thought he should tell his parents as soon as possible about the wedding and their impending grandchild but Mike had held firm: he needed to tell them to their faces.

"We'll talk to mom and dad first, just like we planned. But with so many people here already…" He sighed. "This could get awkward."

"Don't worry about me," Glad said. "I'm a rough, tough, superhero librarian. I take on people like Marie Stahl every day. I can handle your family."

"You threw up on Marie Stahl," he reminded her.

"Vomit is my superpower," she replied primly.

Mike laughed and squeezed her hand, but he still didn't open the truck door.

"I'll be all right," she said. "I've been feeling a lot better lately."

He regarded her. "You're still not a hundred percent. We don't have to stay the whole time or anything."

"I'm okay. I promise." She brought his hand to her lips. "Let's go. I want to meet everyone. Even your mother."

They left the truck and journeyed to the front door. Mike rang the bell and rocked back on his heels, exhaled loudly. Glad slipped her hand into his and squeezed it.

The door was opened by a pleasant looking woman with gray hair and a ruddy complexion. She beamed at Mike and held her arms open.

"Hi, Marta." Mike stepped forward and they hugged.

"So glad you're home again," she said, then released him and gave him the once-over. "You look good. Ohio must agree with you."

"It does." He pulled Glad close. "Marta, this is Glad."

Glad shook the other woman's hand. "It's nice to meet you."

"Marta's been housekeeper here for over ten years," Mike said, then turned back to Marta. "I need to talk to mom and dad before we go in there. Do you think you could get them away for a minute?"

Marta looked towards the open double doors from which talk and laughter spilled. Then she eyed Mike and asked, "Would this have anything to do with you showing up married?"

Glad gasped and put a hand to her mouth.

"What-how..." Mike stuttered.

"Like you could ever get away with anything on my watch!" Marta elbowed him and laughed. "You're both wearing wedding bands, silly!"

"Oh, geez." Mike passed a hand through his hair, then looked down at his ring finger. "I didn't even think."

"He's pretty nervous," Glad supplied.

"How about we put you in your father's office and I'll go-"

"*Feter* Micha!" shrieked a voice from the doorway. Glad caught sight of an excited young face, then the youngster disappeared back into the room, shouting, "It's *Feter* Micha! *Feter* Micha's home!"

"Shit," Mike said.

"Oh, dear," clucked Marta.

"What now?" Glad asked.

Mike pulled her towards the doorway. "Guess we're winging it." They stepped inside to a chorus of *Feter* Micha's and pounding feet.

"You'd better stand back," Mike advised her, then he was pummeled from all sides by an excited gaggle of youngsters. Glad watched as he hugged and kissed one after the other and noticed how he gave attention to each child, asking about school, sports and anything else that came up. She felt a shifting inside, and happiness filled her heart.

He was going to be a wonderful father.

The children scattered after a minute and a man and woman separated themselves from the rest of the group and approached the doorway. The man was silver-haired with glasses and his eyes were crinkled up with obvious pleasure. The woman, on the other hand, looked like she'd been carved out of marble, beautiful but cool and emotionless.

"Showtime," Mike murmured to Glad.

"Go get 'em, tiger," she whispered back.

"Micha," said the man who must be his father. "You're looking well."

They shook hands. "Happy Anniversary," Mike said to them both. He bent and kissed his mother's cheek, then turned and reached for Glad's hand.

"Dad, mom, this is Glad," Mike said. "Glad, my parents, Dr. and Mrs. Kovalski."

"It's so nice to meet you," Glad said.

Dr. Kovalski smiled briefly. "You didn't tell us you were bringing a friend, Micha."

"You didn't tell us you were bringing a *goye*," his mother said, disapproval heavy in her voice. Glad winced.

Mike cleared his throat. "Well, actually-"

"I don't know if we can fit another place at the tables, Micha. You should have said something-"

"Mom-"

"Gloria, please," Mike's dad tried.

People were staring, whispering over the drama at the door. Mike's face flushed and Glad squeezed his hand tighter.

"Lev, this is our anniversary party," Gloria Kovalski said to her husband. She turned back to Mike. "It's for friends and family. You should have asked before you dragged some *shiksa* in off the street-"

Mike's brows smashed together and he said, "Glad *is* family. She's my wife."

A stunned silence fell over the room.

"Your WHAT?" shrieked his mother.

"Mom-"

"Your WIFE?"

She knew it probably wasn't true, but it seemed like the entire room gasped as one. Glad felt her face burn hot, then Mike shifted and slid his big hand around to settle on her hip.

"My wife," he repeated firmly.

Gloria Kovalski sighed loudly and stalked away, exclaiming bitterly in Hebrew.

"Do I want to know what she's saying?" Glad asked.

"No," Mike growled, staring after his mother.

"Well, this is…um…quite a surprise," Mike's father said, ignoring the murmurs all around them.

"I'm sorry," Mike said. "We wanted to tell you in private, but the kids…."

His father waved a hand. "*Zeh klum.* We'll adjust. The other day she was complaining because you hadn't married and given her grandchildren yet." He shrugged. "So, it's a surprise, but a good one. You needed a wife."

"Speaking of grandchildren…" Mike said. He swallowed hard and looked at Glad for help.

"I'm pregnant," she finished, giving her father-in-law a tentative smile. He started, his mouth opened, but then his entire face lit up like a sunrise.

"A baby!" he exalted. "Wonderful!" He pulled Glad into a warm hug, then held her at arm's length for a quick appraisal. "When are you due?"

"In spring-"

"She's PREGNANT?" came an outraged voice nearby. The murmuring in the room got louder.

"Shit," Mike muttered again.

Gloria Kovalski threw up her hands and stalked back over. It was now or never. Glad put on her best smile, stepped forward and grabbed her mother-in-law's hands hard in hers.

"Yes!" she said, smiling even wider. "Isn't it exciting? We can't wait to become parents! Mike's going to be such a great father, isn't he?"

Gloria Kovalski stared at her like she'd suddenly grown two heads. Glad went on, tamping down her panic with a string of babble. "I know, it's awfully sudden, and I'm sorry we couldn't come sooner to share the news with you all. We were talking about marriage sometime next year and then all of a sudden the baby and, well, we decided why wait, you know?"

Glad released her mother-in-law's hands, painfully aware of the exclamations all around them. This was worse than gossip in Mill Falls. Disaster seemed imminent; she could feel her husband's distress radiating off him like fire. She had to do something, say something-

As if on cue, a fresh wave of nausea rolled in and she closed her eyes against it. Gloria Kovalski gasped and Glad felt a concerned hand automatically close over her arm.

Mike's hand gripped her shoulder. "What is it?" he asked.

"She just went snow white," his mother said, her voice hushed.

She opened her eyes. "I think I might…need to lay down for a minute."

"Oh geez." Mike scooped her up. Glad shut her eyes again and concentrated on breathing slow and easy. For all her joking about it, vomiting in front of her in-laws would not make a great first impression.

"Oh, the poor thing!" someone said.

"Can I lay her on the sofa in your office?" Mike asked, walking.

"Of course," his father said, then murmured to someone else, "Maybe a little soup?"

"What is the matter with her?" Gloria asked. She sounded worried. Good.

"The baby's making her sick. She's had it pretty rough."

Then Mike was lowering, laying her down on a wide, comfortable surface and Glad opened her eyes. And saw a dozen faces crowding the doorway.

Dear God, she had an audience!

She managed a small, wan smile. "I'll be all right."

"Do I need to get my bag?" Dr. Kovalski asked.

"She's okay, dad." Mike pulled a soft throw off the back of the sofa and tucked it around her. "Her doctor back home says it'll go away once she hits the second trimester. She's better than she was a month ago. She spent two days in the hospital-"

A collective gasp went around.

"I know, right?" Glad said. "I feel like such a weakling. I mean, women have been having babies forever but leave it to me to get sick. And how embarrassing is this? What a way to meet my husband's family!"

A few laughs, some smiles. She turned to Mike. "You may as well introduce me."

Mike smiled at her, squeezed her hand. "Everyone, this is my wonderful, beautiful wife, Glad." He began to point into the group filling Lev Kovalski's office. "That's my sister Lydia-we call her Lyddie, and her husband Neal, my younger sister Sarah, and there's my brother Ben and his wife Mona, and…"

"I'm so happy you're together," Sarah gushed as they sat together on an elegant loveseat. The party was winding down; most of the remaining guests were part of the family. "Micha was miserable, and then I went and spilled all over you, and then when he told me you thought I was his *date*!" She laughed merrily.

"I wasn't exactly thinking straight," Glad allowed.

She'd rejoined the party after her nausea faded and throughout the evening Mike's extended family had all been kind and welcoming. The children especially seemed to like her and Mike's youngest nephew, a dark-haired imp named Stephen, had latched on to her like a magnet. Currently he was snuggled close, fighting sleep while gripping his well-loved teddy bear in one hand and watching his siblings and cousins romp around the room.

"After Rachel…did what she did, things were upside-down," Sarah continued. "We all thought the worst of Micha at first and by the time it got straightened out he'd left for Ohio." She looked across the room, where Mike was talking with his brother and father. "I'm glad he married you instead of her," she confided. "You're so much nicer. Rachel could be a real witch, especially if she didn't get her way. I hear she's running that doctor husband of hers ragged."

"Mike mentioned that she liked getting attention," Glad said, trying for neutrality. She didn't want to gossip about someone she'd never met.

"Oh, yes. If it wasn't about her she'd make it about her." Sarah rolled her eyes. "Even my mother remarked on it, and she's the queen of drama, as you've seen."

"She's pretty formidable," Glad allowed.

Sarah giggled. "That's one way to put it." Then her eyes went to the doorway and she sighed. "Well, here's where my fun ends."

"What do you mean?" Glad asked.

"See that guy in the doorway?" Sarah asked. Glad nodded and she said, "That's Daniel Blumenthal. Mom wants me to marry him. He's rich, you know."

Glad studied the man, now being embraced by Mike's mother as if he were one of the family already. "What does money have to do with it?"

Sarah rolled her eyes. "Money has everything to do with it. She wants me to have a husband who can give me everything I want. But she doesn't understand-" Sarah clamped her mouth shut and put on a smile as the man in question crossed the floor, a million-dollar grin on his face.

Introductions were made, some polite party conversation followed, then Sarah excused herself for a moment and Blumenthal began his spiel. He was a genius, a whiz with money, could shit gold bricks if he was so inclined. And Glad, trapped by a drowsy preschooler, could only nod and smile politely as the man bragged on, barely pausing for breath. And then he said:

"So you hooked up with the lawn boy, eh?"

"I beg your pardon?" Glad asked, not sure

she'd heard correctly.

Blumenthal *tsked*, a condescending smile on his face. "He dropped out of pre-med to go shovel mulch and mow grass. What a waste."

Glad's mouth dropped. "I happen to be very proud of my husband-"

"Sticking your foot in it again, I see," came a smooth voice behind the man, and Nico Roth stepped into view. He leaned down and kissed her cheek. "Hi, Glad. Good to see you again."

Glad smiled up at him, grateful for the interruption. "It's so nice to see you, too." She watched Nico shake Blumenthal's hand, noted his dark eyes had turned hard with dislike.

"Blumenthal," Nico said coolly.

"Still ambulance chasing, Roth?"

Nico gave the other man a lazy smile. "It has its moments. Still bean counting?"

"It has its moments," Blumenthal returned with a smirk. "I don't suppose you've heard the news? Sarah and I are getting engaged."

Nico paled a fraction and Glad's heart broke for him. She turned her gaze across the room to Mike and summoned him with a tiny jerk of her head. He immediately started over.

"Is that so," Nico replied, his voice carefully neutral.

"Guess the better man won, eh?" Blumenthal gloated.

28

From across the room his wife sent him a panicked look. Mike took in his best friend squaring off against some guy dressed in a suit with slicked-back hair and a sneer. He headed over just in time to hear Nico say, "Is that so?"

"Guess the better man won, eh?" asked the sneering one.

Mike saw Nico's hand curling into a fist and hurried his last steps. He pulled Nico into a hug and exclaimed, "Great to see you, man! Glad you could make it!"

Nico hugged him back and whispered, "Just let me punch that fucker once."

"Not here," Mike murmured and released him. He stuck out his hand. "Mike Kovalski."

"Daniel Blumenthal," the other man said, wincing as Mike gave his hand an extra hard squeeze. Then he smirked and said, "So you're the lawn boy from Redneck, Ohio."

Well, that was easy. He didn't even have to try and like this asshole. "That's right. *Shalom*, y'all," Mike drawled, grinning.

"Quite a comedown from pre-med," Blumenthal went on. "But I guess someone has to mow the grass, am I right?"

Okay, he'd promised himself he wouldn't make any scenes, but this jerk needed a smackdown like yesterday. Mike narrowed his eyes and opened his mouth...

"My husband, Mr. Blumenthal, is a licensed landscape architect, a certified master gardener and holds an advanced degree in Botany," Glad said from the sofa, her voice hard as steel. "His design for the grounds of our public library will be on the front cover of next April's *Library Journal*, an international publication. He also won a design award for the landscaping on this very property."

God, he loved his wife.

"So?" Blumenthal asked, clueless.

"So, for all your pompous talk about spinning straw into gold, you are woefully ignorant of how the real world works," Glad said, glaring at him.

"It also means I don't mow grass," Mike said.

"And your manners could use a little work," Nico added.

Blumenthal stared at them, finally at a loss for words. But before he could recover Sarah rejoined the group.

"Nico," Sarah said, her voice trembling and her heart in her eyes. "I didn't think you were coming."

Nico faced her and Mike saw the same emotion in his friend's eyes. They really did love each other.

"I wasn't going to. But I need to say something and I don't think it can wait."

"Here?" Sarah asked.

"Here and now." Nico took a breath. "Don't marry him. It's a mistake."

This was news. Mike turned Sarah to face him. "Since when are you getting married?"

"I-I-" Sarah stuttered, flushing.

"We've been discussing it," Blumenthal said, a nasty little smile on his face.

Nico rounded on Sarah. "Have you accepted?"

"I...not...yet."

Nico stepped closer. "Listen, he can buy you things, but that's not a good enough reason to be with someone the rest of your life. You need to love him, too. Love and respect him. You know that, right?"

"How dare-who do you think you are?" Blumenthal hissed, outraged.

Sarah's mouth worked but nothing came out.

"Sarah!" Blumenthal hissed again. Her flustered eyes slid his way; she gulped and tried again but no words came.

"I've got nothing to offer," Nico went on quietly. "You know that better than anyone. I'm up to my ass in debt from law school, I spent all my savings bailing out mom and dad after they got took in that scheme. It'll take years for me to get on track again. I've got *nothing*."

Sarah stared at Nico, her eyes filling.

"I can *not* believe this," Blumenthal groaned, rolling his eyes. "Don't listen to him, Sarah. He's just a shyster punk-"

"Shut up," Mike said.

Nico reached out and cupped Sarah's face. "You've got to do what's best for you. And I know I'm miles away from being anyone's best bet. You'd be way better off with…you deserve someone who can give you the world. Just…don't settle, okay?" He leaned forward and kissed her cheek. "I love you, *neshome.*"

Nico turned and walked out, oblivious to the stares and murmurs following him. Sarah turned to Mike, her face a misery.

"Go after him," he urged.

"Please," Blumenthal scoffed. "She knows where she belongs, she's not going anywhere." He grabbed Sarah's arm and turned her to face him. "What would your mother say?" He shook her arm as if to drive his point home. "What would everyone think?"

"Tell you what *I* think: you'd best take your hand off my sister," Mike growled, his expression thunderous.

"How about you mind your own business?" Blumenthal snarled.

"How about I break you in half?" Mike replied.

Blumenthal let go and stalked off. Mike turned back to Sarah. "Mom will be pissed, and she'll cry and scream and there will be drama.

But she'll be even more unhappy if you marry that *schmuck* and are miserable the rest of your life. You love Nico."

Sarah nodded, tears spilling down her cheeks.

"Mom will get over it," he assured her.

"You can probably catch him if you hurry," Glad advised from the sofa.

Sarah gave them both a watery smile, then turned and left the room. It wasn't quite a run, but she was going pretty fast in her sky-high heels. Mike settled next to Glad and Stephen crawled onto his lap with a yawn and a "*Feter* Micha". Mike kissed the top of his little head.

"Have I told you lately what a great wife you are?" he asked.

"Have I told you lately what a great husband you are?" she replied.

***

As expected, there was drama in the Kovalski house when Sarah announced she had no intention of seeing Daniel Blumenthal anymore, then tears and lament when she informed her mother that she was dating Nico Roth instead. But in the end, their mother had agreed with Mike that what she wanted more than anything was for her daughter to be happy.

Gloria also thawed considerably towards Glad over the weekend. She might not be thrilled with a *goye* for a daughter in-law, but she and Mike's father loved babies and were definitely on board for more grandchildren. Within days of their return to Mill Falls, a large box arrived, stuffed with all manner of baby paraphernalia.

"This is crazy!" Glad said, holding up an adorable stuffed bear and a package of bibs. "I'm not even showing yet!"

"This is only the beginning," Mike promised.

Fall plunged into an early winter with snowfall starting in mid-November. Glad left sickness behind and bloomed with good health and spirits. Her appetite spiked and her baby bump grew and soon she and Mike felt tiny movements from within. They shopped for a few big baby items together, bought a crib, a changing table and a rocker and Glad made over one of the empty bedrooms upstairs to a nursery.

Mike developed his portfolio and met with several potential clients for landscaping jobs the following spring. He'd been contacted again by Renny McQueen, who had heard through the grapevine that Mike and Green Spaces had parted ways, and proposed the idea of using Mike as an independent contractor, selling Mike's plans with Sunrise's plants. It would mean making regular visits to Cincinnati, but McQueen's client list was long and Mike's commissions would be high.

Mike also picked up some part time work with Greg Turk, who ran a snow removal business through the winter. It meant working odd hours and sometimes all night, depending on the weather, but the cash in his hand was gratifying.

When he wasn't busy planning or plowing,

Mike and Fonz were tearing apart the kitchen and pantry, as promised. By the end of December, Glad had a new kitchen with sleek and simple Shaker-style cabinets, quality countertops and appliances, a deep, stainless steel sink and thick linoleum tile in a neutral sand color. The puke yellow flooring was gone at last.

January brought childbirth classes and sincere panic for Mike. The breathing exercises were fine, but those diagrams of the stages of labor-including a sketch of a fully dilated vagina-and the birth movie that followed just about did him in.

"I can't do this," he said on the way home from Glen View, where the classes were held.

"I'm the one doing this," Glad reminded him with a smile.

"You know what I mean! I can't watch you in pain like that! And the blood and...and..." He shuddered so hard the truck veered on the road. "Ugh. I do not want to see that. I'll probably pass out or something."

"It's just childbirth!" Glad chided him, laughing.

"It's gross!" Mike said. "I thought I'd be just holding your hand and helping you breathe and all that other stuff would be under a sheet or something! But no, it's all just hanging right out there for the world to see!"

Glad laughed harder. "Oh, for heaven's sake, you've seen me down there!"

"Not like that, I haven't! I can *not* do this, girl."

"Yes, you can."

"Nope. Not happening."

"Mike Kovalski, if you leave me alone in that delivery room I swear I'm telling the Mill Falls gossips what a chickenshit you are."

"You wouldn't do that."

"I'll put a notice on that billboard outside of town." Then she *bawked* at him.

By Valentine's Day Glad had a new downstairs bathroom, cute and cozy with a stand-up shower and pedestal sink. She loved it. Then Mike mentioned that, since now that she had a nice kitchen and bathroom she really should let him off the hook about the whole delivery thing. Glad smiled sweetly, stroked his winter-bearded face and said, "Not a chance."

And she *bawk-bawked* him out of the room.

Winter slowly gave way to some bare ground in early March. Mike began his treks to Cincinnati to go over designs with Renny McQueen and meet with clients. Holly, April and Fran threw a surprise baby shower at the Mill River Inn on the second Saturday and Glad cried over the outpouring of friendship, warmth and support.

"I think we've finally arrived, Mrs. Kovalski," Mike said on their way home.

Glad agreed. "I love this town."

Mike left for Cincinnati again on St. Patrick's Day, getting up before dawn to make the drive. Glad, unable to sleep comfortably for long, joined him downstairs.

"You're close," he said, stroking a careful hand over her belly. "What if something happens?"

"Nothing is going to happen," Glad assured him. "You'll only be gone for three or four days and I have two weeks to go. I'll be fine. My girls are by all the time and Frank and Sal are next door...I probably won't have a minute's peace with them all hovering over me."

"Okay." Mike tried a smile and failed.

"I'll be fine," she repeated. "I promise."

"I'm going to miss you, girl."

"Me too." She stroked a hand down his arm.

"Guess I better get on the road." Mike picked up his duffel, then dropped it and took his wife into his arms instead, kissed her with everything he had in him. Then he laid his head against her shoulder, breathed her in, held her as close as he could. Heaven, every time.

"I love you, Mike," she whispered softly.

Mike held her tight. "I love you, too."

"Call me when you get there?"

"And every night, too. I'll be home Thursday night, probably before you get out of work."

"Good," Glad said. "I'll expect a back rub when I get home."

"You got it." He kissed her again, then moved his hand down and tapped at her belly. "And you behave yourself," he said to it. "Stay in there until I get back home."

The baby obliged with a swift kick. Glad smiled and stroked a hand over her belly. "We'll wait for you."

Mike took a long look at her, memorized her. Even this late in her pregnancy, swollen ankles and all, she was still the most beautiful woman he'd ever seen. He stroked a hand over her hair, kissed her one last time then left the house, dreading every mile that took him away.

***

"Mrs. Kovalski?" It was Sally from Circ and she sounded worried. "I think I just saw Jimmer Hall go by the front desk."

Glad groaned. After the last scene with Jimmer and his subsequent ban from library grounds, she'd hoped he was gone for good. No such luck. And since Chris was, of course, on vacation this week, dealing with Jimmer fell into Glad's lap-what there was left of it, that is. "Did you see where he was headed?"

"I think he went upstairs."

"All right. I'll come out and see what's going on." Glad hung up and pushed herself out of her chair with another groan. Rubbed that ache in her back that had been pricking at her on and off all day. Did she really have ten days left of this? If she got any bigger she'd probably explode.

Glad walked up to Reference. The library was quiet this time of night. She noted only a couple of people on the public computers and Deb alone at the desk.

"Did you see Jimmer Hall come this way?" Glad asked softly.

Deb's eyes widened. "No. But I was helping someone in the 300's just a couple of minutes ago. I could have missed-"

A curse floated out of the stacks, followed

by thumping noises.

"What in the world?" Deb asked, standing.

"I'll get it," Glad said. She headed towards the sound.

Jimmer Hall was standing in the 790's, muttering and pulling sports books off the shelf, shaking them and dropping them next to him. He was breathing heavily.

"Mr. Hall," Glad said quietly.

Jimmer did not answer. He pulled another book out, shook it and dropped it.

"Gotta be here," he muttered and grabbed another, shook it and dropped it. "Gotta be here."

"Mr. Hall," Glad said louder. "What are you doing?"

Jimmer started pulling books off the shelf with both hands, frantically shaking them and dropping them at his sides, oblivious to anything else. Glad sighed and walked up to him.

"Jimmer," she said firmly, and put a hand on his arm. "You're making a mess-"

Jimmer rounded on her. "Where is it?"

"Where is what?" Glad asked, taking a wary step back. Jimmer's eyes were red, his face was flushed and his nose was running freely.

"My amp!" Jimmer grabbed her arms and shoved her against the stacks. "Where is it?" he growled, shaking her. "Where *is it*?"

"I have no idea what you're talking about. Now let me go."

Jimmer stared at her a second, then let his hands drop. But before Glad could even put her next thought together Jimmer brought one hand back up and she was looking down the barrel of a nasty-looking handgun, held in the young man's shaking hand.

"You tell me," he said. "You tell me right now! I had a drop, right here, and it's gone."

"So you are the one," she said. She'd been right all this time, but having her suspicions proved by a gun in her face didn't exactly make this a celebratory moment.

"Where is it?" Jimmer asked again.

"I don't know. Put down the gun, Jimmer."

"No way. You took my amp; I know you did!" Jimmer reached out and grabbed her arm, shoved the muzzle under her chin. "You tell me or I swear-"

"Is everything okay?" came Deb's voice from behind them. Jimmer yanked Glad around, pointed the gun in Deb's general direction and fired. Glad shrieked, Deb dove out of sight and Jimmer fired again.

Chaos erupted. Screams echoed through the building. Jimmer dragged Glad out of the stacks and began shouting. What he was saying was anyone's guess; her ears were ringing from the blasts and she couldn't make it out. She saw Deb and two patrons heading for the stairs, their arms in the air, then she was dragged along and down, Jimmer's gun waving wildly next to her. Glad noted the front doors swinging shut; someone had made it outside and she could only pray they would call the police right away.

"Move it!" Jimmer snarled, yanking her arm. They stumbled down the steps and he pulled her towards a small knot of people.

"You!" Jimmer pointed the gun at Ashley.

"Go lock those doors!"

"Jimmer, please don't do this," Ashley begged. "Please don't-"

Jimmer cocked the gun. "You think I'm playing around? Huh? Go lock the damn doors!"

"But I don't have a key." The girl was sobbing, clearly terrified.

"I do," Glad said to Jimmer. She pulled a key ring from her pocket and held it out.

"Take it!" Jimmer roared at Ashley. The girl scrambled to Glad and grabbed her keys.

"It's number four," Glad said to Ashley, trying to keep calm. "Turn it to the right to lock."

Ashley stumbled to the front doors, weeping. She picked out the key but then dropped the key ring.

"Dumb bitch," Jimmer growled.

"Be patient," Glad said quietly. "She's scared."

"You think I give a fuck what she is?"

Ashley finally locked the library doors and returned Glad's keys, crying all the while.

"Go sit down," Jimmer snarled, then stuffed the muzzle of the gun back under Glad's chin. "And now, bitch, you're gonna tell me where my amp's gone to or I'm gonna splatter your brains all over this library."

29

"Please, Jimmer," Glad said softly, not wanting to give Jimmer any more reason to pull the trigger. "You don't want to hurt me-ow-"

"Shut up!" yelled Jimmer, pressing the gun harder, forcing her head back. "Where is it? I need my fucking amp!"

"I don't-know-where-" She could see the staff, wide eyed and crouched together, patrons huddled in frightened bunches. She could hear a cacophony of voices, young and old, screams of babies, weeping teens. But nothing was louder than the panicked beat of her heart, nothing scarier than a sudden snap inside, nothing more mortifying than a warm flow down her legs. "Oh, God-"

"What the fuck??" Jimmer shrieked, staring at the wet pooling around her feet.

"My water just broke," she told him. It was all clear suddenly; those nagging back pains were labor pains! Good grief! She'd been in labor most of the day!

"What's up with that?" he demanded, gun hand twitching.

"It means my baby's coming. Please, Jimmer. Please let me go."

"No way, bitch. You're my ticket out of here. Soon as I get my shit I'm gone. In your car. And maybe I'll drop you at Urgent Care if you cooperate."

"THIS IS THE POLICE!" boomed from outside. Everyone screamed, even Jimmer. *"WE HAVE THE BUILDING SURROUNDED! PUT DOWN YOUR WEAPON AND SURRENDER!"*

"Oh-ahh-" Glad gritted her teeth against a contraction.

It's early! Too early? I don't know!

"WE KNOW YOU ARE IN THE BUILDING! RELEASE YOUR HOSTAGES AND PUT DOWN YOUR WEAPON!"

"Do it Jimmer. Please-oh-ow-" Glad tried to remember her Lamaze breathing. Completely blanked. She was sweating, cramping, shaking all over.

Mike, are you home yet? Are you close? The baby's coming-

"Take me instead!" Deb stood, eyes snapping fire.

"Take me!" A patron yelled. "She's having a baby, for God's sake!"

"Shut up!" Jimmer yanked Glad around and dragged her over to the nearest window. He broke out a pane with the butt of his pistol and screamed, "You get me my amp now! This bitch is in labor in here and she needs a fucking doctor!

393

You get me my amp and let me outta here and they can all go free!"

"THE HOSTAGES-"

"Fucking get it! Get it now or this baby won't have a mother!"

***

Mike was cruising his radio settings, hoping WGLV, the local station out of the college in Glen View, would come in. But he was still some ways out and reception wasn't the best out here. He pushed the seek button again and there was a bray of static, then: "*-standoff in Mill Falls, local police are-*" and he lost the station.

"What?" he said out loud. He tried the different stations, fiddled with the settings. No use, he'd lost it.

Mike fished his mobile out and pressed his first speed dial. Glad didn't answer her cell. He tried again at her work. No answer.

No answer at her work? It was only seven-thirty. Someone should have picked up.

Mike scrolled down his list and punched Frank Delacroix's number. No answer. He moved to Sal Amico. No answer. Turk. Nothing. Fonz. Nothing.

What was going on?

His options shrinking, he scrolled again and punched Harry Phelps. It rang once. Twice.

"'lo?" Harry grumbled.

"Harry! It's Mike Kovalski-"

"Boss! Where you at?" Harry barked.

"What's going on up there?" Mike

demanded.

"Trouble up Mill Falls way. Some nut has a bunch of people locked up in the library!"

Mike's heart lurched. "*What??*"

"He says he's gonna kill 'em if he don't get what he wants. I guess the cops were investigating some drug ring. It's live on TV right now!"

Damn it! Nothing had happened for months! Glad had thought the drug business was over and done with!

Don't panic. Think.

"Have they said who's in there with him?"

"What? No, no names-"

"Harry. Glad works in there."

"Oh, man." Harry was silent a moment, then he said, "I'm sure she's all right, no one's been reported shot or anything."

"Listen, can you call me in a bit and let me know what's going on? I need to hang up and drive, here."

"Sure, yeah, 'course!"

Mike hung up and focused on the road, focused on eating up the miles between here and home. His guts were in a knot; trouble was brewing and he had the feeling Glad was smack in the middle of it.

***

"Jimmer, please, can I sit down?"

"Don't fucking move."

"Please-ow-ooh-" Glad checked the wall clock. Her contraction times had decreased rapidly the last ninety minutes, from twenty to twelve to seven. Now it was five minutes.

They were waiting for the police to comply with Jimmer's demands. He hadn't asked for much, just a baggie of meth and Glad's car. She'd happily thrown her car keys out the broken window twenty minutes ago and assumed an officer had picked them up. Maybe her car was waiting at the front entrance now-

"JAMES HALL!" the police megaphone brayed from outside. They'd identified him, somehow. *"YOUR VEHICLE IS IN THE FRONT OF THE BUILDING! YOUR PARAPHERNALIA IS ON THE PASSENGER SEAT! YOU WILL NOT BE HARMED! PLEASE PROCEED TO THE FRONT OF THE BUILDING!"*

"Let's go, bitch-"

"Wait-need to-finish-contraction-okay-"

Walking, or more accurately, being yanked along, was agony. Glad felt intense pressure deep in her abdomen. The baby wanted out.

Please, God, let me at least get to the Urgent Care. Please.

Jimmer shoved her in front of him as they reached the front door. "You go out nice and slow. Don't do anything stupid. Got it?"

"Got it." Glad willed herself to remain calm. It was nearly impossible.

She unlocked the front door and they exited to a corona of police lanterns and floodlights trained on them and the library doors. A helicopter chuffed overhead. Glad walked slowly, blindly forward, seeing the vague outline of her car in front of her. Then, from her immediate left came a harsh, loud *"DROP THE GUN!"*

Glad startled and screamed, Jimmer pushed her forward and she stumbled. She felt a hot hand hit her and she fell hard to the concrete. Everything went black.

***

Mike's phone rang. "What's happening?"

"Jesus Christ, they shot him!" Harry hollered.

"What?"

"He came out with a woman, then he pushed her and shot her and they shot him! Holy shit!"

Dread clamped around his heart. "Who was the woman?"

"I don't know, they haven't said-wait, wait-" Silence. Murmurs. Mike heard a muffled "Are they sure?" and "Shit." Then Harry was back on the line. "News just said it was the assistant that got shot."

Mike's vision went completely black for a second or two. *He shot Glad. My wife, our baby-*

"Mike. Is that-"

Mike's phone dropped into his lap. His breath came in harsh rattles out of his chest, his hands shook so hard he could barely grip the wheel.

Glad. Shot. Injured, maybe dead. The baby-

No, no no no. Don't even think it. She'll be fine, she'll be fine. Just keep your head on your shoulders and your eyes on the road. Just get there. Just fifty-eight miles.

Fifty-seven.

Fifty-six.

***

Glad came to in a blurry haze of noise and pain. She was surrounded by uniforms, lights and everyone was yelling.

"-stretcher!"

"-we've got a G-S-W with labor-"

"-perp's dead-"

"-closest treatment?"

"-Urgent Care on Smith-"

"On three! One-two-"

Glad was lifted in the air and Sal Amico's face swam into focus.

"You'll be all right, sweetheart."

"My-baby-"

"Baby's doing great. Keep breathing. That's it, nice and easy."

Glad drifted away from consciousness.

"-going into shock-"

"Stop the fucking bleeding!"

"-you hear me? Glad-"

Pain wrenched her back to reality and she gasped, groaned and writhed on the gurney.

"Lie still, we need to keep your shoulder stable."

"Need to-push-"

"Not yet, not yet-"

"Help me!" Glad fixed on Sal's dark eyes, so much like Mike's. "Help me, Mike, I need Mike!"

Sal dug in his pocket and activated his

phone. A missed call from Mike popped up. Sal redialed.

"Sal! Where's Glad? Is she-"

"We're going to the Urgent Care!" Sal yelled into the phone. "She's having the baby! Get your ass up here!"

"I'm on my way! Is she all right?"

Glad shrieked in pain. "Gotta go!" Sal said.

"Wait! What-"

Sal hung up and clambered up into the ambulance. The doors slammed shut and he bent over Glad, checked her dressing and slid the blood pressure cuff on as the ambulance tore off for the Urgent Care.

**

Glad was having their baby right now. She was early by two weeks or more.

And he was still at least forty minutes away. Damn it!

Mike glanced at his GPS. Thirty-six miles. Thirty-five.

Fuck the speed limit. He punched the accelerator.

**

"We need to stop that bleeding!"

"Is the bullet still in her?"

"BP is one-fifty over ninety-five, pulse one-twenty."

"Sweetheart, you've gotta try and relax." Sal was at her side, guiding the gurney back into the treatment area of the Urgent Care.

"Can't-can't-" Glad gasped. "Hurts-so-"

The team slid the gurney into a treatment room and she was quickly transferred to the exam table. Glad's world swam out of focus for several minutes.

"-blood loss..."

"-cut them off her-"

Cool metal slid up her legs and her pants and underwear disappeared. Pillows were shoved behind her back to prop her up and a warm blanket was laid over her body. She faded out again.

"...ten centimeters..."

"...if the head's down-"

Pain! Glad gave an agonized groan.

"We need to get that bullet out!"

"We can't! The baby's coming now! Christ, she's crowning! Get her legs up!"

Another wave of pain began building and Sal's face was in front of hers. "Okay, time to start pushing, sweetheart."

"Mike-"

"He's coming, I promise. Okay, ready? Breathe, one, two, push!"

Glad bore down with a groan.

"-six, seven, eight! Okay, breathe, you're doing great, doing great, let's go again. Ready? One, two, push-that's it, three, four, five, six, seven, eight-"

Glad was out of her head; the pain was everywhere, deep and stabbing, turning her world into a red haze. Dimly she heard someone calling her name, then she had to push again. And again.

Mike shuddered to a stop in front of the Urgent Care and ran inside.

"Where's my wife?" he demanded of the night nurse.

"Who are you?"

"Mike Kovalski! I need to get back there!"

"I'll need to see some ID-"

"I need to help her!"

"Sir, you can't just go back there-"

"GLAD!!!" Mike yelled at the top of his lungs. This place wasn't that big, she couldn't be too far away. "*GLAD!!!*"

Silence. Then blessedly, Sal Amico's cranky, gravelly voice floated out to the desk.

"Get back here, Kovalski!"

The nurse rolled her eyes and punched a button. The treatment area door unlatched and Mike was through it like a shot.

***

"Push, Glad! Come on, just one more time," the doctor on call said.

"I can't." She'd pushed so many times already. She was losing strength, losing will. Glad squeezed her eyes shut and pushed, huffed, lost it.

"I thought you said you'd wait for me." She opened to sepia brown eyes and thick black brows over her. She smiled through a haze of tears.

401

"Mike-"

"One more, Glad! Push!" came from Sal.

"You're here-"

"I'm here, girl."

"Help me, help-ahh-" Glad emitted a strangled shriek. Mike grabbed her hand in his.

"Glad, you need to push. Mike, help her! Hold up her other leg, like this!" Sal said.

Mike grabbed hold. "What do I do now?"

"Talk to her. Calm her down," the doctor said over Glad's weeping. "She can't push if she's so worked up. This baby needs out now."

"*Neshome,* you need to relax. Everything's going to be fine."

Glad groaned and pushed. No progress.

"You can do it, girl. You can."

"I love you so much," she said, panting.

"I know, baby. I love you, too-"

"Love later. Push now!" Sal commanded.

"I can't-"

"Yes you can," Mike said in his best no-nonsense voice. "Let's do this, girl. Breathe, good, good, push!"

Glad bore down, groaning.

"I can see the shoulder!"

"Count it, Mike! One, two-"

"Three, four, five-"

"A little more! Push!"

"Six, seven, that's it, *neshome,* that's it-"

The pain suddenly left her and she faded, felt Mike's lips on hers, felt his stubbly cheek, the wet of his tears against her face.

A tiny cry filled the room.

"It's a boy!" Sal exclaimed.

EPILOGUE

Mr. & Mrs. Micha Kovalski
are pleased to announce
the birth of their son
Samuel Micha
on the twenty-second of March
7 lbs., 3 oz.

Summer weekends were lazy, spent puttering in the back yard or lounging in the shade of the wide front porch. The air was redolent with the smell of summer flowers and smoky barbecue grills. A cicada called from down the street and another one answered with a long, shrill buzz.

"There we go," murmured a soft voice and Glad opened her eyes to her husband settling in the nearby rocker with Samuel.

"He's up already?" she said over a yawn.

"Just fretting a bit," Mike answered, and began slowly rocking back and forth.

403

Glad smiled, warm with love over the picture they made; her big, burly husband cuddling his tiny baby boy. Samuel was just four months, healthy and strong, his black hair swirling around his tiny head. Mike had taken to fatherhood easily, feeding and changing diapers like a pro. Since Glad could barely move her shoulder for the first ten days after Samuel was born, this had been a godsend.

Mill Falls was returning to normal. The drug ring had collapsed and scattered; several arrests were made and the library-being one of the drop locations-figured prominently in the news for the first twenty-four hours. But in a world ever-hungry for the latest disaster, Mill Falls quickly faded from the limelight and by the time Glad, Mike and Samuel returned home from her hospital stay, the reporters and camera crews were gone.

To be replaced by a deluge of family, friends and other assorted well-wishers, including-to their surprise-Mike's parents in the weeks following Samuel's birth. That particular visit was only minimally tense and Glad was pleased to watch Mike's parents fall completely in love with their new grandson, to the point they mentioned returning again in the fall.

Now Mike was singing softly to Samuel, a lullabye.

Durme, durme, hermosa donzella, durme, durme, sin ansia i dolor, durme, durme, sin ansia i dolor...

"I keep meaning to ask you what that song means," she said softly.

"*Sleep, sleep, beautiful child*," he sang in English, "*sleep, sleep, without worry or pain, sleep, sleep without worry or pain...* it's old, some kind of Yiddish-Spanish. I think they call it Ladino. Bubbe sang it to me all the time when I was little." Samuel gave an indignant cry and Mike smiled. "Right on schedule."

Glad pushed herself off the lounger. "His stomach is his God. I'll get it."

She disappeared into the house and Mike rocked Samuel, cooing at him, tickling him under his chin. Fatherhood was, aside from his wife, the best thing that had ever happened to him.

Glad returned to the porch, bottle and cloth in hand. "Do you want me to feed him?" she asked.

"It's all right. Hand it over." Mike flipped the cloth onto his shoulder and tilted the bottle down. Samuel latched on immediately.

"Greedy little beggar," he said, chuckling.

"Like father, like son," Glad said with a smirk.

Mike eyed her, doing a slow perusal that made her blush all over. "You just wait 'til I get you alone later."

Glad gave him a sly smile and leaned down for a kiss.

"I love you, Mr. Kovalski," she said.

"I love you, Mrs.-who's here?" A dark red sedan slowed and pulled into the driveway.

"It's a rental," Glad said vaguely, watching the car roll to a stop.

Mike sat forward and peered over the rail. The passenger door opened and his sister stepped out into the summer heat.

"Surprise!" Sarah said, smiling and waving.

"What are you doing back here?" Mike put the bottle on the table next to him and moved Samuel up to his shoulder. Two taps and the baby obliged with a lusty burp.

"Well, we were on our way back and thought we'd stop and visit for a couple of days," Sarah said.

"We?" Mike asked suspiciously.

"Back from where?" Glad asked, going down the steps.

The driver door opened and a tall, lean man stepped out. Mike heard Glad gasp and he began to laugh, delighted.

"Vegas," Nico Roth said.

Dear Reader,

I'm so glad you decided to check out Mike and Glad's story, and I hope you liked it-I had a great time writing it! There's more stories coming from Lord County; I'm hard at work on the next book in the series, starring April Fonzi and that mysterious bar owner, Matt Slade. I hope to have it finished and ready to publish by the end of August 2016. After April and Matt, our local "Farmer McHottie", Jim Ascher, will have an unexpected reunion with a love he lost long ago. And there's more stories simmering on my back burner for Holly and Turk, John Fonzi and more!

If you enjoyed *Something to Talk About*, or have any questions, please drop me a line through the contact page on my website, www.bethdonaldsonwrites.com. I'd love to hear from you! You can also review my work on Amazon if you'd like; I'd sure appreciate it!

I have a blog on my site, where I'll wax on about anything that comes to mind-and drop all kinds of hints for my characters and stories! There's a link to my Pinterest, where I keep pasting inspirations for my characters and stories, and a link to my Twitter as well. I try to update weekly if I can.

Thanks again for reading, and we'll see you again soon!

Beth

Made in the USA
Lexington, KY
10 January 2016